Consequences of Being

Chris Sheerin

a book by

darkWolf Press

darkWolf press, 5 Orlan House,
Strand Road, Derry, BT48 7AB.

Tel: 07597 691377

Email: chrissheerin@live.co.uk

About the author

Chris Sheerin was born in England, but has lived in Derry, Ireland since 1969. He was educated in St Columb's College and Magee University.

Other books by Chris Sheerin include:

Chasing Shadows (Marino Press, 2001)
Days of Rain (Guildhall Press, 2003)
Three Wolves (darkWolf press, 2011)
One Year from Today (darkWolf press, 2014)

Poetry Books by Chris Sheerin include:

Forgotten Flowers (darkWolf press 2010)
Affinity (darkWolf press 2011)
No Strings (darkWolf press 2012)
Blue Gods (darkWolf press 2013)
Puzzled Hearts (darkWolf press 2014)

For Damian Devlin

PRELUDE

If anyone had thought to ask the vagrant known as Miles Kivlehan where he was on the morning the Stranger arrived in Craiglann, he wouldn't have hesitated in telling them. He had been sheltering from the rain inside the Old Man's newsagents, his nose pressed to the window and his gaze lost in the heavily-puddled Crissom road as a small tsunami of water was suddenly upcast against the pane by a removal van braking hard outside. Miles may also have added that the rain had all but abated by then, though a brooding ache of clouds still marched over the small town towards the west of Eire, staining the sky dark as obsidian.

Precisely why he recalled the Stranger, Miles mightn't have found as easy to relate: After all, the man was but one of an infest of customers who'd used the shop since his own arrival one hour earlier. In retrospect, Miles guessed his interest may've been sparked by the half-filled removal van's contents–a few tattered suitcases and several loosely-wrapped electrical appliances–all of which instantly suggested that someone new was moving into town. That, and perhaps the fact there was currently only one uninhabited property of any note within Craiglann's grey epicentre – the old farmhouse up on Pheasant's Crest.

It had been suggested more than once that the old farmhouse was haunted, and Miles supposed its eerie facade, the crock of dilapidated outhouses upon its periphery and its encompassing briar fence granted some credence to that rumour. Still, the vagrant surmised it was equally possible the old farmhouse had remained vacant for near a year now because it stood on the same hill–Albeit directly over the road–as both St. Augustine's chapel and the disreputable Mission Home of Adullam. So, with these thoughts in mind, he found himself watching with vague interest as the Stranger stepped from the van and stared ponderously at a small map for a few moments, before refolding it, returning it his jacket pocket and moving slowly into the Old Man's shop. The Stranger was tall and grey-eyed, with drawn cheeks and strong hands – that Miles quickly noted. Nor did he say much – he merely grunted and pointed to various items upon the shelves. And the Old Man, too ensnared in his own toil to deduce who'd temporarily employed him, served the newcomer without engaging in even the most general conversation, no doubt thinking him merely another customer who'd no wish to exchange idle chitchat about a rainy day which would hardly be exorcised by discussion.

So, on that fateful morning the Stranger was just another customer; and Miles guessed the man wouldn't have spoken at all had he not been a newcomer in town. What the vagrant considered more alarming, however, was that, when he did speak, the Stranger's enquiries were directed solely at Miles himself.

Miles pulled himself away from the tens of destroyed tears of rain which had pooled deep in the window's putty fractures and realised the tall man had asked him for directions to the farm on Pheasant's Crest. Filled with a sudden lowly pride that he'd at least been correct about something on this dull winter's morning, the vagrant pointed out of the window in the direction the van was already facing. The tall man raised a quizzical eyebrow and Miles sighed deeply, realising he'd have to expand upon his reply. So, the vagrant stuck his head outside the door beneath the leaking awning and the *For Sale* sign above it to point to the broken lot of outbuildings on the right-hand side of the distant hill, explaining that the farm's entrance was just a little beyond that. Miles startled visibly then as a large black mastiff suddenly thrust its head out of the back of the van and barked unnervingly. The newcomer smiled reassuringly, telling him the dog was friendly and that he could pat it if he liked. The vagrant, however, shook his head in turn and dropped his gaze, unused as he was these days to more ordinary people entering his world in anything other than a neutral or unfriendly manner.

As Miles was about to step back into the shop, he felt his eyes being drawn downward to a coin the Stranger had pressed into the centre of his left palm. The man spoke again, an unlikely smile creasing his lips as he suggested the coin might be enough to put towards a small dream. Miles frowned at that statement, so the Stranger quickly added that it was a saying where he came from. As Miles feigned understanding, the other man winked solemnly at him before climbing into the van and passing the instructions on to his driver. The vagrant then watched the vehicle driving up the Crissom road for a few moments, before putting the coin into the breast pocket of his shirt and buttoning it.

And the coin hung there close to his skin, like evidence, a witness and an amulet all in one. There to be put towards a dream–albeit a small one–if he'd have it so, or to be kept as a reminder that not all coins were donated out of pity, without thought or to lessen some personal guilt. But then it was also a coin, Miles would discover several days later, perhaps worth far more than its monetary value because it had been given to him by a man whom everyone in Craiglann would soon come to know as the Murderer.

O N E

Had he been handed a golden doubloon that day, Miles couldn't have purchased even the palest of his dreams, for they'd departed the world some nine years before along with his wife and children. Indeed, these days the vagrant rarely craved the sanctity of subconscious deception, by now fully convinced that men did so only when most beset by angst, and, too, that the inherent tragedy of all dreams was not their brevity but their lingering promise. This being so, he currently gave greater stock to grim reality, and his deepest concern was raising enough money to buy the cheap bottles of wine he drank daily in an assortment of darkened lanes and corners in a bid to blur the present.

Like many others, of course, the Old Man who owned the newsagents was too busy chasing fiscal spectres to deduce why Miles viewed all dreams as lies. That same morning he'd ushered the vagrant from his shop at the first lull in his work, even as he muttered under his breath that Father Joseph Ryan–Adullam's sole administrator–should make it compulsory for each of his charges to bathe at least once a month. In his now usual manner, Miles had nodded vacuously at that remark, before making his way back to the Mission Home. There, lunch awaited–a creamed chowder and soda-bread to stave off the cold–supplied by Nan, the Father's solemnly disposed senior-housemaid. The vagrant was too early for lunch, yet no one seemed to mind. Or no one seemed to care: These days, it wasn't all that easy to determine which.

Miles was ignored by most people, and no one in Craiglann had ever asked him about his dreams, or even if he had any. He'd been one of the town drunks for eight years, by choice a loner who at times sang duets with an imaginary friend – or several, they cruelly joked within earshot, if he felt especially lonely. In those early days he'd even been a source of amusement, but that was at the start. They'd soon learned to blank him, their consciences alerting them over time that he was slowly becoming their moral responsibility. So, now, they occasionally flicked a coin at him in order to ease both his and their pain, before turning quickly away as he passed by to avoid being reminded fully of their duty.

Miles, once a person himself, always recognised the signs of discomfort as he approached, bottle in hand, melancholy tune upon his lips, his clothes often rain-sodden and reeking of stale drink, or worse.

He'd never wanted to impose upon anyone, yet it had become increasingly difficult to avoid doing so. At the start, he even offered each benefactor a whispered thanks, yet that always brought uneasy frowns and made them think they hadn't done enough. So these days, when he'd begged enough to sustain him, Miles purchased his wine and vanished down a nearby lane, there to dwell as a Cimmerian shade in almost perpetual darkness. Because it was for the best, he now felt, if everyone supposed he lacked clarity of mind during the long moments when circumstance forced those most temporary of unions.

The townspeople, however, were wrong to think as they did. Even when drunk, Miles saw more than they imagined. He knew that the town–they called it a town, but Miles believed it to be no more than a large village–had been founded in the valley upon the scar of a deserted riverbed just over a century before. Now, the River Hart weaved a higher course through the nearby hills, as yet closely circumventing the town-proper, but held there in safely meandering equipoise by a low aggregate of natural rock and unnatural brick walls. Over time, the town's periphery had also expanded, with the surrounding valley's original contours still being dug away and desecrated at every viable opportunity. The town-planners, having little in common with Nature other than that they too abhorred a vacuum, ever ensured that.

Conversely, the town-centre hadn't changed much at all. True, the Crissom Road had been upgraded many times. But the six side-streets which forked off its length were lined with the same century-old buildings–now home to newer shops and businesses–interspersed by stone houses, cracked and whitewashed, in which many generations had sprouted, seeded and died as so many deep-rooted blooms. Craiglann's later constructions–the factories and warehouses–had been consigned to the smaller roads upon the periphery; and, just beyond the river on either side of the townscape, the hills were rich and fertile. Worked to farmland in summer, harlequin fields of golden rape pressed against squares of jade-green potato drills or rectangles of rich brown rye. And behind Pheasant's Crest–a mile or so beyond St Augustine's and Adullam, in the midst of an unbroken horizon of hills thick with Christmas firs–a double-peaked mountain, Cara Mor, fought for dominion of the sky against near-perpetual banks of grey-black cumulus.

Miles stared in that direction now, oblivious to scenery he'd once deemed unblemished and pacifying. It would rain again soon, but he didn't care. One day was much as another in Craiglann, the weather rarely changed things. Life here was nutrient-deficient and stunted. Worse still, her people were decades behind the rest of the world in their attitudes and beliefs, in their dull aspirations and gently waning hopes.

Nothing moved on – except those in the Mission Home. Spurred on by either intolerant locals or the Father, everyone in Adullam was forced to eventually leave after an allotted period of grace. Unless, that was, they adhered to the mainly unspoken wishes of the majority and became a ghost.

Miles passed Mullan's Bar at a saunter, the gaudy yellow exterior bright and inviting, the dishevel of lunchtime customers making their way inside regarding him as an apparition who existed but momentarily, before vanishing in a blink. He would've liked to have gone inside and sat close to the glowing peat fire that the straight-laced Dave Mullan stacked high in the grate, summer or winter, yet that indulgence was beyond him today as the few small coins he had in his pocket would barely buy him ten cigarettes, never mind a pint of beer. Besides, it would probably be late this afternoon before he'd gathered enough money for a small bottle such as the half-empty one he now had tucked away in the inside pocket of his coat.

He walked ponderously on up the Crissom, pulling his coat tighter to his ever-thinning frame as the wind blew a splatter of rain against him. Several yards on, just across the road, was Mullan's only local competition, The Drunken Duck, owned by the scruffy Dan McGinty, whom, it was generally agreed, ran that unruly emporium like a modern Last Chance Saloon. In his youth, McGinty had apparently declared it his sole ambition to make millions and then retire to Mayo, but three decades of chequered reality in the bar-game had distilled that plan to a fleshless whim. Nowadays, it was believed he would've contented himself with abject poverty if the same were to be inflicted by some beneficent deity upon the slightly younger Mullan–himself just two decades into the bar-game, and therefore a virtual newcomer–whom McGinty openly declared his self-appointed enemy of both business and pleasure.

Miles crossed the road as a convoy of cars congested the roundabout, passed the Friendly Bank and stopped in front of Molly Devine's hairdressers, The Hair Lair. The senior-hairstylist doubled as the local fortune-teller, a heresy frowned upon by the Father as it clashed with his own creed, yet the priest always relented on that judgement come summer and gave her a great spot in his parish fete for her Tarot reading and crystal-ball gazing. By all reports, Molly's youngest daughter was getting married in a few weeks time, just shortly after her 18th birthday, and it was said the senior-hairstylist predicted great things for the couple. Their first born–a son according to the crystal, though Molly admitted it didn't always have the clarity you'd need for a correct vision–would have swimming and painting in his blood. The second child, Molly believed, would be a beautiful wee girl with brains to burn. Aye, Molly would proudly tell anyone who cared to listen, her youngest daughter was getting hitched to Con Logue's son, a great wee lad who was himself very nearly 20 years-old.

Miles stared idly in through the cutting-shop window for a few moments, then moved on, recalling how he'd thought the couple a bit young for marriage when he first heard that story. He'd seen them strolling up the mainstreet a few times, caught a whisper of their affection on a cross-breeze, seen it in their eyes. They hadn't seen him, of course, even though he'd passed within a shadow's length and even though they'd tossed him a coin or two. But they were a nice wee couple, Miles supposed, and he'd be the first to agree that maybe he was the one out of touch with modern thinking.

The vagrant walked on down the road past another burst of public services, firstly bypassing Con Logue's garage–Con-by-name and Con-by-nature, they surreptitiously called him–and then the *Garda Siochana* station and the Great Wall Chinese restaurant, the latter two buildings starkly contrasted, if, in another sense, conveniently placed. Convenient in the sense that Pete Wong would never have to take flight after a non-paying customer, and, too, in that the officious Vinny McIntyre–Craiglann's Chief Guard and peacekeeper, if much-possessed of a debatable arbitrary wisdom and an often unfathomable methodology–was always liable for a free meal if he ever tired of his or his subordinates' cooking. Which he did quite often, it was said, and more often than was perhaps comfortable for his ever-expanding waistline.

Past the Post Office – robbed but once in its long history and the suspects eventually rounded-up by Vinny and his subordinates, before being tried and sentenced by the elderly, but now retired, Judge Laverty. Past the Galloping Gourmet cafe – a busy little place the day long, now owned by the Raffertys, who'd bought it from the previous owner six months back. Past the hardware store, the clothes shop, the delicatessen – the traits and opinions of the owners of all of those establishments known equally well to Miles as those he'd just passed, despite the vagrant having had little or no conversation with any of them over the years. Then on towards the small hump-backed bridge which straddled one of the River Hart's two ancillary brooks: That same inviolable isthmus which, once travelled, fetched you into the Father's consecrated hunting-ground, with the responsibility for being there resting entirely with no one but yourself.

Having had something of a fateful history with that particular bridge, Miles crossed it quickly, then stopped behind a high hedgerow at the roadside. There, he took the bottle from the inside pocket of his coat, uncapped it and took a long swig, then another, the last he'd get until after lunch. His vision swam almost instantly, and he revelled in the fleeting bitter-sweet satisfaction. But the familiar heaviness of heart and limb found him as swiftly as he tucked the bottle away, and it bore down upon him in fathomed depths as he walked on towards Adullam.

He paid scant interest to the old farmhouse on his right-hand side of the road and felt the familiar knot in his stomach as he neared the entrance to St Augustine's, all too aware that there, within these two acres of consecrated ground, the tenets of Christendom were as firmly set as those in ancient Palestine. One man was responsible for that, and had been for as long as all thereabouts could remember – Father Joseph Ryan. Or Father Joseph, or the Father, to grant him the only other titles he'd accept, for he'd never been known to anyone as Joe – not even his mother, they said. In the Father's opinion, life was a gift from God and there to be savoured, and this he often preached in his morning and evening Masses. However–and Miles had picked this particular bit of philosophy from the Father's daily actions moreso than his sermons–you should never look as if you were enjoying that gift too much, for then God would see that you weren't taking life seriously at all.

Miles stared at the hulking chapel, the brazen white facade now tarnished by the greyness of rain, and the burnished copper cross set high atop as if to ward off more-predatory gods. The chapel had been built over a century before on the crest of the hill, but the more recent Mission Home–a mere 80 years old, and joined to the chapel by an underground tunnel–made it appear older still. The surrounding front gardens, tended carefully in summer, had fallen to the ravages of approaching winter, with the lawns now thinly concealed beneath a mat of cinnamon and umber leaves. The skeletons of silver birch trees along the perimeter, however, were dwarfed as fledglings by the Great Oak which stood in the private cemetery at the topmost end of the chapel. That particular oak had been there perhaps as long as the chapel itself; and, despite its age, still bloomed thick with sweet-scented acorns each summer.

Now, Miles noticed a man in the chapel grounds as he moved through the gate, his black uniform instantly revealing his identity. The vagrant cursed inwardly as he followed the gravelled path up towards the door of the house.

The Father was a tall man, just over six-foot, and his face was an abundance of adipose contained in extra chins and thick ruddy jowls, yet his eyes were sedulous and coldly intelligent. He stood beside a flayed alabaster statue of the Virgin, hands clasped behind his back, examining the superfluous run of water which had fawned after the hill and seeped into the ruined flower-beds to drain all too slowly into the pebbled base below. The priest sighed wearily as he observed the slaw of muddy twigs and leaves he'd have to go at some time later in the day with a trowel. The drainage had been set wrong, the pebbles too tightly packed – he'd told the gardener this many times over. But the gardener was a very busy man who moved from parish to parish at the command of the Bishop, so obviously had no time for being told his business. Thusly, once again, this winter's storm waters had shifted dormant bulbs out of the soil to lie like three-week-old onions upon the saturated bed.

More work for the Father and his trowel, Miles chuckled inwardly, glad to see he wasn't the only one having a bad day, a bad week, a bad life. And the priest with a fishing rod lying angular against the chapel wall, all ready to make for the Hart – such a shame!

The Father was sighing audibly when Miles passed slowly by, yet he turned and nodded evenly just as the vagrant reached Adullam's front door. Miles returned a small nod, recalling a time when the priest would've put his greetings into words. Still, it was a greeting of sorts, and Miles couldn't really blame the Father for having virtually given up on his inmates, most of whom had blatantly misused so many chances over the years to better their lives under his austere guidance.

'Make sure you wash before lunch, Miles.' The Father didn't even look back at the vagrant, hypnotised as he seemingly was by the cratered flowerbeds.

Miles mumbled a sullen aye, then entered Adullam, thankful for the heat. Lunch wasn't even going to be a surprise as he'd caught sight of the menu before going out this morning; and, as the Father was perhaps no longer going fishing, the meal would pass as a ritual. Wracked with those despondent thoughts, the vagrant moved upstairs to the bathroom, where he removed his coat and hung it on a nearby hook, taking care to secure the half-bottle in his inside pocket. Then he proceeded to wash the morning away, seldom looking into the mirror as he did so, his lavabo accompanied by a low whistle which sounded loud even to him in the Trappist silence of the house. Having done this–and aware he'd have to affect a speedy retreat after lunch–he pulled his damp coat back on and went downstairs to the azure-painted dining area, the walls of which were hung with several Sacred Heart and Virgin icons, their accusing eyes covering every nook and recess. Here, six tables were neatly set as if a sudden vagabond army might tumble in to dine under the baleful glares of the celestials, yet Miles had never seen any more than two in full use during his time in Adullam.

The vagrant sat at the table cradled in the sunlit recess of the largest bay-window which overlooked the entire crest of the hill. From there, he could see not only the unworked spread of Adullam's back garden, but the chapel further up the hill and the topmost boughs of the Great Oak.

Similarly, if he lifted himself up in his chair, he could see over the old farm's briar fence across the main road: No visible life there at the moment, however, her many secrets hidden still. Lacing his fingers, Miles watched Nan going about her work in the kitchen through the hatch, listening as she dismissed her temporary staff, even as she testily reassured them that she'd do the unwashed dishes herself later. Miles smiled wryly: He'd been press-ganged to assist Nan with the dishes many times and it was a bothersome chore. There was, of course, no escaping the ultimate chore–evening Mass–but he didn't want to think about that yet. He supposed it wasn't an unreasonable request, having to attend mass twice a day, once at 9-00am and again at 6-00pm, yet he was sure it was simply Father Joseph's way of showing the local community that the church still had high hopes of breaching an untapped seam of goodness in those who'd temporarily placed themselves in its care.

The sudden downward turn of the door handle caused Miles to startle. The Father appeared and the vagrant frowned darkly, before slyly tucking the wine bottle deeper into his inside pocket and screwing the cap tight to prevent precious leakage. Lunch was about to become a chore, a silent façade in which you pretended to savour your food until the enjoyment was sucked out of it. Worse again, the Father had probably contributed to the chowder and would lord over the meal as if it were a minor loaves and fishes tale. The priest nodded at Miles once more, then sat directly across from him, where he took a small notebook out from his own jacket pocket and began to read.

Miles sighed inaudibly, content with the diversion. For a few moments he concentrated upon the tablecloth, after which he stared up at the ceiling and then the icons on the wall: The icons knew too much, however, so he quickly averted his gaze. But, as if magnetically drawn, his gaze eventually alighted upon the Father.

'You're starin', Miles.' The priest's tone was neutral.

Miles nodded evenly. 'So I was, Father.' He paused momentarily. 'Sorry about that. Just wonderin' where lunch is, that's all.'

'It'll arrive, Miles. It always does. Have you ever known it not to?'

In your eight years with us, the Father may well have added. From the look upon his face, Miles could see he wanted to say that, yet the priest would never be so uncouthly direct. Miles nodded meekly, dropping his gaze. 'Shame about the bulbs, Father.' Changing the subject, or wishing to – it rarely worked.

Father Joseph paused, as if plundering his inner bible for response. 'God gives and God takes away,' he replied curtly. 'He always has his reasons for doin' so.'

'Aye, Father, he probably has good reasons for doin' everythin' he does.'

Miles bit at his lower lip, wondering why the priest always had to fire off a Parthian shot as he moved away from a subject not of his choosing. *They're gone*, Miles, he might well have added: *They're gone forever, so maybe it's time you picked yourself up and got on with it!* But then, distracted by a sudden commotion in the hallway, the vagrant pushed those bleak thoughts from his mind. He tried not to laugh as Pele, Brian and Wing-Ding entered the dining room and moved towards his table. The three men ceased chattering amongst themselves directly upon espying the Father, an enforced reverence washing over them as a tide as they each pulled out a chair and sat down.

Miles chuckled softly, recalling Wing-Ding–the youngest of Adullam's current habitués–earlier that morning with a calcified build up of porridge around the thin slice of his lips, looking as if he'd roughly applied a lineament for countless cold-sores. Miles shuddered at the thought, feigning disinterest as Brian–the oldest and broadest man there– winked at him. Father Joseph looked up from his notebook, and Miles whistled softly in a feeble attempt at disassociation.

'The construction of this Mission Home,' the priest began, 'was funded by our very generous community eighty years ago.' He stared between the men until each meekly surrendered their gaze. 'You, Peter, do you know *why* it's called Adullam?' The tall, unassuming man, surreptitiously known by the others as Pele shook his head. 'Well, it's because Adullam was the cave in which David sought *refuge* when he fled from Saul. It was there he offered *succour* to all those in debt, distressed and *discontented* with the world. The people of Craiglann had much the same idea when they built this place – Miles, are you listenin'?'

Miles removed his fork from the tangled brocade of the tablecloth, set it on the tablecloth and nodded dimly. 'Adullam,' he repeated. 'Refuge. Saul.' Splodges of rain spattered heavily against the windows and he wondered if it was worth going back down the main street this afternoon to get a peaceful drink, or whether he should take a chance and hide in or behind Adullam's sheds with the little drink he'd saved from this morning.

The Father nodded evenly. 'But now the distressed, the poor and the *discontented* don't want to come here any more. Do you know why that is, *Wing-Ding*?' The priest winced as he did each time he'd cause to say that name, and yet it was the only one which drew any response from the callow youth.

Wing-Ding shook his head. The 19 year-old youth had the look of the hunted, always glancing furtively around him as if a posse was in close pursuit. His ebon hair stood in disjointed ropes upon his head, greasy and lacklustre, and his clothes were worn, but clean, the only real sign of his poverty being the drawstring he used to secure his trousers in place of a belt, tied at the front in something of a Gordian knot. The youth had received his nickname in a nearby town because he kept talking to trees and lampposts – perhaps, Miles supposed, needing a focus for his disjointed ideas at times. He'd skipped that town about six months back when reality threatened to expose itself, seeking haven in Craiglann. But he'd insisted on keeping the nickname, and so suspicions as to his mental well-being had circulated as soon as he stepped off the bus, telling the driver who he was and where he was going. It wasn't his fault though, Miles had been told that. The name had been given to him firstly by his peers, who'd realised he wasn't so quick on the uptake, then by others who should've known better. Sadly, he'd been institutionalised through time into believing he'd no other.

'Then I'll tell you,' Father Joseph said, pedantically. 'It's because the sons of Bachus roam freely through her halls at all hours of the day and night.' The priest switched his gaze back to Miles. 'Sometimes they hum songs in drunken revelry.' He turned, drew a bead on Brian, the hammer of his gaze cocked. 'At other times, they bay for no particular reason at the moon. Isn't that right, Brian?'

Brian was about fifty-years-old, close to ten years older than Miles himself. He'd been a businessman once, a dealer in jewellery and watches. But his business, a success at first, had folded as he took to drinking the profits. Then he'd apparently lost his wife to another man, someone younger, better looking, wealthier. And so, as he'd one day informed the others in a fit of pique, without a good woman to guide him it had been a matter of time before he'd turned into a horse-dung Midas, whereby everything he touched turned to shite. Still, he didn't really care anymore, he added sombrely, and most believed him. Now, however, he suppressed a devilish grin, his right eyebrow arched high. 'Only when it's a full moon, Father.'

The priest stared at him until the laugh dissipated into a respectful frown of subservience. 'But it won't happen again?' More an order.

'No, Father. Not this month for definite. No more full moons, y'see.'

'Good.' Father Joseph's head turned at the rumble of the trolley as it skirted the mat. Nan was at the helm, her concentration fixed upon the soup tureen, the white soup dishes precariously rumbling a clatter as the wheels took each small tor of carpet. Brian's grin returned, albeit thinly.

'Good!' Father Joseph repeated. He allowed an appreciative smile to Nan, watching as she skirted the table, doling out dishes in her first methodical lap, then ladlefuls of a pinkish cream soup in the second. 'Good!'

Miles raised a hand, the other cradled his belly. 'Not too much, please, Nan,' he said, softly. 'Stomach's not the best, y'know.'

Nan's gaze was anything but sympathetic, her dearth of compassion due to her having served a ten year sentence in Adullam with no remission. She placed three plates of scone bread in the centre of the table, then moved the trolley around until it was behind Miles. She drew out a suspicion of mosaic soup with her first ladle, waiting patiently for Miles to tell her she was being ridiculous as she emptied it into his bowl. He simply shrugged, so the second ladleful was fuller, a bubbling lava of cream supporting thin parings of fish atop. Miles toyed with his spoon, before exchanging knowing looks with the other three men as Father Joseph returned to his notebook. No one smiled; it didn't look very nice. Nan, however, proudly examined her Epicurean handiwork for a few moments, before pushing her trolley off towards the kitchen, seemingly content with her small contribution to the world of the poor. Father Joseph clasped his hands in prayer and Miles instantly steepled his fingers, his eyes half-closed. The priest mumbled a quick Grace in Latin, before urging the men to begin their meal.

'You're not eatin'.' Miles was aware of the priest's voice on the periphery of his mind. He startled, aware the smell of the bisque was making him nauseous.

'Don't blame him, Father,' Wing-Ding said in a low voice, rarely speaking any other way. 'Looks like the Red Sea, what with bits of stuff floatin' in it. Too much salt, that is. Too much salt is bad for the heart, that's what they say.'

'As is too much drink.' The priest's head didn't even leave the page.

Miles winced and lowered his eyes, knowing that anyone with any sense would've seen that pointed jibe approaching from a thousand yards out. Wing-Ding, however, seemed oblivious to its meaning. He chanced a sip at the soup, his eyes haunted. 'Tastes better than it looks, lads,' he whispered. 'Give it a chance.'

Miles felt his stomach heaving. But, under the priest's cold gaze, he began nibbling at something that had once been nibbling peacefully at something else in the nearby River Hart. He tried to concentrate on getting it behind his gullet, swallowing it before a sea of stale drink threw it back up. It went down, stayed down – he wasn't sure it would. 'Mmm, not too bad,' he lied, toying with a piece of scone bread. He broke it, then slipped half into his pocket as the Father ruminated within his manual. 'Quite good actually. Hardly eat another bite.' Maybe it was too early to say that, he mused, toying with another spoonful. 'Mmm! Where would you ever find the like of it?'

'In the Red Sea,' Brian replied, dryly. 'But mmm! Quite good!' The older man took another spoonful, raised an eyebrow. 'Mmm, quite good.' Miles ignored the dark mimicry, as too did the rest. 'Went there once,' he continued, his mocking tone disappearing as he fell under the Father's sledgehammer glare.

'Where, Brian?' The Father's reply was tolerant, his book temporarily forgotten.

'The Red Sea, Father. It's thick with salt. You could float an elephant in it, though it probably wouldn't live long. Right enough, the ex-wife survived that time, more's the pity. And she floated too, but then life's strange at times.' Brian paused thoughtfully for a second. 'Y'see, everythin' in it is dead because of the salt, Father. Same as this soup.' He pouted, took another spoonful. 'Stuff floatin' in it, and all of it dead as a big, salty maggot. Mmmmm!'

'Mmm!' The Father's turn now, his own soup an interest, having finally cooled to the correct temperature. 'I personally think it's very nutritious.'

It was then, in that rare moment of tranquillity, that it happened. The bottle, not as securely tucked into his coat pocket as it should've been, fell down across Miles' lap and onto the floor as he went to scratch his ankle. Miles went to retrieve it quickly, his heart in his mouth. His head, however, was one of two heads under the table when he got there, and the Father's head wasn't very happy at all.

'You know the rules, Miles.'

Miles nodded forlornly – he did. They all did. And, while this was not an excommunicable offence, it was one punishable by labour; the scrubbing of floors or pots and pans, all under the austere scrutiny of Nan's emasculating smile.

Unless you got in there and played an ace, that was. Tomas had taught Miles that. Tomas, the only vagrant to have left Adullam and Craiglann with a semblance of dignity: Tomas, the eternal joker, Tomas the chess player, a man forever three moves ahead of the rest. Do or say something they don't expect–anything–but do or say it with confidence, the other man had often told Miles with a wink. True, the Father was intelligent, but he *could* be thwarted, anyone could.

'Near empty, Father.' Miles shook the half-full bottle. It sloshed a fiduciary slosh, over half-full. 'Just about to bin it when you came in – forgot.'

'Let's go above the table, Miles. Things always look different up there.' They did, and the Father held out a hand. 'I'll bin it then, shall I?'

17

Miles nodded, cursed inwardly and handed the bottle over. He bit hard at his lower lip before licking quickly at the top one, knowing he'd spend the afternoon in the kitchen if he didn't play that ace. 'You've seen the new neighbour then, Father?' The priest raised an eyebrow, bidding him to continue or get off the pot. 'Over in the farmhouse, he's there now. Seen him comin' into town earlier, forgot to mention it. Had a chat with him and he said one or two things.' Miles lowered his gaze to avoid the priest's visual polygraph, yet he spotted an ignition of interest in the reptilian eyes before he did so, wondered if it was enough.

'A chat, Miles?' Gnawing at the bait, eyeing the hook, cautious.

'Aye, Father. Shifty looking character. Strange eyes. Said one or two things I couldn't quite get to the bottom of, if you understand. Shifty. *Sly* as a fox.'

'There's a lot of that about, Miles.'

Miles took another spoonful of soup. 'Mmm!' he sighed. 'Beautiful, really was.' He eased himself out of his chair and stretched, catlike, the dining room door a million miles away, the off-licence at the furthest end of town a mere ten minute jaunt beyond it.

'One or two things?' The fleshy barbels sinking over the bait, hook in the mouth.

'Aye, Father, but I, ehm, have to go to the bathroom a tick. Sure, you'll all be here when I get back.'

The Father rifted softly into his hand, then dropped his napkin into his near-empty soup dish, clearly having had enough to eat. 'Aye, well, I'd appreciate it if you did come back, Miles, because you'll be helpin' in the kitchen this afternoon, as that's the price we pay for disobeyin' rules.' Miles nodded, cursed inwardly again. 'And I'll be around to make sure you've no trouble doin' so. Is that alright?'

Miles nodded again, unconvincingly. 'Aye, Father,' he replied morosely. 'Of course. I, ehm, wouldn't have it any other way.'

T W O

With the dishes and the cleaning having been completed under Nan's austere scrutiny, Miles wearily made his way up into the dormitory. Alone in the room, he lay upon his bed, mentally tracing pictures in the leaden sky through one of the skylights, even as he attempted to decipher the moans of the wind as it churned through the chapel's bell-tower before fading away in the eaves. He was fine to begin with, the first hour passing almost too easily. But then his joints and bones began to ache, and a dull heaviness in his chest made him feel as if an ardent succubus had climbed astride him, intent upon draining the life from his body. Sore now, very sore, he melted under the reproachful gaze of the clock–high upon the wall and encased behind heavily-dented wire mesh–as her secondary arm lashed out protracted moments of time. Within moments, the vertiginous dizziness struck him as a hammer blow and he fought to keep the bile from rising in his throat. The panic would have ensued almost instantly had he let it, but sometimes he could just about keep it at bay by wilfully casting his mind back through time.

***

Miles had just turned nineteen when he met up with the unhurried and rather plain Sarah McGill, she being some four months his junior. Nevertheless, even though they were both living away from home for the first time and had enrolled for the same Greek and Roman History and Philosophy degree, they'd little else in common. Due to her outwardly serious disposition, Miles even deemed Sarah a prudish and socially inept character, whereas he was, self-admittedly, outgoing and fully resigned to undertake all freedoms previously denied him by authoritarian parents. Too, as the homely Sarah was averse to drinking, smoking and partying, Miles automatically presumed she'd no true zest for life and that she'd perhaps only attended university because her rich, farm-owning father made her do so. The perceived differences between the two, therefore, were enormous in his young mind, so he dismissed Sarah as a potential friend, lover or suitor almost instantly.

More dissimilar yet were their backgrounds. Whereas Sarah–an only child–had seemingly enjoyed a stable upbringing under the protection of her widowed father, Miles was the youngest and shyest of three brothers, which caused him to be plagued by many self-confidence issues in his early youth. A late developer, slight if quite intelligent, it soon became clear to him that intellectual acumen invoked little interest in girls infatuated with only the roughest and toughest of their male peers. So, shunned, shunted and of a perpetual Omega status, he retired to the hazy perimeters of that adolescent hunting ground, thereafter only attracting girls who mirrored his lack of self-esteem. Several spited remarks from those same girls about his scrawny body and abnormal lack of confidence –which apparently relayed itself as an insurmountable mental deficiency– rapidly diminished his trust in females even further, leading Miles to conclude the fairer sex weren't too fair at all. And despite his instinct informing him that he wasn't as ugly or mentally stunted as some, that lack of esteem would track him through the ensuing years, ever-after confirming what he now supposed a fact: He wasn't worthy of love. And yet, throughout this same period, his intellectual prowess would profit from that shortfall in female adulation: Having little else to do, Miles spent all his spare time at his studies.

Still, by the time his college years came around, Miles had begun to recognise his blossoming intelligence as an asset. Too, he'd grown taller, he was involved in athletics–both sprinting and hurdling–and he was starting to notice that girls now noticed him. Despite this, a deeply-imbued lack of confidence in women wasn't easy to shake. In fact, as he aged, Miles still found it hard to believe girls could be romantically drawn to him: It was, he grimly supposed, more likely they just wanted help with course-work or an empathetic ear as they discussed all occurring elsewhere in their lives.

So, resigned to the fact that no female would ever accept him for what he was, Miles decided to opt for a single life; and yet he was also possessed, in the way of all young men, by a strong desire to attain immortal recognition of one sort or another. Somewhere in his second year, he read an article that would define his expectations, and this concerned a particular soldier who'd died during a recent Asian battle, only to have ten sobbing girls attend his funeral, each claiming to love him more than life itself. Recognising this particular form of immortality also had the added benefit of less responsibility, Miles vowed to enjoy himself from that moment onward with as many girls as possible, while mentally distancing himself from each in a bid to prioritise his sporting pursuits and studies. Moreover, he promised himself that he'd never get involved in a serious relationship until he considered the time correct.

After all, bitter experience had now taught him that girls were basically the same; and so, if or when the time came to enter a permanent relationship, he'd simply choose the one who best suited his needs at that particular time.

So, adopting this plan, Miles spent the first year of his university life dating, and juggling, as many girls as he could. His first date with Sarah, however, was something of a by-product of another date which turned sour. Having been dumped by one particular young lady who'd grown wise to his game, he felt impelled to quickly restore that dent in his ego; and, upon discovering from mutual friends that Sarah fancied him, he asked her out, thinking her an easy catch and someone he might possibly bed quite easily.

She'd definitely liked him at the start – that was obvious from Sarah's guileless attitude. But Miles would soon discover she wasn't the sort of girl he might bed on their first, second or even third date, despite the fact he'd taken her to the cinema that first night, for a walk along a scenic country vista on their second, and for a drink on the third night in the hope she'd succumb to his well-practised charms as easily as one of his regular dates. Not only that, much to his consternation, Miles had also had to listen as Sarah discussed her country upbringing, her favourite pets and various other topics which did little to stir his imagination. So, as far as he was concerned, the whole exercise had proven a waste and he didn't have much choice in the end: He unceremoniously dumped Sarah at the end of that third date, concluding that she wasn't even slightly interesting and certain he'd never go out with her again.

In fact, it wasn't until Miles saw Sarah dating a sports rival–a sprinter from a nearby university called Mark Brady, who'd bested Miles many times over at several inter-university athletics meetings–that he finally changed his mind. The reason had little to do with Sarah; after all, she was no more special than any other girl he'd dated. But to let Brady better him at something else as well – Miles could never stand for that.

So Sarah became a challenge. And, despite the fact Miles had never met a girl whom he considered worth running after, he knew he'd have to get her back, even if for the worst of all possible reasons.

***

Miles startled awake, breathing as heavily as if he'd been chased from one end of Craiglann to the other. Forcing himself to backtrack a little, he realised he'd been dreaming of how he met Sarah, only to have those precious thoughts hijacked by vicious nightmares of that final day with his wife and their twins. Abruptly, he made himself take a deep breath, then another. Above, the sky poured through the skylights as an amethyst veil, smothering the dormitory in a mantle of indigo and violet. Moments later, the vagrant slowed his breathing, hoping to alleviate the tension in his pain-wracked body. But he startled again as he caught sight of something to his front, and his breathing stalled as he noticed Pele hovering over him like a grim delusion.

'Mass, Miles,' the other man urged, pointing towards the clock. 'It's five-to-six. You'd need to hurry.'

Miles, feeling torpid and lacking the will to rise, regarded Pele for a moment. The tall man was roughly thirty-five years old, or maybe a little younger or a little older, it was hard to tell. The name was a nickname, of course, given to him by past friends who'd jokingly compared him to the world's greatest football player due to his former handiness with a ball. But, as with everyone, the past had vanished for Pele, and the visibly atrophied muscles in his legs declared you didn't need to see him kicking a ball to know his gifts had vanished too. Now his belly was bloated by drink, his skin sporular and his nose that of an insistent boxer who'd taken on most of the crowd after the bell. Miles would've felt sorry for Pele, but the drink was a vulture which fed, Promethean-like, upon all of them, and he'd really no time for others. He nodded and rose despondently under the other man's concerned gaze, one hand against the bunk as he forced himself up straight.

'I'm ready,' he replied, wearily. 'Let's go.'

Some three minutes later, the two men entered the chapel. A series of naked lights were slung low along the length of the aisle, thin stalactites brightly lit here on this mid-winter's night. The rosaceous oriel windows behind the altar were dimmed, their Cherubim, Throne and Seraphim stories muted and distorted; and, evenly spaced along the chapel walls, the twelve stations of what Tomas had once jokingly termed 'The Mythography' were depicted in shadowed bas-relief. As with most week-nights, only a handful of the townspeople were present, yet only Wing-Ding and Brian were thus far in compulsory attendance. The two men were seated near the back of the chapel, and Miles and Pele moved into the pew directly behind them. The Father entered the chapel moments later. Almost immediately, the priest stared sombrely down in the direction of his charges. As he did, Miles fiddled with a prayer-sheet, waiting until the Father relinquished his gaze. But by now the world was yawing, and, even though Miles was sitting down, the haloed stalactites above him were beginning to sway unnervingly.

'I need a drink,' he told Pele, his agitation rising. He had to get a drink, he knew, or the cold sweat upon his forehead would soon be running along his face in rivulets. Still, when he wiped at his forehead moments later, he found it wasn't overly cold or warm, that it wasn't even wet. 'You anythin' on you at all?'

Pele glanced about him, dropping his head as he met a few peeved glares, and only lifting it again when he was sure no one was watching. He waited for the Father to chant another dull prayer, then nodded. 'Some,' he whispered, as if reluctant to impart the knowledge. The epicarp of orange peel that was his face broke into a strained grin as he furtively revealed the bulge of a bottle in his inside pocket. 'A little. But you'll have to give me money. Not a lot,' he added softly, as if seeking to be fair despite his angst. 'But some.'

Miles nodded wearily. Mass was blurring, the world turbinating at speed, someone in front of them shushing the two, their anger subdued but firm. Miles took some money from his trouser pocket, quickly counted it and handed it to Pele; the other man sneaked the bottle to Miles. The transaction complete, both men then inched apart in a feeble attempt at disassociation. And Miles, wishing time on as usual, turned to impatiently wait for the Father to finish saying Mass

Less than an hour later, Miles lay again upon his bed, staring off through the skylight into the nigrescent sky as a gibbous moon broke through the clouds. After Mass, he'd hurried around to the sanctity of the back sheds and gulped down the drink, realising he'd paid a little over the odds for it in that crazy underworld of laissez-faire, but not caring. The drink–a viscous lard of rum and whiskey–had been well worth the money, despite the physical effort required to hold it down in his stomach until the gravitating effects kicked in. It had also saved him a trip into town and would hopefully tide him over until morning.

Now, he watched as splodges of rain dashed off the skylights, and he listened once more as the wind blew the drain-pipes as melancholy oboes. Across the room, some forty-feet distant, Wing-Ding lay upon his bunk in the corner. That particular corner was bare and solitary, and the younger man had chosen it on his first day in Adullam. Protected on two sides, the youth often sat there staring at the other men, his arms wrapped around his knees, a near-catatonic misanthrope who seldom let another near. Presently, though, he lay under the blankets, seemingly lost in the blackest realms of a nightmare, his face emerging from a shadow of bedclothes every now and then to suck lamely at slightly fresher air; just enough for Miles to see that, even in his slumber, he was forever evading demons. Pele and Brian's beds were empty, the two having left Adullam just after Mass. If they were smart, they'd be back before curfew, in just under an hour.

**

The two men returned shortly before 10pm, half-stewed but wise enough to recognise that Adullam was a refuge for one half of a day, an open-prison for the other. Despite the sudden onset of vertigo, Miles kept his eyes firmly shut as both clumped to the furthest side of the room, and he feigned sleep even as they feigned concern. Brian cast his boots into a corner, giggling as he did so. Miles grated his teeth, wondering if the older man would sing to the moon before he went over. From Pele there was less noise, yet loud sighs occasionally escaped his lips, signifying the exact moment each article of clothing was removed and tossed to the floor in a heap. Pele was in bed no more than five minutes later, and asleep in perhaps another two. Insensate and stupefied by drink, his snores were soon his secondary voice.

Brian undressed down to his shorts and lay upon the bed, the heat of the room apparently suffice to warm him. 'You saw the fellow who took over the farmhouse then, Miles?' the older man said moments later, his voice none too quiet. It was as if he knew, or perhaps sensed, Miles was pretending to be asleep.

Miles waited a second, bluffed a snore and threw it in amongst the others. Brian laughed almost derisively. 'I'll sing a wee tune or two, Miles. You know me well enough by now. That, or howl a fuckin' dirge.'

Miles sighed, raised his eyes to heaven. He knew Brian alright: Fond of *the language* when it suited was Brian, yet the older man never employed such slang in front of the Father, no one did. Brian seemingly hadn't a care in the world, his indocility brought on by drink and sometimes by the ripening of the moon, but moreso by those cruelties life had inflicted upon him. He was as arrogant as Tomas had been too, yet nowhere as intelligent. At times that made him very annoying – like now.

'Aye, I saw him,' Miles whispered. 'Now go to sleep.'

'You said he was mean lookin'. You said there was somethin' you didn't like about him. That right?' Brian asked. 'Sly and shifty – that what you said?'

Miles frowned, trying to remember. He couldn't recall if those had been his exact words, yet he felt they may've been. Still, he didn't want to debate the subject just then and certainly hadn't the energy to argue. 'Aye, I did.' He shrugged indifferently; his opinion didn't count, after all, for he was just a non-person speaking to another non-person in the solitude of a communal prison cell. 'Aye, shifty. Sly as a fox. Mean as hell.'

'We'd hardly want that sort around here,' Brian remarked seriously. 'Sure, there's more than enough of us in Craiglann already, eh?'

'Aye.' Miles closed his eyes, praying a dreamless sleep would find him quickly. 'We'd hardly want that.'

'You reckon he'll be frightened off then? By the rumours, I mean.'

Miles forced his eyes open. Despite his tiredness, he found himself recalling those stories he'd heard about the farmhouse being haunted. Some said an evil spirit lurked within the stones, there to remain until someone performed an as yet unspecified deed, in which case it would be released. Others said it was the ghost of a young boy, because they'd seen him running up through the fields each night to tend the wild goats which grazed there. And still others said it was an old man, for they'd seen him sitting upon the roof of one of the outhouses one night as the heavens stormed, shouting his head off and shaking his fist at the sky.

Miles smiled sadly. He would've welcomed such a distraction, but there was no ghost in the farmhouse. The young boy had neither been young nor a ghost – that had been Miles himself. Young looking? That was debatable, yet he'd always liked the way they'd stuck that bit in. Urged on by the indefatigable Tomas, Miles had brought the goats down through the farm one night to feed at the Father's flower-beds as a bit of a joke. The farm was in-between owners then, her gates wide to the world; thereafter, for obvious reasons, they always remain locked. The Father hadn't appreciated the jest, of course, but the rest of the inmates had feasted upon it for days. As for the old man, he'd been called Sean Allen. He'd climbed the gorse in the throes of drink, then somehow clambered onto an outhouse roof because he wanted to tell God exactly what he thought of Him – or so he'd told the Father when members of the local Fire Brigade finally coaxed him down.

Sad about Sean. He'd died of cirrhosis some two months afterwards, never really giving up on life until the day he just gave up. Miles recalled that particular morning well, for he'd been awoken by the stench of recently eviscerated bowels. He'd stared at the dead man for several moments, before dressing hurriedly and leaving Adullam to go for his usual walk in town, far angrier that day than usual, though he didn't know why as Sean hadn't been anyone special. When Miles returned later that afternoon, Sean's bed had been freshly made, his locker cleared and the room saturated in air freshener – Sean might never have been there at all. Shame about Sean, because he'd stayed in Adullam for two years before moving straight in to the graveyard further up the Crest. Pity about Sean, as Miles would've liked to have liked him, had it been safe enough to do so.

Miles quickly returned his thoughts to Brian's question. The older man may well have asked if it'd be long before Adullam's inmates scared the new owner away. Miles could see the problem. In principle, it had been a fine idea to build Adullam next door to the chapel so the resident priest could keep an eye upon his charges. Practically, however, that umbilical attachment imposed heavily upon the local farming community. After all, running a farm meant filching an undisturbed five or six hours of sleep a night before arising at cock-crow. Now, not only would any potential owner of that farm have roosters to awaken them at dawn, they'd have the occasional drunken werewolf to keep them on their toes throughout the night. No, Miles thought wryly, you could hardly blame the new owner if he decided to leave as soon as that particular problem made itself apparent.

'Aye, he'll not be stoppin' long,' Miles mumbled, eventually. 'You, ehm – there much happenin' in the town tonight?' He'd been going to ask what Brian had been doing tonight, but he knew Brian's routine as well as Brian knew his.

'Not much – too wet. Anyway, most people are savin' their money for Christmas, and then this weddin's comin' up. Molly what's-her-face's daughter is marryin' the wee lad she started goin' out with last year when she fell out with that other fellah she was goin' with – or I think that's the gist of it. You know the lot I'm on about?'

'Aye.'

Miles, very tired now, hadn't heard what Brian had said, but he felt that saying aye was the correct thing to do. After all, he'd a half-chance of being right.

'Then I tried to get into Mullan's, but Big Sean wouldn't let me in. He said I was too noisy, but, sure, you lot have heard me noisier.'

'Aye,' Miles sighed. He'd definitely heard that.

'But he said I was, so I wasn't for arguin',' Brian grinned, his teeth reflecting in the waning moonlight. 'Didn't like me singin' my songs.'

'I wonder why,' Miles muttered under his breath.

Brian turned onto his side, dragging the blanket up around him. 'Me too,' he laughed. Within moments he was sleeping, his snore a torturous rasp.

The snoring kept Miles awake for an hour afterwards. Though, when the vagrant finally fell asleep, he was tortured by indistinct flashes of darkness, smoke and fire. The same nightmares, always the same, and he'd once ironically believed they might ease somewhat over time. But they were never going to go away, he knew that now, and these days he considered that only just and fitting.

***

The Father was going fishing. He explained that to Nan in the hallway– loudly, so everyone could hear–and his voice dutifully rounded the stairs and carried that message up into the dormitory. Half-awake, Miles gazed at Pele, Wing-Ding and Brian in turn, and each seemed equally puzzled as they all knew it was time for Mass. Moments later, Brian shrugged and grinned broadly.

'What's happenin'?' Wing-Ding asked fearfully, his eyes dulling over. In his mind, the Father–whom Wing-Ding now considered his last hope at salvation–had obviously given up and was leaving to make a better life elsewhere. As a result, the place would fall to wreck and ruin, and they'd all die unnaturally horrible deaths.

Yawning loudly, Miles watched neutrally as the youth nervously searched the floor around his bed for his clothes. But, after a small time, he willed Wing-Ding to relative calm simply by raising a palm. Miles then rose from his bunk, dressed quickly and made his way to the door. 'You wait there. I'll go see.'

Brian closed his eyes and turned upon his side. 'We'll be here when you get back, Miles. So make sure and take your bloody time!'

Nan was standing there as the front door closed behind the Father. Miles halted midway down the stairs in case he'd misheard, waiting for the Father to reappear and say it was all a mistake. Presently, the vagrant stepped down to meet the housekeeper. Upon seeing him, she merely fixed him with an almost cat-like stare, before walking sternly off towards the kitchen area.

'No Mass today?' Miles chanced hopefully.

'Leak in the chapel roof,' Nan called back in telegram. Not one given to surplus chatter, she often time-saved. 'No Mass. It'll be fixed. Leak.' Stop, she might've added, though she didn't.

Miles made his way back upstairs. Wing-Ding was the only one awake and he was more anxious than usual. The youth's hair stood in thinly-tangled ropes, giving him the look of one who'd been half-electrocuted before the fuse had gone.

'The roof of the chapel,' Miles explained, wanting to go telegram himself, but holding back as Wing-Ding could transubstantiate from liquid subservience to iced stubbornness in seconds. Besides, words easily spoken seemed to quell him, and Miles didn't usually find that such an effort. 'It leaked, so there's no Mass today.'

Wing-Ding still looked worried, as if he believed they'd soon be repairing the chapel roof with stones dug fresh from the supporting walls as he sat watching, helmet-less, in the pews.

'You can go back to sleep again…' Miles paused, thinking maybe he should add a clause, just in case the Father returned and blamed him personally for this lethargic mutiny. 'Well, I suppose,' he added lamely. 'Because no one said any different.' He shrugged and turned towards the dormitory door.

Wing-Ding stiffened. 'You aren't goin' back to bed, then?'

Miles half-turned and attempted a reassuring smile. 'No, I'm not really tired. You get yourself some rest. Everythin' should be fine.'

Miles went to the bathroom. Feeling a little braver today, he dared his stare to linger on the man in the mirror as he washed and shaved. The eyes, once bright and iridescent, were now flecked with tinges of flint – at least, he saw them there. Filled with sorrow too–that was a definite fact –even though he tried to conceal that from the world. The skin on his face also had little flesh to prop it and sagged beneath his cheekbones where once it had been tighter, yet Miles consoled himself that it was probably nowhere as bad as the Father's.

He sighed heavily as he dried himself, wondering just how much of himself he left in that mirror each time he walked away. Soon after, he went downstairs and ate breakfast, feeling slightly better for the fullness in his stomach, after which he sat around for a time in the dining room, his thoughts adrift. The clattering of pots and pans resounding from deep in the kitchen was comforting only because he wasn't the one creating that noise. He smoked two cigarettes and rifled through the daily paper, before leaving the house and walking down towards the bridge. The day was chill and he drew his coat closer, the sky scumbling red to orange around a slowly awakening sun, a smog of weak cumulus seemingly two towns distant.

The Father hated missing Mass, Miles knew, for he too had his own routine and would have felt disturbed by change. Everyone of years did, Miles had once been told, and now he knew that to be true, for familiarity brought succour as well as breeding contempt. He paused on the bridge, shivering as he stared into the loquacious brook as the cold grey waters stuttered to her banks. The water was now six, maybe seven feet deep in places and ran at a pace, moreso this winter. Miles found himself thinking back to the time he'd jumped from there in a fit of despair, amazed now at the ease with which he'd done so. He'd been lying on his sodden bed when he had heard the voice, a lack of drink having already turned the shadowed dormitory around him into a surreal world inhabited by creeping, stalking nightmares. The words had come from nowhere, and eased their way too simply into his brain: *Do it, Miles - come to us and we'll be waiting! Free yourself from your pain, because you've borne it now for four years and God has no right to ask any more. Come to us, we're waiting!*

Miles would never recall exactly how he reached the bridge that day, yet it always struck him that he'd jumped over the low wall just as the Father's car was coming down the Crest. The vagrant had been standing there one moment, and in the next he'd jumped straight into the coagulated mud, the stream at low ebb, maybe three-feet deep where he landed. Back in Adullam, he'd bathed and changed into some warm clothes, before going downstairs and pulling a seat close to the sitting room fire. 'I fell, Father Joseph,' he'd explained as the priest sat down silently at his side. 'It was an accident and I fell in, swear.'

The Father had frowned heavily. 'I'm goin' to believe you, Miles– *this* time–because it's my job to have faith and give all men a chance. Sayin' that, I can't treat it as an *accident* if it happens again.' The priest's tone softened as Miles nodded his understanding. 'I know you've had a hard time in the world, and I won't pretend to know the level of your sufferin', as it's somethin' you've never fully shared with me. But I *do* care what happens to you. And, even if you *think* I apply the law around here a little harshly at times, that's my job, and *someone* has to do it, otherwise there'd be no *discipline*, and both you and the others would suspect nobody *cared* about you at all.'

Miles hadn't actually needed the priest's penchant for emphasis to help him understand the Father's sincerity that day: After all, the priest had given him the benefit of the doubt, when he could've simply thrown him out onto the street or passed the buck by recommending psychiatric care. Moreover, the Father had also taken Miles into Adullam initially without fully pressing him for his reasons for being there, and that, too, required a certain amount of trust. Despite this, Miles had always felt that nobody, including the priest, would ever cauterise the ceaseless stigmata in his now near-empty heart.

Miles shunted that painful memory aside and continued down the Crissom towards the town, the route diurnal, his feet attuned to every ridge and pothole. Overhead, a shadow of rooks broke from the rooftops and made for the trees on the brook's embankment as Hugh Rafferty rolled up the iron shuttering outside the *Galloping Gourmet* café, now bright with graffiti from the previous night. Across the road, the Great Wall restaurant was still closed, but in the Garda station shadows flitted against the frosted windows, the pale orange light in the backdrop casting wanly out onto the scatter of take-away boxes now littering the forecourt. Miles laughed uneasily at the thought of how life in Craiglann never seemed to change, even as he fumbled a jangle of coins around in his pocket. He suddenly wondered if he'd enough left from his barter with Pele last night to buy a half bottle, and who'd be the first person today to throw him a coin.

A double stream of cars cut through the puddles on the uneven road and the vagrant stepped close to the wall of a nearby garage, yet was unable to completely avoid the splash. Shaking droplets of dirty water off his trousers, he cursed loudly. The rain had fallen heavily in the night and the town's drainage system clearly refused to deal with the overload, leaving the place a mire which would take the day to dry out. Despondently, Miles moved on through the slowly awakening town towards the off-licence, turning the coins out from his pocket as he did so and wincing as he realised his tally was a little short of the price of a half-bottle. He licked at anxious lips, before peering furtively in through the off-licence window and noticing young Michael on the till. Miles exhaled in relief, then went in through the door. The boy lifted his head from a newspaper.

'A half bottle,' Miles told him dolefully, re-counting the coins as if they might suddenly multiply. 'One half, that's the lot.'

Big Michael suddenly appeared around the inner door to the house and Miles cursed under his breath. The older man was drying his hands on a tea-towel, yet the look upon his face said that he'd soon be washing them again – of Miles.

'Miles.' The greeting was as uncompromising as the stare.

'Mr Doherty.' Miles dropped his head. 'Sir.'

'A half bottle is it, Miles?' the older man asked neutrally. He ushered the wee lad from the shop into the house, then set the tea-towel on the counter between himself and the vagrant, a small but definitive barrier.

'Aye,' Miles replied uneasily, moving the coins from one hand to the other. He screwed his face as if debating calculus. 'Might be a wee bit short.'

Big Michael stared down into the vagrant's shaking hands. 'Or more.'

'Aye, Mr Doherty, maybe.'

The older man sighed audibly, lifted a bottle from the shelf and took the money out of the vagrant's hand. 'It's comin' to an end, Miles,' he warned with a stern wag of an index finger. 'All of this shite, it's comin' to an end! And soon, mind, soon.'

Miles nodded gratefully, took the bottle and turned towards the door. 'They say the world's comin' to an end,' he replied, softly.

'Only for some of us, Miles. Only for some of us.'

'For some of us, aye,' Miles agreed solemnly, realising the man had probably never said a truer word. He nodded his thanks, left the shop and took to the lane behind the bus shelter, ignoring the swarm of freshly scrubbed faces in the jumbled queues. He sat in the shadows on a dustbin, no longer disturbed by the cracks of his crepitating bones, and sipped from his bottle until he grew oblivious to the morning chill. When he was sufficiently warmed and temporarily immunised against both his own thoughts and the day, he got up to watch yet another bus leaving the station. Bright yellow-white lights above the seats, suitcases and bags in the racks; off to the office, to university, to school, to live.

Miles would've envied them had he the time. But he was far too busy. He had to walk up and down the Crissom, to vicariously enter into– yet remain tightly upon the periphery of–a host of other lives to ensure he didn't have to closely examine his own.

So, several minutes later, he moved out of the lane, out of the depot, and took to the road again, not realising then, in that early morning hour, that this day was going to be the start of something less than ordinary occurring within his own life. Nor too did he know that, in the course of the coming week, quite a few of those who regularly pointed out his seemingly endless personal faults, would very soon have that unwanted favour returned.

T H R E E

The rain came on just after 10-00am, and Miles spent the rest of the morning in Mullan's, even though it wasn't strictly open for another hour. Tucked away in a dim corner, he sat alone, sipping at a pint, the setting evocative of days when the drink had merely authorized time with others and he'd been able to test his every trouble through laughter. In more recent years, of course, Miles had begun to feel like Tantalus, son of Zeus, standing in waters which ever-receded as he neared. The difference was slight: Miles could always scrounge a drink nowadays, yet it only filled the void in his bloodstream, never the void in his mind.

Molly Devine and a few of her apprentices came in for lunch just after 12-00am, their break, as always, manoeuvred about a surge or dearth of appointments. Molly, viewed as a good woman in the main, had suffered the hardship of seeing her husband run off with a younger girl a few years before – a girl from her salon, sadly enough. Whispers suggested he'd headed to Cavan, taking half their property and most of her savings. She'd motored on with the business, though, prim and stalwart despite her pain. And she'd kept at the cards and the crystal-ball gazing; just to pass the time, she insisted, yet many felt she still hoped to foresee her spouse's eventual return. A good woman, that was how people viewed Molly, as she'd relay only the nicest parts of her sibylline prophecies–they were 'a cert' to happen, you just had to keep your chin up and wait–and she'd skirt around the bad stuff by claiming that nothing was written in stone and that everyone had the power to alter their destiny. If they really wanted to, that was; because you had to want to, since God only helped those who helped themselves.

She was as beautiful as Aphrodite, too, Miles had always thought that, and her all afluster these days as her youngest daughter was getting hitched shortly after her 18th birthday. Still, Molly didn't seem worried that the prospective bride was just a teenager–Miles surmised this from her breezy chatter–yet he supposed that was because she spent so much time with her apprentices and her own youth remained. Just then, Mullan wordlessly set a pint in front of the vagrant. Confused because he hadn't paid for it, Miles stared about the bar, realising he was now momentarily visible to someone. Seconds later, Molly nodded primly in his direction, but only Miles noticed that. He nodded back, but no one–maybe not even Molly–noted his acknowledgement.

She talked on.

The lad–wee Eddie Logue–was good to her Marie, Molly smiled, and that was why she'd agreed to the wedding. Always buying her stuff, never leaving her side, you'd swear the two were joined at the hip. Last night, sure, Marie hadn't returned home; but then, Molly admitted ruefully, even though she didn't encourage *that* kind of thing, well, times had changed, hadn't they? And the girls, some of them red-faced, giggled at her enlightened approach as they tucked into lunch, most only fresh from school themselves.

No, things definitely weren't the way they'd been in her day, Molly repeated, so you had to try *that* stuff, didn't you, because she wished she had. She wished a whole lot of things now, she added wistfully, like maybe having known that bastard–God forgive her!–before he'd laid a finger on her. Her sixteen and thinking herself a queen because he'd given her a lift home in his dad's flashy car – Molly up-turned her eyes and shook her head as if unable to credit her memory, yet her pale smile remained. And him turning the heating up, before suggesting she could take her top off if she was too warm, and he'd help her if she liked. Christ, had she been naive or what?!

The girls laughed a chorus and Molly joined in. Miles would've liked to have laughed too, but that wouldn't have been right. People could tolerate you sitting next to them, and they'd even put up with the smell, the occasional twitch or the fact you sometimes glared into the fire as if it had done you a personal wrong. But smiling was overstepping the mark. So, the vagrant quelled a grin as Molly talked on about how she'd advised Marie to postpone the wedding until June or July, the more traditional months. But her Marie was–and here, Molly upturned her eyes again–Aquarius with Taurus in the ascendancy, y'see, and Taureans were stubborn and pig-headed on their worst days; traits, no doubt, she'd picked up from her father. Saying that, Marie was dogmatic and determined, too, and those gifts she'd definitely claimed from her mum. Still, Molly said she had to be thankful for small mercies: After all, Marie had called off her engagement to that other toe-rag she'd been dating, and he hadn't a patch on Eddie Logue. And a year of going out with Eddie was definitely enough, Molly concluded sagely, as she'd seen a great future for them in the cards, so it had to be true, hadn't it? And the girls clucked their agreement, for they knew as well as anyone that Molly was good at the cards, so it had to be true, of course it had.

Miles listed slightly then; only slightly, but enough for Mullan to grant him a reproachful scowl. Instantly, the vagrant forced himself board-straight until the barman's glare diminished. Moments later, Vinny McIntyre, Craiglann's Chief Guard, entered the bar, his appearance inspiring muted chat amongst Molly and the girls, little of it in any way good. Although on duty, Vinny had just popped in for his lunch. As he approached the bar, he diligently scoured the room, nodding firstly to Molly and then Old Jack at the end of the bar–both of whom nodded curtly back–before removing his heavy blue Garda coat, now fleshed thick with rain, and hanging it under the counter to allow the droplets to pool upon the cobbles. As he took off his cap, shook it and lightly deposited it upon the counter, Vinny turned his attention to Mullan: It was raining a bucketful, the Guard declared, and unlikely to get better, too, the whole country was in for one hell of a winter, he was sure of it! The Chief Guard then eyed the scotch and the half of black that Mullan set in front of him as he scanned the menu, undecided. Then he asked for his usual, and Mullan relayed the order to one of his kitchen staff.

As the barman did so, Miles smiled gently: Mullan often worked sixteen hours a day and knew as much as any tapster about people and their foibles. He'd known Vinny would order his usual, yet he'd known not to pre-empt the Guard as he'd most likely go awkward and order something different. Aye, Mullan knew enough to keep the money rolling in, Miles supposed, and that was a gift the feckless Dan McGinty over in the Drunken Duck had perhaps always envied.

New man in town, Vinny said, sipping at the black and then looking quickly around him – him on duty, after all. As Mullan nodded evenly and said he'd heard, Vinny added that nobody had seen the stranger yet, but then, if the fellow was wise, sure, he'd keep himself to himself, because everyone knew everything about everyone in this God-forsaken place, didn't they? And, sure, you couldn't pick your nose but the scandal of it was over Craiglann!

Again, Mullan nodded agreeably, picking out the nuggets in Vinny's every sentiment, even as he awarded him an appeasing lunch. As he watched this, Miles felt his stomach rumbling and realised he'd have to leave soon in order to make it back to Adullam for his own. He gulped back his drink, trying to concentrate upon what Vinny was saying - the stranger, no one had seen him since his arrival.

Miles smiled wryly: I've seen him, he wanted to say. Had a chat with him a few days back, or maybe it was a week ago, or yesterday, I can't recall. Remember what he looked like though - tall and sly as a fox. Or, at least, that's what I told Brian so he wouldn't howl at the moon. And I think he was mean and shifty – or that's what I recall saying to either Brian or the Father. Or did one of them actually say that to me?

The world yawed familiarly. An alarm bell went off in Miles' head, a sensor: A Mullan-sensor. The vagrant rose carefully, pulled his coat on and left under both the barman's and Vinny's austere glares. His own lunch came and went shortly thereafter– braised beef, just as the majuscule script upon the menu had promised. And, with the Father absent, the meal passed off unceremoniously. But, shortly afterwards, the priest returned and lunch was quickly forgotten.

***

The fish had obviously been hiding, clinging frigidly to the under-surfaces of rocks with hooks and sucker cups, plainly having no wish to play an allegorical role alongside some scone bread. Still, if an empty knapsack had been the Father's only problem, Miles supposed he'd have graciously accepted his lot. But from the way the priest brusquely entered Adullam and curtly asked Nan to join him in his office, he'd obviously other concerns. Feeling it was a matter of time before these became widely known, Miles went up to the dormitory and quickly revealed his fears to the other three men. And, just seconds after he'd finished, his instincts proved correct, for the Father stood centrally in the opened doorway, with Nan close behind. All four men knew what was coming: A holy shake-down had been ordained, no doubt qualified by some loosely-scribed passage of the Good Book. Still, this was but one of the many sporadic searches the priest carried out to keep his charges on their toes. The vagrants were, of course, allowed the usual few moments to re-order their affairs, yet this was an irrational courtesy in a sense, as any such affairs would involve the hasty secretion of alcohol. If the Father and Nan really wanted to play fair, Miles mused, they should've at least turned their backs and counted to ten.

Miles so wanted to blame the priest's unsuccessful fishing trip for this unnecessary trespass. But Brian, now staring resentfully at Miles, clearly believed him responsible. Coming reeling into the chapel the way he'd done the previous evening, giggling at nothing throughout Mass, sure, Miles must've known the Father had seen him and Pele playing shop in the pews. But the Father wasn't for naming names, yet an accusation was tacitly expressed by his gaze, which lingered upon Miles a second longer than anyone else. Aye, the vagrant mused as he dropped his head, it was as plain as the big red nose on your face to all hereabouts precisely who was to blame for this situation.

Nan flicked a few switches to life and light splashed instantly into even the deepest corners where only a Stygian darkness once dared thrive. Standing close to the bottom of his bed, Wing-Ding shifted from foot to foot, even as the others stood impassively beside their own beds, experience having taught them all that this was the best thing to do. The Father nodded to signify he was ready, then went to Miles' bed, where he ran a sweeping hand firstly beneath the blankets, then through the locker and under the frame, before shaking out his extra boots – though not too near, the smell repellent. The next bed, Pele's bed, had the mattress lifted –the seams checked for signs of tampering, for removed stuffing, for its replacement–then the pillowcases out-turned. Brian's section of the dormitory, on the other hand, always took a little more scrutiny as the Father knew the vulpine Brian was full of *the craft*. The Father, however, wasn't so slow himself, and Brian wasn't the first Brian to have boarded in Adullam.

The locker, the bed, the seldom-used washbasin nearby – these the priest quickly scrutinised, yet all were much too obvious for a man with Brian's talent. The Father's eyes worked the area hard, then turned to meet Brian's wry gaze, firm-set above a lycanthropic smile. The priest held it momentarily, waiting for it to provide some clue, which it did after a while: He then turned to the radiator on the wall, a heaven-sent afflatus there as a spark in his eyes. He took a glance down the back, certain he'd find what he was looking for. But nothing. Now, as the priest rose, Brian's eyes were diamond-cut, and his raised eyebrow silently asked: What are you looking down behind there for, Father?

Lips tight again, yet taking it very well if you didn't know him, the priest strode towards the door, turned back again. 'The hole in the chapel roof has been temporarily fixed,' he declared sternly. 'Tomorrow mornin', everythin' will be as it should be.' He left then in a subdued fit of pique, all fish, big and small, having shoaled away from his rod that day. Nan flicked off a few of the lights, as if she too was happy to see only as much of the dormitory as she had to, before following him dutifully downstairs.

With the Father gone, the men relaxed as much as it was possible for those four to do. Aware that Brian's eyes were still trained coldly upon him, Miles blanked the other man and lay upon his bed, a sudden ennui corrupting him to laziness. After a time he lit a cigarette, though didn't offer one to anyone else: You never did that either, for, being a separate entity, nobody expected it. He looked up amidst the stuccoed cornices and mouldings, blew a tinged pall of smoke in that direction, then a few smoke-rings. When the smog had cleared, his eyes sought out something new in the shadows – a spider, a shadow, anything. Discovering nothing, he stared up through the skylights as rips of black cumulus bloated the sky and tiny missiles of rain struck the glass before racing noisily into the outside drains. Some minutes later, Brian got up from his bed and crept softly into the hallway. When the older man finally ascertained they were alone, he returned and drew the door back from the wall, then removed a bottle from behind it. He grinned victoriously and almost spitefully at Miles, before uncorking the bottle and draining its contents in one go. Wordlessly, he then secreted the empty bottle behind the door again, before lying back down upon his bed.

Miles stared at the door, seeing the empty bottle clearly in his mind. Grating his teeth, he was tempted to curse both Brian and God for that unfairness, but he fought down his anger. He noticed Wing-Ding had sought the solitary retreat of his corner and was, once again, clinging limpet-like to his bed. Pele had begun walking in an agitated scuttle up and down the room, his head held low as he regarded his Judas legs, his body a joggle of bones.

Miles frowned heavily, needing a drink. He wondered whether he should go into town now–which meant braving the rain–or wait patiently until after Mass. He should stay, he knew, for then the little money he had left would last him the night. But staying there meant listening to Brian's rambling, or watching Wing-Ding rocking upon his bed and Pele scrutinising his feet. Miles could, of course, distract himself by seeing how many times he could walk the length of the dormitory, thereby staving off his own compulsion. Besides, if he managed today, he'd manage tomorrow and the day after, then maybe forever. Saying that, forever was a long time, if you thought about it – maybe the longest time of all.

As was, at all times, an hour.

He was halfway downstairs when he noticed the local woman known as Mrs Gorman standing in the hall beside the Father, her handbag clutched to her waist with liver-spotted hands, her face cast in appropriate subservience. Frowning deeply, she stooped in doleful reverence as if relaying a beatitude to the Stations. The Father, equally confessional, stooped to meet her, yet the words between them were paled by the drone of the vacuum cleaner in the background. Miles moved past them into the sitting room. There, he grabbed at the remote control, sat down and flicked the television to life. He muted it as soon as the vacuum engine died, however, straining to listen into the conversation.

'She's missin', since late last night, and it's now near four in the afternoon,' the old woman said contritely. 'And her supposed to be getting' married soon, too. What d'you think happened to her, Father?'

'She'll be *fine*, Mrs Gorman. Sure, it's only been a night.' The priest's voice was smooth with trained compassion. 'She might've taken a *bus* out of town after a *tiff* with her fiancée. She could be in a *friend's* house. She...'

'Aye, but her mother is worried out of her mind,' the old woman interrupted softly. 'She hasn't spoken to her daughter in twenty-four hours, and the wee lad said she didn't stay with him last night. Apparently, they'd both been in the Drunken Duck, then he'd left her off at the traffic lights before headin' on home himself.'

Miles, fidgeting the remote to smoothness, took a brief inventory of the details. He'd been a smart man in his day. Back when he was a man, that was. Back in the old days, when the world turned smoothly within the hands of Atlas and Miles Kivlehan clung tightly to the handrail, content to watch life drift by. He'd taken A-Levels in Physics, History and English, then completed both a Degree and a Masters in Greek and Roman History and Philosophy. A smart man, Miles had even taught part-time in his local university for four years. So what do you do, Miles? they'd ask. And casually, proudly, he'd tell them. The looks of admiration would follow, the eyes gathering respect deep in their centres: Must know a thing or two – that acknowledging nod said it all. A watered-down Aristotle, Socrates or Plato, with the philosophies of ancients upon his lips, the precepts of wiser men at his recall – how could you not like him, trust him, respect him? Because people like him deserved respect, as nothing could break them, nothing at all.

Aye, Miles had considered himself intelligent once, yet he didn't anymore. Still, to his surprise, this situation caught him up temporarily. Molly Devine's youngest daughter, he concluded, assembling the clues. Missing, out all Tuesday night, and Molly had thought she was staying at wee Eddie's house. The vagrant shrugged, thinking it no big deal. Instead, he flicked the television's volume higher, even as he mentally staved off an angry rumbling in his stomach. He didn't recall falling asleep then, yet when he startled awake he noticed Wing-Ding in the armchair opposite, reaching furtively over to free the remote from his grasp. Miles pulled it back sharply. 'Give me that – I'm watchin' that!'

'You were sleepin'!' It was almost an accusation, but timorously applied. Somewhat strange coming from the normally placid Wing-Ding.

'No I wasn't!' Miles was hungry now, the acid in his stomach dissolving the lining. He flicked the volume up, feigning a sudden interest in a cookery show until the youth conceded all rights with a shrug. As Miles changed channels, however, a sudden memory stirred, detached and invoked by no recognisable stimuli. He recalled waking the previous night–yet another nightmare wrenching him from his slumber–

and sitting bolt upright in a bid to ease his thoughts in another direction. It had been raining heavily and he'd looked around and noticed Wing-Ding wasn't in his bed, but he'd supposed the youth was downstairs or in the bathroom. Still, Miles had remained awake for the best part of an hour after that and the youth hadn't returned.

'You got out of bed last night,' Miles said, accusingly. 'You were away for ages. Where did you go to?'

The youth shrugged and flicked through a newspaper, obviously unhappy about conceding the remote.

'Go out, did you?' Miles persisted, knowing that there was no way he could've done so, as Adullam's doors were locked strictly at 10-00pm, and the only outdoor fire-escape was in full view of the Father's bedroom window.

Wing-Ding didn't reply, so Miles sighed heavily and lightly tossed the remote into the youth's lap; it was only a mild concession after all.

Wing-Ding grinned broadly and discarded the paper. He grabbed the remote, flicked a different channel into life, then another. 'I did go out,' he confirmed, timidly. 'And I stayed out for a while, too.'

Miles raised a very sceptical eyebrow. 'And how'd you do that?'

'I crawled out the kitchen window.'

'And no one saw you?' Wing-Ding shook his head and smiled wanly, as if the posse had been thrown temporarily off the scent. Miles bit at his lip. 'You go anywhere in particular?'

Wing-Ding shrugged. 'Not really. But I saw him. From the roof.'

'Saw who?' Miles raised an eyebrow as he recalled the rain thumping off the skylight windows the previous night, audible even above the howling of the wind. 'And from what bloody roof? What are you goin' on about?'

'The neighbour. The *stranger* in the farmhouse. Out at the river. I saw him last night from the roof of our back sheds.'

'What the hell are you talkin' about, Wing-Ding?'

'He was out last night beside the river,' Wing-Ding said softly, his eyes wide and innocent. 'He seemed to be puttin' somethin' *into* the water – I don't know what. He had his back to me, y'see. I sat on the roof and watched him.'

'You sat on the roof in the rain?' Miles glared sourly at the encumbrance that was Wing-Ding and wished a double-portion of dinner on him. The callow youth nodded. 'What was he doin'?'

Wing-Ding shrugged. 'Fishin,' maybe, though I didn't see a line. Bendin' over, puttin' somethin' *into* the water, watchin' it sink. Somethin' *big*. I saw him.'

Momentarily distracted, Miles cocked an ear as he heard the Father talking loudly to Nan in the hall: The priest was saying he'd be back soon, that she should go ahead with dinner if he wasn't, and that he'd get himself a sandwich later. Miles sighed, wanting to find out more from Wing-Ding, but feeling he had to move about as his stomach was killing him. He got up and went upstairs to wash himself, hoping to kill the remaining time before dinner.

At 5-00pm, Brian and Pele returned to Adullam, having met on the Crissom. As they entered the dining room, Brian smiled a rosy-cheeked contentment. 'He won't be joinin' us, the Father. There's a problem in town.' He sat at the table, grinning as Nan entered the room, pushing the bain-marie to her front. 'I'll be sayin' grace,' he said, winking at the housekeeper. 'Seein' as how the Father isn't here.' Nan sighed tolerantly, and Brian clasped his hands to his front. 'For what we are about to receive,' he said, piously, 'we shall very soon grieve. Amen.'

Pele and Wing-Ding suppressed a grin as a scowling Nan moved speedily around the table, doling out ladlefuls of stew. Miles smiled thinly, having heard the thwarted blessing before. Her work complete, the housekeeper then moved off into the kitchen, seemingly glad to be getting out of the way.

'Bit of a commotion in the old metropolis,' Brian said, after testing the stew and giving the thumb to Nan through the hatch. 'Molly Devine, she...'

'Her daughter,' Miles cut in, abruptly. 'She's missin' since last night. *We know*.'

Brian looked at him, aggrieved. 'Word travels fast,' he snapped, blowing upon his spoon. 'But the wee girl's probably just got a touch of weddin' nerves.' He winked at Wing-Ding and the youth smiled uncertainly. 'That's what I'd do if it was me,' he snorted loudly. 'Not natural, marriage – wantin' to throw all your baby-cement in the one mixer, not right. Take it from me, I've worn the strait-jacket there.' As he spoke, Miles shook his head firmly to signify his disagreement. 'What?' the older man rasped after a moment.

'She didn't run off,' Miles frowned, not knowing know why he'd said that, but somehow unable to stop himself. 'Why would she bloody do that?'

'Because she's wiser than her years, that's why.' Abrasive, getting tucked into his stew.

Miles shook his head forcefully once more. He just felt like annoying someone. That it happened to be Brian was coincidental; it could've been anyone.

'She might've run away, Miles,' Wing-Ding agreed, innocently. 'I did. Once.' He shrugged, dropped his head. 'I was told not to come back. Ever.'

They all regarded the youth neutrally, not too used to his input. He often reminded Miles of Echo, who'd wasted away to a voice and was thereafter doomed to repeat the words of others. Miles shrugged, allowing the youth his say, even if he didn't actually agree. Across the table, Pele shrugged undecidedly too, and Brian seemed set to render yet another strong opinion when there was a commotion in the hall. The front door opened and a brisk wind blew hollowed notes from the wooden chimes above the opening. Miles shivered, spoon heavy in his hand as he waited to see who'd fill the doorframe. He knew there was a good chance the Father had returned, but he hoped it might be someone else.

His prayer was half-answered. The Father entered the dining area, shaking the rain from his coat. Close behind, physically wider and therefore possessed of a greater coat, was Vinny McIntyre. The Guard removed his cap and the ragged collection at the table regarded the officer uncertainly, their meal temporarily forgotten.

Vinny was a big man. Towering above them, Miles could tell from the breadth of his shoulders that he'd laboured hard in his early years before securing the cushy position now his own. It was easy to picture him, axe in hand, chopping down Christmas firs in the hills which overlooked the town, or working his way up and down potato drills, back hunched, gathering spuds on a cold morning. Or boxing: His nose, ridged and slightly off centre, told tales of a time when reason died and brutality was all that remained. The eyes, of course, said more. Even here, cap in hand and feigning piety in this extension of the house of God, his eyes told you he was used to winning battles, verbal, physical and mental. He was bigger than the scrawnier men who habituated Adullam, bigger and scarier. No one regarded him for long, except Brian, who might once have been nearly as big.

The Father cleared his throat. 'Gentlemen,' he said, without any outward sign of irony. 'Mr McIntyre has come to Adullam on a bit of business. One of the girls in the town–I doubt any of you'd know her–hasn't been seen for a time. Molly Devine's daughter, Marie. I could give you a description...'

'Five-foot-two,' Vinny interrupted gently. He waited for the Father to step back, his rugose frown indicating slight concern. 'Near eighteen-years-old, eight stone, black hair, brown eyes, pretty wee thing. She's been missin' since last night...'

Vinny stopped talking and scanned the group. Eyes meeting eyes, that was his job. The searching of pupils for glimmers of darkness, the upturning of slabs from over darkly-sealed souls to see what wicked creatures scurried about beneath, pained by the sudden light. He locked his gaze steadfastly on Brian, but the older man smiled a minatory grimace, held him out for it.

Brian was too old to let others stare him out – he'd told Miles that once in the dormitory. In the older man's opinion, there were no true dangers in the world if you didn't care, only more opportunities to test the ever-increasing frailty of the human condition.

'Seen nothin', Mr McIntyre,' Brian said, eventually. 'Seen nothin', done nothin', heard nothin', like the good wee monkeys we are. We know her to see,' he added, before Vinny could thicken his frown. 'Pretty wee thing. But none of us have seen her.' Brian scanned the table, toyed with his spoon, lifted a wedge of stew, blew on it, put it down. 'At least, I haven't.' He downturned his gaze, then went workman-like at his dinner. 'Though the others may've done, right enough.'

The Father sighed and looked between them. 'Did *any* of you see her about today, or late last night?' he asked, evenly. 'If you recall where you were, you may be able to help. Of course, you might have to think about it for a time, but...'

Fidgeting with his cap, Vinny coughed politely as if to beg forgiveness for his second interruption. 'If you can be of any help, gentlemen, I'd be grateful. You can call into the station any time. You all know where it is, I believe.'

The four men regarded each other with thin smiles: They'd all taken their turn in the station, but only to help in matters which concerned them directly. Vinny lowered his head, obviously feeling his journey a waste. The Father sighed again, before showing the officer into the hall. Seconds later, a gust of wind flung notes from the chimes and the Chief Guard was gone.

The Father returned to the table. There, a muted conversation, which had sought life in his absence, died instantly. The priest accepted a bowl of stew from Nan, then sat adjusting his cutlery, allowing the food time to cool. He stared off through the front window for a time and seemed to be listening to the cacophonous drum of the rain as it lashed the window panes, though his eyes pained slightly as if his thoughts were actually elsewhere. Moments later, the priest returned his gaze to the present, before turning to Wing-Ding.

'You were out last night, weren't you?' he said to the youth. Mildly asked, but, from the reproachful tone, the Father seemed certain of his facts.

Wing-Ding looked as if he was considering a lie. But then his face took on that familiarly haunted look. The youth dropped his head, not wanting to stare in the direction of the approaching posse. He nodded cautiously.

'You were out for about an hour or so,' the Father added, evenly. Another statement of fact. 'Did you go anywhere near the town?'

Wing-Ding nodded innocently, his eyes liquescent and pitiful. 'For a while, Father,' he replied, fawningly. 'Just for a walk, nothin' else.'

'But you definitely went down into the town?'

'Only half the ways down. Then I came back. Straight back.'

Miles noted the younger man had omitted to add he'd been sitting on top of the back sheds for a time, though that was hardly surprising. The Father would've frowned even moreso upon that strange action, before putting it to the youth–in the way he did when considering a spring-clean of inmates–that maybe Adullam wasn't the right place for him, that maybe he needed the help of more resourceful others. Such as those who dressed often in white coats, perhaps.

'So you came in around one.' A third statement of fact. The Father would've been in his bed by then, for his routine rarely changed. Though Miles now guessed the priest had probably heard the youth leaving Adullam and sat up awaiting his return.

Wing-Ding returned another cautious nod. A definite aye, though nothing else. Which was unusual for him, as he was steadily used to vacillating between one statement of certainty and its contrary in an ever-ongoing bid to please.

'Then I think you should maybe tell Vinny that,' the Father said, evenly. 'You should go down the station and speak to him in person. He's understandin', is Vinny. Just in case things don't bode well in this... *thing*. Not that there's anythin' wrong as yet,' the priest added quickly. 'But...'

The statement hung there, pendulous, an idea arrested in its infancy. Wing-Ding nodded expectantly, still unable to comprehend just what the Father was getting at. Nevertheless, Miles saw from the exchange of concerned glances that the underlying accusation was equally obvious to Pele and Brian as it was to him.

'Sometimes it helps to get your story in first,' the Father continued, with a slight shrug. 'That's all I'm sayin'. And then there's the matter of your punishment for disobeyin' house-rules. Dishes – two days worth. Is that alright with you?'

Wing-Ding nodded, having no choice but to do so. A piquant vigour momentarily lit the youth's eyes, only to be as swiftly replaced by carefully fostered doubt.

He faded then, as always.

FOUR

There was an agitation in Craiglann throughout the next few days hitherto unknown in the small town. The Garda station, normally worked by a skeleton crew except on parade-days and the like, was manned by six full-time officers, with Vinny taking the lead-role in an as yet informal investigation. Dressed in his blue-black dreadnought and cap, and seemingly impervious to the cold, bludgeoning rain, the Chief Guard was seen walking along the Crissom that Thursday morning towards Pheasant's Crest. Momentarily, he lingered at the traffic lights beyond the Drunken Duck–as if envisioning Marie there as she said good-night to her fiancée–before walking solemnly on towards Adullam and the old farm. Just a little before the stone bridge, forking off to the right and closely bordering the lower perimeter of the old farm, was Inislae Brae. The Devine home was midway along that street, and, normally, Marie would've turned down there. Some fifty or sixty steps later, she would've been in her family home.

According to hearsay, Vinny conducted the first part of his investigation in the station, his phone-based enquiries restricted to Marie's family and more intimate friends. Achieving little with that, he'd then despatched officers to the bars, the off-licence, the community-centre and other businesses within the locality. But nothing turned up. Phone calls to relatives outside of town also came to nothing, as did an appeal on the local radio. Despite this, not many people seemed overly concerned as yet about Marie's disappearance, for it was generally agreed that people went missing for many reasons and not all those reasons were necessarily bad.

Now, Vinny stood pensively upon the corner of Inislae Brae, seemingly unaware that Miles Kivlehan had passed him by; yet there were days too, Miles knew, when the Guard hadn't the time or energy to believe in ghosts. Unspeaking, and gazing slowly around at everything and nothing, Vinny was a Maigret or a Poirot, with the troubles of Craiglann–his own investigative sphere–weighing heavily upon his shoulders. Miles walked on towards the town-centre, his head declined into the wind, and not for a second then did he envy the officer his task.

***

On the third day of Marie Devine's disappearance–the Friday, and therefore one of the busiest days of the week–Vinny and his men were a show of force in the town-centre, leaflets in hand. Had anyone seen her? This was what she looked like, though the photocopy was slightly blurred as the photo was taken two years ago outside the local secondary school. Still, you'd probably recognise her from around, what with the town as small as it was, and were you anywhere near the Crissom at midnight on Tuesday? Some help was forthcoming, yet little, it had to be supposed, was of true relevance. Nevertheless, in the three days following Marie Devine's disappearance, Father Joseph also did as much as he humanly could. A surfeit of prayers were offered in the daily Masses in the hope that God might keep the wee girl safe and well; and these were followed by the hawking of the usual parish bulletins, now with an additional memo asking people to help out the Gardai and Molly Devine in any way they possibly could.

People were glad to see Father Joseph doing his bit – Miles hated admitting that, yet it was evident from their open acknowledgements or the silent appreciation in their eyes. Throughout the last six months, for example, the priest had stood at the chapel gates every Sunday after midday Mass, no matter the weather, collecting for St. Augustine's refurbishment. People gave generously to the Father, shook his hand and congratulated him on doing a fine job, even if he was looking for 150,000 euros, which, most quietly agreed, was a lot to expect from a small community. Still, to give the priest credit, he'd raised the bulk of it through collections, raffles and charity auctions, and the restoration would go ahead in March. And so, with the Father and God on their side, Miles could understand why people believed the wee girl would turn up safe before long.

Miles Kivlehan, however, chose not to involve himself directly in the dark affair of Marie Devine's disappearance; after all, his opinion didn't count, so why would he? Instead, he'd spent the last few days as he spent every day; cadging a few coins as he walked the Crissom, sitting out the rainier hours in a corner of the Old Man's newsagents or Mullan's, or passing over a few coins short in the off-licence. As always, he was ignored by most, but during his travels he ascertained two topics of discussion were currently in vogue. The weather, ever a topic anyway, was the first. The weathermen had promised a stormy December with sleet or snow at Christmas; and few doubted it, the drab inclemency of the last few weeks enough to convince all around that, for once, the reports were likely correct. Yet that primary subject always gave way to the disappearance of Marie Devine. It was gruesome conversation, Miles mused, yet fascinating in that it allowed even those with little or no imagination to explore new depths of their subconscious and come up with all sorts of loathsome theories.

The wee lad, Eddie Logue–and he'd always been called 'the wee lad' as he was slight and thin–was the first to be slandered. In sibilant whispers they now berated him for leaving his girlfriend at the traffic-lights, which, most concurred, wasn't a gentlemanly thing to do. And even though Eddie's parents confirmed he'd arrived home some ten minutes after he left Dan McGinty's bar, most dismissed that alibi as inconsequential. After all, Con Logue was a businessman, so he'd probably pass a polygraph if he told you he'd just got back from Mars. And his mother, Deborah, was a good woman, but a mother still...

All theories implying the young lad's possible guilt were explored in their entirety, believed by some in degrees, but doubted by most. Yet all were fudged by Vinny McIntyre, who apparently saw clues otherwise concealed from lesser people, even if he wasn't directly forthcoming with them. According to the Chief Guard, Eddie Logue had told the truth: He'd left wee Marie at the lights in the same way he'd done many times before, then he'd gone straight home. From there, Marie had made her way up the Crissom towards Inislae Brae; and this was confirmed by a local taxi-man who'd noticed her walking alone in that direction as he drove out of town on a fare. But that was all that was known for sure. Still, despite Vinny's affirmation, the blackening of Eddie's name was soon made known in the Logue household. And the diminutive Con Logue, never one to lie down, responded by asking why no one was blaming the lad Marie dated *before* Eddie. After all, he was a serious drinker in his day and forever fighting in the community-centre discos; and, sure, it was well known he'd also beaten Marie up once for looking at someone else. To Con's displeasure, Vinny refuted that argument almost instantly: The other lad, young Geoff Harkin, was a rogue, sure enough, wild on the drink and running with other girls, whatever. But, as to his involvement in Marie's disappearance, it wasn't possible, as he'd headed to Dublin about three months ago to find himself work in the travel industry

In Mullan's, Old Jack mused that they–whoever *they* were, but on that he wouldn't be drawn–had taken Marie up Cara Mor, the mountain on Craiglann's perimeter. But Mullan refuted that, saying it was much too bleak up there and far too treacherous a climb. Slyly, Jack then suggested that Father Joseph should go up for a look anyway; after all, he viewed it as his private Mount Pisgah, from whose crest he often cast a kingly eye over Craiglann, his Promised Land. Jack chuckled gleefully at that, before glancing warily about to see if anyone was listening, for he didn't need that getting back to the priest. Luckily enough, no one but Mullan was within earshot; and Miles, of course, but Miles didn't count, even amongst small numbers. The vagrant finished his beer then, leaving the bar as the subject of Marie Devine's disappearance was broached once more.

Later that Saturday afternoon, the vagrant shambled into the off-licence. Along the length of the queue, chatter about the girl was also rife. The river was to blame, one perm-haired woman claimed; sure, the Hart had claimed many lives in the past, albeit a long time ago and she couldn't recall any names off-hand. A silver-haired woman behind her nodded forcefully; true, she trumped, and, sure, hadn't one of those ne'er-do-wells in Adullam once tried to end his life in the brook? The perm-hair raised an eyebrow, before turning to stare dimly at Miles. Paling visibly, Miles suddenly envisioned her locks manifesting, Gorgon-like, into a slithering mass of snakes, so he quickly downcast his eyes, fearing what might ensue if he held her gaze too long.

It seemed an eternity before Big Michael broke that spell by politely coughing the queue forward, and, soon afterwards, he and Miles were in the midst of their perpetual routine. This was the very last time Miles was getting away with this shite – the off-licence owner simply used a doleful shake of his head to deliver the umpteenth in an ongoing series of final warnings.

Miles nodded his thanks, then secreted the bottle in his inside pocket before moving outside. Pity about the girl – they were the last words he heard as the women made their way down the road. Beautiful girl as they recalled her, lovely eyes, not a bad word on anyone. Junoesque they might've added, and so beautiful that Zeus might have ordered her swept up to Heaven to serve as his personal cup-bearer. Miles shrugged sadly, recalling Marie as rather plain, yet he knew why others thought like that. It was the beauty of loved ones you recalled the most. It was the sparkle in the eyes, the funny things they used to say, but more especially the way they made you feel. Aye, Miles thought sadly, he understood why people thought like that as well as any man half-alive.

The vagrant brushed those sombre thoughts aside as he neared the bus terminus. Momentarily, he considered seeking solitude in the lane behind it, yet the talk of the last few days had aroused a foreign interest in him, so he glanced down the street amid a small scattering of pedestrians, wondering where he might go next to learn more. A familiar figure, however, was moving in his direction.

Flustered, Miles retreated quickly into the lane, where he hid behind a bin, waiting for Pele to pass. It was, Miles knew, a childish action, as he'd never avoid Pele in Adullam. But then, in the Mission Home, necessity made the inmates stick together to resist the Father urging them either singularly or collectively into the world; and such a federation required little input as it was compelled more by selfishness than anything. But outside Adullam, life was different. Here, people measured a man's worth by his reliance upon others: The self-reliant gained the most respect, whereas the needier were afforded the least. This unscribed law applied throughout society, and even those who begged upon street corners were granted a muted respect if they refrained from overly encroaching upon others.

Moreover, Miles knew well how the other inmates whiled away their private hours, and, in truth, their interests didn't warrant any further external interaction. Despite being teased by the children who gathered in the community-centre, Wing-Ding spent his days there, fussed over by one of the proprietors, a caring spinster named Mrs Malhaffey. As for Pele, he was often seen around the river, idling with local fishermen and discussing football or days recalled without pain. Brian, contrarily, was more secure despite his inner demons. The older man passed time in the Drunken Duck, travelled into nearby towns or, at times, spent a night in the Garda station, depending upon the depth of the anger in his soul. Brian was a deep man and Miles had more in common with him than the others, but Brian was also volatile and hadn't yet realised that fighting fire with fire usually ended up with everyone getting burned.

The vagrant took a long drink of wine and directed those sobering thoughts away. Minutes later, he stepped warily from the lane. Edging alongside a grumbling bus, he moved back onto the Crissom and began walking towards Adullam. A small time later, he was relaxing in the living room, his mind frazzled and unwilling to continue setting logic against uncertainty. A fire burned in the grate, thick cuts of pine scenting the room, a spume crackling at their sawn-off ends. The heat leeched what remained of the vagrant's energy and he closed his eyes, only to feel himself once again slipping uncontrollably back through time.

***

Upon discovering Sarah McGill's new love interest was a sporting rival named Mark Brady, the younger Miles Kivlehan knew he had to win her back, or at least deter her from seeing Brady again. Naturally, Miles realised getting Sarah to see him again would be problematic due to the way he'd unceremoniously dumped her at the end of their third date. And yet, after due reconsideration, he reasoned that he hadn't mistreated Sarah during their brief time together: He'd taken her on three dates, spent a reasonable amount of money on her and half-listened to everything she had to say. Moreover, he was now prepared to take her back despite the fact she was dating his sporting rival – something, he suspected, she was only doing to make him jealous anyway. This latter concession, in his opinion, was rather generous. Yet there were limits as to how far he would go, for Miles couldn't risk tarnishing his pride or showing vulnerability. In the end, there seemed but one way forward – he had to launch an all-out assault against Sarah's emotions.

This decided, Miles began by trying to indirectly embarrass his sports rival at their next inter-university athletics meet. With the racing over, and Miles having beaten Brady in the 100 yard sprint, the young athletes and their admirers retired to an on-campus bar for their usual liquid refreshments. A short while later, when everyone was in a state of relaxed inebriation, Miles dared a friend to secretly squirt some lighter-fuel into Brady's pint of beer. This had the desired effect: Brady, red-faced and instantly unable to control his bowels, was forced to make his next 100 yard dash to the toilets. Nearly everyone present had fallen about laughing at this, and a smirking Miles had keenly watched Sarah's reaction, yet the look upon her face wasn't the one he'd expected. Staring coldly at Miles and his friends–who all quickly denied responsibility– Sarah departed the bar, her demeanour one of obvious anger. Miles was confused by what he'd seen: What was she thinking? Hadn't she seen what an idiot Brady was? Why did she want to be with a loser, a no-hoper? Had she no shame or self-esteem?

A bewildered Miles found himself questioning Sarah McGill's values after that incident, yet he was still determined to separate her from Mark. He knew, however, that the situation now required a more direct approach. So, judging jealousy as the hardest of all emotions to conceal– as well as, perhaps, the quickest entry into Sarah's heart–Miles began wandering around campus with girls he'd previously dated; girls who still liked him, yet in whom he no longer held a romantic interest. These seemingly spontaneous but well-timed meetings would cause Miles to bump into Sarah often, during which times he'd flirt outrageously with his acquaintances. As a further provocative gesture, Miles attended the same bars or night-clubs as Sarah and Mark, acting out little snapshots of his now fabulous life in order to make her pine for him. There could only be one possible outcome to this, he believed – Sarah would soon be his once again. But Sarah didn't react as he expected. She simply smiled when they met, after which she politely and openly asked him how he was getting on with his life, his studies and his latest girlfriend. Miles found this difficult to deal with: With his ego deflating rapidly and Sarah seemingly oblivious to his efforts, he began to wonder if she'd ever truly fancied him at all. And finally, surmising that he'd been duped, he allowed a very deep hatred for her to grow in his heart.

That hatred, of course, inflamed a desire for further revenge, and Miles knew he had to somehow poison Mark and Sarah against each other. So, a few weeks later, Miles had yet another colleague spread a rumour around the university that Sarah McGill and Miles Kivlehan were still crazy about each other, and that she was only using Brady to win Miles back; which was obvious, the rumour expanded, as she kept turning up at the same bars and night-clubs Miles frequented. At the same time, Miles sought to convince Sarah that Brady was seeing other girls behind her back. Of course, Miles let Sarah know that he hated having to tell her this, yet he couldn't watch a good friend being used.

Sarah hadn't believed him at the start. Mark wasn't like that, she frowned: He took her out, he was kind and he listened to her. Miles shook his head: But that was just his way of getting her into bed, wasn't it? Sarah frowned again: But Mark hadn't mentioned bed yet, she explained, and they'd been dating several weeks. A very relieved Miles allowed his smile to broaden: No, Mark was just using her–*everyone* was saying it–and he'd probably dump her when he got what he wanted. Sarah's eyes narrowed at that: Was Miles jealous of Mark, was that it? Miles snorted indignantly: No way, he wasn't the type! Sarah smiled broadly then: Miles was jealous, she was sure of it, because he now knew he never should've let her go. Upon hearing this, Miles shrugged indecipherably; the sort of shrug that suggested she may've been correct, or the sort that said she could believe what she wanted. It was a non-answer, a half-answer, and it allowed him to keep his pride intact.

Besides, Miles felt he wasn't actually lying to Sarah. In fact, in one way, he'd told her about the ways of all men; and, in another, he'd fought to regain her. Couldn't she see that? Didn't she recognise that they'd *both* made a mistake and that Miles was actually giving *her* another chance?

Sarah smiled self-confidently then, seemingly having made up her mind. Then she leaned over and whispered into Miles' ear that she'd instinctively felt–from the moment they'd met–that she and Miles were meant for each other. Miles nodded happily upon hearing that; a simple nod, a simple non-answer once more. And, within hours, Sarah finished with Brady and began dating Miles again. Of course, Miles wasn't going to tell Sarah she wasn't his type and never would be, as her everyday interests were too slow, too easygoing and much too considered for him.

But staying with Sarah meant depriving Brady of one more victory, and Miles Kivlehan knew that was more than enough for the meantime.

***

A short time later, Miles came awake to the sound of muted squabbling. In a stupor, he noticed that Brian, Pele and Wing-Ding had settled into the seats around him. The men were midway through a rather heated and disjointed debate, yet Miles couldn't discern what it was about. Then he heard Marie Devine's name being mentioned and he nodded dreamily: There they were, he mused idly, rabbiting on about the same old subject.

As sharply, Miles opened his eyes, a cold inner admonishment forcing him to do so. *Old subject, Miles? God, how hard have you become? And how sad is it that, after all the pain you've experienced in your own life, you now believe the wee girl's never coming back.*

Wing-Ding seemed agitated – Miles received that impression, despite the draining heat which weighted his bones and appeared to make the heavy spattering of rain bouncing off the windows seem so far away. The Father had said something while saying something else – that was the gist of a conversation now dominated by Brian. The priest had asked Wing-Ding to go down to the Garda station and explain that he'd spent the whole night–or part of it–up the town.

But Brian was saying he hadn't liked the sound of that. He's bloody accusing you, the older man said angrily. He's more or less saying you'd something to do with the disappearance of the wee lass, and you sitting the storm out on the roof at the time, innocent as hell! Brian paused then, placing a firm hand on Wing-Ding's shoulder as the youth made to rise in panic. Of course, the older man soothed, you've actually fuck all to worry about, because even if you *were* sitting on the roof watching the storm, so fucking what? That's your prerogative, because you can sit wherever you fucking want, can't you? Free world, free speech, you can sit in the middle of the road the whole day long if you've a mind!

Wing-Ding silently raised a hand at the end of Brian's free-world and free-speech monologue. The youth's owl-like eyes said he wanted to feel free to say something – if it was alright with everyone else, that was, if it was alright with everyone else? Brian nodded magnanimously and Wing-Ding continued: He hadn't been up on the roof watching the storm *all* night, that was all he wanted to say. He'd spent fifteen minutes up there, maybe half an hour, aye, but then he'd gone for a walk down to the bridge, a little beyond it, needing the air. But, aye, he repeated meekly, aye, he'd spent some of the night up there, aye.

Brian nodded patiently, waiting for Wing-Ding to de-valve so he could go at his own free speech again, so rudely interrupted. Well, that didn't really change things, the older man declared, Wing-Ding's reason for being up on the roof, did it? But, then again, he further reasoned, it didn't have to, the truth being the truth and all...

Pele cut in then. Not really a talker, more a listener, he cut in anyway. He recalled the *reason*, he said, pausing as a series of deep frowns questioned both the interruption and his sanity. The *reason*, he repeated, the *reason* Wing-Ding was up on the roof in the first place. Watching – wasn't that what the younger man said? Watching the new fellow down at the river?

Wing-Ding, his eyes dream-filled, nodded and grinned inanely. The new fellow, the youth echoed softly; aye, the new fellow down at the river. Brian clicked his fingers and Miles nodded, catching Pele's point.

'What exactly *was* he doin'?' Miles asked the youth. Inwardly, he wondered just how many people in Craiglann would bother fishing during the middle of the night. There was the Father, of course, and one or two others. But in the middle of the night, and it raining a bucketful? Maybe not so many at all.

Wing-Ding nodded as if all purpose was set to be revealed, then shrugged sorrowfully, his dreams suddenly replaced by nightmares. Obviously having little faith in his story, he'd replayed it in his head, only to hear the flaws resound loud as drumbeats in his conscience. Like Cassandra, doomed always to tell the truth but never to be believed, he didn't want to say it out loud in case it sounded utterly ridiculous – which, Miles reasoned, it actually did.

As it was, the youth didn't actually get the chance. There was a noise in the hallway, a forewarning breeze breathing life into the chimes as the front door opened. Miles shivered as the Father showed an officious Vinny McIntyre into the room, after which the priest returned meekly to his office. The Chief Guard wished the vagrants a neutral good-day before turning to stare directly at Wing-Ding. Miles realised instantly that the youth mustn't have given a statement to the police officer as the Father had suggested.

'Father Joseph was sayin' that maybe one or two of you could be of help in the, ehm, investigation,' Vinny began. The Guard seemed uneasy with having to say that final word, perhaps because he now realised a certain legitimacy had taken hold, yet his eyes remained firmly upon the callow youth. In the ensuing silence, Brian coughed, drawing Vinny's attention temporarily away to the left.

'The new fellow,' Brian said loudly. Vinny re-focused on Brian, said nothing, but raised his chin and asked anyhow. 'The Stranger – did you talk with him?' Vinny stared wordlessly at the other man for a few moments, before shaking his head; a raised eyebrow asked why. 'Maybe you should,' Brian suggested easily. 'Our young friend saw him actin' mysteriously down at the river on the night the wee girl disappeared. It was a bad night, as I recall, and an odd night to be down at the river. Still, my wee friend needed to get out a while. He dodged the *curfew*, needed the air.' As the other vagrant's suppressed a giggle at his emphasis, Brian shrugged impassively. 'Might be worth checkin' out, eh?'

Vinny regarded Wing-Ding once more. 'That right?' the Guard asked. The youth nodded uncertainly. Vinny pursed his lips thoughtfully. 'Well, I might just do that,' he replied non-committedly. 'Anyhow, young man, don't you forget to come see me. Soon.' Wing-Ding nodded once more, then Vinny wished the men an expressionless goodbye before leaving Adullam.

As Wing-Ding began faltering for breath and seemed set to lose control of his senses, Brian placed a settling hand upon his shoulder, raised his thumb and winked conspiratorially to let the youth know it would be alright. Seconds later, the Father entered the sitting room, and, standing there in his cassock and surplice, it was obvious what was coming.

'You'll do as Vinny says, aye?' the priest said to Wing-Ding.

The youth nodded somewhat ambiguously. 'Aye. I will, Father.'

The Father nodded, then regarded his watch. 'Alright. Anyway, in ten minutes time we're holdin' an extra Mass for the wee girl. It's a chance to offer up a few prayers and light a few candles. Is that okay with everyone here?'

Miles regarded the clock upon the wall, as too did the others: It was 2-30pm and the priest was saying that word again. The four men looked between each other, then consented dismally, having no real choice.

***

Vinny had never been one for listening to rumours. In the tradition of every great detective–with which he rightly or wrongly identified himself –he chose to rely basically upon evidence and not so much on hearsay. Though he'd certainly listen to hearsay if it was interesting enough, he'd always put that about too. By late that Saturday afternoon he'd heard a host of disjointed theories, ranging from the half-considered to the ridiculous. Phantom truckers had driven through the town–that was a favourite–as had an assortment of mac-wearing dirty old men in their seedy little cars. They'd lifted her, abused her and kidnapped her – Vinny had apparently heard variations on that theme at least ten times already. The brook - that was the second favourite. She'd taken a couple of drinks –less than she could normally handle, her fiancée had said, though she may've been tired–and she'd fallen into the brook. So, having been carried off into the estuary outside of town by the racing waters, Marie was now fish-food, dead and gone, never coming back. Vinny, however, scotched each of those rumours in turn. Truckers and seedy little men in cars? Sure, the wee girl had been too wise for that. And, sure, somebody would've spotted someone like that in town – because very little, the Chief Guard added acidly, ever escaped the townspeople's attention.

The brook was a different matter, and not one so easily discounted. For this reason, the Chief Guard spent an entire afternoon walking his men up and down the course of it, scouring the banks and peering into the fetid waters for any sort of a clue, no matter how small. But even after spending hours poking it with sticks, they found nothing beneath the water-moss, the cat-tails and the algae. Rumour also had it that Vinny was going to dredge the entire river when the weather evened up. Yet the Chief Guard quickly put paid to that rumour as well: After all, the Hart would've been way out of the wee girl's way, because she'd either have had to cut through the old farm to get there, or go on half a mile past her home by road to reach the main section, and the fact that the local taxi-man saw her near the corner of Inislae Brae made that very unlikely.

Pele said that he'd also seen Vinny McIntyre going up to the old farmhouse early on Saturday evening, and he said the Guard simply walked up to the gates and waited for the Stranger to come out. The two men then stood talking for a time, after which they shook hands and Vinny left.

The Stranger seemed friendly enough, Pele shrugged, and he'd been patting his monstrosity of a dog and pointing here and there as if telling Vinny about his plans for the land. Easygoing and informal, that was the way Pele described that particular meeting, yet Miles knew the same thing couldn't be said about the atmosphere amongst the locals anymore. The search, hardly frenetic, was gathering concern with its lack of speed. The longer Marie Devine was gone – well, they all knew what that meant. Nice wee girl, poor wee girl – it didn't look good for her at all.

***

On Saturday night, at about 9-30pm, just shortly before his return to Adullam, Miles heard another rumour. Passing a small group of weekend revellers outside the Drunken Duck, someone remarked that there'd been a phone call to the Garda station–at least that was what Seamus Brown, one of Craiglann's trainee Guards, apparently told someone else only minutes before as he passed on foot-patrol–and it basically implied that, on the night wee Marie Devine vanished, the Stranger had been seen dragging something heavy out of his front door and down to the Hart. Word spread quickly after that, a garrulous chirping which dissoluted by osmosis and worked its way through the town like wildfire. Privileged information it was, but word always got around in a town as small as this, people always found out.

Who made the call, no one seemed to know. All they knew for certain was that Vinny and four officers had travelled back up to the old farm in a Gardai car. Upon hearing this snippet, Miles scurried up the Crissom, reaching Adullam just as the Guards were exiting the old farmhouse, their faces grim and gaunt. Moving unobtrusively in behind a few of the locals, Miles noticed the Stranger standing at the farm's gateway. Visibly perplexed and wan of pallor, the newcomer somehow managed to wish the officers a good night, before closing the gates and returning up the gravelled path into his own private world.

Inside Adullam, Miles went straight to the dormitory. There, Pele and Wing-Ding were quick to fill him in on the missing details, but there was little new to report. The only other thing of interest was that Brian hadn't returned, missing the curfew as he did now and then. Still, that wasn't too unusual – Miles supposed the older man had found some alternative company for the evening.

So, with that subject dismissed, Miles, Pele and Wing-Ding resumed their primary conversation. After a few minutes, Pele braved the first presumption: The Guards had obviously been searching for Marie's body over in the farmhouse and they'd found nothing. To the two men sitting before him, Pele reiterated that it would have be a body they were looking for by now, because the chances of her being alive – well, he was going to say it straight because everyone else in town seemed to be skirting around it:

She was dead now, wee Marie Devine. She had to be.

F I V E

Sunday morning mass passed as a humdrum blur. But, just before the closing prayer, Miles sneaked out of St. Augustine's, certain the Father intended setting him to work with a collection bucket at one of the exits. With barely a backward glance, the vagrant hurried down Pheasant's Crest towards the Old Man's shop, where he hoped to remain until lunchtime. It was 10-00am and a heavy mizzle came on as he reached the Crissom, yet he slowed and began scouring the pavements and drains for coins that passers-by may've lost on their way to or from town the previous night. As he did so, Miles smiled thinly, realising that only an absurd delusion could've convinced him that the priest would let him anywhere near money meant for the chapel renovations. Trust issues aside, why would the Father do that when he'd never done so before?

Regaining perspective, Miles supposed that sudden irrationality had either been brought on by a lack of alcohol or because mounting depression had again skewed his ever-wavering perception of reality. That it was Sunday didn't help, for, on this day when God supposedly entered more fully into a man's life in order to ease his pain and isolation, Miles often felt more alone than ever. With no crowds around to beg from or avoid, he was forced to compare his life to the lives of those who actually had a life; and, by engaging in such comparability, his own misery was increased a thousand-fold.

A small time later, Miles entered the newsagents. There, the Old Man greeted him neutrally, indicating with sharp eyes that he move into the corner out of the way. Miles did so, then watched in silence as the vendor restocked his shelves, even as he half-listened to the radio furnishing a bleak report of more inclement weather to come. Gazing outside, he realised the downpour had grown heavier, but allowed himself to be distracted by a tumbleweed of old fish- and chip-paper rolling along the road with the local road-sweeper in extremely idle pursuit.

As usual, Mrs Daly was the first customer to enter the shop. She was middle-aged and rather Amazonian of nature; the sort, Miles wryly surmised, who mightn't have thought twice about lopping off a breast to aid her bow arm. Mrs Daly gave Miles the impression that she looked down her nose at most men, yet she was fond of the Old Man–as were most locals–because he was inoffensive and would always help you out in times of trouble. She greeted the newsagent affably, said something about the weather, ordered her papers, then got straight into it about the noise in the street the previous night. Well, she'd been sleeping soundly, she began, used as she now was to a certain level of revelry as she lived just two doors down from the Drunken Duck. But she'd been awoken just after 2-00am by the sounds of screaming, and it sounded like someone was getting murdered. Mrs Daly crossed herself then, made a quiet remark about the wee girl Devine, and said she hoped they'd find her soon, God bless her! Then she resumed her conversation, saying she couldn't exactly see who'd been involved in the ruckus, what with the street-lights not being as bright as they should've been–and she'd been onto the council about that, too!–though she'd definitely recognised Con Logue.

The Old Man raised an eyebrow, as if to check he'd caught that right. Oh aye, Mrs Daly confirmed, it was Con Logue alright, for she'd have recognised his voice anywhere. And, even though the garage-owner was far too small for fighting, there he was, punching the head off some boy – though, again, Mrs Daly hadn't seen who. Then Frankie Devenney –aye, him with the bad leg he'd got in that crash years back–well, he'd stuck his nose in, as had that other eejit, Neil Martin, who was forever selling dodgy goods in the Saturday market! Still, to be fair, Mrs Daly backtracked, Frank or Neil may've been trying to break the fight up for all she knew, though chances were they'd actually started it. And, seconds later, the whole thing escalated into a god-awful brawl, with the local taxi men and a couple of the wee girls who worked for Molly Devine sticking their noses into it as well.

The Old Man had fished out Mrs Daly's usual Sunday morning groceries at this stage, knowing her purchasing habits so well she just had to nod at certain fridges or shelves. So what happened then? he asked, wide-eyed. Where were Vinny and his squad when this was happening? Everyone in Craiglann paying taxes for that lot to sit in their nice warm station, you'd think they'd do a wee bit in return at times, wouldn't you? Alright, they had their hands full looking for the wee girl–the Old Man's pause was almost one of remembrance–but, Christ, you could hardly let the town go to pieces as a result, could you?

Oh, he'd arrived *eventually*, Mrs Daly sneered, along with five of his men. But it'd taken them half an hour to settle the row down – and that was only with the help of Dan McGinty and a few of his more sensible patrons. And, sure, didn't an ambulance arrive then, yet there was nobody hurt enough to get into it. Oh, there were lots of black eyes and cuts, Mrs Daly confirmed, and a few bruised ribcages and busted noses. But there was definitely no need for an ambulance, and the driver had been annoyed about that, giving off to everyone thereabouts and asking who'd phoned it, though no one seemed willing to say.

The Old Man shook his head despondently and forced an interlude in Mrs Daly's monologue, stating emphatically that it was never like that in his day. One-on-one, that was how it was back then. You had a problem with someone, you took them into a lane and went at it. And you didn't use weapons, just your hands or feet. But these young fellows, y'see, they hadn't the same moral fibre. Mrs Daly nodded, agreeing to that: Moral fibre, she snorted as she left the shop, they were definitely lacking in that, and she wished they'd bring back the birch!

Miles spent the next few minutes trying to recall if they'd ever used the birch in Craiglann or, indeed, anywhere in Eire in his day. Then he gave up and focused upon the next bedraggle of customers to enter the shop, watching impassively as they gathered their papers and groceries into little plastic bags before running out again into the rain. The Old Man had brightened at this stage, the bulk of his work done. And so, those customers who knew more about the fight, he eagerly extracted gossip from, his knowledge growing fuller all the time; and, those who knew less about the fight, he plied with all the latest information.

The verbal disagreement had started in the Drunken Duck, that much now seemed certain. But the fist-fight had been elicited by Mullan's doorman, Big Sean Flaherty, who'd seen the argument starting in the street and thought to quell it by throwing the first punch, the result of which was a quickening vortex of people pulling and hauling each other. Still, no one was too surprised as Big Sean was a hectoring bully of Boeotian dim-wittedness at best, yet now his thoughtlessness had turned a small argument into a vendetta, with half the town swearing the other half hadn't seen the last of it. But then, Big Sean's involvement aside, it was all *his* fault, that was obvious – Mrs Stewart was the first to throw that accusation into the ring, adding that she'd go up to his place herself soon if something wasn't done about him. She wasn't going to say a name, she continued acidly, but then she didn't have to, as his name was now on everyone's lips – even though, she candidly admitted, few, if any, actually *knew* his name. Still, that aside, people knew *exactly* what he'd done, and that was all that mattered.

Aye, Mrs Stewart sneered, because of *him*, wee Marie wasn't coming back; and because of *him*, poor Molly Devine, usually so outgoing in her modish clothes and with her perfectly coifed hair, was living an almost purgatorial existence. They were saying Molly wasn't speaking to anyone, Mrs Stewart opined angrily, and that she was starving herself to death in Inislae Brae. Aye, *he* was responsible for this!

No, no, she continued, raising a hand to stall the Old Man's frictionless input, it had to be said, and it had to be said out loud – it was *his* fault, and everyone knew it because he'd been acting suspiciously down at the river that night of her disappearance, putting *something big* into it. So it was obvious, wasn't it?

The Old Man didn't reply to that, his silence equally condemning. And about an hour later, when a small tide of late Sunday morning risers found themselves queuing in the newsagents, that accusation would firmly take hold.

***

The Stranger entered the shop around 10-30am. There, amid the throng he stood, unnoticed at first as he was wearing a rain-spattered overcoat with the hood drawn around his face. But then someone spotted him and like the Red Sea they parted, their scornful, accusing glares directed against him. The Old Man, however, didn't say a word, even if his narrowing eyes declared his thoughts. The Stranger, his cheeks reddening as he stared about him, hastily took a pint of milk from a nearby fridge, set a few coins upon the counter and mumbled a quick thanks to the Old Man. He then scurried back into the rain, climbed into an old pick-up and drove off towards Pheasant's Crest. He was scrutinised by everyone as he did so, with some even daring to stand closer to Miles to get a better look. Moments later, one man muttered that the pick-up looked just like the one someone had said they'd seen, if not on the night of the–well, on *that* night–then on a night either side of it. Then someone else urged him to say it out straight as everyone was thinking it anyhow - the night of *the murder*, wasn't that what he meant? The local man was a private sort who rarely voiced an opinion, but he nodded sadly, dropped his head, mutely saying aye. He'd thought it, he admitted sadly, and so did everyone else hereabouts if they were to be honest.

The Old Man coughed to regain everyone's attention: Aye, they were all thinking it, he agreed, and he'd had many similar conversations that morning. So, he was going to do something about it. Not that he usually got involved in stuff like this, he declared: No, that wasn't his form. But you had to have scruples, for if you hadn't those, you'd nothing. So, he was going to suggest an embargo by which they'd deny the Stranger goods to show him what they thought of him – and it was entirely up to everyone else in Craiglann if they went along with it or not, as it was only a suggestion. The Old Man wasn't going to talk to him again either – not that he'd done so anyway, he snorted, for the Stranger was an ignorant bastard, and God forgive him for saying it, but he was! Though nor was he going to tell the Stranger exactly *why* he wasn't getting served, because Irish slander laws were dodgy at best. Anyway, the Stranger was wrong for this town – the Old Man said he'd had a feeling about that from the start, the way you did with some people. Take, for example, the first day he'd come in here, he hadn't opened his mouth: He'd just grunted and pointed to this and that, ignorant as hell! Though he said something to Miles, didn't he, Miles? He said something to you, didn't he?

Miles had been drinking surreptitiously from his bottle when he heard his name somewhere on the blurred periphery of his consciousness. He nearly choked, the wine running out of his mouth to gather ripe as a bloodstain on his coat. Thinking at first he was being chastised, he screwed the lid quickly back onto the bottle, before slipping it back in his pocket, nearly dropping it in the process.

'Isn't that right, Miles? He's ignorant as hell! Isn't that right?'

The vagrant frowned heavily, confused that the Old Man had spoken to him calmly and clearly, especially with others about. Expectant faces regarded Miles now, not too harshly for once, so he nodded unsurely, unaware of what he was agreeing to, but feeling it correct to do so. Smiling thinly at that modest victory, the Old Man regained everyone's attention with another small cough: There, they'd heard it from two people now, he said, so what more was there to say? So, it was only right, doing what he was doing–what they'd all be doing soon if they'd a conscience, mark his words!–and he'd be the first to start it all off.

The chatter continued in the same vein for a time, but Miles didn't take it on. Instead, he spent several moments trying to work out what he'd agreed to. The answer wouldn't come, so he let it go: It didn't matter, after all, for he was a non-person and his opinion didn't really count. Besides, by acting so stand-offish, the Stranger had to be guilty of something, and people didn't just make harsh judgements about others without evidence. No, people lived and let others live, that was how people were.

Miles reflected sourly upon those unsettling thoughts as he left the shop, moving with the wind at his back towards Mullan's. Someone had kidnapped, or maybe even murdered Helen of Troy, he mused idly, and now the Greeks and the Trojans looked set to go to war, though who was who was anyone's guess. People were also offering a surfeit of sympathy to Molly and none to the Stranger, the latter of whom they were now even prepared to openly blame for murder, despite most not even knowing his name.

Greek against Trojan – Miles smiled wanly, recalling how, in his university days, he'd Hellenized certain friends or ongoing relationships as a mnemonic aid to help him through exams. One of his philandering uncles, for example, he'd likened to Zeus, who often seduced comely human maidens; and a cuckolded neighbour he'd likened to the blacksmith god Hephaestus, who once caught his wife Aphrodite in bed with her lover Ares, God of War. In such a way, Miles had been able to learn the names of not only every mortal hero the ancient Greeks and Romans invented to explain the ongoing struggle of mankind against the heavens, but a vast array of gods and demigods who seemingly thrived upon perpetual discord, vengeance, unsavoury dalliances and other ungodly behaviour. Despite the work involved, it had proven an immensely enjoyable task in the end, and Miles had grown to envy the simplicity of those arcane belief systems. Simply put, the ancient Greek and Roman gods didn't promise you undying love and help, only to have you realise over time that you were on your own, no matter how much you dared hope otherwise. They merely gave you an ideal to live up to and an ear in times of need; and, if you didn't like the attributes afforded to one, you simply chose another and offended no one.

A game, it had been a game to Miles at first. Now, to his surprise, he actually found himself half-playing it again.

Big Sean Flaherty was sitting at the bar talking to Mullan when Miles went in, the doorman's short-sleeved tee-shirt–hardly winter wear–reminding people they'd best keep their opinions of him to themselves. Big Sean's face was at least superficially contrite, and Miles guessed he was now trying to justify his part in the previous night's debacle. Propped idly against the counter, however, Mullan was impassive enough, though he may simply have been distracted by the trickle of people filing in for Sunday lunch. Miles ordered a drink from the barmaid, before finding an unoccupied stool in the corner.

Mullan, of course, had long since made the vagrant aware that he'd have to surrender his seat if anyone ever needed it. Still, knowing that wouldn't happen for a while, Miles relaxed and eavesdropped in on nearby patrons, with those conversations he listened into–some by accident, but some by design–concerning either the fight or the girl, or how one half of the town now had it in for the other. Names were mentioned–some Miles knew, some he didn't–and transgressions dragged up, with those committed the previous night weighted by past deeds to add spice. One such tale took Miles a little, if not fully by surprise, the author not having the forethought to scrutinise exactly who was sitting next to him. Or, more likely, not caring. Someone else had been involved in the fight, someone whom the author was sure lived in Adullam. An alcoholic, burly, maybe fifty years old – did anyone know him? But from the frowns and the general shaking of heads, no one did. Of course, Miles would've known it was Brian despite the description. Brian drank in the Drunken Duck, sometimes fought for nothing at all, sometimes slept it off in the Garda station, and he hadn't returned to Adullam last night. Miles shrugged inwardly, not truly concerned: Brian was his own man, so therefore big enough to look after himself.

That lunchtime, there was more news for Miles when he returned to the Mission Home. Semi-inebriated, tired and racked with an unfathomable pain in his knees, he wasn't really interested in hearing anything else about the events of the previous night. But Wing-Ding and Pele were in the dormitory as he entered, and they seemed eager to share their news. Miles lay down heavily upon his bunk as the two men approached him, sitting down one on either side of the bed.

'You hear about Brian?' Pele said.

Miles nodded, closed his eyes. 'Drunk,' he said. 'Fightin' in town.' His reply was telegrammic, all he'd energy for at that moment.

'They had to take him to hospital this mornin'.'

'Why?' Half rising, a cramp in his belly, the myalgic pain thick in his legs.

'When they took him to the station he got violent.' Pele grinned at Miles' nothing-new-there frown. 'He had to be restrained. At least that's what they said. You don't think he'd be stupid enough to hit a Guard, do you?'

Miles shrugged: It was possible, even likely. 'Is he alright?' he asked anyway. But that was probably a stupid question too, he mused, as Brian always seemed to come through things like that relatively unscathed.

'He has a fractured skull,' Pele frowned. 'They had to make him stay awake all night in case he slipped into a coma – at least, that's what the Father said. They might keep him in a few days.' He managed a broader grin. 'The Father was down the Garda station this mornin' – he put in a complaint, as far as I know.'

Miles frowned again. The Father defending an inmate of Adullam? That wasn't so likely – and that, Miles would've liked to have seen for himself.

***

It was Monday morning and the rain, as heavy as it'd been throughout the previous month, was now accompanied by a rousing wind that blew a subdued blurt of a gale around town. Slates were dislodged on roofs, small trees set fast at permanent angles, and the corrugated sheeting on some sheds and garages blown off and away down winding country roads. There'd been one car crash in the locality because of something like that in the last few hours, and another near-miss according to news reports. The weather was growing increasingly worse, and the local radio was advising people only to go out into the streets if they really had to.

Miles hadn't slept well that Sunday night; intermittent flashes of that last afternoon at home with his wife and children some nine years ago had seared into his subconscious, forcing him once more into a shadow-world where surreality ever-presented itself as given fact. Sarah had been smiling in his dream, telling him she loved him despite everything he'd ever put her through. But then the nightmares had begun, a maelstrom of jerky, acidic memories forcing him wide awake, only to leave him clawing at his pillow, teary-eyed and gasping for breath.

Proper sleep evaded him after that, and, lethargic and snappy, he'd taken a couple of verbal swipes at Pele and Wing-Ding during morning Mass, before retreating into the sheds behind Adullam. And yet, with no drink there to soothe him, and more tired than he'd have believed possible, he found himself hacking lumps from the shed's wooden frame with a screwdriver he found lying on the windowsill. It was something to do, something to help, but it didn't help even slightly. He sat down on an untidy stack of old boxes as his energy left him, then rose to suddenly kick at an untidy stack of old paint cans as cold anger rejuvenated him, prising off their lids with the screwdriver and stabbing wildly at the thick shell of pungent, coagulated paint before painting staining pictures on the greasy wooden floor.

It was the sort of thing you'd have chastised your children for, he thought darkly. If you had children, that was, if you had them.

Angrily, he threw the stick away, moving to the window to watch as the rain drove bitterly hard into what remained of the flower-beds, as the wind lashed the willows to life, and as it blew hard at the unrepentant oak behind the chapel, barely shifting its full upper limbs. Miles wished it would all quickly abate and allow him to return to what remained of his life. Several hours later, he picked at lunch, during which time he gazed constantly outside to see if the stormy weather was about to draw to a cease. Supposing it wasn't, he left Adullam anyway. The Crissom, seemingly longer now as the wind challenged his every step, was heavily puddled, with only an occasional car moving towards town. No one stopped to give the vagrant a lift, but then they never did. Rammish smelling, sodden, and wearing scuffed shoes that were beginning to leak, as well as a grimy coat and a tea cosy of a hat he'd bought years back, how could he really blame them?

When he'd purchased his bargain bottle, he made his way back to Mullan's. Thoroughly soaked, he melted under Mullan's reproachful gaze and was relieved when the barman resumed his conversation with one of the bar's elderly patrons. The pint of black was slow in coming, and Miles, feeling vulnerable there in the open, fidgeted with his sleeve, anxious to return to the sanctity of a corner. The elderly man was talking, saying he'd heard about the Stranger up in the old farm, as well as the embargo they'd more or less put on him; he then asked Mullan if he thought the Stranger was guilty of anything.

Mullan shrugged thoughtfully, working methodically at the pint. There hadn't been anything like this in town before, he replied after a time. But then a young girl disappears, and the Stranger is seen down at the river at the same time, not fishing, just putting something into it – what was he at? So, if he was unable to account for himself–and there was no evidence he had–then starving him out of town was fair justice. Of course, Mullan shrugged, it *seemed* as if the Guards weren't doing much about wee Marie's disappearance. But there was no body and no murder weapon, y'see, and you needed either or both, that was how that the law worked. And they'd searched the Stranger's farmhouse, but, sure, the river had probably carried the wee girl's body to the ocean by now! The elderly man shivered briskly, even as Mullan took the money from Miles, counted it–it was the correct amount–and handed him his pint.

Mullan was tolerant, Miles had long since learned, yet the bar-owner would brook nonsense from no one.

Miles found a seat and considered what was happening. Fabian skirmishes were now being employed by more and more of the townspeople; and, deprived of victuals, the Stranger would eventually starve or flee. And this was necessary, according to common consensus, as Vinny wasn't doing enough. But then the Chief Guard would never do enough, Miles mused wryly, not even if he did everything he could, which he probably was. No, people wanted their pound of flesh now, for the longer wee Marie was gone, the longer anarchy would prevail. Anarchy – that was another word they were using. People were being abducted and perhaps even murdered, gangs were slugging it out in the streets, and the good people of Craiglann were more or less under curfew. It was easy to see, most now concurred, how bloody civil wars started! Christ, where was it all going to end?

Miles would've loved to have corrected more than one of them. Anarchy? Abduction? Murder? Gangs slugging it out? They made it sound as if there was some sort of a Hellenic soap opera going on right under their noses. Still, the vagrant didn't say a word to anyone, believing such ridiculousness would blow itself out in the next few days. But later than afternoon, as he listened into yet another conversation, he wasn't too surprised when he heard about the meeting.

There was talk of it everywhere around 5-00pm. The Old Man from the newsagents had organised a delegation to go see Vinny in the Garda station for an informal chat. It wasn't a protest – the Old Man made that clear from the start, because there was nothing for anyone to protest about as Vinny and his men were working the case hard, day and night. But the wee girl had been missing since last Tuesday night, and the townspeople wanted to know *exactly* what the Guards had turned up, and if it was safe to allow their own offspring out at night. They needed to calmly raise a few concerns and have Vinny tell them what was happening. And everyone was welcome to attend, the Old Man declared easily, because that way there'd be no misinterpretations or scandalising about what was being said. Which was important, he concluded, because Craiglann was full of bloody rumour-mongers who just couldn't mind their own bloody business!

The meeting was arranged for 7-00pm and Miles considered attending it for a time, recalling the elation he'd felt when he'd been involved in demonstrations in the past. Anti-vivisection, Anti-abortion, Save the Rain-forest, Ban the Bomb – he'd been into those sorts of things back when he'd been alive, they both had.

He allowed himself a wry smile, then drank deeply of his drink and slipped back to the safety of the present. No, maybe he wouldn't bother going, he decided. Maybe he'd just return here after dinner, sit in a corner and slip into a conversation, a mute with ears; part of everything going on, yet, as always, part of nothing.

***

He'd had a feeling about the meeting, and he might've discussed it had anyone asked. The locals calmly putting their ideas to Vinny McIntyre about how the investigation was going, and about what was being done – Miles could never have seen that happening, as there were far too many hotheads in Craiglann. It had also been agreed that the meeting would last less than an hour, but Miles had an opinion about that too. Meetings like that never met schedules: They were drawn-out affairs in which things were said and nothing was said, in which things were agreed-to and nothing was agreed, and in which everyone said something and nobody said anything.

Still, it would be interesting to hear the outcome, and, one way or the other, Miles intended to do so. But then, shortly after the conclusion of evening Mass–so shortly that you might've thought he missed it on purpose–Brian returned to Adullam, a bloodied bandage wrapped around his head, another around his right hand, and him looking for all the world as if he'd been smote down with half a stigmata, yet he was otherwise full of smiles. The Father was there to greet the oldest of Adullam's habitués at the front door with a semi-courteous nod and words which– while not truly empathetic–offered Brian a small ray of hope for the future as to things 'being done about it all'.

Brian sat amongst the others in the dining room for a time, milking more sympathy from the other habitués. The older man took tea from Nan and cigarettes from Pele, before eventually explaining just why he was totally innocent of everything they were considering charging him with. Brian then hurriedly explained to the Father–who, upon hearing something about 'charges', was on the verge of distancing himself–that it was *only* common assault and, sure, he'd been done with that many times over. But this time he was innocent, swear! Y'see, Father, he'd been trying to help one of the wee girls up after she'd fallen down in the wet as she tried to jump on someone's back. And then some bugger–God forgive him, Father!–had hit him full in the face with a can of *his own beer*, and, sure, he'd had to retaliate, Father, hadn't he? Sure, that was what happened to the hand, Father, may God strike him down if he was lying. Self defence it was, Father, sure, he'd no choice but to defend himself, swear!

The Father uncomfortably circumvented that one by calling Nan back into the sitting room and asking her to fix Brian a late snack as he'd missed dinner. As the priest did so, Brian began informing the other inmates in a whisper about what some of the local women were saying. The Devil was coming to Craiglann–Brian said that was the latest rumour –and the coming storm was heaven-sent, too. It was God's retribution against the sinners of the world – or so the wee woman in the post office had told him. Aye, God was exacting revenge by sending an apocalypse– a small one, mind–just to warm us up for the big one we'd be getting in 2032. Brian lifted his head, aware the priest was listening: It's what everyone's saying, Father, swear! They're quoting Nostradamus, talking about Judgement day just as in Exodus, something to do with the wrath of God, swear!

Needless to say, all of this was quickly dismissed by the Father, who solemnly declared that Brian shouldn't go listening to all that end-of-the-world-is-nigh *tat,* as it was simply the confounding nonsense of born-again Christians, Jesuits and Jehovahas! *And,* the priest added sharply, he'd be pleased if Adullam's guests wouldn't go *spouting* it in public and getting everyone's hackles up, thank you very much!

Miles left Adullam shortly after that, returning straight to Mullan's where he ordered a pint of black, intending to take it easy so he wouldn't miss anything when the rest of the townspeople returned from the meeting. He ended up taking another three pints, however, as the clock struck 8-00pm, then 8-30pm, then 9-00pm, for there was still no sign of anyone. Then, at roughly 9-10pm, Old Jack blustered in through the door, near-breathless, his features paler than normal and him speaking a commotion. Miles, taking advantage of this distraction, moved closer to the small group now gathering around the older man so that he too could hear what Jack was about to say.

There'd been a whole carry-on down the Garda station, Jack declared loudly, and he looked about him then, saying he was surprised no one had heard it up here. Dave Mullan, immediately forsaking another customer mid-order, gave Jack a quick short of whisky to keep his tongue fluid before bidding him continue.

Well, Jack said after a swallow, it'd all started innocent enough, with about a dozen locals setting off to the Garda station. Laughing and joking, they'd been aiming to get things sorted out before getting home out of the rain. But, sure, Vinny wasn't there when they arrived, and that led everyone to conclude the Chief Guard didn't care what people thought. Naturally, a few angry words were uttered, yet the crowd retained a sense of calm even then. But, sure, hadn't wee Con Logue arrived in at that, and him all agitated as nobody had mentioned the meeting to him. And hadn't the garage-owner started on about what people were saying about his son – which was a bit rich, Jack snorted, as that subject hadn't actually come up until then.

But then Neil said something–Neil, the markct-trader whom Con was fighting the other night–Neil Martin, was it? As Mullan nodded and raised his eyes to heaven, Jack continued, explaining how Neil had informed Con that everyone was there to help clear wee Eddie's name, yet Con had retaliated sharply by saying his son was innocent, so why would he need his name cleared? Still, no actual punches were thrown at that stage, as everyone was crammed into the reception room and there wasn't room enough to swing a cat. The fight didn't actually begin until Vinny and two of his men arrived and began asking everyone to move outside into the rain as they were creating a fire-hazard. Of course, Jack snorted, what with everyone then getting soaked through to the skin, there was nearly a riot in the hall, with people throwing sly punches over each other's heads and the Guards in the middle of it threatening violence. God, it was awful, Jack mumbled, the worst he'd ever seen or heard, and he'd seen some scraps in his day!

Mullan shook his head in disbelief. So, was it over? he asked, beating everyone to the bite. Jack vehemently shook his head. *Over?* Christ, it was only beginning! For now people were talking–(and when pressed as to *who* was talking, Jack wouldn't say)–about going up to the farmhouse and hauling the Stranger out. Of course, Vinny was quick to respond that he'd jail anyone caught doing that, as the Stranger's was innocent until proven guilty. But that, Jack said, was all he'd heard, for he left shortly afterwards, feeling things were getting way out of hand. Still, just before he went, he'd heard Vinny on his walkie-talkie, ordering in his part-timers and some Guards from somewhere up the country, though the latter were apparently too busy helping the overwhelmed Fire Brigade clear a few fallen trees. Vinny hadn't exactly been trying to raise a riot squad in the strictest sense, Jack surmised finally, yet everyone knew he wasn't the sort to tolerate public disorder for very long.

As Old Jack concluded his tale, Miles returned to his corner seat. There, he chuckled lightly under his breath, realising he'd guessed the meeting's outcome from the start. He sank the remainder of his drink, musing that it was time to go home and forget this crazy world for a time. He waited until Mullan was distracted at the bar, then lifted a few half-empty glasses from a nearby table and poured their contents into his own glass. He watched numbly as the mixture settled into a thick tar of a drink. But, as he waited, he realised that, somewhere in his mind, he'd just called Adullam his home. The Mission Home, with its papyraceously thin curtains, its spotlessly white walls, its crazy inmates and the Father – time had finally institutionalised Miles Kivlehan into calling it his home.

Angry at himself for even letting such a thought broach his consciousness, he quickly picked up the drink and sniffed it, wincing at the smell. Then, holding his breath, he hurriedly swallowed it down, remaining there in his seat for another minute or so to see if his stomach would reject it. Near certain it would settle, he then rose unsteadily, pulled his coat from behind the curtain and put it on as he moved towards the door. Years ago, he knew, he'd never have imagined how easy it was to do some of the things which now came so easily to him.

Still, years ago Miles Kivlehan was a completely different person. Years ago, he used to fight for his own rights and the rights of others – they both did.

But then, of course, that was years ago.

S I X

Miles was groggier than usual when he awoke that Tuesday morning, prised harshly from a sombre dreamscape by a series of loud, disconnected commands resounding up from the downstairs hall. He slowly determined the voice belonged to Nan, who was brusquely informing her charges that it was time for Mass. The vagrant tried lifting his head from his pillow, but couldn't, before recalling the near-incapacitating cocktail he'd gulped down in Mullan's the previous night in a bid to draw himself into the deepest of sleeps: *Drink from the Underworld River Lethe and forget your time on earth before you cross into Hades – your dreams shall vanish, and peace shall be yours forever.* It was a legendary Greek ritual which you were supposed to perform upon the moment of your death, though Miles had long since learned the Lethe could often be poorly substituted in life.

Naturally, there was a price to pay for that most fleeting of comforts. Today, his bones ached, his chest was constricted and his thoughts bleakly cloyed. Despite this, even as he eased himself slowly and painfully out of bed, it soon struck Miles that only he and Wing-Ding were present in the dormitory. The youth–already washed and dressed, but with his hair in its usual snakelike tangle–wordlessly watched Miles pulling on his clothes, after which the two men slowly made their way out of Adullam and into St Augustine's.

When they arrived, Pele and Brian were seated in their normal pew, but the chapel was otherwise half-empty. Miles glanced quickly up the right aisle; his usual seat behind the stone pillar which he favoured solely because it concealed him from the Father's view–now lay untaken. The vagrant eased his way into it and sat down, with a pouting Wing-Ding trailing noisily in his wake. The chapel seemed colder this morning, even though the heating was probably up full, so Miles drew his coat in close to his body. Moments later, he closed his eyes, supposing he still had a few minutes before the priest arrived to hypnotically ease his flock into yet another day.

***

The barriers of time vanished and Sarah was sitting upon their favourite bench in the grounds of the local park as he arrived, seeking shade from the afternoon sun beneath a verdant canopy of maple and elm as she studied a translation of Homer's *Iliad*. As Miles sat down beside her, he pleasantly reflected that several weeks had now passed since his small romantic coup, with the interim having granted him a further boon of two successful sprinting victories over a spiritually-defeated Mark Brady. To add to his satisfaction at this upturn in his sporting profile, Miles felt buoyed by Sarah's revelation that she'd had 'a feeling' about the two of them from the start, for he now knew their romantic interlude was his to own for as long as he wished, and, too, that he'd no need to worry about her running back to Brady.

Still, despite Sarah's doubtlessly sincere disclosure, Miles as yet considered theirs a temporary relationship. In his mind, she was just another girl to whom he'd impart fleeting happiness before moving on. And, in truth, Sarah made it easy for him to feel that way: She always seemed content to be with him, no matter what he suggested they do; she would openly discuss most aspects of her life with him, even if he was purposely reticent about his own; and she even accepted and forgave his bleaker moods, the latter of which made Miles suspect Sarah had always played a secondary role in romantic affairs and was therefore prepared– and even quite willing–to settle for whatever was thrown at her.

Comforted by such certainties, Miles spent more time with Sarah over the ensuing weeks, attending seminars with her on study days, going for long walks with her in the evening, or, if they'd money to spare, to the cinema, local bars or nightclubs. Naturally, with the campus as small as it was, Miles had to refrain from seeing other girls during that time, but he was prepared to suffer that loss just then. And yet, one morning soon afterwards, it struck him that something was wrong in his life. For several days and nights he'd felt edgy and unsettled, and that mood had pervaded all aspects of his academic, social and romantic life. It was only upon noticing the date on his alarm-clock that he understood: He'd been seeing Sarah for three months now, and his self-imposed time-limit with any girl was about six weeks. At that moment, Miles felt crowded and an inner voice insisted he get out while he could. Besides, his greatest sporting rival had long since been despatched, and Miles had not only won Sarah over but bedded her too.

Supposing he'd no real choice, Miles decided to ditch Sarah, but he knew he'd have to be careful how he did so. After all, because Miles was viewed as a charming rogue on campus, he couldn't be seen to have openly duped Sarah, who was by then equally popular amongst her peers for her kindly ways and quirky personality. Knowing this, Miles reverted to a 'dumping strategy' he'd used in the recent past. Basically, whenever he felt pressurised by any of his conquests, he'd sought out the positive aspects of their union and destroyed them. If a girl enjoyed walking on the beach, for example, he'd cease doing it; or, if she liked going to the cinema, he'd cease doing it. Each time he'd recognised a commonality of deed, thought or purpose, he intuitively weeded it out, thereby placing an immediate onus on his partner to find alternative ways in which to please him. Naturally, each of these alternatives would soon be met with the same rebuttal; and, in this way, Miles soon convinced his partners that they'd little in common, before dumping them and moving swiftly on to his next conquest.

So Miles tried such an approach with Sarah over the ensuing two weeks, yet Sarah–ever-compliant and seemingly oblivious to his scheme –sought to re-accommodate him in every way possible. Frustrated by this, Miles next attempted to make it appear as if the gradual breakdown of their relationship was solely Sarah's fault. He'd accuse her of turning up at his apartment at unusual times of the day because she didn't trust him–(after all, he was popular with other girls, he declared coldly, and she perhaps couldn't deal with that)–or, on those nights when Sarah wanted to go out with her friends, he'd accuse her of putting them before him. In addition, he'd find fault in everything she did; he'd stop confiding in her, thereby leading her to suspect she wasn't worthy of his trust; and he'd expect her to know what he was thinking, then storm off when she didn't.

It was a cold process, he knew, and he'd eventually have to blame her for ending their affair, yet hopefully they'd talk again in the future. But then, wasn't he actually doing Sarah a favour? They had very little in common after all, so it was best she moved on. And wasn't this what you did when you liked someone? You let them go, after firstly considering their welfare before your own.

Nevertheless, when the time came to actually finish with Sarah, it hurt Miles more than he expected. It was a summer's day, they were studying in the park, and he simply told her he wanted to end it because they hadn't been getting on for too long, and he knew in his heart it wasn't going to work. His tone had been arrogant, and he'd raised his head to let her know his word was final, seeking an agitation to supply him with a further excuse to say 'I told you so'. And yet, struck inarticulate and staring soulfully into his eyes, Sarah hadn't said a word in reply. She'd simply nodded her sad recognition of the situation and walked away. Miles had frowned at that, unable to comprehend what she was thinking. Didn't she care enough about him to fight back? With other girls there'd been arguments, the placing of blame, something he could snap back at with a carefully considered response – but what had happened here? There'd been a slight recognition in her eyes, a notion, perhaps, of what was going on in his head, or of how he'd manipulated the situation to his own advantage.

But just walking away – hadn't she said she'd had a feeling about the two of them? Miles didn't understand.

The days would pass slowly after that, with Miles wondering where his formula for romance had failed. Sarah, however, would never intentionally avoid him after that day–attending the same university course, it would have been much too difficult for her to do so–yet she was never the same with him again. And, when Miles heard from her closest friends that she was talking about quitting university and going home to nurse her sick father, he'd find himself experiencing the strangest emotions he'd ever known in his life.

***

Now, Miles startled awake, only to discover that the Father had begun Mass, and yet the priest's tone was strangely condemnatory. Miles straightened, aware that one particular sentence was forcing its way into his brain. There'd been a *shot* fired outside the Stranger's farmhouse late last night – the Father was repeating that over and over, while staring accusingly into his congregation as if each person there was solely responsible for firing it. The priest paused momentarily, before solemnly adding that the events of the previous night were a downright *disgrace*. Everyone running up to the farmhouse after causing a *near-riot* down in the Garda station – whatever had they been *thinking*?

Miles stared around, quickly realising there were many more people present in the chapel than usual. The diminutive and now panda-eyed garage-owner, Con Logue was here, as was his wife, Deborah, and his son Eddie. Sitting directly behind them was Vinny McIntyre, Mrs Malhaffey from the community-centre, the Old Man and countless others who never usually attended morning Mass. Still, Miles was more surprised to espy the elderly Judge Laverty in the back row: Something of a recluse these days, Miles couldn't recall the last time he'd seen the retired judge in chapel. The vagrant felt his interest peaking and he sat bolt upright in case he missed anything.

Up into the *air*, that was where the shot was fired, the Father continued, and, sure, wasn't it a good job! Of course, if everyone had *listened* to Vinny in the station last night and stayed *away* from the Stranger's farm, that *wouldn't* have happened, would it? The priest raised a hand as mild whispers swept through the congregation, and he apologised then for not knowing the newcomer's name, but it was pronounced in the Gaelic, apparently, and he'd never been good with the native language. That aside, he said with a dismissive wave, it was hard to credit that, last night, some of his parish actually threatened to *lynch* the man if he didn't come out and answer the charges being levelled against him. Still, that wasn't the worst of it, the priest frowned, for when the man *had* come out to talk, nobody *wanted* to listen. The mob–and they *were* a mob, for only *mobs* acted as such–started clambering over his gates and throwing bricks at him and his dog, forcing them both to rush back inside and close the door. And, sure, hadn't that same mob then tried breaking his door down, causing the Stranger to react by firing off one *defensive* shot from his shotgun?

Up into the air, of course, Father Joseph repeated wearily, but, sure, God almighty, wasn't that *understandable*? The Father raised his hand higher as yet another spiked susurration swept through his congregation, yet this time it took slightly longer for the gathering to quieten. Alright, the priest reasoned, so everyone here *knew* what this was about: Wee Marie Devine had been missing a week now. *Sad* it was, and, sure, no one felt it as much as he did as she was a member of his flock, a *lovely* wee girl whom he'd baptised, given first-communion, confirmed and had even planned to *wed* to her beau here in St. Augustine's, *but*...

The Father took a deep breath, then began patiently explaining that the Gardai were investigating Marie's disappearance full-time, *and*, just because the Chief Guard hadn't *yet* imparted his findings to the public, it didn't mean he wouldn't do so *eventually*. Y'see, leads were followed *surreptitiously* at times–that was how policing went–and investigations took *time*. Furthermore, what would *Molly* say if she saw the way people were going on? She wouldn't like it one bit, the Father declared, and he was *absolutely* certain about that. The priest paused, allowed a mantle of guilt to settle, then stared momentarily between Con Logue and the Old Man, after which he dropped his gaze and remarked that *no one* in particular could be blamed for instigating last night's sorry affair, because *no one* knew for certain *who'd* roused the mob into firing stones at the Stranger, nor *who'd* been the first to call the man a murdering...

Well, again, that wasn't important, the Father sighed. What *was* important was that everyone realised the Stranger was an *ordinary* man who'd bought the farm on Pheasant's Crest with the intention of cropping it, and *nothing else*! So, why didn't they stop blaming him for Marie's disappearance and concentrate upon *helping* Molly and the Gardai in any way they could? Besides, there was a big storm approaching and apparently it was going to be *really bad*, making the wind of the last few nights pale in comparison. So why didn't everyone *focus* upon that? Of course, it would perhaps be for the best if everyone *stayed at home* tonight, for then the emergency services would know where everyone was if the worst came to the worst. But *if* things got tight, Adullam had a few extra beds.

The Father raised a hand again then and said there was just one more thing to mention: Weather permitting, both he and Vinny were holding an *official* meeting in the community centre that afternoon at 2-00pm, and all were welcome to attend. But this time, as the meeting was *official*, there'd be *dignity* about the whole thing. This time, everyone would be *seated* and they'd have to put their hand up if they wanted to *speak*. And, this time, the *Stranger* would also be asked to attend...

Miles stared around as the disgruntled murmurs peaked at that unexpected declaration, before turning back to regard the Father, who now stood with his head raised high as if to declare that the meeting would still go ahead, no matter the level of dissent. The vagrant then watched with bated breath as the priest–seemingly unfazed by the simmering furore–dropped his head, joined his hands and prayed that God watch over Marie Devine wherever she might be, before quickly closing Mass.

Several minutes later, as the church de-flocked, the vagrant sat shaking his head in mild disbelief: The Stranger confronting the hotheads of Craiglann in the community centre – what was the Father thinking? The priest obviously didn't seem to understand he was playing with fire.

***

Later that morning, Miles was sheltering from the driving wind and rain in a doorway beside the off-licence when an elderly local farmer, Emmet Harley, and his middle-aged son passed by. As he stopped at the doorway and rummaged for change to give to Miles, the older man mused that, although he hadn't agreed with everything that Father Joseph had said earlier that day, the priest had been correct in one regard: There was a big storm coming, and, if it was anything like the Big Storm of '58, they were in for a lot of trouble. At this, Emmet's son pursed his lips thoughtfully, saying he'd never heard of that particular storm.

Well, his father explained, the main problem back then was that the river hadn't been as well-secured as it was now, causing it to flood its banks and sweep down from the surrounding hills into the town. Naturally, those living on the Crissom–the Hart's original course–had been forced to abandon their homes as the river flooded the entire road, even as it short-circuited the power-cables and phone-lines, leaving the whole town in darkness. Of course, the army had stepped in at the height of it; they'd had to, as it was a national emergency, and they'd even had to evacuate scores of people in boats. Christ, that'd been really bad!

As the two men moved inside the off-licence, Miles quickly counted his scran and moved in behind them. For once, the vagrant was thankful that there were another four or five people in the queue ahead of them, as he once again found his interest peaking.

Aye, Emmet reflected, it was a bad storm, yet St. Augustine's had remained undamaged due to its position on the Crest. But the graveyard on the lee of the hill behind it hadn't escaped as easily. Y'see, the earth up there was very boggy at the time, due to a lack of drainage. As a result, the ground soaked up thousands of gallons of water, which led to countless graves being flooded and disinterred by the force of the wash. Aye, Emmet continued sombrely, it was said that many of the corpses were never found, and that others were dismembered and thrown back into the first casket the council workers came across. Of course, everyone knew that St. Augustine's was protected by God and so immune from the wrath of angry spirits. But the old farm, well, that was too close to the graveyard to remain unaffected. And, if you thought about it, Emmet pouted, over the last few years every successive owner of the place had stayed there a shorter time than the last. Sure, that hardly made sense: You bought a farm and you worked it for twenty years at least! So, maybe all the previous owners had been driven out, and maybe they'd been afraid to say what happened for fear of being ridiculed. Or maybe they'd simply been possessed by malevolent spirits. And, of course, there was always the chance this Stranger was weaker than most, and that he was now being impelled to do all manner of crazy stuff, just like Jack Nicholson in that film about the shiny thingamajig...

The two farmers collected their order, thanked Big Michael, then left. Miles was now the only customer and the off-licence owner regarded him neutrally for a moment, before taking a half-bottle from a nearby shelf. Big Michael held out his hand and Miles smiled thinly as he handed over the money. There was a look of genuine surprise on Big Michael's face: The right money this time, Miles? And a bit over to pay of some of your debt, too? Very nice indeed!

The vagrant's heart skipped a beat, yet he didn't say anything, not having a leg to stand on. Big Michael quickly noted the look upon his face, however, and sighed loudly, before taking another half-bottle from the shelf. He handed both to Miles, who, in turn, nodded his genuine appreciation and carefully tucked the bottles deep into his inside pockets. The vagrant then left the off-licence and the wind ushered him up the Crissom towards Adullam. As he walked, Miles kept his hands very firmly fixed around his prize: To drop even one bottle of the precious ruby-red liquid now would mean one hell of a lot of pain later on.

Back in Adullam, Miles realised that none of the other inmates had as yet returned. Nan, too, was busy in the bathroom and the Father was nowhere to be seen. Miles seized that opportunity and sneaked out to one of the back sheds, where he deposited his cache behind a pile of old boxes. Going back inside, he then made his way upstairs, where he changed into fresh clothes. Lunch passed as a formality a small time later, with the other inmates having little to say and the Father reigning supreme over the meal. Soon after, Miles returned to the dormitory, where he intended to lie down, but Wing-Ding stood in the doorway.

'The, ehm, community-centre,' Wing-Ding hedged. 'You goin' over there?'

Miles had forgotten all about the meeting. His only real concern now lay with his wine: What if it was discovered when he was away? A fearful caprice suddenly struck him and he was momentarily undecided. He could take a chance on going into town, he supposed, because it wasn't as if he could actually do anything if Nan chose to conduct yet another sporadic shakedown. Besides, if his cache was discovered, he'd be left with nothing, no matter where he was. On the other hand, if he attended the community centre, he might well scrounge some more money from one or two sympathetic locals.

Wing-Ding smiled as Miles nodded, his decision made. The older man then pulled on his coat and damp hat, knowing the latter would afford little protection, yet hoping it would warm him slightly. Minutes later, the two men left Adullam and walked towards the town with their heads declined as the rain attempted to cut sections out of them. They reached the centre about ten minutes later. Inside, Mrs Malhaffey greeted them warmly, saying the Father and a few others had turned up. Vinny McIntyre hadn't arrived yet, though, and Mrs Malhaffey implied that wasn't good, especially with the events of the previous week. Wing-Ding responded to each of her comments with a small nod, before fugitively suggesting the weather may've had something to do with the Guard's absence. The wee woman smiled kindly, saying she hadn't thought of that – which would, Miles knew, have sounded sarcastic coming from someone else, yet it sounded kind from her.

Miles and Wing-Ding entered the main hall. There were perhaps a dozen people present in all. The Father acknowledged the inmates' arrival with a brisk nod, before turning to talk to Con Logue and a small knot of parishioners. As Miles moved further into the hall, he unobtrusively homed in on what the garage-owner was telling everyone about Saturday night's fight in the Drunken Duck, and Monday night's disturbances in both the Garda station and outside the old farmhouse. Con was stating loudly that, fair enough, in hindsight he probably shouldn't have gone up to the farmhouse and offered the Stranger out to the road for a clean fight, and yet the scurrilous accusations being laid against his son, Eddie, had messed his head up to no end. Still, he hadn't orchestrated the charge on the farmhouse: No, the bunch of parasitic hyenas who'd followed him up the Crest had done that! So why was his name the only one being bandied about, Father? What about Mullan's henchman, Big Sean, who was about as reasonable as Lizzie Borden on acid? What about Frank Devenney, who–bad leg aside–could incite a crowd better than anyone bar Hitler? What about George Harkin, Neil Martin and countless others he could mention? Of course, Con harrumphed, their involvement hardly mattered, did it? Because the people of this town were more into innuendo and speculation than fact. And, Con declared, they didn't seem to realise it was a fact the Stranger was in this thing up to his neck! A fact, because the guilt was written all over him and he was afraid of being found out for what be was!

The Father hmm-ed and haa-ed uncomfortably as Con paused for breath, before quickly regarding his watch and explaining that this was why they were holding the meeting. Everyone's doubts would soon be *erased*, the priest smiled thinly, and all of their, *mmm, theories* would soon be openly aired, with the *real* facts laid bare for everyone to see.

Miles listened to Con Logue's abstruse arguments for a further few moments, then moved further up the aisle, unable to fathom the logic applied. He saw several rows of chairs lined before a raised dais–upon which were set a table and three chairs–so he took a seat in the last row, sighing tolerantly as Wing-Ding sat beside him. The vagrant half-listened to the youth's incessant chatter–much of which was a repeat of their last few conversations–and nodded occasionally, lost in his own vague thoughts. But he startled suddenly as Wing-Ding poked him in the ribs. Coming out of the toilets was Molly Devine, flanked by her two oldest daughters and three of her young apprentices. The senior hairstylist was pale and nervously disposed, perhaps uneasy at the imminent prospect of having her life's troubles laundered in public.

Coming through the front door at the same time alongside an infantry of followers was the slightly crippled Frank Devenney, and he immediately gave Con Logue a spiteful glare, before edging into the middle of the second aisle. The farmer Emmet Harley, the Old Man and

Dave Mullan entered as a group, followed closely afterwards by Brendan Harper, the accountant for whom Marie Devine had worked full-time. Molly Devine greeted everyone in that small group with a faint smile, before being side-lined by the accountant, who sorrowfully explained that he'd been away on holiday for the last fortnight, only to arrive back this morning and hear the dreadful news. Several minutes later, the Rafferty family came in, as did the elderly Judge Laverty. The town's former judge gravitated immediately to the Father, declaring in not-so-hushed tones that he'd been sitting at home with nothing to do and thought he'd pop over. Still, everyone wasn't to go getting on edge because he was here, he explained, because he wasn't a judge anymore, and this was just an informal sort of a hearing anyway.

Miles felt something akin to pity for the Stranger then, feeling the man was in for a hard time of it when he appeared. The vagrant watched the door for a time, expecting more people to show, but no one else arrived. The gathering now numbered some two-dozen in all. Time passed slowly after that and everyone sat there complacently, with only low whispers escaping their lips. But at roughly 2-30pm, Miles noticed Mrs Malhaffey approaching the dais, whispering something to the Father and pointing him towards her office. The priest left the main hall for a few minutes and, when he returned, appeared ill at ease. He stood upon the dais, coughed uncomfortably and said he'd just had a phone call from Vinny McIntyre. The Chief Guard had asked the Father to forward his apologies as something had *come up* and he wouldn't be able to attend the meeting; it would, therefore, have to be *postponed* for now, if that was *alright* with everyone present.

Well, it was hardly alright – a general shaking of heads and a disgruntled buzz told the Father this before he'd even finished speaking. Con Logue, however, was the first to say it openly.

That said it all, the garage-owner thundered: Vinny hadn't bothered his arse showing up at yet *another* important meeting, proving once and for all he was a law unto himself! Still, Con spluttered, at least the Chief Guard *had* phoned. The Stranger, on the other hand, hadn't phoned *or* turned up, which meant he was just sitting on his arse, in his farmhouse, guilty as sin! The man was afraid to come in and let the law-abiding people of the town question him; or afraid, more likely, that Con Logue would crack him, Con declared thickly, because he could personally tell when anyone was lying; it was all there in a man's eyes. So, in retrospect, was it any wonder that even the more decent people of the town were now calling the Stranger the Murderer?

Several other vociferous comments were voiced after that, none too different in the main, and then a series of pointed questions were aimed at the priest. Why wasn't Vinny coming, Father? This thing that had 'come up', did it concern the wee girl? Couldn't a couple of Vinny's men still escort the Stranger down to the centre instead, Father, just so everyone could get this mess sorted out? And, with respect to Molly, Father, was there even any hope of ever seeing the young..?

That last question was left unfinished as everyone, including Miles, turned to regard Molly Devine. She'd retained her composure until then, but now there were tears in her eyes because someone had attempted to openly deny her hope. Still, the vagrant's gaze was drawn suddenly away from Molly as a hailing breeze cut up the aisle and a tall figure walked in through the door. Miles was the first to see him, and he nudged Wing-Ding hard in the ribs; he was also the first to see the Father turning, and genuine surprise registering upon the priest's face.

Wing-Ding didn't recognise the man standing in the doorway. But then he wouldn't have, Miles mused, because Tomas had left Adullam some years before the youth's arrival.

Now, Tomas stood calmly at the community-centre door, a small rucksack thrown across his back. He was about 33 years old, six-feet tall and thin. His hair was longer than Miles remembered, and his face was unshaven, his clothes dishevelled. Moreover, despite being thoroughly soaked through, it didn't seem to bother Tomas that he was allowing all the warm air to escape the hall, nor did he seem fazed by the wind which blustered around him, sending a detritus of old sweet papers and a chunder of cinnamon and russet-brown leaves in across the polished floor and under the seats. Tomas seemed oblivious to all this, and he remained in the doorway as if awaiting an invitation to join the gathering. Upon espying Miles, however, he smiled familiarly and strode towards him. As he approached, Miles turned again to regard the Father, who was torn between comforting Molly and frowning his displeasure upon noticing his nemesis had returned to Craiglann.

Miles stared once more at Tomas; he chuckled softly as he noticed one of the other man's shoes was missing, with a heavy wrap of four or five socks replacing it. But that was Tomas, Miles mused, totally dismissive and unconcerned about everyone and everything.

The smile remained with Tomas as he walked down the aisle centre. He dropped his rucksack on the floor, ignored a frosty look from an old woman across the way, then sat in the chair next to Miles. Tomas looked around the hall as if keenly assessing the situation, before smiling broadly once again; and his smile was so alluring it drew a similar one from Miles almost instantly. 'Good to see you again, Miles.'

Miles nodded thoughtfully. 'Aye, and you too Tomas.'

Tomas' face was studious. He surveyed the crowd for a few moments, before nodding. 'Bit of a meetin' goin' on here, I see! I noticed all the cars outside, and thought I'd take a look in before goin' on up to Adullam.'

Miles nodded, inwardly amazed at the way in which Tomas could just pick up on life here in Craiglann as if he'd just been away for an hour or less. Seconds later, Miles felt his ribs move; Wing-Ding was pressing a gentle elbow into them.

'Who is he, Miles?' The youth's voice was a hushed whisper, his tortured curiosity that of a small child who craved immediate attention. 'Who is he?'

'Tomas,' Miles told him with a thin smile. 'Tomas, this is Wing-Ding.'

Not in the least put out, Tomas nodded hello, as if used to meeting people with strange and fanciful names all the time. Wing-Ding did the same, if cautiously, as if he'd taken to patting a strange dog.

'Bit of a meetin' goin' on then?' Tomas repeated, nodding matter-of-factly before relaxing deeper into his seat.

'There's been a murder,' Wing-Ding informed him in a rush of breath before Miles could reply. 'A *bad* murder.'

'A murder, y'say?' Tomas seemed to reflect upon that for a moment. Then he pursed his lips thoughtfully. 'Mmm, sounds bad enough, I'll grant you that.'

'A bad murder,' Wing-Ding repeated, his eyes wider, near impossibly so. 'But there's no body and no weapon, and now we're having a meetin' about the killer who's sittin' on his arse at home in his farmhouse and won't come out.'

'A meetin' you say.' Tomas nodded reflectively again as he placed his feet on the end of the seat in front. His shoed foot dripped muddy drops to the floor; the one swathed in socks seemed to melt against the seat, a swampish ooze dripping from it. 'And a meetin' about a murder at that.' Tomas didn't seem overly impressed. 'With God's Geldin' at the head of it, too.'

'Aye,' Miles said. 'There's a wee girl missin' and the Father is tryin' to do somethin' about it.' Miles was aware that Wing-Ding was nudging him gently in the ribs again, the youth's impercipience clear in his frown.

'God's Geldin'?' Wing-Ding was searching the top of the hall with narrowed eyes for someone he may've missed. 'Who's that?'

'The blood-quaffin', Holy Vampire up there,' Tomas told the youth evenly. 'The Father – he was neutered for God. Had his balls cut off – not allowed to use them, y'see. Don't know if he ever really had them anyway, right enough.'

80

Visibly disturbed, Wing-Ding frowned darkly and slunk behind Miles. Miles shrugged evenly, before becoming aware that the Father was still staring down at the three men as if they were a foul pot-pourri of troubles. The priest was looking especially at Tomas, who'd dared to rest both of his feet upon the chair in front. Miles tried to make himself small in his seat.

Tomas smiled broadly once more, before folding his arms and closing his eyes. 'A bit of a meetin', eh?' he repeated for a third time. 'And God's Geldin' at the head of it. Aye, that'd be just about right.'

Miles dared himself to look up again a few moments later. From the look upon the Father's face, he could tell the priest was perhaps thinking he'd spoken too soon when he'd chastised Brian for saying the Devil was coming to Craiglann.

Miles shivered briskly, recalling the legend of Jason and the Argonauts: The king, Pelias, had been warned about the imminent arrival of a stranger who'd bring trouble to his court. Now, the words of that warning returned to Miles from somewhere within deeply buried depths.

Beware the arrival of the single-sandalled man!

S E V E N

Miles, Tomas and Wing-Ding stood in the community-centre door-way, watching as the Father gently ushered Molly Devine's young apprentices across the car-park towards his car through an assault of rain. Miles supposed that some people might've viewed the priest's offer to drive the girls home as his way of ensuring he didn't have to transport his own charges back to Adullam. But, to be fair, the vagrant had overheard the Father firstly offering Molly a lift. She, in turn, had softly explained that she'd be taking a lift from one of her daughters, although she was sure her apprentices would happily take him up on his offer.

As Molly scurried to her daughter's car, Miles studied her carefully. Lost and alone now, she resembled Melpomene, a Muse of tragedy, sagging like a snow-laden willow beneath her troubles and unable to discard that excessive weight. Molly's hopes had to be fading, the vagrant supposed, and today's failed meeting hadn't helped. Not only had Vinny reaffirmed his unreliability, but the Stranger had forsaken a chance to repudiate the heinous charge being laid against him, thereby compounding his guilt and further distancing himself from what little sympathy remained in the town. Now he was no longer the Stranger, but the Murderer, and how could he ever expect to come back from that?

The vagrant sighed heavily, feeling that Craiglann would know more trouble before this dark matter was settled. He then watched quietly as the locals filed from the centre, occasionally listening in on snatches of their conversation. The Chief Guard was mainly to blame for the ever-worsening situation–that was very much agreed upon–yet what Miles considered more alarming were underlying whispers which now declared the Father was also partly to blame. People were saying the priest's attempts at passive mediation, far from being constructive, were actually dragging the matter out. The Father, according to common consensus, would need to climb off the fence very soon and decide whose side he was actually on.

Minutes later, when the car park had emptied and the community-centre was being locked for the afternoon, the three vagrants moved outside at the gentle behest of Mrs Malhaffey, and they stood in the doorway for a time, watching solemnly as the walls of the centre were pounded a hassled grey by the rain. It was obvious that the weather wasn't going to improve; the sky was blotted ink-black and, if anything, the storm was picking up. Accepting this inevitability, the three men took to the Crissom, avoiding a frothing spume that seeped from the over-clogged drains to run as a gurgling tide against the kerbstones, giving passing cars no choice but to send the poisoned water forth as a spray. Miles braced himself as they hurried along, waiting for a drowning that thankfully never came. Minutes later, the men crossed the bridge and moved up Pheasant's Crest into the grounds of Adullam.

From the bottom of the gravelled drive, they espied the Father spectrally haloed against the brightly-lit sitting room window, his hands firmly clasped behind his back. The priest appeared to be scrutinising the topmost boughs of the Great Oak behind the chapel, no doubt empathising with that tree because, like him, it gave little even under the greatest duress. Upon espying the three men moving up the drive, however, the priest's forehead seamed heavily and the look upon his face said he'd more than enough troubles for now and didn't need Tomas to compound them. Presently, the front door was opened by Nan, who instantly granted Tomas a discordant stare, having disliked him intensely since the time he accused her of being a nun who hadn't the guts to go the whole way. Despite this frosty reception, Tomas bade her a cheery hello, before breezing into the hallway and casting his rucksack into the corner like a man who felt relieved to be home. As Miles and Wing-Ding followed along, the Father exited the sitting room and stood wordlessly to their front, chin raised and hands clasped firmly behind his back.

A leaden silence fell upon the small gathering and Miles subserviently took a backward step, unsure as to what might occur. His primary suspicions were that the Father would allow Tomas to stay for several reasons. Firstly, the priest would hardly send anyone out into the approaching storm, no matter how much he abhorred them; and secondly, Tomas had long since served his temporary banishment. Now, Miles supposed wryly, in something paralleling the ancient Roman rules of postliminy, Tomas had the right to have his civic privileges restored, and all–or most–of his sanctions and curfews revoked. Of course, he'd also have to agree to undertake some form of Carthaginian Treaty, whereby his mischievousness and joy were permanently exorcised – the Father's eyes said all this and more.

All Tomas had to do was declare in true biblical fashion that he'd finally seen the light.

Tomas, however, didn't appear in the least bit intimidated by the situation. Relaxed and smiling indifferently, he reminded Miles of Momus then, the Greek God of Mockery who'd been cast from the heavens for his criticism of the other Gods. Noting this apathy, the priest released a prolonged sigh and nodded at the knapsack in the corner. 'You've no drink in that bag, Tomas, I presume? No stimulants, pills, or anythin' else of the like?'

Tomas smiled tolerantly, lifted the bag and held it up close for the priest to inspect – too close, perhaps. 'Wouldn't be so stupid as to offend you on my first day back, Father Joseph,' he replied easily. 'A few cigarettes, nothin' more.'

The Father nodded, not looking directly into the bag, yet it was obvious his enforced trust derived more from the fear he might appear a fool if he searched it and found nothing. 'Aye, well, go get yourself a wash,' the priest replied flatly. He allowed his gaze to fall to Tomas' feet. 'Miles or someone may have a pair of shoes for you to borrow. If not, Nan will find you some later.'

The Father turned and walked off into his study, his cushioned challenge withdrawn. Miles grinned nervously at that unexpected anticlimax. True, the Father had hardly been going to break out a fatted calf for the prodigal son's return, yet the vitriolic stares he'd granted the three men on their long walk up the drive had suggested there was far more to come. But then nothing, nothing at all.

Strangely relieved, Miles led the other men upstairs to the dormitory. There, Pele and Brian lay upon their beds, Brian smoking, Pele gazing long into the past. Moments later, there sounded a cracking report of thunder. It was the last thing Miles expected to hear and he startled visibly. Tomas patted him on the shoulder and moved easily into the ill-lit room, joking that this was what usually happened in horror-films when the demon arrived. Miles half-smiled at that, recalling an adage about there being more truth in jest, before staring up through one of the skylights to see shrouds of black cumulus masking the sky. The room darkened perceptibly and a jagged spear of lightning lanced towards the earth seconds later, yet it was impossible to know if it had sundered its target. An onslaught of rain thundered almost instantly off the windows; loud, very loud – the loudest Miles believed he'd ever heard.

'Looks like it's goin' to be bad,' Tomas said casually above the din.

Miles nodded grimly. 'Very bad,' he agreed, moving towards his bed.

'Well then,' Tomas grinned, 'I may just take a wee nap before it gets too serious.' He moved along the central aisle, checking out the untaken bunks. He finally chose one on the opposite side the room, almost directly across from Miles. 'This alright?' he asked, looking at Brian who was slowly savouring the last puffs of a cigarette.

The older man regarded him momentarily through wolf-eyes, as if keenly assessing the level of threat he presented, before shrugging dispassionately and turning away. Wing-Ding, now sitting upon his bed with his hands clasped around his knees, haltingly informed Tomas that no one else slept there.

'Good, then I'll make it my own,' Tomas smiled. He lifted his bag, shook out his belongings and set them in his locker. He then removed his single shoe and the build-up of socks from his other foot, before going to the bathroom. Removing his own coat, Miles lay upon his bed and lit a cigarette, watching as Pele–deeply unsettled by the commotion–got up and started pacing the room. Minutes later, Tomas returned, wandering stark-naked and with an almost Adamite innocence towards his bed, his wet clothing rolled under one arm. He left the bundle on the floor, drew back the blankets and climbed into his bed. For long moments he languished there, pressing his head deep into the pillows and smiling contentedly as if he hadn't known such luxury in a while. After a small time, Miles caught his gaze.

'Great to see you again, Miles,' Tomas said, fixing the blankets under his neck, before tucking his hands beneath them. 'Aye, it's good to be back.'

'Why did you come back?' Miles asked. He stubbed his butt in a nearby ashtray, after which he took another cigarette from the pack on his locker and lit it. 'There must be better places than this, and you've been gone long enough.'

The other man's grin broadened. 'Ah, I just came back to see the storm, Miles, nothin' else.' Tomas closed his eyes and his arms reappeared suddenly, only to be tucked up behind his head.

There to cradle that impossible grin, Miles thought idly, like the Golden Bowl upon Ocean that holds Sun each night. 'That has to be as good a reason as any,' he replied softly. He took a deep drag on his cigarette, then added uncertainly, 'I suppose.'

The other three men looked amongst themselves, saying nothing.

***

An hour passed and Miles lit his umpteenth cigarette, wondering when he'd be able to snatch a drink in the back shed without attracting any undue attention. It might be a while, he supposed, for the Father and Nan were downstairs; the housekeeper perhaps preparing dinner upon the worktop beneath the window overlooking the yard, the priest no doubt formulating a sermon in his study, the window of which also faced in that direction. Beset by a rising agitation, Miles tried focusing upon the shrieks of the wind as it rendered shrill notes from the outside guttering. But, when he realised the effect of this was less than pacifying, he turned his attention to the still-sleeping Tomas, forcing himself to recall the day they'd first met some four years before. It was the day Miles had attempted to take his life in the brook, the same day–less than an hour after speaking with the Father–that the vagrant realised he'd have to take his next attempt more seriously.

It had been a winter's night much like this one, and Tomas had arrived in Adullam shortly after 6-00pm. Having been excused Mass so that he might 'collect his thoughts', Miles was warming himself at the sitting room fire when there was a knock at the door. Seconds later, Nan answered it and Tomas wandered casually in out of the rain as if he'd lived in the Mission Home all his life. He then shook himself off like a dog and asked the bemused housekeeper if he was too late for dinner, before pouting sadly as she confirmed he was. Soon after, as he unpacked in the dormitory under the morose scrutiny of both Sean Allen and Miles –the only two vagrants in residence at that time–Tomas jokingly asked who'd died. Sean, never a great one for secrets, explained that Miles had tried to commit suicide a few hours earlier. Almost instantly, Tomas brazenly opined that Miles obviously had deep-rooted issues with the Christian concept of eternal damnation, because if he'd *truly* wanted to kill himself, he'd have thrown himself off St. Augustine's bell-tower – something that Tomas then darkly implied he was more than willing to help Miles out with the next time, if that was what he *really* wanted. Besides, Tomas added wistfully, what had Miles actually got to lose by taking his life anyway? He'd just be exchanging one hell for another, so what was God going to do – punish him again?

Somewhat naturally, Miles had been incensed by Tomas's attitude: Who was this arrogant newcomer to lecture him on anything? Still, as he'd lain in bed that night, Miles had replayed the botched suicide attempt over in his mind. Moments before he'd jumped into the brook, he'd reasoned that no hell could be as bad as that in which he currently resided, for how terrible might it be to wander evermore through grim Tartarus alongside the noble Titans? Or how awful might it be to be consigned–like the daughters of Danaus, king of Argos–to eternally carry water in bottomless sieves to fill a leaking pot? Indeed, what hells were they in comparison, for in their grim issue there was at least the removal of ever-fatiguing hope.

Nevertheless, just moments after he'd jumped into the brook, Miles broached the water's surface, certain his lungs had betrayed him or that an innate compulsion to fight for life had kicked in, the way it did with all creatures, base or otherwise. But, as quickly, it struck him that those weren't the real reasons at all. In truth, when the water had seemed set to fill his lungs, the vagrant suddenly realised that he'd hardly be awarded a hell of choice upon his demise, but the one he feared most. And, as his greatest fear in life was continual isolation and rejection, then surely he'd be condemned to eternal loneliness, which would, in turn, mean that his wife and daughters would not be there to greet him in death so that he might at last beg their forgiveness. So, as that dark realisation struck into him, Miles understood that he could not afford to take his own life. He had to live out the rest of his days–as mentally and physically fatiguing as they were–until death took him naturally. Nor could he ever again afford to deny even the lesser tenets of Christianity, for to do that might also ensure his eternal doom.

Tomas, as annoying as he had been on that first day, had actually been correct. And now, as Miles recalled that moment with a strange fondness, it struck him that, although Tomas had made light of his suicide attempt back then, he'd eventually become as much of a friend to him as was possible for two men in their particular situation, because, although neither man had ever once discussed how they ended up in the Mission Home, they'd at last accepted each other without judgement or reproof. At other times, Tomas had also proven a somewhat pleasant distraction, what with his unwillingness to be constricted by Adullam's unchained vassalage, his playful japes and his often brusque and startling neology. But then, some three months later, he'd left as suddenly as he arrived, proclaiming simply–and somewhat irrationally–that the world needed him and he needed the world.

Miles smiled thinly, realising Tomas was perhaps the nearest he'd ever met to a modern-day Odysseus: *Much travelled, he saw many cities and knew the ways of many men.*

Of course, Homer had surmised that there was nothing worse for mortals than a wandering existence, yet Tomas seemed unaffected by such a lifestyle. Miles allowed his smile to broaden, for some reason very happy Tomas had returned, yet unable to comprehend why. Lying there contentedly in the arms of Morpheus as if he'd partaken of the lotus and succumbed to a luxurious distaste for active life, Tomas seemingly had no worries. Still, how could he rest peacefully as globules of rain struck the windows with such deafening resonance? Without the drink to numb his incubation, he had to be restlessly scouring his dreams for cures to his real-life troubles. And, despite his outward bravado, he had to be possessed of pain and at odds with the world. Why else would his relationships with others remain in continual flux? Why else would he allow himself no respite from wandering? And why else would he return to Adullam? Was it because he simply had nowhere else to go now that

87

his problems were resolved? Or was it because he wasn't exactly the person he was portraying himself to be?

Miles felt his adrenaline rising as questions tumbled into his mind. How could Tomas–sober as he most certainly was–lay sleeping as the sky imploded and the heavens wrangled? Hadn't he mentioned something about the way lightning always struck when the demon arrived? Miles felt a coldness seeping into the pit of his stomach as he recalled exactly how Tomas had left Adullam. The younger man had walked westward to the top of Pheasant's Crest, just as Sun dipped into the great Copper Bowl that held her upon Ocean. West: According to Greek legend, both Hades and its infernal region, Tartarus, lay in that direction and could only be approached from the east.

Now, Miles felt his panic rising and he licked at dry lips, realising he needed something to keep his thoughts in check.

'Who is he?' Wing-Ding whispered, further unsettling his nerves.

'Tomas,' Miles replied shortly, taking a deep breath. 'I told you that already. Now go to sleep – you'll waken everyone up.'

'If we sleep now we won't sleep tonight,' Wing-Ding replied softly, repeating something the Father usually said to him. 'Tell us about...' His voice dropped to a whisper. '*Him.* Why doesn't the Father like him?'

'He was here before you, a few years ago,' Miles said tersely. 'Then he left. He was excommunicated for his beliefs.' A wry smile somehow eased its way through his angst. 'For believin' he could do or say what he wanted – that's a better answer.'

Wing-Ding, however, wasn't happy with that reply; he wanted to know what excommunication meant. Miles sighed tolerantly and very softly explained it to him.

'I arrived shortly after he left last time,' Brian said, opening his eyes and stretching cat-like, before dropping back exhausted onto his bed. He turned his gaze to the roof as the dormitory suddenly darkened and the wind rose up. Flashes of impotent lightning momentarily lit the room, and, when they'd vanished, the dim fluorescent bulbs on the ceiling provided an inadequate, lesser light. 'They say he was a bit of a rebel,' the older man yawned. 'Maybe a rebel without a clue!'

Miles, midway through another cigarette and hating the strong taste of the nicotine in his mouth, nodded just to keep the peace, even though he wanted to rebuke Brian for the latter half of his declaration and tell him that it a wee bit like the kettle shouting black-arse at the pot.

'I'm surprised the Father didn't strip-search him today,' Brian continued, acidly. 'What with him threatenin' to steal the silver from the chapel, the way you said he did the last time. Wild man back then, was he, Miles?' The older man narrowed his eyes and stared almost accusingly over at Tomas, who was still deeply asleep. 'I'd say he hasn't changed much. Bet he hasn't changed at all.'

'Probably just needs someone to believe in him, same as the rest of us,' Miles replied, wondering why he felt as if he had to defend the other man. After all, he was bound to suffer if he kept doing so. Seen as a co-belligerent by the Father, and as Tomas's only friend, Miles was bound to incur the priest's holy wrath somewhere along the line.

'I don't need anyone to believe in me anymore,' Brian sighed. 'For years I used to believe in myself when nobody else did. But then, that's the easy part.' He smiled a crooked smile. 'No one ever believed in me when I had nothin', but I was still one of the happiest men alive. Then I became successful. Christ, the problems I had then! Tryin' to believe in other people now they suddenly believed in me – you want to try that. And you wouldn't think it'd be like that, would you? You'd think money would patch over all differences.'

Miles frowned thoughtfully, but didn't reply. He stubbed out his cigarette, turned over onto his side, and, some indeterminable time later, fell asleep.

***

Rain dashing forcefully off the skylights brought him quickly awake. Jagged spears of lightning flashed the sky clear for three, four seconds at a stretch. Terrified, Miles sat bolt upright. He noticed Wing-Ding, Pele and Brian were awake, their eyes trained upon the windows, though Tomas slept on despite the erratic din. Miles took several deep breaths, seeking to reassure himself with fable: Lightning strikes were merely the jagged spears of Zeus, an unending supply of which were hammered into shape within a forge upon a lonely island in the Aegean by a Cyclops; and thunderstorms were simply giants being tortured to death, nothing more. The vagrant forced his shoulders to drop and, after a small time, his breathing slowed and he lay back down, wondering if anyone had noticed him about to go haywire because of simple thunder and lightning.

'Hard rain there,' Brian commented above the racket. 'Seen rain like that years back. Those skylights will never hold out to it.' His forehead had taken on a freshly ploughed look. 'They'll never hold out to that pressure, no way.'

Groggy, and his mouth dry, Miles tried to croak a reply, but he couldn't get his tongue to shape the words. He watched as Tomas stirred awake, stretched his arms and blinked several times to get used to the light. Smiling agreeably, Tomas said, 'They probably won't. Still, they're not supposed to, are they?'

'Of course they are,' Brian frowned. 'What sort of a bloody statement is that?'

'It's just my opinion,' Tomas shrugged, not even looking in Brian's direction. 'I take it I'm allowed one, this still bein' a democratic house of sorts.' He got up, took some fresher clothes from his locker, kicked the damper bundle aside and began dressing slowly. 'Dinner still at the same time around here?' he asked no one in particular. He scratched at his belly and belched loudly, his smile returning as Wing-Ding confirmed it was. 'Good, because I could eat a young pony. Haven't had a meal since last night, and late last night at that.'

'What brought you back?' Brian asked, as if not fully happy Tomas had returned.

Miles sat up, yawned a stunted yawn; tempted to lie down again, he regarded the clock – 4-45pm, only fifteen minutes until dinner. He noticed Tomas scrutinising him momentarily, before directing his attention at Brian.

'I got fed up wanderin',' Tomas replied easily. 'Sometimes it happens. Sometimes you just can't run far enough away, y'know, because the world catches up with you. So I came back to Adullam.' He grinned broadly, pulling on his trousers. 'And sometimes you just like to go where you've got friends.'

'Friends?' Brian snorted. 'You could've fooled me. The Father fuckin' hates you! You saw the way he looked at you in the hall. Hates you! And he can get right and nasty with people he hates. He dislikes me, too. Wouldn't say he hated me, right enough. But, even so, he dislikes me enough to get a dig at me now and then. Christ, he likes Miles, and you want to see the way he talks to him!'

Miles found his voice in anger. 'That's a lie! He hates me – he always has done!'

Brian regarded him darkly for a moment. 'He might hate you very soon right enough,' the older man replied with a grin.

Miles looked at him. That retort had been cryptic, but he wasn't in the mood for playing word and mind games. 'Why'd you say that?'

'I saw him goin' out to the sheds a time back, on one of his treasure-hunts,' Brian pouted. 'You, ehm, haven't anythin' *secret* goin' on out there, have you?'

Miles felt his heart skipping a beat. 'I was just gettin' some air, that's all.'

Brian shrugged dismissively, lit up a cigarette. 'Aye, whatever.'

Tomas looked at Miles, grinned. 'You still drinkin' out in the sheds, Miles?'

Miles shook his head vehemently, suddenly angry with both Tomas and himself. 'I'm goin' downstairs for a while,' he said, caustically. 'I'll see you later on. The noise of that rain is doin' my bloody head in!'

He almost strutted out of the dormitory, moving quickly down into the sitting room. It was bright there in that room with its windows facing out into both the front and back gardens, and Miles stood for a time, smoking and staring down the drive in the direction of the bridge and the town beyond. A thick wash of rain now blurred the middle distance, the last light of day eroding into a coalition of deeply-meshing shadows. The wind was gathering, too, blowing a mournful threnody in from the south and south-west, the first signs as always visible in the young willow which flopped fitfully about at the bottom of the garden in-between a younger but steadier growth of birch and elm. At the top of the Crest, Miles could see the Great Oak looming impassively and almost arrogantly above St. Augustine's. He wryly supposed the Dryads that dwelled within her felt safe from harm at the moment, despite the growing ferocity of the wind and the rain.

The tree's actual torso was as thick as five men, or so they said, and Miles guessed that was true. Her topmost branches also reached out for some fifteen- to twenty-feet in every direction, yet these were bare now, their spring and summer dressing of jade and lime lying in an umber mulch upon the spoiled grass beneath her. There were no birds upon her branches either, and Miles felt his heart sinking as he recalled Ovid's words: *Magna fides avium est, experiamur aves* – Great faith is put in the birds, let us try the birds! It was an augur of old, and by simply listening to the sounds of the birds, by watching the way they drank–or refused to– or by studying the way they perched upon branches, the ancient Romans and Greeks had been able to divine the weather for the approaching days and nights. Similarly, it was said that the will of the gods could be deduced from a bird's choreographed flight across the heavens, by the way it weaved circuitous arcs upon the backs of warm air thermals, or from how it described ever-dwindling configurations upon the back of cold down-drafts.

Before tonight, Miles had noted that the Great Oak was a constant haven to rooks and crows, no matter the weather. But now he saw no birds at all upon her high branches, none within her protective radius, and none in the surrounding sky. Not one bird, the resulting divination of which could only be bad fortune. He was pulled away from that gloomy thought as he heard the kitchen door being pulled open and quickly closed. Seconds later, the Father entered the sitting room, a cold breeze preceding him. The priest was soaked through to the skin and had obviously been in the back garden.

Miles stared quickly down at Father Joseph's hands, fearing his cache of wine had been discovered. The priest's hands were empty, yet Miles knew that meant little. While it was true the Father often revelled in parading his catch in front of the inmates, there were times, too, when he simply poured his reaved spoils away without telling a soul, making the unlucky owner of the drink believe his hoard remained intact. Filled with uncertainty, Miles stared distractedly through the windows again as the priest approached the fire and stood upon the hearth-stone, in silence, his hands clasped behind his back. A while later, Tomas wandered into the room and he moved immediately towards Miles. The Father didn't say a word; he simply allowed his eyes to journey between the two men, seemingly none too pleased with that bold association.

'Bad evenin',' Father,' Tomas smiled. 'It's rainin' a bucketful out there, isn't it?'

'I've noticed, Tomas.' The priest's reply was tolerant, though barely so.

'Semen of the Gods they call it, Father.' Tomas raised a hand to ward off any ill reply. 'In some cultures, that is.'

The Father paused for a moment. 'Are you, ehm, plannin' to stay with us for long this time, Tomas?' he asked as diplomatically as he could.

Tomas pursed his lips studiously, considering his reply for a little longer than was perhaps necessary. 'No, Father. One night, probably no more than that.'

'You picked a fine night for it then, didn't you?'

'I did indeed,' Tomas grinned. 'But then, I love the sort of storms that rage outside your head – they're so much easier to comprehend.' He stared out of the window for a time, watching bright-eyed as the wind whipped the once flaccid willow down the garden into a frenzy. Then he turned and winked at Miles, before adding, 'Aye, Father Joseph, I'd say we're all in for a hell of a night!'

***

For a long time that evening it seemed as if the much-promised storm was going to blow itself out, and the radio and television warnings to stay indoors appeared little more than unnecessary media hype. Earlier weather reports had warned of winds running at between nine and ten on the Beaufort Scale, which apparently resulted in anything from slight structural damage and partial flooding to temporary power loss, widespread flooding and collateral damage. Still, the reports also added that there was definitely no need to panic or stockpile massive amounts of food–though it would be advisable to store some water–for the storm would definitely last no longer than one or two nights at best.

Of all those in Adullam, Brian appeared the least daunted by the gloomy weather reports. The older man was certain that the forecasters were simply delivering a worst-case-scenario to cover their backs, and so now–because evening Mass had been postponed–he was even talking about wrapping up well and going into town a little earlier than usual. But then, shortly after dinner, the wind picked up with such ferocity that it startled everyone within the sitting room into taking immediate notice. Pele and Wing-Ding, who'd been dozing in front of the fire, came sharply awake as the window-panes rattled in their housing and the church bell clanged a disjointed chorus in the middle-distance. The two men rose from their seats and joined Miles, Tomas and Brian at the window facing into the dimly-lit front gardens. The five men watched in silence for a time as the evening waned slowly to darkness, each of them studying the sky like so many grim Magi and listening as the rain spat stones up from the gravelled drive in its fury.

Brian was the first to speak: Nobody was going anywhere after all, he declared dismally, because the storm was definitely on for the night. Upon hearing that, Tomas shrugged casually, his eyes as wide as those of a child on Christmas morning; and, lighting up a cigarette, he replied that he hoped it was, because the sheer bloody noise and mayhem of it let you know that you were really and truly alive!

Some time later, the doorbell sounded. Nan, with her right foot and shoulder tight to the door in case it blew in on top of her, edged it cautiously open to allow entry to Vinny McIntyre. The Chief Guard's cap was wrapped in a thin plastic covering, and his blue dreadnought was thick with rain. A fluorescent orange baldric was also looped from his shoulder to his Sam Browne belt, into which was tucked a waterproof flashlight. The Father exited his study a few moments later, the look upon his face one of genuine concern, and he extended his hand in greeting.

The inmates had moved towards the sitting room door at this stage. Not brave enough to open it fully, they took turns in staring out through a narrow gap to see what was going on. Tomas, ever the mordant wit, whispered that Vinny was here to ask the Father to build an Ark and lead the locals into it, two by two. The other inmates smiled at that, but Miles warned Tomas to keep it down as the Father heard everything, even when you thought he was otherwise preoccupied. Tomas shrugged casually at that and lit up another cigarette. In the ensuing silence the inmates then listened as Vinny firstly apologised to the Father for not showing up in the community-centre earlier on that afternoon, though he said he'd explain exactly why he hadn't done so later on. The Guard then went on to inform the priest that the town was being steadily dispeopled–it had been all evening–though, earlier on, a few had chosen to remain at home. Still, the rain was getting up and those who'd hung around–about two or three dozen or so–now realised their houses weren't safe enough. So would it be all right, Vinny asked respectfully, if they were to take shelter in Adullam for the evening? The Father smiled generously, saying that wasn't a problem – he'd made that offer this morning and it stood strong as ever. So, when were they coming up? And, also, what was the current situation in the town as they spoke?

Nan returned with a cup of tea and handed it to Vinny. He took a quick sip of it, before replying that the Hart had already breached its banks and the Crissom was now under roughly a foot of water, as the drains were clogged-up and unable to take the excess. Still, Vinny said he wasn't so sure how much damage the wind was doing. There were countless trees down, he'd heard that on the radio, but he'd be clearer on everything when he returned. The Chief Guard then handed the half-filled cup back to Nan, stuck his cap firmly back on and apologised for not being able to drink all the tea as it was the best he'd had all day. As he was about to leave, the Father asked Vinny to remind the townspeople to bring a few blankets and maybe some teabags and food to tide them through the night. Vinny said he would, and, with Nan again edging the door slightly ajar, the Chief Guard forced himself, head down and hand tight to his cap, into the night. The engine of his patrol car was barely audible above the screaming wind as it set off down Pheasant's Crest.

Nan wasted no time in barring the men from using the dormitory just shortly after that, telling them that if they'd any business upstairs they were to get it over with now, because once she started cleaning the dormitory, that was it – no one was getting in! And it had to be cleaned, she said, because *people* were coming to stay in Adullam, *people* from the town. Real people, she might've added, though Miles noted she at least had the decorum to refrain from doing so.

Shortly after 7-30pm, the housekeeper returned to the sitting room, muttering something under her breath about things she'd found in corners of the bedroom. Toenails, old and mildewed–they must've been there years, she snorted–as well as board-hard underwear and old socks. And in one corner, she'd apparently found something that disgusted the life out of her, though she wouldn't say what it was, only that she'd have called the fumigation people in if the weather wasn't as bad. She then sternly informed the inmates that she'd aired the place as best she could, changed the remaining beds–eighteen in all–and made the place half-liveable. So, it would be nice, she added pedantically, if they'd all leave it that way for a while without thinking they had to wreck it immediately – the way they always did! The Father, standing behind her, reinforced Nan's sour rebuke with a firm nod; and, when the housekeeper had finished, he asked the men to remain where they were for a moment as he'd something to add.

The Father began by saying that, by now, all of Adullam's regular habitués were aware of the *situation* with Molly Devine; how her daughter had *disappeared* and how things had been a bit of a *muddle* for the last week or so in town, with tempers reaching a *crisis* level and people doing and saying things they *didn't* mean. Of course, the priest continued gravely, he realised how *difficult* it was going to be for everyone present, what with a load of relative *strangers* about to invade their privacy. Still, Adullam was a *sanctuary* for *all* and he couldn't turn people in *need* away. So, if *everyone* present would take these factors into *consideration* and try to remain on their *best* behaviour until morning...

The priest looked amongst the five men, letting his last sentence hang, and the inmates nodded varying degrees of understanding. The Father nodded grimly then, his lips tightly pursed, before leaving the sitting room to seek the sanctity of his study.

'We can do that, can't we, Miles?' Tomas said neutrally. He was sprawled across the sofa, remote-control in hand, casually flicking fuzzed stations in and out of the ether.

Miles, sitting down in the armchair furthest from the sofa, stared at the other man for long moments, before shrugging uncertainly.

'Of course we can,' Tomas grinned facetiously. 'Of course we can.'

Having travelled up Pheasant's Crest in a small convoy of cars, the evacuees bundled noisily into Adullam's hallway. Peering unobtrusively through the sitting room door, Miles noticed the rain-lashed figures of Mrs Gorman, Mrs Malhaffey, Mrs Daly and Mrs Stevens spilling inside as a shivering gaggle, only to be lightly hectored on through by the irascible brood of Dan McGinty, Big Sean Flaherty, George Harkin, Neil Martin, Frank Devenney and the Old Man. Trailing behind, a more genial composition–comprising Big Michael Doherty, Dave Mullan, Hugh Rafferty and the accountant Brendan Harper–shouldered off the bitter rain and bravely awaited their turn at entry. Several less prominent locals were also present, all soaked to the skin and equally in need of shelter. But the Father and Nan greeted each there as a kindred spirit, taking their sodden coats and ushering them gently towards the sitting room in order to make way for the next incoming batch.

Realising their sanctity was under threat of imminent invasion, Miles huddled alongside the other inmates in the recess under the front window. Presently, the invaders edged tentatively into the room, only to herd warily at the door and regard the vagrants with defensive uncertainty. But that icy stale-mate melted away as Molly Devine and her two daughters cut unconcernedly through the divide and moved towards the fire. Encouraged by this, the interlopers began easing into the nearest seats and chairs, allowing yet another passive influx entry to the room, this small group inclusive of Old Jack and the elderly Judge Laverty and his wife. As everyone made themselves comfortable, Miles noticed that most people were reluctant to sit beside Adullam's regular habitués; and yet, his growing discomfort aside, the vagrant felt slightly vexed by this display of reticence, deeming the locals hardly in a position to choose. Still, when the diminutive Con Logue, his wife Deborah, and their son Eddie, finally showed up, Miles was grateful for that disparity of esteem. Scowling darkly, the garage-owner firstly extended a scything glare around the living room, as if daring people to meet his gaze, before loudly declaring that he was going to the dormitory to secure a few beds for his family. Aye, Miles decided dismally, if anyone was Factor X in this strange equation it was Con Logue, and the regular habitués were perhaps better having nothing to do with any of the new arrivals at all.

As Con stormed upstairs, his red-faced wife wrapped a protective arm around her son's shoulder before quickly apologising to everyone present for Con's behaviour. Her husband wasn't normally like that, Deborah explained; he was just sick of people intimating that Eddie had been involved in wee Marie's disappearance. Not only that, his business concerns had been getting to him for a long time now: What with the bigger conglomerates cutting prices, Con had at last been forced to put his garage up for sale, yet he still hadn't found a buyer. Of course, the Logues weren't the only ones falling foul of the multinationals, Deborah shrugged, seeking an ally in the Old Man, who was standing nearby.

Sighing heavily, the Old Man nodded, saying that, aye, he'd been trying to sell his shop for the same reasons. Deborah seemed relieved by that affirmation, yet she still wore a deep frown as she turned to ask Molly Devine how she'd been keeping since they spoke on the phone the previous day. Molly, barely retaining her composure, replied that she was keeping her chin up: Marie was alive–her mother's instinct told her that– and God was looking after her! The Father, entering the room at that point, nodded sagely: True enough, he agreed, God *would* be watching over Marie tonight–*wherever* she was–as well as hopefully keeping an eye on those who'd *chosen* to spend the night in Adullam!

Miles gazed around the room upon hearing that declaration, sensing an underlying lack of confidence within the ragged assembly, despite the fact most were nodding in agreement. Still, the Father seemed pacified by that consensus and he further informed everyone that Nan was going to make them tea while he went and secured the chapel bell, which, as they could all hear, was clanging away like mad. As the priest left the room, Adullam's latest guests settled as best they could, some drying themselves off with warm towels, some huddling around the fire, and others moving upstairs to the dormitory or the bathroom. All the while, the five vagrants looked on in silence as the newcomers traded theories and suppositions about the storm; and Miles, seeking to keep himself distracted, switched his brief attention span from one brisk tale to another in a bid to keep his mind off the drink.

The Crissom, already awash with a suet of gravel and clay, would soon resemble a floodplain–that was widely accepted–and the torrential rain guaranteed few buildings would escape flood damage. Muted talk was then exchanged about the inevitable ruination of carpets and linoleum, with each person there calculating how much the storm might cost them personally. But then the conversation switched track, with someone darkly inferring that the Hart was intent upon reclaiming its old course because Man had interfered with Nature and Nature was getting even, even as someone else added that the wind sounded like a banshee in mourning for someone either dead or about to pass on! At this, the Amazonian Mrs Daly shivered briskly, saying she pitied anyone out in it as it was strong enough to flench a whale, though it was probably nothing in relation to the winds God had planned for the End of Days! As she spoke, Mullan winked playfully at Big Sean, before replying that Mrs Daly could quote anyone she wanted, but, as far as he was concerned, the truth was there in the prophecies of Nostradamus! Which had the desired effect, of course, as Mrs Daly quickly retorted that he was talking nonsense: If you wanted the truth, she hissed, it was all there in the Bible, and the writings of Nostradamus were nothing but bloody riddles!

Big Michael, espying a gathering frown upon Molly Devine's face, was the first to point out that all that negative talk wasn't getting anyone anywhere: It was only a storm, the off-licence owner stated evenly, and they'd all seen storms before, even though this one was definitely going to get worse before the night was over! And such was the prophetic certainty with which he spoke that all other conversation died away as everyone turned to the front windows in a bid to gauge the determination of the storm. Out in the front garden, the willow and the elms were being ferociously pounded by the rain, and the thin white fence was under notable pressure too, a mere plaything for a rising gale that churned up a sodden leaf-storm around it, even as it hammered hard at the chapel bell further up the Crest. Seconds later, Judge Laverty's wife noted that Father Joseph had obviously secured the bell as it sounded duller now, yet she was quick to add that she didn't actually mind the noise as the toll often comforted her when she was feeling low! Molly Devine smiled sadly upon hearing that, again gently remarking that she hoped her Marie was in somewhere safe from the storm, wherever she was.

Unnoticed by most, the Father had been standing in the doorway for several moments. He shook his head and then smiled a gentle, yet reproachful smile. Now, now, he soothed, there was going to be a *bit* of a storm, and *maybe* it'd be the worst they'd seen for a long time. But it was *only* a bit of a storm, and, at every single moment in time, there were *thousands* of storms occurring all over the world, many far much worse than this!

Upon recognising the stark truth in the priest's statement, the general negativity dissipated almost instantly; and, shortly after 8-00pm, Adullam's latest guests had settled as best they could. A dozen more chairs were brought into the sitting room, the fire was stoked impossibly high and steaming bowls of chicken soup and tea were handed out to all present. Fully sated and seemingly tranquillised by the heat, the newcomers allowed their conversations to grow small as the evening progressed, granting the growing ferocity of the storm precedence. The inmates, too, began chattering softly amongst themselves, but Miles didn't join in. He lit a cigarette and stared out through the black window panes, attempting to decipher an adumbration of shadows and reflections in the Tartarean night to keep himself from remembering just why he needed a drink so badly. But the past, he soon realised, was never going to let him even briefly forget.

***

On the morning Sarah left university, Miles didn't say goodbye. He simply stood at his bed-sit window in the Halls of Residence across the campus and watched her climbing into the front seat of a taxi. For a moment–even though they were some 300 yards apart–he was certain her eyes fleetingly picked out his window, but then the car turned quickly around and she was gone.

Since they'd broken up, Sarah had approached Miles only if she needed help with course-work, as well as quite willingly aiding him if he needed similar assistance, but as for reconnecting on a personal level she wasn't interested. In fact, Sarah finally admitted to Miles that he'd done the right thing by ending the affair before it turned sour, thereby enabling them to retain their friendship. But Miles hadn't replied to that. He'd simply nodded uncertainly, after which they went on with their separate, if subtly intertwined lives. Still, even though Miles dated other girls in the following weeks–which again didn't elicit any outward signs of jealousy from Sarah–something at the back of his mind wouldn't allow him to fully move on.

Sarah had affected him, even if he couldn't decide how, and every girl Miles now met reflected in pale comparison. In the past, he'd adhered to a strict romantic formula, but with Sarah things hadn't gone to plan. It wasn't as if she was the most beautiful girl he'd ever dated–even though he'd grown to believe her far prettier than when they'd first met–and, looking back, their relationship had been far been perfect. In fact, apart from having a core of commonalties they were different people, and this ultimately reflected in their lovemaking, which was satisfactory and never in the least bit wild. Of course, Miles grudgingly accepted he'd never been with Sarah for the correct reasons, and, despite the fact she'd never known that, he wondered if it was some form of mild remorse which now caused her to be incessantly on his mind.

It was possible, of course, that Miles was 'in love', yet he was sure it wasn't that. In the past, certain girls had expressed their love for him–

more often in the throes of passion–yet he was certain that what they claimed to have felt was something else. In his mind, love wasn't an all-consuming feeling of 'forever' that beset you when you first met your 'other half', nor a suspended moment in time during which you were struck dumb by your heart's treason, incapacitating you for days thereafter. No, true love was perhaps more of a slow realisation that your life's main search was over; a discovery which, no matter how joyous, you were better withholding from all but the object of your affection so as to avoid open ridicule. But then, no matter love's definition, Miles was firmly convinced that forsaking the attentions of many for one was a dangerous gamble and he was certain that he'd never in his life do that for anyone. He did, however, feel as if he'd been given something and had it snatched away before having time to fully evaluate its worth. This being so, Miles eventually concluded that he'd have to see Sarah at least once more, if only to ascertain precisely what she meant to him. Besides, he felt it would do no harm to break his own rules for once, because, even if they got back together, it wasn't as if she'd try to force him in a direction he didn't want to go.

And so, determined to settle his internal dilemma once and for all, Miles found out Sarah's address from the school register and took a taxi to her father's small farm on the city outskirts. But, as his car drew up at the entrance, Miles realised he couldn't have arrived at a worse time. From the steady procession of cars filing into the small estate and the grim looks upon the visitor's faces, it was obvious Sarah's father had lost his battle for life. It was an hour before an ashen-faced Sarah McGill dragged herself away from her painful duties, and, after Miles extended his genuine sympathies, she haltingly asked him to accompany her on a stroll around the farm. They walked quietly for a time, before Miles softly suggested that it must have at least consoled Sarah to see so many of her father's closest friends attending his wake. As he spoke, Sarah sat upon a low stone wall near the gateway, where she quietly considered his words. Then, moments later, she told him why she believed so many people had called to pay their respects.

Sarah began by saying her mother, Carol, had taken her life when Sarah was two-years-old, yet nobody–including her father, Bernard–had discovered why until recently. It turned out that when Carol was sixteen years old, she'd dated a boy of a similar age who lived nearby; and, even though it was a childish and meaningless affair, Carol unfortunately fell pregnant. Sadly, Carol grew up in a time when young, unmarried mothers were virtually societal outcasts; and so, after much heartfelt consultation with a discreet and empathetic midwife about the stigma she'd face if she went through with the birth, she decided to have her pregnancy terminated. It was a hard decision to make–though, again, no one would know this until years later–but at the time, Carol believed it the correct one, so the termination took place.

Several months passed, after which Carol was introduced to nineteen year old Bernard through a friend. Carol, a firm believer in Fate, somehow recognised Bernard–a gentle youth from a deeply religious family–as the person with whom she wished to spend the rest of her life, yet she determined never to divulge her past to him for fear he'd reject her, which was the last thing she wanted as she loved him dearly. Two years later, Carol and Bernard married, and a year later Sarah was born. But Sarah was to be the McGill's only child as Carol became consumed by guilt shortly after her daughter's second birthday. Struck by the realisation she'd once denied life to an unborn child, she began harshly and silently judging the youth she'd once been, little realising that, in adulthood, she'd never apply the same judgement against any girl in a similar situation. Carol told only one other person of her angst – the midwife who'd helped her terminate the pregnancy. And, even though the older woman gently explained that all people tend to judge themselves more harshly than any God ever would, and that repressed feelings have no choice but to intensify, Carol was convinced it would hurt Bernard more to know of the monster she'd once been, thus she decided that the burden was, and always would be, hers to bear alone. The midwife disagreed, of course, and yet, realising she'd never change Carol's mind, she swore once more to keep her secret. Nevertheless, the older woman's words proved true: Because the past returned to haunt her more fiercely as each day passed, Carol's despair grew, until, at last convinced she was worse than any person she'd ever known, she eventually took her life.

Naturally, Bernard was beset by grief at the loss of his wife, which was further compounded by guilt; after all, he'd known nothing of her past, and, perplexed as to why she'd committed suicide, he felt somehow to blame. He wasn't, of course, but with similar unobjective harshness he became more introverted over time, judging himself unfit to add anything but the fruits of his labour to the local community. Years passed, and, even though Sarah realised the strength of her father's love through his actions moreso than his words, others weren't as understanding. Bernard's neighbours soon became entangled in the immediacy of their lives and they failed to realise that, not only can tragedy alter a man's perception of time, but the dual sorrows of grief and guilt have the power to nourish each other limitlessly. Resultantly, Bernard became a virtual recluse, believing that either Fate or God had granted him a concept of eternity as punishment for his sins, and time passed slowly for him thereafter. As for his neighbours, they merely watched his gradual withdrawal, thinking his decision odd, yet accepting he'd made his choice.

However, six months ago, when Bernard was walking in a nearby lane, he chanced to save a young boy's life by knocking him out of the path of an oncoming car which was speeding around the bend towards them. But, as he did so, Bernard was struck by the car, contracting severe external bruising – injuries which, due to their slowness to heal, alerted specialists to performing a series of tests which led to him being diagnosed with bone-cancer. Still, two positive twists resulted from this dark episode: Bernard's neighbours, realising they'd mistaken his ongoing grief for apathy, would afford him their utmost attention and care after that; but, more importantly, during this same period, Bernard received an elderly female visitor into his home, and this woman sadly explained that she was the midwife who'd helped Carol terminate her first child. The woman then told Bernard exactly why Carol had made her decision, about her ongoing angst, and of how the young girl made her swear never to tell anyone, especially a young man called Bernard, whom Carol was sure she'd one day marry. Upon hearing of Bernard's deteriorating condition, however, the elderly woman had chosen to break that promise, realising she should've perhaps done so years before. Rather ironically, Bernard told the woman that she shouldn't judge herself too harshly, for, like Carol, she'd made a decision influenced by events of a specific time, after which she'd stuck by it, believing it correct. Bernard further explained that he was just so happy to have discovered the answer to his greatest question during the time of his greatest pain, thereby easing his mind completely. As a result, he was often dismissive of his illness in his final weeks; and, two days ago, he'd died happily, knowing he hadn't failed any of life's tests and certain he and Carol would soon be united.

So, Carol had killed herself because she was afraid Bernard would reject her if he discovered what she'd done, and she'd even been prepared to face the uncertainty of death to show how much she loved him. And then there was Bernard, who'd lived life as best he could, only to one day find himself at odds with the world because people couldn't understand his grief – until the day, that was, when he instinctively performed an act of virtue which again earned him a place in their hearts.

So, Sarah asked Miles somewhat wryly, were those people who'd turned up to pay their respects really good? Indeed, they were nice people –charitable, kind and sympathetic–but why hadn't they gauged the reason for her mother's pain when she was alive, or the reasons for her father's ongoing sorrow after his wife's death? Weren't there always clues in a person's actions or conversation, and wasn't there always a tell-tale look in their eyes? And if only one of those neighbours had thought to ask the correct questions, mightn't they have changed both her mother's and her father's future for the better?

Miles hadn't been able to provide Sarah with an answer to any of her questions that day. He'd simply shrugged, before sheepishly explaining that he'd acted rashly by finishing with her and very much wanted to see her again when she returned to university. But Sarah shook her head, suggesting it was better they remained friends because Miles was correct – there was something missing from their relationship, and she wasn't the sort of girl who wanted to settle for less than she was worth, only to wake up in two decade's time to the realisation that she and her husband should both have waited a little longer for the right person to come along. She wanted more, she explained, even if she couldn't yet define what 'more' was, and despite the fact that she still fancied him madly. And Miles had simply nodded his acceptance of that, relieved in one way that he'd once again experienced something of a near-miss, but wondering why he felt as deeply regretful as he did.

***

Feeling an elbow digging abruptly into his ribs, Miles turned. Still in something of a stupor, he realised it belonged to Tomas, who'd gently edged Wing-Ding aside in order to sit closer to him. 'Y'hear that, Miles?'

Despite his darkening mood, Miles allowed himself a moment to isolate the tormented screams of the wind from the incessant thud of rain pummelling the windows. Those prevailing noises aside, he could hear nothing but the muted toll of the chapel bell and the evacuees babbling chatter, the latter of which buzzed around the room like a bee in a jar, all too alert to its boundaries. Perplexed, he shook his head, wondering what Tomas was talking about.

'That sharp crack,' Tomas smiled. 'It sounded like a rifle shot, but it was the fence at the bottom of the garden. The wind ripped a bit of it off just now.'

Tired and having somehow missed that small episode, Miles shrugged evenly. Tomas regarded him keenly, even as he drew a packet of cigarettes from his pocket and offered them around. Wing-Ding, the only non-smoker in the small group, automatically declined his offer; purely on reflex, Miles and Pele did too, as did a scowling Brian, who was keenly unsettled by all forms of extension.

Unoffended, Tomas smiled easily and lit one up. 'Hey, Miles,' he said suddenly. 'You mind the time I took the horse from the old farm?'

Miles raised an eyebrow, trying to think. The memory was there on the periphery of his consciousness and he tried centring it, somewhat vague about the entire episode but recalling the more absurd parts. He smiled thinly, nodded.

'I took it for a jaunt up the Crissom one night, face into the traffic,' Tomas explained to the other men in a perfidious whisper. 'The last owner of the farm, y'see, he kept it tied up, day and night. So, I decided to race it up and down the main road for an hour because the poor thing needed the exercise.'

'You stole a horse?' Wing-Ding gasped, incredulously.

'I set it free,' Tomas grinned, as if savouring rich memories. 'It even out-raced its owner's tractor back up the Crest, and I felt like I'd won the Derby! Hey, Miles, and mind the time I took a walk over the new wooden floor in the Father's study with a pair of golf shoes. He thought God had tested him with a plague of wood-worm, didn't he?' Miles chuckled darkly. 'And that mornin' I typed a few choice paragraphs from *Penthouse* into his sermon before he said Mass, you mind that?' Miles frowned, not recalling that particular incident. 'You not remember that?' Miles shook his head. 'Your memory not the best these days, then.'

Miles couldn't tell if that was a question or a statement of supposed fact. 'I remember some things,' he replied solemnly, dropping his eyes and sitting bolt upright. 'Some things I remember.'

Tomas nodded contemplatively. 'Aye, well, I suppose we all do that.'

'What did you *really* come back to this shit-hole for?' Brian asked him suddenly, his red-rimmed eyes searching, aggressive. 'You must've found a better place than this in your travels. You get yourself thrown out of everywhere else, or what?'

'I just came back to see the storm,' Tomas shrugged. 'I told the Father that, and he seemed happy enough with that explanation. If he can be fuckin' happy that is!'

'He fuckin' hates you,' Brian exclaimed suddenly, an underlay of venom in his voice. He fumbled with his own packet of cigarettes, a slight tremble there in his hands. Miles looked at him, supposing that Brian–like the rest of them–was fully aware of the darker implications of not being able to leave Adullam this evening. 'And you hate him too,' Brian continued, acidly. 'That's fuckin' obvious!'

'I don't hate him,' Tomas shrugged. 'I just don't like the way he hides behind his dog-collar, or the way he makes out he only lives to help others. His do-goodedness – what's the word for that again, Miles?

Miles thought hard for a moment. 'Altruism. His altruism.'

'Aye, his altruism,' Tomas said abrasively. 'Alright, he mumbles a few prayers and says the odd kind word to his parishioners. But why shouldn't he? After all, *they* pay for his food and lodgin's and look after him all year round.'

'They aren't all bad,' Miles sighed, not in the least disturbed by the fact that Tomas seemed to thrive upon forever sticking his fingers into the suppurating wounds of Christ. Still, his instinct told him it might be better to curb the other man now, before either the locals or the Father overheard what he was saying. 'Some priests are alright. They don't all make out they're better than us.'

'Of course *some* of them are alright,' Tomas agreed. 'I'm on about the ones who aren't. This feigned altruism of theirs is just a selfish pension scheme designed to gradually earn them a place in Heaven, even as they live continually off the backs of others here on Earth. But I can see that clearly, and the Father doesn't like me for it. That's what his problem is with me.' Tomas pointed to his chest. 'But me – I've no particular beef with him.'

'Sounds like it,' Brian shrugged, closing his eyes. 'Sounds like you don't have a beef with anyone this side of the stratosphere, right enough!'

Tomas acknowledged that touché with pursed lips, even as he continued smoking his cigarette. He remained quiet after that; all the inmates did: They just sat in a mildly companionable silence, ghosts to all except each other.

Shortly afterwards, there was a knock on the door. At first it was ignored, for the door-knocker had taken to beating a tattoo of its own accord just over an hour before. But eventually a pattern was discerned which couldn't have been the work of the wind, and the insistent rapping was answered by Nan. Seconds later, Vinny McIntyre and Seamus Brown shuttled hurriedly into Adullam. Now off-duty and dressed in soaking casual clothes, Seamus gratefully accepted a towel from Mrs. Malhaffey before entering the sitting room. Seemingly forever on duty, however, Vinny remained in the hallway, schooling the Father about something in a professional whisper for a few moments before finally entering the sitting room. As dozens of expectant eyes turned towards him, the Chief Guard instantly felt obligated to relay the latest news. 'That's most of the town sorted now,' he declared, accepting a cup of tea from Nan and using the cup to warm his reddened hands. 'Seamus and I have checked the place out – everyone is indoors and hopefully no one will venture outside until mornin'. Still, we'll obviously not know if they do, as quite a few of the phone masts are down.' Vinny paused then, as if sensing he was just about to be inundated with questions. 'So, ehm...'

105

A pained Mrs Malhaffey launched the first pointed enquiry: Had the community-centre suffered any real damage? Before Vinny could reply, a Spanish Inquisition came at him thick and fast. How were things on the Crissom? Was there any sign the flood was drawing to a cease? What about their houses, their businesses, their factories, their shops?

Vinny raised a calming hand, and–apparently fine with that particular fielding–fired off a volley of answers. The community-centre was fine, he said, but the Crissom was now under a wash of water two-foot deep. Aye, the Hart was still spilling over; and aye, it looked set to do so for hours yet. Aye, he'd seen slates flying about all over the place as he drove up to Adullam, but no, he couldn't tell exactly which houses had been damaged. Aye, a few cars had crashed in the vicinity, but no, nobody had been seriously hurt – as far as he knew. Aye, there'd been similar damage all over the county, but no, there'd been no fatalities as yet. And aye, he'd seen one or two water-rats swimming along the Crissom, but as for otters, beavers and seals, ehm, well...

The Father, watching this impromptu question-time from the sidelines, was the first to notice that a pent-up Con Logue was set to once again employ his wrath. Just before the garage-owner could do so, however, the priest quickly clapped his hands together and informed the gathering that the dormitory was now *ready* for use, and that *everyone* could make their way there whenever they wanted. In an overriding tone, he quickly added that there were *only* eighteen spare beds–though there were plenty of blankets and several sleeping bags too–and so it was a case of *first-come, first-served*. As several of the evacuees moved towards the sitting room door, an outmanoeuvred Con Logue realised he'd merely seconds to decide whether he should pursue his attack upon Vinny or go upstairs and ensure no one purloined the beds he'd secured hours before. Clenching his jaw tightly, Con chose to do the latter, but, as he stared between the Father and Vinny, his eyes relayed his thoughts: This matter wasn't over yet, and he'd be back!

Shortly after most of the locals had made their way upstairs, Miles began to feel restless. He got up and went into the unlit dining room. There, a sudden impulse told him he might be able to sneak out to the sheds now everyone was otherwise distracted. As he was considering whether it was worth the risk, the vagrant searched the top pocket of his shirt for his cigarettes. But, as he did so, he discovered a coin; the actual coin that the Stranger had given him a week ago, and the one he'd slipped into his buttoned-up pocket only moments after the man's departure from the Old Man's shop. Taking it from his pocket, Miles turned the coin between his fingers; it was an ordinary coin, yet the Stranger had initiated a conversation when he handed it over, perhaps indicating he'd donated it with genuine concern. Very few people did that anymore, Miles reflected: In fact, thinking back, he couldn't honestly recall the last time it had happened, or if it had ever happened at all. He frowned and returned the coin to his shirt pocket, putting those thoughts from of his mind: The Stranger was no longer his concern, he decided darkly: He'd gotten himself into this bloody mess through his own volition and he could bloody well get himself out of it the same way!

Miles was distracted from his thoughts as someone suddenly loomed unnervingly out of the darkness at him. It was Tomas, and the other man had a grin firmly fixed upon his face.

'Don't go out there,' Tomas whispered. 'Nan is creepin' about like a wraith – look!' He pointed through the hatch into the dark scullery, where Nan was heating several pans of water on top of the range. Then, with a curled index finger, he indicated that Miles should quietly follow him into the hall. 'You'll have to wait, Miles, if you're goin' on your wee errand.'

'What I do is my business,' Miles snapped. 'It's got nothin' to do with you.'

Tomas raised his hands, mock-defensively. 'Hey, I'm just tryin' to help. I could even try and distract her in a while, if you want.'

Miles, smoothing his thumbs with his forefingers, nodded uncertainly. 'And what do you want for that?' It was out before he had a chance to hold it in, and he downturned his gaze, knowing what Tomas would say.

'Nothin',' Tomas grinned, handing him a cigarette. 'Just tryin' to help you out.'

Miles wanted to snap that people always had a reason for helping others – even priests! But he bit his lip, ignored the cigarette and moved back into the sitting room, carefully easing his way past those at the door-end towards his adopted patch of carpet near the window. The Father, still deep in quietened discussion with Vinny McIntyre, looked up from where he was sitting and Miles felt the priest's orbs drilling distrustfully into him as he sat down.

Time seemed to slow for the vagrant after that, even as he sought an uneasy solace in pale conversation about the town and the weather. But, shortly after 9-30pm, that spell of timelessness was broken by a loud, shattering noise. The noise appeared to come from the dormitory, and it was swiftly followed by a cry of terror. The Father, Seamus Brown and Vinny McIntyre were the first to react, rising quickly and racing out into the hall and upstairs. Presently, several others followed along behind. Miles was about to get up too, but Tomas held him back, saying that they should wait a while to avoid getting caught in the rush.

Moments later, when the two men eventually went upstairs and stared into the dormitory, it became instantly apparent what had happened. The skylight windows had caved in, several dislodged slates having beaten at them so severely that they'd exploded into shards and fallen into the room's centre. Now, a very shocked Mrs Laverty was in the process of being comforted by Mrs Stewart beside the door, and Seamus Brown was trying to drag sodden sleeping bags out from under a deluge of rain which had nothing to dissuade its forceful entry: That was a visibly futile gesture, of course, and Seamus merely succeeded in getting soaked in the process. The rest of the locals huddled in the doorway, darkly entranced as the downpour lacerated the beds, saturated the sleeping bags and drowned the carpet. As another flash of lightning streaked the sky, Vinny McIntyre quickly took control of the situation, warning everyone to stay away from the beds. The frames were made of metal, the Chief Guard rasped, and so likely to attract lightning; which meant, sadly, that they'd have to leave their possessions where they were until morning. Vinny then urged everyone to return to the sitting room, and Miles took a last look into the dormitory before the Father closed the door, wondering if the growing puddle of water on the carpet would soon find its way downstairs.

Deborah Logue was comforting a very distraught Molly Devine when Miles and the others entered the sitting room. Poor Marie, the senior-hairstylist was sobbing, what if she was out in that weather? What if something really bad had happened and she was hurt, with nobody to help her? As she spoke, Molly sobbed convulsively and Deborah drew her closer, her own expression as mournful. The diminutive Con Logue was standing impotently at the side of the two women, drawing himself up to his full height, his hands tightening into fists and his chest inflated, as if daring anyone–anyone–to say anything. His angry stares found Neil Martin, Dave Mullan and Big Sean more than most, and, from his stance, it was apparent that the fight which had taken place outside the Drunken Duck had yet to undergo a nasty sequel.

Miles averted his own gaze, fearing Con Logue might yet turn his wrath upon any one of the inmates just to release the pressure in his head. The vagrant was surprised the garage-owner hadn't done so already. The reprobates in Adullam - Con could've blamed any of them for wee Marie's disappearance, and it was perhaps only a matter of time before he did, especially if he heard that Wing-Ding had also been outside Adullam on the night in question, which the garage-owner obviously hadn't as yet.

The Father stepped in to soothe Molly and Deborah; and Dave Mullan–spotting the barely dormant volcano that was Con Logue–took the garage-owner aside and sought to engage him in pacifying conversation. Nan, needing no further cue, took to the kitchen and made yet another round of tea, for Molly first and then for the others, but for the regular habitués last of all. As Miles settled into his spot under the window, he was advised to move back by Brian. 'That glass is goin' to come in, too,' the older man warned him. 'The putty is too firm, y'see.' He pointed to the frame, but Miles–seeing nothing but putty–shrugged his incomprehension. 'There's no real give in it, and that's what happened upstairs,' Brian explained, his tone serious. 'You watch, Miles. They'll come in yet – you mark my word.'

Miles noticed that quite a few of the evacuees had overheard Brian, yet no one said a word as they stared at the windows, mentally attempting to gauge the strength of the panes. Nan, upon seeing this, tutted loudly and quickly went over to the front windows, where she drew the curtains tightly together before moving to the back end of the room and doing exactly the same.

Miles retreated a little down the length of the wall, where he lit up yet another cigarette with trembling hands, the windows the last thing on his mind. He needed a drink and suddenly felt a longing for his wine stir within him. He could see the rubicund nectar clearly in his mind, and imagined it in his mouth, sweet and potent at first, with a bitter aftertaste as it traced down along his throat into his stomach, there to fuel his body, his spirit, his mind. He needed it badly – if it was still in the back shed, that was, if it was still there.

But whether it was there or not he had to take the chance. The wind was only the wind, after all: Blown straight out of the cave of Aeolus, tumbling and playful, it was often nothing more than that. The lightning, too, was nothing more than the spirited work of Summanus, the thunderbolts no more than the mischievous work of Zeus. And this storm was no more than a blurt of a storm which would die away very soon. It was only a storm, and storms apparently occurred in every corner of the world all of the time, so the danger wasn't in any way real at all.

At least, Miles didn't stop to consider it as such until a large section of the white fence surrounding the front garden surrendered to yet another rifle-shot tear and broke free from its mooring, only to fly at the front windows of the sitting room with such velocity that they came crashing in around him.

NINE

The long subterranean tunnel which led from Adullam to St Augustine's reeked of must, and its mouldering ceiling was tracked by a vine of ancient wiring that bled one dim bulb at its centre. And yet, as the Father carefully guided the evacuees through the umbra towards this faint light, his attention was alarmingly drawn to several fast trickles of water running down the wall just inches from the electrical mains-box which supplied both buildings. Urgently retracing the leaks to a small number of as yet tiny breaches high in the crumbling stonework, two things became apparent to the priest: Firstly, if the storm persisted at its present rate, the tunnel would flood quickly during the next few hours; and secondly, with the threat of electrocution now prevailing, once everyone entered the chapel tonight, there'd be no turning back. So, after hastily shunting the evacuees and the vagrants into St Augustine's, the Father locked the door to the slype, pocketed the key and flicked at a nearby panel of switches, sparking the low-slung lights along the aisle into gradual life. He then suggested that everyone sit in the pews nearest the altar, before softly bidding Nan to turn on the heating. As the small crowd settled, the priest beamed a pacifying smile, telling them not to worry, because, *despite* the storm's severity, St Augustine's had stood on Pheasant's Crest for over a century and was the *safest* place around, even if it wasn't yet one of the warmest; though that secondary factor, he smiled, *would* soon be remedied. Moments later, as promised, the heaters grumbled into life and the chapel slowly began to warm.

The regular habitués had, as usual, retired to a pew several rows behind everyone else. Miles, struck by a sudden chill and craving solitude more than ever, moved to the furthest end. Things couldn't get much worse, he decided then: He'd no drink, his stomach was acidic and a dull ache pulsed through every joint, sinew and tendon in his body. It may've been psychosomatic, he supposed, yet, as always, it felt real enough to him. The ongoing noise was also jangling his already frayed nerves. Despite the chapel bell having finally been secured, its muted clanging still reverberated down through the walls to bounce echoically from every corner; and the wind's predatory screams served as a solemn reminder that life was but a momentary illusion, with the future pledged to none.

Miles shivered briskly as he recalled a conversation he'd overheard somewhere concerning the Big Storm of '58 and the spirits which supposedly haunted the old farm. He had never believed in ghosts, despite Homer's thought-provoking descriptions of the shadow worlds of Hades and Tartarus, eternal home to the breathless dead. Still, the vagrant grimly supposed that if there was a time for them to exist, it was now. His mind was suddenly filled with visions of elementals and manes rising from their graves, breaking down the chapel door and overwhelming everyone within, oblivious to the fact St Augustine's was supposedly sacrosanct and inviolable. He shivered again, urging those terrifying thoughts aside, only to find his heart skipping several more beats as the chapel lights flickered momentarily and then went out.

Miles jumped to his feet in the near-pitch darkness. Deeply unnerved by a host of startled cries and exclamations, he felt a similar angst overwhelming him, yet somehow refrained from adding to the clamour. The Father's authoritative voice could be heard above the noise, stating that there were *hundreds* of candles out the back, and, if everyone would *please* sit back down and *remain calm*, he'd go and fetch them. The priest then borrowed one of several cigarette lighters which were sparked aflame, utilising its pale light to guide him out to the sacristy. As he did so, a number of evacuees moved warily into the ambulatories, where they methodically lit those candles already there. Presently, the darkness was soothed to a tolerable orange-grey light and dozens of fresher candles were placed around the chapel; some in latten candlesticks upon the altar, and some upon the wooden pews, to which they were welded by drips of quick-cooling wax.

Miles stared about him, the ambience darkly hypnotic. He'd never seen the chapel like this. In daylight, it was a comparative Minoan palace, bedecked in bronzed oak and copper mahogany, with a central altar of polished marble and honeyed-wood. But now the entire place was a corruption of formless shadows that leeched fast to the arched windows, to the periclinal ceiling and the ribbed vaults of the roof. Now, the incuse depressions of the Stations-of-the-Cross flickered to stunted life upon their dark sealstones as so many caricatured negatives, the altar appeared tarnished and sullied, and the many carved wooden columns along the aisle–once reassuringly spaced–clustered momentarily atop each other or swayed vertiginously apart, dependent upon the whims of a host of twinkling flames. The vagrant wasn't so sure he liked the effect: In fact, after a short time, he was certain he didn't. He shivered again, his mind running wild. Once more, he envisioned coffin lids being flung wide in the graveyard and phantasmal spirits bearing upon the chapel, zombie-like, in order to satiate a primeval urge too occult to contemplate.

'Christ!' he found himself muttering. 'I need a drink. I really need a bloody drink!'

Tomas, seated but inches away, turned to assess him keenly and placed a reassuring hand upon his arm. 'Hey, calm down, Miles,' he whispered. 'I'll get you a drink–trust me–but you'll have to wait. You can do that, can't you?'

Miles gritted his teeth, beset by internal angst. Trust required patience and confident reliance upon others, he knew, yet he wasn't sure he possessed even a rudimentary amount of either quality any more. Still, as an echoic boom of thunder rattled the chapel windows, he nodded an exaggerated nod.

Beside him, Tomas smiled enigmatically. 'Have patience, Miles. I swear, before this night is over, I'll grant you your every earthly desire.'

**

It took several minutes for everyone to realise the power-cut also meant an end to the heating, with cold gusts blustering in under the chapel doors and through undetected seams in the window-frames necessitating that observance. Nan was fast on hand, pointing out that there were two kerosene heaters in the sacristy which had last been used a few winters back when the snows had all but blanketed the town, and these were soon brought out and lit. The housekeeper then led a small procession of local women out to another small room behind the altar, saying there was a gas stove there upon which they could make some tea – although there weren't many cups around, so would everyone mind taking it in turns? A general shaking of heads implied most didn't seem to mind at all. And, soon after, the tea was made and the smell of flaming kerosene emanated from the glowing heaters, with an insufficient but welcome heat reaching out to warm those seated in the first two or three pews.

Sitting down upon the altar step with his fingers steepled under his chin, the Father watched in ponderous silence as the evacuees gradually resettled. Then, during a lull in their conversation, he apologised for the stark conditions of the chapel, saying he *truly* wished he could make things more comfortable. Of course, he joked, the storm and resultant flood would in no way reach the diluvial proportions described in Genesis, which meant everyone here was *perfectly* safe tonight. Too, on a more philosophical note, there was no point in worrying anyway because the storm was an *act of God*, and therefore beyond anyone's control. And, of course, *everyone* faced the occasional ordeal in their lives, only to usually look back upon it in retrospect and realise it had made them even more *appreciative* of all they currently possessed.

As most people nodded and smiled their agreement at these wise words, the Father then surmised that some might've used the unpredictability of this *brief* interlude to spout prognostications of doom at their enforced audience: Many a priest from the *old school* would've done so, he admitted, just to reinforce their *authoritarian* brand of Christianity. Yet *modern* religion didn't encourage such tactics, the Father frowned, for the Church had discovered over the years that installing religious fervour through fear was a *barbaric* conduit which eventually destroyed *all* societies, no matter the strength of their financial, political or cultural structures. No, the best way to preach God's word was by *example*, and through love and *tolerance* of others. And this was *especially* important nowadays, for to completely negate, harm or provoke anything or *anyone* served only to amplify your *own* fear of their existence – any philosopher could tell you that.

Which was all a bit deep, the Father said with a nonchalant wave of his hand, and this perhaps wasn't the right time to get all philosophical. Besides, what everyone needed *now* was a *ray of hope* – the Father said he knew this because he *knew* his parishioners, having been their priest for twenty-three years. Aye, *twenty-three years*, he smiled, eliciting mild gasps and remarks about how quickly time had passed. Still, during that time, he'd learned a lot from the *very wise* people of Craiglann – from both the present population and those who'd sadly passed away in recent years. And he recalled one *important* thing about their departed brethren: When they'd been alive, they'd been *survivors*, every last one of them. And *so*, all everyone here had to remember tonight–to quote yet another philosopher–was that anything which didn't kill you made you *stronger*.

The Father nodded contentedly then, as if realising from a host of pacified smiles that his impromptu sermon had struck deep into his flock. Then he paused expertly–as if aware most were still considering his words before slipping into a conversation with a couple of women in the front pew about the outrageous prices of carpet and linoleum.

In a bid to distract himself from his growing discomfort, Miles regarded the Father neutrally, torn between a grudging respect for the priest's devout beliefs and disappointment that he had–for the umpteenth time that evening–used cliché-ridden rhetoric to pacify his temperamental flock, all of which incessantly implied that things would work out for the best, no matter what. Too, the Father seemed equally certain that two profound truths would work to his advantage. The first was that, because people were social beings who needed to be accepted and liked, they'd often attempt to meet the expectations of their peers in order to gain respect. And secondly, the Father was aware that when you asked someone for their trust, you indirectly implied that you'd chosen them above others because *you* trusted them, a factor which often flattered people into assisting you in order to further boost their own self esteem.

After forcing himself to deliberate upon these ideas, Miles decided that–his grudging respect for the priest aside–the Father hadn't actually clambered onto a virtual limb by asking for the evacuees' trust. But, as the vagrant smiled grimly at this realisation, he was startled back to reality by the unexpected sight of Con Logue, George Harkin and the Old Man standing, as one, in the second pew. A few moments of silence ensued, which even the very storm seemed to acknowledge, then Con Logue began to speak.

'What about the Stranger, Father Joseph?' the garage-owner asked loudly. 'We all want to know why we're bein' forced to spend the night in this leaky and draughty chapel–no offence to you–while he's allowed to sit it out in his nice wee cosy farmhouse?'

'Aye,' George Harkin bleated. 'And after him doin' what he did...'

'What he may've done, Father,' the Old Man quickly intervened, staring apologetically at Molly Devine and her daughters. 'Or, what circumstances now state he probably did – that's what we mean.'

A sudden, fragmented argument broke out in the first three rows, with some there openly agreeing with this skewed rationale, and others decreeing such a topic should be debated only at a more suitable hour and venue. His own thoughts temporarily sidelined, Miles wondered how this dark subject had arisen from the comparative price of textiles, and how anyone could view the old farm as a relatively better place to spend the night than the chapel, which was equally secure despite its lack of heat and light. Still, from the way in which the Father stepped hastily up onto the dais, it became apparent that the priest intended to quell all mention of either wee Marie Devine or the Stranger before the discussion became too heated.

'Now, there's *no* need for that sort of talk on this awful winter's night,' the Father said evenly. 'We've all troubles *enough* right now, and we should attempt to get through this evenin' with the *least* possible friction.'

As Con Logue was about to issue a reply, the Old Man placed a hand upon his arm and calmly asked him to sit down, before doing the same with George Harkin. 'We don't mean to offend Molly, her family, or anyone, Father,' the newsagent said softly. 'But, as George so rightly said, the Stranger has now had ample time to clear his name and he hasn't done so, meanin' he must have somethin' to hide. Besides, as a week has now passed since wee Marie's disappearance, we think it's time Vinny told us if the Stranger has an alibi for what he was doin' on the night in question, and if he's a prime suspect in the ongoin' investigation.'

Miles studied the Father for a time, before concluding from the priest's defensive body-language that this was one rational argument for which he'd obviously no formulaic response, yet nor could he fudge the issue as it would seem as if he too had something to hide. Nevertheless, as the Father turned to seek support from the Chief Guard, yet another volley of questions came at them both from every angle. Aye, Father, did the Stranger have an alibi? And why didn't Vinny bring him down to the centre earlier as promised? Was the man simply snubbing the law, or had Vinny simply not bothered to tell him to turn up? Exactly what leads were being followed, and who had Vinny already eliminated from his enquiries, and why? And didn't both Vinny and Father Joseph have a responsibility to set the community at ease by disclosing their findings, thereby ending the general breakdown in law and order in Craiglann? In fact, wasn't it all Vinny McIntyre's bloody fault, in a way, because of his incredibly poor communication skills and the fact he was incapable of doing the job he'd been bloody well paid to do?

Standing to the left of the dais, a frowning Vinny McIntyre appeared to be gravely considering each of those questions, including Con Logue's stinging accusation that it was all his bloody fault! Then, just as it seemed he'd been stricken dumb by that barrage, the Chief Guard strode purposely onto the dais to stand beside the Father. For long moments, Vinny stared coldly at the more belligerent evacuees, and only when they'd regained their seats did he reply.

Alright, the Chief Guard said eventually, so they all wanted to know what was happening – fine! Well, he'd been on an errand this afternoon, actually, and it had been something to do with the case. *But*, he wasn't at liberty to disclose the purpose of that errand just yet. What he could say, however, was that the Stranger had cooperated fully with the police, yet certain unforeseen circumstances–which, it had to be said, weren't the Stranger's fault–made it impossible to fetch him down to the meeting. Still, as to the man being a suspect, Vinny shrugged, well, technically he wasn't, as nobody had proven there was anything to suspect anyone of as yet. Not only that, Vinny declared as he drew back his dreadnought to reveal a holstered gun at his hip, there would definitely be no more breakdowns of the law in Craiglann!

As Vinny raised his chin to emphasise his conviction, the slightly crippled Frank Devenney eased himself gently from his seat, stating that there were a few points he wished to clarify. Firstly, was Vinny issuing veiled threats here, or was he seeking everyone's wilful cooperation? Because cooperation was one thing, Frank frowned, but martial law was another! And–apart from the fact everyone present knew Vinny had never fired a shot in anger in his life–didn't the Chief Guard realise it was communal respect for the law, and not fear, which ultimately served it best? After all, Frank mused condescendingly, fear–as Father Joseph rightly pointed out–was a barbaric conduit which eventually destroyed all societies. So, weren't the most successful laws those which rarely, if ever, had to be physically enforced?

'You're twistin' my words!' Vinny replied hotly. 'What I meant was, I'll do my best to ensure no harm befalls anyone here tonight - nothin' else!'

Shrugging uncertainly, Frank admitted there was a slight possibility he may've picked Vinny up wrong. Still, the crippled man sniped acidly, maybe he'd picked up on *exactly* what the Chief Guard meant, because maybe Vinny now felt he'd no choice but to resort to empty threats, seeing as how he'd lost the trust and respect of his community. Take the events of the last week, for example: Couldn't a press-conference or a radio interview have prevented the general dissent? In fact, Frank added sharply, had his *own* personal pain been necessary on Saturday night outside the Drunken Duck, when he'd simply intervened on behalf of the Guards, who'd somehow taken half an hour to drive up from their station, less than a few minute's walk away? Frank shook his head dolefully: No, it *hadn't* been necessary, he declared, but then that was the law in Craiglann, wasn't it? Sure, even the new judge–that what's-his-name fellow from Galway, who'd recently replaced their own revered Judge Laverty–hadn't a clue! No jail-sentences for him: It was fines for muggings, for vandalism, for burglary, for everything! Sure, Frank sniped, all anyone had to do these days in Craiglann was rob a place and pay the fine out of their takings in order to leave themselves with a healthy profit!

Those last remarks were met with an appreciative nod from Judge Laverty, but with titters of laughter from everyone except the Father and the Chief Guard. The two men stood together at the altar rail, wordlessly and seemingly at a loss as to how the recent calm had suddenly evaporated into a barely subdued revolt.

For a time, there followed an uncomfortable silence, and then Con Logue lit up a cigarette. 'You don't mind?' he asked the Father dismissively, blowing out his match and throwing it casually beneath the pew. The Father shook his head and replied that he didn't, yet Miles could see the priest wasn't too pleased with this indirect breach of his authority. As if taking this as a cue, Brian lit up a cigarette and the Father regarded him hollowly, before tightening his jowls and looking quickly away. Miles shrugged inwardly and followed suit, giving one to Tomas simply because he owed him one and for no other reason.

Tomas lit the cigarette up, inhaled deeply and gratefully blew the smoke up into the cold chapel air. 'Some storm this, eh?' he grinned at Miles. 'Way more than a storm in a teacup, isn't it, eh?'

Miles didn't reply: The other man might well have meant the storm itself, he mused, but he might also have meant the uncertainty of their situation. It hadn't even turned 11-30pm, yet it was obvious both the Father and Vinny McIntyre had a tenuous handle, at best, upon this ever-simmering predicament. For a time, Miles sat there smoking and wondering what lay ahead in the night. Some ten minutes later, both he and everyone else would find out.

***

It was the loud report which startled everyone to silence: It sounded like a gunshot according to some, yet no one was able to determine exactly what it was, the noise coming so suddenly after a flash of lightning. There then sounded a second loud crack, equally distinct amidst a slow grumble of thunder and seemingly amplified by the charging wind. As fevered speculation swept through the gathering and the evacuees grew notably agitated, Vinny McIntyre raised his hands. 'It's alright,' the Chief Guard shouted. 'Sit down, for God's sake! That wasn't gunfire! Despite what some people think, I *know* the sound of a gun when I hear it and that wasn't it!'

'Aye, well you should,' Con Logue snapped, just loud enough for the Chief Guard to hear. 'What with the way the Stranger was able to fire his gun off into the main road last night without being taken to task for doin' so!'

Vinny McIntyre's face was a study in controlled rage. 'For your information, Con, that wasn't what happened! The Stranger fired a legally-held shotgun into the air–once–above his own land. But he was entitled to do that – it was self-defence. Or, sorry, it would've been self-defence if all the brave people there to confront him hadn't run off before he'd a chance to fire off a bloody second round!'

Con Logue was about to cast fuel onto the flames of that argument when there followed yet another loud report. As all talk quickly ceased, the Old Man cocked an ear, saying it sounded like wood splintering, and a large amount of wood at that! The Father nodded his stern agreement and steepled his hands. It was the tree, the priest said in a muted whisper:

It was the Great Oak at the topmost end of the chapel - it could only be that!

Big Sean stood up. Then, after spending several seconds immersed in thought, Mullan's bouncer loudly suggested he should go outside to see if it was indeed the Great Oak. At this, the Father shook his head: No, the priest replied firmly, it wasn't too safe out there at the moment, and even Big Sean–big as he undoubtedly was–couldn't withstand the ravages of the storm. Big Sean stood on anyhow, formidable as the Colossus of Rhodes, with the strength of his stance alone declaring that he'd have no trouble taking on the storm.

The Father shook his head again and said that if *everybody* would just wait a moment, he'd go look through the sacristy window, for the tree was visible from there. Angst-ridden, Big Sean deflated into his seat and the Father made his way out to the sacristy, only to return minutes later. Aye, it was indeed the Great Oak, the priest confirmed dismally: Lightning had struck at the tree's very heart, and, as far as he could see, the oak had suffered substantial damage. The Father shrugged lamely then, saying he was near sure the force of the blast had also uprooted the tree, and that it was now slightly tilted towards the chapel. All of which, he dismally hypothesised, probably wasn't for the best.

As all there considered the gravity of his words, the Father suddenly clicked his fingers as if struck by divine inspiration. The priest scanned the small crowd intently, before beckoning a thickset man called Gerry–whom Miles knew by sight as a local contractor–up from the second pew. After a brief, whispered discussion, the two men disappeared into the sacristy for several minutes before returning to the chapel proper, where the Father again keyed open the door to the arched slype. After peering intently down into the tunnel for a time, the Father relocked the door, before asking Gerry to address the increasingly agitated crowd.

At this, Gerry stepped obligingly up the altar steps. Alright, the contractor began, it looked as if lightning had indeed struck the Great Oak several times, but it also looked as if the tree had suffered no substantial damage so far – that evident from the fact it as yet remained upright. Of course, Gerry mused, appearances could be deceptive, and his perception may've been skewed by the irregularity of the weather, the distortion of shadows in the wind and the darkness, or by the fact the sacristy windows were made of concave and bevelled glass which hadn't been cleaned in ages. However, Gerry mused, there were certain immutable facts which didn't rely upon personal perception: The storm showed no sign of letting up, everyone was stuck here in the chapel for the night, and, if it was badly damaged, the Great Oak presented a formidable danger. As to why the oak posed such a threat, the reasons were these: The oak was perhaps the thickness of six men, it stood close to sixty-feet high, and its lower and middle limbs spread weightedly out for about twenty feet in any direction – meaning it weighed several tonnes. More importantly, it stood approximately ten-feet from the chapel wall, which was probably the worst place it could stand. To a host of confused frowns, the contractor quickly explained that, should the tree succumb to any more lightning strikes, it would become further destabilised, and, given its theoretical mass and its gathering velocity as it travelled rapidly over that ten-foot stretch...

'You're sayin' that, if it falls, we'll all be bloody hammered into the ground!' Con Logue blustered. 'That's what you're sayin', isn't it?'

Gerry nodded gravely. 'That's what I'm sayin'. Y'see, if it does fall– and I'm talkin' hypothetically here, as it's been standin' there well over a century–then it'll fall straight through the altar wall behind me. Now, you'd think with the chapel havin' an apex roof, the tree might hit it and slide off. But, y'see, an apex, despite the fact its strength lies in the high part of its triangular frame...' Gerry paused upon observing Con Logue's ever deepening scowl. 'Well, it probably wouldn't stand up to a big tree smashin' side-on into it, that's all!'

'You mentioned the main problem,' Mrs Malhaffey said, raising a quizzical eyebrow. 'Does that mean that there's a second problem, or a third?'

Gerry nodded sternly. 'There's another problem, aye. The tree isn't incombustible, which means lightnin' might spontaneously ignite...'

'It might be set on fire by lightnin',' Con Logue seethed. 'Before fallin' into the chapel, settin' the place on fire and killin' us all stone dead, is that it? God, speak plainly, man, and stop makin' out you know more than you do!'

'Can't we just return to Adullam?' the Old Man suggested. 'We'd be safer there, surely, and maybe we could board up the windows.'

Gerry shook his head. 'The tunnel's flooded and the water-level is now close to the electrical mains-box. And, alright, the electricity is out for now, but we don't know when it'll come on again, so we can't take that chance.'

'We're hammered then!' Con Logue declared with a frown.

Gerry sighed wearily. 'That's about the height of it, aye. But only hypothetically.' He shrugged uncertainly. 'That's if the tree falls onto the chapel wall. We can't say it will for sure. There's a chance it mightn't.'

His own senses heightened, Miles stared about him, aware that everyone was now considering the gravity of the situation. Still, as he took stock of the dilemma, the vagrant gradually concluded there was nothing to worry about as yet. True, the Father had declared the Great

Oak to have been stricken by lightning at least once or possibly twice; and yet the priest had trusted almost entirely to his senses for that observation, without allowing that the senses were often misleading. The building contractor, on the other hand, had weighed knowledge provided by visual perception against logic deduced from personal experience over the years, after which he'd forwarded a more rational–if sceptical–analysis.

Naturally, Miles understood why both men had focused upon the worst potential outcome from this scenario: Any rational person, when weighing all possible gains against all possible pitfalls in a potentially dangerous situation, would be driven by survival instincts to consider their fears above their hopes. What was more of a mystery to Miles was why the Father and the contractor had chosen to impart their fears to the gathering. The vagrant supposed they'd done so from a sense of duty, yet their reasons may as easily have been rooted in a sense of fair-play or some other ethical obscurity.

Still, Miles didn't want to dwell upon the moral dilemma of whether it was better to inform someone about what was going to occur in such a precarious situation–thereby inhibiting their immediate happiness, but allowing them time to prepare for the worst–or if it was best to allow them to retain peace of mind until the end, especially if the eventual outcome couldn't be changed. What the vagrant did want to consider was a piece of knowledge few people were aware of, and one which was perhaps–out of everyone now gathered there in the chapel– particular to him alone.

In his university days, Miles had learned that storms were common in the Northwest of Greece, particularly around the mountain areas. In Dodona, the site of an ancient oracular shrine to Zeus–who imparted omens by rustling the leaves and branches of trees–there stood one particular oak which had been struck more frequently by lightning than any other. As far as Miles knew, that same tree remained as yet upon its mountain site after being struck hundreds of times over, its biggest threat currently the discriminatory whims of motorway planners. This being so, Miles decided there was a good chance the Great Oak might survive several lightning strikes without toppling over. Moreover, if the tree should be set aflame, there was a strong possibility the storm winds and rain would extinguish the fire almost instantly. And lastly, it had to be remembered that the Great Oak had stood upon Pheasant's Crest for over a century and had perhaps survived many similar storms.

Of course, on a more negative note, Miles knew that Nature also abhorred stereotypes, and for this reason the Laws of Chance never allowed any two moments in time to be exactly the same. As a result, new things constantly occurred in the world, and sometimes–as awkward as it might now prove for everyone here in the chapel–trees of all sizes were felled upon occasion by lightning.

Miles smiled at the irony of it all. Over the last four years, he'd deduced from listening in on a myriad of conversations that the Great Oak had stood as a sentinel to Craiglann's residents, its impressive size and all-encompassing branches as inspirational as the chapel itself. Yet now it hovered like a modern Sword of Damocles over St Augustine's, sharpening the evacuees' every sense and drawing out each renegade moment of time in order to show all there how ephemeral life could be. How ironic, Miles decided. Until tonight, the tree had led people to believe its longevity could only provide succour as time moved on, yet now that role had been completely reversed by one storm, and that same tree threatened to wipe out everyone's lives within moments.

Miles startled as Con Logue suddenly jumped up on top of the pew. 'I say we go over to the farm,' the garage-owner declared. 'That... animal...is safe as a row of houses over there, and we're about to get crushed or even burned to death here! I say we drag him out, or at least take him prisoner and use his farm until the storm is over. I say we do it, and we do it now!'

At this, Vinny McIntyre walked confidently along the length of the altar rail. 'I'll go see him when the storm lies off a bit,' the Chief Guard said thickly, slowly tucking his hand into his belt only inches away from his gun.

'He has a gun,' Mrs Stewart sharply reminded the officer.

'He has a shotgun,' Vinny sighed audibly. 'A legally-held weapon which is technically not the same thing. You're makin' him sound like a gunman holed-up somewhere. He's not. He's a farm owner, and most farmers own legally-held shotguns for the shootin' of vermin and such.'

'A gun is a gun!' George Harkin said. 'So, what would you do if he pulled that gun on you?'

Vinny looked around, all eyes trained upon him. He patted his holster. 'He won't be pullin' a gun on anyone, especially me. Besides, I've a gun too, and my gun is more accurate than his.'

'The Stranger's denyin' us our right to life,' Con Logue fumed. 'Somebody will obviously have to take that gun off him before this night's over.'

'You seem to forget, Con, that there's a storm ragin' as we speak,' Vinny replied, thickly. 'It's not as if we can all go saunterin' up over the field. Sure, half of us would be cut down long before we got there.'

'Storms don't maintain the same consistency throughout,' Con replied, as if meteorology was a personal hobby. 'It'll ease off when the eye of it passes over the town, and then we can all get the hell out of here!' He waved his hand angrily. 'Anyhow, when that happens, are you prepared to lead us over there?'

Vinny seemed at a loss. 'I– that is, we–haven't determined if that's the proper course of action as yet.' He stared between the Father and Judge Laverty as if seeking some moral and judicial support. 'And nobody is goin' anywhere with the storm as it is. But if it eases off...' He shrugged uncertainly. 'Well, that, ehm, has as yet to be determined.'

'And who determines that?' George Harkin snapped as Vinny stood there, seemingly at a loss. 'Have you even determined who determines things around here?' Again no answer was forthcoming, and George shook his head in disgust. 'You can't even determine that, can you, you big gallump!?'

'I'll go with you, Con,' Big Sean said, standing and inflating beyond his usual height and girth. 'He didn't come with us earlier, but he'll not resist again.' Sean stopped speaking then and sat down, his face a blush of crimson. The Father regarded the bouncer quizzically, before asking him what he meant. Big Sean shrugged painfully. 'I met Vinny on the Crissom earlier,' he mumbled. 'And he said he was off to see the Stranger, so I said I'd go up with him. But, ehm, there was a bit of a scuffle, and...'

'And it shouldn't have happened,' Vinny interrupted sheepishly. 'I went over to the farm and told the Stranger I was escortin' him to the community-centre for safety reasons, so he went inside for his coat. But then Sean, thinkin' he was goin' to get his shotgun, made a grab at him. So yer man, in turn, thinks it's a trap and dives back inside, locks the door and starts shoutin' that everyone around here is mad in the head.' Vinny sighed deeply. 'Now, he says he wants to see another delegation of Guards in the mornin'. Guards from another county, he says, because the ones around here are all...'

'Mad in the effin' head?' Con offered sourly.

Vinny nodded, fixed Big Sean with a withering look, then lowered his head. 'Aye, so he locked himself in there. And he said he isn't comin' out–no matter what–until the other Guards arrive to collect him.'

'Mad in the head,' Con Logue nodded, fixing the Chief Guard with a glare. 'You can see where he's at there, the murderin' bastard, can't you? Forgive me Father Joseph, but as mad as this Stranger is, he's obviously able to spot that same trait in others. And, despite what Vinny said earlier, he is a gunman holed up somewhere! So Vinny, havin' now been proven a liar several times over, are you *still* prepared to put your neck on the line for the good people of Craiglann as you swore to do in your oath?

Or, when the storm subsides slightly, do we have to go over there to the farmhouse ourselves?'

'Now, now, Con,' the Father said, with a wag of his finger. 'I think you're goin' too far. What you're thinkin' of doin' is wrong in both the eyes of God and the law. Vinny is in charge here, and what he says goes.'

Con shook his head, a strange glint in his eyes. 'Well, it might be wrong in the eyes of the law, Father Joseph, but you can't stand there and tell me it would be wrong in God's eyes. It's utilitarian, that's what it is – the consideration of the many above the one. Y'see, we can't have the guts of fifty people dyin' here tonight because one man has locked himself in a farmhouse, and him most likely a murderin' bastard at that! So, all I'm sayin' is, if Vinny doesn't uphold the law here in Craiglann to the best of his potential tonight–and he can't even decide who makes the decisions around here, for God's sake!– we'll be forced to take that power back from him.' Con stabbed a finger into his own chest. 'And I'm sure that when I go over to the farm, I wont be on my effin' own!'

In the uneasy silence which followed, Miles sought to rationalise the situation. It was true, he supposed, that both the Father and Vinny McIntyre were the current physical representations of the law in Craiglann. Yet, despite having accrued great respect over the years, both seemed oblivious to the fact their overall governance was held firmly in place not by order or legislation, but by the faith, trust and the goodwill of the people. However, if each of these perceptions now deteriorated, the only outcome would be growing unrest. The vagrant frowned heavily, realising Con Logue was only stating the obvious: Despite being under an obligation to obey the laws of society, every single individual ultimately had a higher obligation to save not only their own lives, but the lives of their immediate families. All of which meant, the vagrant concluded unhappily, that it was perhaps only a matter of time before this gathering decided to take the law into their own hands.

Miles pushed those nasty ideas quickly from his mind. And, as a small susurration of voices regurgitated and chewed over the most important parts of Con Logue's latest argument, the vagrant once again sought comforting refuge in his own past.

T E N

During the days which followed his visit to Sarah's country home, Miles spent most of his time studying for his imminent second-year exams. And, to while away the few hours he allowed himself off during that same period, he either attended track-events with friends or spent dull evenings alone in his bed-sit, watching television or listening to music. Dating other girls merely for the sake of doing so no longer appealed to him, however, as Sarah was constantly on his mind. Why, he mused sadly, wouldn't she go out with him again? After all, he had freely admitted that he'd been wrong to finish with her, and she had told him that she still fancied him madly.

Miles guessed his confusion stemmed from the conflict between Sarah's words and actions. When she'd spoken of her ongoing attraction to him, he'd seen the truth in her eyes, yet when she'd refused to see him again he'd sensed regret in her tone – it didn't make sense. Still, as Miles pondered this dilemma, he recalled how, during her father's wake, Sarah had said there were often clues to a person's deepest concerns in all they said or did. So, thinking she may've already revealed the reasons for her angst to him–either unknowingly or wittingly–he tried to recall how she'd described her upbringing, her mother's tragic suicide and her father's loneliness in the years ensuing his wife's death. And, after much thought, Miles surmised that Sarah's greatest fears were rooted in issues of distrust and poor communication–issues which most likely evolved from her mother's inability to trust that her husband might forgive her one terrifying secret, and from her father's inability to communicate the sense of loss he felt upon the death of his wife to those around him in any way other than the primary, but often overlooked language of physical action.

Miles relaxed a little as he lay there upon his bed, happier because he'd pinpointed Sarah's deepest concerns through rationalisation, yet concerned because those deductions gave rise to equally many questions. Firstly, why did he still need to understand what Sarah thought of him? Was it because he truly valued her opinion? Or was it because he knew she was slipping away, and that such knowledge–if used correctly–might somehow bring her back? Miles wasn't sure, yet knew he had to find out. So, upon Sarah's return to university two weeks later, he again spent as much time as possible in her company by 'bumping into her' in the local park, the library or elsewhere on campus in a bid to determine her thoughts. Still, all attempts to elicit answers from either her conversation or her body-language proved futile, and Sarah became increasingly introverted as the days passed. Miles, though, had no intention of giving up: Stubborn to the point of failure, he now felt he had to ask Sarah at least once more if she'd go out with him again. And yet, on the day he intended doing so, he made an interesting discovery.

When they'd dated previously, Miles and Sarah had spent many evenings in the local park. And, upon the perimeter of the park's two-mile walkway, was a certain bench they preferred as it sat within the shade of a ring of elm and maple trees, affording it protection from both the rain and the sun. Miles knew Sarah still visited the park most afternoons, yet she currently chose to study upon the open lawns in order to catch the sun. Still, on the day Miles planned to meet up with Sarah in yet another 'chance encounter', he inadvertently found himself walking behind her along the main trail. As he was about to call out her name, however, a voice in his mind urged him to wait; and so, for several moments he discreetly followed Sarah towards the park's centre. Then it happened: As she neared the ring of maple and elm, Sarah stepped off the trail and walked towards the bench they used to sit upon, after which she traced a slow finger across the back-rest before eventually returning to the trail and continuing on her way. Miles, watching discreetly from a distance, was instantly overwhelmed by a strange elation, for he knew she'd performed that action in order to briefly reconnect with her recent past. He allowed another few moments to pass, and then, as the sun ripened overhead, hurried to catch up with Sarah, now certain that–should he approach the subject tactfully–she'd date him again. But, only moments after he'd declared it a coincidence them meeting there, Sarah told him softly that there was no such thing, but that she was glad to see him as she'd something to say. He shrugged happily, feeling it could only be good news, but then she told him she was going away after their exams and it was unlikely she'd return the following year. Her father's business was now her prime concern, she explained sadly, and, even though she planned to keep her family home and one or two fields, it would take several months to oversee the sale of the rest of the land.

As Sarah spoke, Miles was again struck by a sense he was being robbed of something very precious. Their final exam was two days away, and, should Sarah not return to university, he'd probably never see her again. Sarah must have noticed the disappointed look upon his face–even though he tried to hide it–because she then asked him if he wished to accompany her upon her stroll. Miles nodded solemnly, suddenly understanding how loss could change one's perception of time; and he walked through the park alongside her for an hour in virtual silence, un-warmed by the sun and unaware of anything but the soft feel of her shoulders beneath the weight of his arm.

The next two days passed as a blur and the exams came and went, their usual terror now lost to Miles Kivlehan, who'd willingly have taken them over again every day as a trade with time. And, on their last evening together, Miles and Sarah returned to the park, where they sat upon their favourite bench and watched the sun extinguish itself behind an unearthly blaze of hills upon the horizon. It was twilight before Miles at last found the courage to tell Sarah he felt cheated, and how he realised he now held no true control over his present or his future. But, as he talked, Sarah hugged him tightly, telling him everything would be alright: If you believed in God, she smiled, then all you had to do was trust and pray for his grace; or, if you believed in Fate, you'd realise that, even though they resided a thousand miles apart, those destined to share their lives could be drawn together by nothing more than a single strand.

But Miles had shaken his head at that: No, he replied sadly, his studies of philosophy had shown him that God was nothing but a necessary creation used to bind people to synthesis, until, at some point in the future, mankind recognised it had moved beyond tribal existence. And Fate was merely a way of shifting responsibility onto the whimsical laws of coincidence. Besides, Miles asked, how could anyone claim to believe in predetermination–call it Fate, Providence, God's plan, or whatever–and then declare true freedom of choice? After all, if people truly acted out their lives in accordance with the set plans of a higher power, then surely they should follow their basest instincts and indulge in their every selfishness throughout their lifetime, for how then could that same higher power judge and punish them for actions over which He or She had always maintained the ultimate control?

Sarah had laughed at that theory, telling Miles he was a true cynic, an intelligent man who'd learned to suppress the voices of instinct and his heart so he might listen to the cold voices of logic and reason in an attempt to gain dominance over his existence. But relying solely upon logic and reason was dangerous, she chided, for if you followed each to their ultimate conclusions, how many risks would you take? Logic would deem your only goals to be personal happiness and an extended life, meaning you'd only ever exert yourself if it made you feel good; and reason would warn you to follow only tried and tested paths. Too, if you truly believed you had complete control over your life, how could you comprehend the beauty of such spiritual qualities as love, hope, faith and trust – qualities which transcended all logic and reason?

Miles shivered upon hearing Sarah's words, knowing she was right in one regard: For all their benefits, reason and logic– along with custom, tradition and institutionalised thought–often sounded out the voices of instinct and the heart, leading man to live in a false state of consciousness. Now, the truth struck into him as an arrow: In his youth, Miles had learned to rationalise everything in order to exert dominance over his world. Fear had made him do so, and he'd gradually convinced himself that love and trust had to be earned, that hope was simply an admission of defeat, and that faith had its calculated roots in fact. Sarah had obviously recognised these beliefs in him yet never questioned them, even though she'd perhaps known that such justifications could only ever destroy their relationship in the end, for each allowed always for the judgement of others above the self.

Miles hung his head, finally aware that, despite the many walls he'd constructed around himself, Sarah had seen through him all along. And now the source of her inner conflict was apparent: Despite being able to accept him for what he was, she'd reached a stage where she had to protect herself from further emotional harm. Miles didn't know what to say and so he just sat there silently for the rest of the night, offering her his coat as it grew chill, and wishing ghost wishes beneath a ghost moon as it progressed slowly through a haze of clouds towards its zenith.

It was raining that next morning as Miles accompanied Sarah to the local train station. And, as they sheltered under the platform canopy he bought her a packaged rose from a florists shop nearby. Smiling wistfully, Sarah took it and asked him if he knew the flower's true symbolism. He shrugged uncertainly and listened as she explained that the rose–a traditional gift for lovers–was supposed to represent *agape*, which was spiritual or unconditional love. And yet, Sarah smiled, as roses were stripped of their thorns before being packaged, they were also symbolically stripped of the very pain which necessarily cradled that beautiful virtue, thereby devaluing its essence. Miles frowned, unsure of what Sarah was trying to say, but then he kissed her deeply before she boarded the train, not wanting to let her go. As she was about to enter her carriage, however, Sarah reached into her handbag, pulled out an apple and casually threw it to him. Smiling ruefully, she then said that everything was probably for the best. Miles nodded sadly, oblivious to the growing downpour as the train pulled out of the station, and quite suddenly overwhelmed by the enormous realisation that he loved her and would probably do so forever.

***

A venomous rage of thunder drew him back to the present and Miles stiffened in his seat, aware that all talking in the chapel had suddenly ceased. But, after a weaker display of lightning had shredded the night-sky, yet another squabble broke out in the pews, with Con Logue, the Old Man and many others directing their wrath at Big Sean and Vinny McIntyre. Feeling his own adrenaline surge, Miles attempted to calm his nerves by breathing deeply and closing his eyes. A sharp slap on his knee, however, shattered any attempts at concentration, and he turned to see an animated Tomas laughing gleefully as the Father feebly intervened in the ongoing diatribe, telling everyone there was *no need* for their current behaviour, and that it could all be sorted out *amicably* if they'd all just stop shouting. Still, sensing the priest's words might not be enough, an exasperated Molly Devine stood and ordered an immediate halt to the madness, suggesting that Judge Laverty be allowed to comment upon what should be done: After all, he'd administered law in Craiglann for as long as anyone could recall, and this incessant bickering was getting nobody anywhere. A begrudged calm took hold as most respectfully consented to her idea. Then, after a little coaxing from his wife, Judge Laverty rose warily to his feet.

His features grim and discerning, the elderly judge stared momentarily around the chapel, before authoritatively clasping one lapel of his jacket. This was a strange situation, he stated evenly, and unlike any he'd ever encountered; so, before he rendered an opinion, he wished to make several points clear. Firstly, he was no longer the town's judge, which meant that–despite the fact he'd administered local law for over three decades–he wasn't speaking in an official capacity. Secondly, he'd possibly make a few points that not everyone would agree with - which was to be expected, obviously, given the challenging nature of the topic. And thirdly, and most importantly, it had to be remembered that Vinny McIntyre was still the law in Craiglann; and so, no matter those opinions expressed, the Chief Guard's decisions would ultimately prevail.

His opening words were met by several mumbles of dissent, yet these were swiftly overwhelmed by many more affirmative comments. Unfazed, the elderly judge continued, saying he'd now briefly deliberate upon the dilemma facing those in St Augustine's. And the dilemma, to reiterate, was this: No one could leave the chapel for the duration of the storm as the tunnel leading back into Adullam was flooded; and, barring a miracle, outside help could probably be discounted until morning as the phone-lines were dead and the masts down. Moreover, because the Great Oak had been struck by lightning, there was a strong possibility that the tree could topple into the altar wall at any moment, the effects of which would be catastrophic. Yet, these facts aside, there was one place of relative sanctity on the other side of Pheasant's Crest – a sturdily built farmhouse which could possibly be reached should the storm temporarily subside. Still, Judge Laverty sighed, these physical problems were–as everyone knew–further exacerbated by rather more complicated human factors. And there was one person whom it would seemingly be quite necessary to discuss here tonight more than any other – the latest owner of the old farm, who, because nobody had actually bothered to get his name, was now being called the Stranger. And the need for this discussion was obvious: This same man was currently, if unwittingly, denying everyone here very necessary access to his property. But, while such a choice apparently favoured him, it also severely limited the options of those now sheltering within St Augustine's.

Now, Judge Laverty mused, while it would seem a simple matter for one person to approach the old farm during a lull in the storm and converse with this Stranger, all evidence suggested otherwise. For a number of reasons–which had yet to be substantiated even slightly–a strong link had been suggested between this man's presence in Craiglann and the disappearance of wee Marie Devine. So, before any proposals were forwarded as to how a mutually satisfying compromise might be forged with him, it was perhaps best to firstly give brief consideration to the disposition of the Stranger.

They knew relatively nothing of the Stranger, the elderly judge confessed, except that he was *persona non grata* – a person not favoured. In fact, it was possible he was completely innocent of all the charges being laid against him; and here, with deference to Molly and her family, they were talking about either possible abduction or murder. Yet another consideration was that the Stranger might be *non compos mentis*, meaning he was perhaps insane, fully or temporarily, and so totally unaware of the wrongfulness of these particular acts. This said, it was also possible the Stranger was indeed guilty of the heinous charges laid against him, though here too there were varying degrees of guilt. His crime could well have been a case of manslaughter–which was the killing of another without malice aforethought–or even of First-Degree or Second-Degree murder, each of which required a different sentence under the rule of everyday law. *But*, Judge Laverty declared implicitly, there was *no* clear and indicative evidence to support such suppositions of guilt as yet. There was no motive, no concrete forensic evidence, no written or verbal confession, no murder weapon, no actual body and no material witnesses. Nor, the elderly judge frowned, had the accused been caught *inflagrente delicto,* or 'in the act of committing' the supposed crime. And so...

He paused as a distraught Molly Devine took a handkerchief from her eldest daughter, deliberately waiting until she bade him continue.

And so, the elderly judge repeated uncomfortably, if everyone thought about it clearly, the Stranger's supposed guilt had been determined by either the *fact* he hadn't yet said a word in his own defence, the *fact* someone had phoned the Guards saying he'd been dragging something heavy down to the Hart on the night of Marie's disappearance, or by a physiognomic study of his face – which basically meant that nobody liked the look of him! Still, as ironic as all of this was, Judge Laverty shrugged, this man's guilt or innocence was now a secondary consideration, as the safety of everyone within the chapel had become the ultimate concern.

Naturally, the elderly judge continued, there seemed to be one sensible option open to them tonight, this being that someone approach the farm during a comparative lull in the storm and ask the Stranger for communal sanctity. A promising outcome to this option would, of course, depend upon several factors. If the Stranger was guilty of any of these alleged crimes, for example, then chances were he wouldn't want anyone entering into his abode; furthermore, he might even go so far as to shoot at anyone who dared ask such a favour. On the other hand, if the Stranger was innocent, it may well be supposed he wouldn't be too concerned about letting anyone stay the night – yet there was also a problem with this latter supposition. Because of ongoing allegations, this man had been treated as a virtual pariah over the last week, and what had begun as a general shunning had culminated in several attempted attacks upon his person. Therefore, given this man's belief that he was now in grave danger from everyone hereabouts–and even if he were totally innocent of the primary charges being laid against him–he might still forcibly resist letting anyone into his home because he now entertained great fear for his life. However, momentarily placing each of these possible outcomes aside, this still left the problem of who should approach the farmhouse, if or when it was decided someone should actually do so.

Judge Laverty rubbed hard at his forehead, before stating that there were two police officers in the chapel – Vinny McIntyre and young Seamus Brown – the former of whom was on-duty and uniformed, and the latter of whom was off-duty, un-uniformed and a trainee.

So, because Vinny was more experienced, because the situation was a precarious one, and because the Chief Guard was on-duty, he would, by law, be required to engage in any negotiations – and yet the problem was the Stranger no longer trusted either him or the law in general. So, bearing this in mind, if Vinny were to confront the Stranger in order to ascertain his current train of thought, what were his chances of success? Not only would the Chief Guard have to make his way quickly across the Crest in order to lessen his chances of falling foul of the weather, he'd also have to get close to the farmhouse so as to present his case to the Stranger. Yet, by making his way over there at speed, mightn't it seem to the Stranger as if Vinny was launching another furtive attack? And, in such circumstances, mightn't the Stranger shoot Vinny and then claim self-defence in a future court of law, possibly drawing nothing more than a verdict of misadventure, regardless of the outcome? An alternative solution, of course, could see the Chief Guard waving a white flag and loudly declaring his peaceful intentions as he approached the farmhouse, but mightn't the Stranger, given the events of that afternoon, also perceive that as a trick designed to draw him into the open? And if the man opened fire upon Vinny in that particular instance, might this not again be viewed as self-defence?

So, Judge Laverty said pensively, the case was indeed a tricky one. In short, the chances were that if Vinny now approached the farmhouse, he'd do so in the belief that the Stranger was going to eventually open fire upon him. Moreover, if the Stranger now saw Vinny approaching his home–in the dark, in the midst of a storm, and for seemingly no good reason–he too might instantly perceive himself, once again, under serious threat. With this mutual distrust presiding, and with both men being armed, it might only take one false move on either side to instigate a situation in which someone could very well get hurt and possibly die.

Judge Laverty frowned gravely as yet another tumultuous growl of thunder clamoured in the heavens, yet he retained his calm as one massive bolt of lightning struck out sharply at the earth somewhere beyond Pheasant's Crest. And then, in the fading brilliance of that blinding light, the elderly judge turned to Vinny McIntyre, declaring that a good judge usually conceived of a situation quickly, before ruminating upon it slowly and eventually passing judgement. Yet this situation required a different approach, he mused, in that he could only proffer a quick analysis of the situation before passing all authority back to the Chief Guard, whose business it now was to decide the best course of action. Still, if Vinny would allow an old law-lord another few seconds, there were a few pieces of philosophical advice he'd also like to dispense – and this he'd rather do in public to show everyone that the law was impartial and had nothing to hide. Judge Laverty paused then, awaiting Vinny's approval to continue, and this was granted unwaveringly.

The first piece of advice, Judge Laverty began, was that the law governed man, and yet reason governed the law. In essence, this meant the human face of the law occasionally had to shed uncompromising legislature and recognise that, no matter how great man's ability to conceive, he could never fully transcribe rules governing eventualities such as the one now presenting itself. Another unfortunate shortfall of the law was that it couldn't fully persuade where it couldn't fully and justifiably punish: To realise the truth in this, one only had to reflect upon the way a person's primary consideration was how they might best avoid breaking the law for fear of serious repercussion, rather than how they might best obey it for reasons of personal satisfaction. And again, Judge Laverty declared evenly, at no time did this latter truth apply more than when the lives of good and decent people were at stake–and, in this particular instance, he could be talking about both the people of Craiglann *and* the Stranger–for who'd be even partially persuaded by laws which promised them varying degrees of punishment for their compliance?

This, Judge Laverty decreed, really only left two options open to the Chief Guard: He could enforce the law to the letter or he could place the law in the hands of the locals and leave all further action to a majority vote. In the current situation, the best option might seem to be the granting of a vote; or, to quote a piece of advice offered to his Emperor by the Roman philosopher Cicero, *Salus Populi* - let the welfare of the people be the chief law. *But*, the elderly Judge warned, if such power was granted to the people, they'd have to be aware of the immense responsibility–both moral and legal–which accompanied that choice. And, in such an eventuality, should they then decide upon a verdict *ad hominem*–or, according to personal feeling–they might later wish they'd adhered sharply to the written letter of the law.

As Judge Laverty sat down in his seat, Miles studied the reactions of the locals as they stared indecisively between themselves. In some ways, the former Judge had spoken wisely, the vagrant decided, with his avocation that the law be placed into the hands of the citizens paralleling long-forgotten strains of Athenian justice: In Athens, when the law existed with the full consent of the people, jurymen took an oath to abide and vote by it accordingly; but, at times when the law was resisted by the majority, jurymen were expected to judge each case upon its merits.

Still, even though Miles understood the benefits of such a common-sense approach, he also recognised the drawbacks. By presenting the locals with an option to vote, Judge Laverty had shown them they were still a democracy, yet he'd also undermined Vinny McIntyre's authority, thereby leaving the Chief Guard in an awkward position. If Vinny now agreed to go along with whatsoever decision was reached and something went wrong, he'd bear personal responsibility afterwards; and yet, if the

Guard refused to hand authority over to the people, he'd immediately be perceived as an enemy of democracy.

Fighting off a sour feeling in his gut, Miles wondered what the locals would do if granted self-governance. In his opinion, the sudden presentation of an untamed democracy would lead to widespread panic, as a strong leadership would still be necessary to stave off needless anarchy. For this reason, Miles felt it might be best if Vinny asked the locals whose guidance they might agree to adhere to should they be granted self-governance. Would they adopt the Rule of One, whereby the Father, Judge Laverty or the Chief Guard adopted a supreme role and enforced that ruling using the strongest people at hand? Would they agree to an oligarchy, which would see the priest, the judge and the Guard enjoined in a Holy Trinity of an alliance to ensure the smooth transition of that potentially fatal recourse? Or would they agree to a tyranny, whereby Vinny would use his firearm and people such as Seamus Brown and Big Sean to implement his decisions?

Considering each of those options in turn, Miles concluded that a short-term oligarchy was perhaps best, in that it would allow all aspects of morality, physical law and legislature to govern the people fairly in this time of their greatest trouble. And, in a way, such a ruling would adhere strongly to the classical oligarchic argument of Sparta, which deemed that the better classes should always oppose true democracy, because commoners–who'd little or no education and no self-discipline or principles–would legislate unfairly and improperly if granted power. Contrarily, the better classes would always have the utmost respect for the law, morality and all the higher values of life, and were thusly more suited to legislate properly for the good of all. When that argument ran to its logical conclusion, therefore, the masses would always be unworthy of the same rights as the few.

Miles was considering this argument further when, out of the corner of his eye, he noticed Tomas standing up. Instinctively, Miles shuffled away from him, a stranger feeling now in his gut than the one previously there, and he watched as the other man carefully extinguished his cigarette.

'We're having a trial then,' Tomas said, casually addressing no one in particular.

'Please sit down, Tomas,' Father Joseph told him pointedly.

'Just sayin' a few words, Father,' Tomas smiled. 'Everyone else here is, so I thought I might too. Is that alright – if I say a few words?'

'We aren't havin' a trial, young man,' Judge Laverty said evenly. 'I'm just givin' my opinion as one who has practised law for thirty years. I'm a judge no longer.'

'You sound like one,' Tomas said. 'No disrespect intended, but you sounded as if you were layin' down the closin' arguments before the trial has even begun.'

'That's enough,' Father Joseph said, glaring darkly at Tomas. 'You've no right to talk to Judge Laverty like that. He's simply tryin' to make the best of a bad situation. And I don't think your input will be of any real help.'

'I've no right to talk you mean, Father Joseph. Bein' who and what I am, I've no right to a say, is that it?'

'That isn't it at all, Tomas,' Father Joseph returned thickly. 'We're all havin' a rational conversation here. So, if you don't have anything rational to add, then I'd rather you just sat down and remained quiet.'

'It's just that our lives are at stake here too, Father,' Tomas replied, sweeping a hand in the direction of Miles, Pele, Brian and Wing-Ding. 'I thought maybe you might've recognised that. Despite us bein' what we are, and all that.'

The Father was about to reply, but Judge Laverty raised a hand. 'Let him speak if you would, Father Joseph,' he said, softly. 'If he has somethin' of interest to say, then I think we should hear it. Everyone here has a right to free speech after all.'

'Aye, let him speak,' Molly Devine agreed. They all turned to look at her. 'I'm not very comfortable with the fact you're all so willing to judge this person we're now calling the Stranger without him ever having said a word in his own defence.'

The Father seemed taken aback by the senior hairdresser's words, yet he nodded almost immediately, before sitting silently back down against the altar rail. Miles smiled thinly at the uncomfortable expression upon the priest's face, receiving the distinct impression he'd rather have fiddled elsewhere as Rome burned. Or fished – maybe the priest would simply have preferred to have gone fishing.

Tomas sat upon the edge of a bench, one foot on the pew to steady himself. He lit up a cigarette and watched as the smoke eddied and swirled for a moment before being dragged off by a cold breeze.

'You can say it any way you want,' he said, after a moment, 'but we're havin' a trial. And it seems to me we have ourselves a ready-made lynch-mob.' He proffered a hand towards the first three pews. 'And, over here, a Judge and a prosecutor rolled into one.' This time his hand turned to Judge Laverty. 'So, I think it's only fair the Stranger is represented in this court by a defence.'

Con Logue laughed out loud and then regarded Tomas as if he was something he'd found under his shoe. 'Who is this fool?' he snapped. 'And why are you all listenin' to him? Him sittin' there astride his pink elephant with a smug look on his face, thinkin' himself head and shoulders above the rest. Huh, he's as full as a bingo bus and he doesn't even know what this whole effin' thing is about!'

Tomas shrugged lazily, before smiling as if totally unoffended. 'I'm not drunk,' he said, dragging deeply at his cigarette. 'I actually haven't drank since yesterday.'

'Well, good for you,' Con barked. 'But this is no concern of yours. You know nothin' about the situation at all.'

'Well, maybe I don't know all that much, but I do know one thing.'

'Aye, and what's that?' Con returned, bitterly.

'You're sendin' Vinny over there to murder a man,' Tomas explained. He raised a stalling hand as Con went to object. 'You can say it any way that you want, but, if Vinny doesn't get this man to willin'ly hand over his farmhouse, he'll have to murder him. And everyone here in this chapel is goin' to be complicit in that.'

'No one said anythin' about murder,' the Father said, his eyes reptilian.

'They don't have to,' Tomas said. 'They're votin' it in with their silence. That's the funny thing about people – they'll tell you it's human nature to put your own survival before that of others. But, isn't human nature just a way of excusin' yourself of personal responsibility and blamin' the worst excesses of your humanity on a negative, communal gene which has never been proven to exist?' Tomas shrugged as if unsure. 'Anyway, all I'm doin' is proposin' a short trial, or hearin', in which certain people forward the reasons for thinkin' the way they do, instead of bayin' like a pack of wild dogs in each other's wake.'

'That's an interestin' point,' Judge Laverty said, rising to his feet. 'And it's one I myself would agree with. But it would need to be a short hearin'. And then there's also the problem of who'll defend this Stranger. Seein' as how nobody actually knows the man, well, that might prove rather difficult.'

'I will,' Tomas smiled. 'I'll defend him.'

His response was met with much dry laughter. Judge Laverty raised a hand. 'I'm sure you mean well young man, but what experience have you of courtroom defence?' He raised an eyebrow. 'Have you any at all?

'Some,' Tomas said, putting a hand upon his lapel and drawing a laugh from Wing-Ding, Pele and Brian, though frowns from Miles and everyone else.

'Are you familiar with the law?' Judge Laverty asked, patiently. 'If you want me to take you seriously, you too must treat me with respect. So, again, do you know how a court operates, and of the rules which must be adhered to therewithin?'

'I've defended people before, aye,' Tomas said.

'You can understand why people aren't takin' you seriously, I suppose,' Judge Laverty said, regarding the bleak looks upon the faces of the gathering. 'You have to understand the scepticism your outburst has provoked.'

'Of course I do. They're judgin' a book by its cover – it couldn't be any clearer.'

'Then you don't mind if I ask you a few questions in a bid to ascertain your credentials?' Judge Laverty asked, walking towards the central dais. 'Because I'll have to presume it's been a while since you've stood on the other side of a dock.'

Tomas laughed easily, feigned a search of his pockets. He pulled an old handkerchief from one, a few bits of paper from another. 'It looks like it might have to be the questions,' he smiled sheepishly. 'I seem to have left my credentials in my dress suit.' His reply drew more frivolous laughter from Brian and Pele, much to the annoyance of the Father and most of those seated in the front pews.

'You aren't actually going to take him seriously?' the Old Man said angrily. He stood and slammed a hand into the wooden rest to his front. 'This man is wastin' our time.' His call was hailed with several vociferous shouts of agreement.

'He has as much right to speak as anyone else, so why should I not?' Judge Laverty said above the din. 'And, if the law is to be seen as impartial, I must listen to everyone, no matter their demeanour, their perceived facade or the state of their apparel. This situation is most irregular, and this man is correct in a sense. If I send Vinny up to the farmhouse to take it over, he might end up havin' to murder a man or get killed himself, and that isn't somethin' I'm comfortable with. We could go with a majority vote, too, but then can we really vote to kill a man who doesn't want people on his property, especially in light of everythin' that has occurred over the last week?' The elderly Judge shook his head firmly. 'No, a trial or a hearin'–no matter how inadequate and brief– might actually be the best solution.'

'We haven't got time for a trial,' George Harkin sneered. 'We'll all be killed stone dead! I say we go over there, and we go now!'

Miles watched in disbelief as another five, then ten, then fifteen people stood and began shouting angrily in the direction of the Father, Vinny McIntyre and Judge Laverty.

All authority and respect for the law and the church in Craiglann seemed to die right there as a wave of panic began to grow, and Miles had a feeling it was going to expand within a very short space of time to almost pandemic proportions. Seconds later, however, Vinny pulled out his gun and raised it into the air. The Chief Guard's face, a flushed pink until just moments before, was now calciferous and completely drained of blood.

'No one is goin' anywhere,' Vinny barked, his steel-eyed glare compelling mostly everyone to quickly regain their seats. 'Frank was correct earlier on, Con, when he said I'd never used this gun in anger. But there's a first time for everythin', believe me. And you're entitled to your opinions, every last one of you. But, so help me God, if you try takin' the law into your hands again tonight I'll do everythin' in my power to help you meet your maker!'

Miles noticed that there were few there, it seemed, who doubted the Guard. The Father moved to Vinny's front then, reiterating that mob-rule wasn't the *answer*, and nor too incitement. *Nothing* had happened yet, the priest added softly, and so if everyone would just *relax* then they could all reach a *decision* between them. But they would all have to *remain calm* - that was a very *necessary* precondition.

The priest then stared directly into the eyes of those as yet standing until they, too, sat down once again. Moments later, a semblance of calm had been restored.

'Right,' Judge Laverty said uneasily. 'Seein' that we have now regained a measure of control, we should begin again. So, what is your name, young man?'

'Tomas.'

'Tomas - mmm. Well, Tomas, have you a second name?'

'I prefer to be called Tomas only.'

'Very well then, Tomas. Now that everyone is seated, let us continue.'

E L E V E N

Tomas casually ground his cigarette stub into the tiles underfoot, seemingly unaffected by his generally frosty reception. 'I must first apologise for how I looked earlier,' he explained loudly. 'I was hitchin' a lift this mornin', y'know, and some fellow ran his car over my shoe – nearly took my foot off in the process. Anyway, if you bear with me, you'll see I'm well up for the task in hand.'

'Aye, well, hurry up!' Con Logue snapped, staring coldly between him and Vinny McIntyre, who now sat framed in shadow upon the altar steps, gun in hand. 'Because, in case you haven't heard, we don't have all bloody night!'

Judge Laverty stepped onto the dais and stood directly in front of the altar. 'Alright, Tomas,' he said, 'I'd like you to define some terminology for me. If you've had any contact with legal procedure, you should know what I'm talkin' about. If you don't, then I trust you'll sit down and not disturb us again.'

'You *will* do that, Tomas, won't you?' the Father reiterated pointedly.

Tomas nodded easily. 'Of course, Father. That shouldn't be a problem.'

Judge Laverty frowned contemplatively. 'Very well, young man, if I told you that I was a *judge emeritus*, what would I mean?'

'That you've served your time, and that the position is honorary only,' Tomas replied, seemingly totally unfazed by that question.

Judge Laverty nodded grimly. 'Do you know what I mean if I say that I am presentin' you with *prima facie* evidence?'

'Evidence assumed to be true until proven otherwise.'

'*De jure* - do you know what that means?'

'By right, or accordin' to the law.'

As Tomas spoke, Miles watched the proceedings through slitted eyes, both unnerved and angered by what he was hearing. Tomas, whom he'd once viewed as both Momus and Odysseus, had now adopted a new, unfathomable persona. The vagrant clenched his jaw hard, trying to work out exactly why this annoyed him. Was he simply jealous because Tomas had concealed his true self from everyone in Adullam more skilfully than Miles? Or was it because Tomas had played everyone, including Miles, for fools from the very start? The vagrant nodded soberly at this latter realisation, that deception rejuvenating a long-forgotten vulnerability within him. He noticed, however, that Judge Laverty and many others seemed visibly impressed by what they were hearing.

'Sub judice?'

'Under consideration by a judge and a court of law.'

'Very good,' Judge Laverty said, honestly. 'You are clearly a man of learnin', Tomas, that I must admit. But there is still one question I must ask.'

Tomas pursed his lips. 'Ask away – in the Latin or French, whatever.'

'No, no,' Judge Laverty frowned. 'I'd rather know why you wish to defend this man. After all, your motive must be personal, seein' as how you've only arrived in town and have no knowledge of this Stranger. You do have a motive, I presume?'

Tomas took out his cigarettes and lit one up, before edging past the other vagrants into the centre aisle. Walking slowly to the bottom of the dais, he turned and addressed the gathering. 'My motive is simple,' he said eventually. 'Y'see, I just can't grasp this idea that it's better to sacrifice one man–no matter his perceived crimes against humanity–in order to save the lives of others. It may be utilitarian, but it's not very Christian, is it?' Tomas turned to regard the huge wooden cross above the altar, then smiled as if suddenly enlightened. 'Or maybe it's very Christian, I d'know. Still, I'd like to defend this man because I believe even an alleged murderer should have his day in court. True, I don't know much about him, yet doesn't that make me impartial enough to act as his defence? And, as I speak on his behalf, we may–hopefully, and time permittin'–even arbitrate a solution which favours everyone here tonight'

'Aye, and maybe we'll discover the meanin' of life too,' Dan McGinty snapped.

'We might indeed,' Tomas grinned. 'Anyway, my reasons are also utilitarian. Because, when you walk out of that usurped farmhouse tomorrow mornin' over the body of the Stranger–safe and well, and ready to move on with your own lives–you might feel better for at least discussin' beforehand exactly why he had to die.'

'A clear conscience never fears a knock on the door at midnight,' Mrs Stewart said primly. 'So, if the Stranger's a truly good man, he won't shoot at Vinny, and Vinny won't have to shoot at him. And, if this man trusts in God, then he'll know that everythin' will work out alright for him in the end.'

Tomas laughed dryly. 'I'd have to disagree on several points. Firstly, anyone forced to defend themselves against physical violence in a lawful and free society may do so with a clear conscience – and this would apply equally to the Stranger. Moreover, you're sayin' that God–should He exist–never subjects good people to needless cruelty, and that He always discriminates in favour of the righteous – a highly debatable point at best! Still, if this is so, then shouldn't we–good people that we are–just sit back and trust Him to guide us safely through this storm?

'You're just bein' facetious,' Frank Devenney muttered. 'And all of this talkin' is puttin' our lives in jeopardy. Listen to that storm.' The semi-crippled man shivered briskly as the wind drove a torrent of rain against the chapel's windows and doors. 'We're all goin' to die, and I hope that everyone on that platform can live with themselves after it.' He paused, realising what he'd said from the nervous laughter which ensued. 'You know what I bloody mean, and you're all thinkin' exactly the same, so what the hell are you gigglin' about?'

'I know what you mean,' Mrs Stevens frowned. 'And I also know Vinny McIntyre was granted his position in order to show strong leadership. So, if he doesn't want to go over to the farmhouse, he should empower young Seamus Brown to do it.'

'But what if either man gets shot, and perhaps injured or killed tonight?' Judge Laverty interrupted. 'Will that rest easily upon your conscience?'

'They're paid to take such risks,' the Old Man said, abruptly. 'Don't get me wrong – I don't want to see anyone hurt. But they took an oath to defend the people of Craiglann in times of danger, and it's now their duty to do just that.'

'We took an oath to defend people, not attack them,' Vinny seethed. 'And with respect to Seamus, I'm the one legally empowered to approach the farmhouse. Nor does he have a uniform at the moment, which would make him look like a civilian carryin' a gun – which, as you may agree, would hardly end well. No, it's all down to me, and I'll do this only if there's no other option. However, if I do end up killin' this man tonight, then the blame shan't be mine alone.'

Tomas nodded reflectively. 'I agree that no one should be above the law,' he said. 'But this Stranger has been subjected to all sorts of discrimination, harassment and physical threats over the last week. Now, he's very afraid and fear will always force a man to arm himself against the world.' Tomas looked at Mrs. Stevens. 'Have you ever been afraid?' he asked her, easily.

Mrs Stevens folded her arms defensively. 'Aye, but I've never thought about killin' anyone. This man's guilty – that's why he locked himself away.'

Tomas suppressed a laugh. 'Well, we'll know that soon enough. Still, the best I can do now is argue in his defence – sort of like a Devil's Advocate, if you would.'

'I'm prepared to go over to the farmhouse,' Frank Devenney snorted angrily. 'I've no qualms about shootin' a murderer. If Vinny's afraid to go over, then I shall!'

'You're an arse, Frank!' Vinny retorted hotly. 'You act first and think later. It was the same on Saturday night in the mainstreet. You just kept interferin' in that fight, even when I told you we'd the whole thing under control. You're a bloody arse!'

The Old Man stood and raised his hands as Vinny and Frank Devenney were about to intensify their argument. 'What more is there to say?' the newsagent said angrily. 'Tomas has made us aware of the Stranger's position, but he's also ignored the fact there isn't a civilised country in the world where the law would place one normal man's right to life above that of the many. Besides, if this Stranger is prepared to resort to violence before listenin' to reason, then he obviously doesn't have a right to live in our society.'

'My argument precisely,' Tomas smiled. 'Reason *before* violence. Wow, you're actually gettin' way ahead of me here!'

'You're just a bloody strife-riser!' Con Logue barked at Tomas. 'You haven't even met the bloody man, so how can you argue in his defence? What the hell is your game anyhow, and who are you to judge us?'

'I haven't even begun to defend this man yet,' Tomas replied easily. 'Everythin' I've said so far is just an openin' argument, and the best is probably still to come. Besides, who's anyone to judge anyone? You're actually gettin' well ahead of me here, too.' He pointed between Con Logue and the Old Man. 'Are you sure you both wouldn't like to get on my team, as it were?'

Clenching his fists tightly, the simmering Con Logue exploded to his feet, only to be held back by his bewildered wife and the Old Man. Vinny McIntyre stood at the same time, stepping defensively in front of a bemused Tomas. Con and the Old Man relented momentarily, yet their eyes promised Tomas all sorts of retribution.

'That's enough,' Judge Laverty said. 'I understand both arguments here. The odds have been stacked against this Stranger from the start, so I understand why Tomas wishes to act in his defence. Still, I too am bewildered as to how anyone can present a further case on behalf of someone they don't know. So, bearin' this in mind, we shall have our hearin' and it shall hopefully last no more than an hour at most. Though I shall also reserve the right to stop the proceedin's at any time, should they become in any way ridiculous.'

'In that hour we could all be dead,' George Harkin snapped, pointing between the Chief Guard and the Father. 'This is nothin' more than martial law. And you, Father Joseph, are allowin' this travesty to take place in your chapel without sayin' a word against it. You should be fuckin' ashamed of yourself!'

Miles sat bolt upright in his seat, chilled by the fact someone had dared to go at *the language* in front of the priest. As the storm raged violently in the background, the vagrant noticed everyone staring with bated breath between George and the Father. The priest fixed George with a withering look, yet the other man's glare was uncompromising.

After several protracted moments, the Father dropped his head and spoke, his solemn tone designed to draw penitence from stone. 'This is the strangest *situation* I've ever encountered, George,' he began. 'And only now do I realise that both *God's* law and the law of the land can sometimes *conflict* heavily. Still, *my* moral guidance will not get us through this situation, nor will Vinny's strong *physical* policin'. So, now we must look to legislation to *decide* our actions. And, as Judge Laverty has already said...'

'Judge Laverty isn't a judge anymore,' Frank Devenney interrupted. 'And this *isn't* a trial. Nor is Tomas a defence solicitor, and nor is this a bloody courtroom. Which means it's all nothin' but a bloody farce!'

'I agree with Frank,' Con Logue added sharply. 'So that would mean anythin' said here tonight isn't legally bindin'. And Frank, I'm goin' to take this opportunity to apologise for kickin' you the other night outside The Duck...'

'So it was *you* who kicked me when I was down! You...you..!'

'Aye, it was me,' Con Logue replied nonchalantly. 'Look, as Vinny said, you were makin' a bloody arse of yourself. And I thought you hit the wee girl from the hairdressin' shop, so I stuck the boot in you. Now, in hindsight, that might've been wrong. Besides, I had the whole thing under control and I was just throwin' a few punches, man-to-idiot, with Neil Martin over there...'

The market-vendor rose quickly to his feet. 'Idiot, is it, Logue? I'll show you who the idiot is if you care to step outside.' As Big Sean gently eased him back into his seat, Neil pointed threateningly over at the garage-owner. 'I swear, Con, should I have to swim the length of the Crissom in the mornin', I'll have you for that...'

'You'll have to wait,' Frank Devenney seethed. 'I'm havin' him first!'

'Gentlemen,' Judge Laverty called above the ensuing squabble. 'All this bickerin' is gettin' us nowhere. We've business to attend to, do we not?'

'Aye, we do,' Con Logue frowned. 'So, as I was sayin' before I was so rudely interrupted, Judge Laverty isn't a judge anymore, and so...'

'But Judge Laverty has been a judge for many years,' Father Joseph said in exasperation. 'And he only retired a couple of months ago, so I think his record stands for itself in that respect...'

Judge Laverty raised a hand. 'I think, Father, we should address that particular point. Mister Logue is correct – whatever is decided in this room tonight shall be in no way legally bindin'. But, that same decision will hopefully give us a clearer picture of our objective. So, to the rules. Firstly, brevity is critical. Secondly, witnesses shall be called to take the stand, and they shall come forward, one at a time, and tell us–without interruption–what they know of this strange situation. Thirdly, Vinny McIntyre and young Seamus Brown can act as bailiffs.' Judge Laverty examined the dais for a time. 'And I shall use the altar as my bench. Justice shall be done, *deo velente*.' The elderly Judge looked expectantly down at Tomas.

'God willin',' Tomas said easily

'Very good, very good indeed. We definitely have one man of learnin' amongst us. That, unfortunately, is the only thing of which I am certain here this night.'

'There is, of course, one more thing,' Tomas said. Judge Laverty raised his head and eyed the other man wordlessly. 'We also need a jury. Four or five people, no more. And not just anybody at that, as most of the people here in this courtroom...'

'It isn't a courtroom,' the Old Man chastised him. 'It's a chapel, and very few people around here seem to have any bloody respect for that fact!'

'Very well,' Tomas grinned. 'Most people here within this *chapel* seem to be directly involved in this case, so I say we pick people who are *tabula rasa,* whereby they possess minds un-subjected to, or relatively free from, outside experience or influence.'

Judge Laverty scratched thoughtfully at his head. 'Well, prudence deems that a limited jury would prevent squabblin'. But we'd need people who can consider both sides of this argument objectively.' The elderly Judge peered over his glasses and scanned the pews. 'And in that respect, Tomas, you seem to have set yourself a tall order. Whom would you suggest perform that task?'

'Those untainted by the facts, and those who haven't sided one way or the other in this case so far.' Tomas stared down at the seventh pew, to where Wing-Ding, Pele, Brian and Miles were sitting, and Judge Laverty followed his gaze. 'I can see quite a few people here who haven't been allowed to have an opinion for ages.'

'They are to be your, ehm, jury?' the Judge said. His tone was one of almost disbelief, though he refrained from sounding too incredulous at the last moment.

'Why not?' Tomas shrugged. 'They're impartial. In fact, speakin' plainly, you could even say that they don't really care one way or the other.'

It was then that Con Logue rose angrily, saying he'd heard enough. The sound of the hammer clicking back on Vinny McIntyre's gun, however, returned him to his seat. Judge Laverty called everyone to order. 'I'd like to discuss this with Father Joseph and Vinny McIntyre if I may,' he said then, his frown deepening.

Tomas raised his palm-heels. 'Not a problem. I'll just take a wee walk and allow the blood to circulate in my poor achin' feet.'

***

Several minutes passed. Up in the front pews, Con Logue and a few of the townsmen confederated darkly, reminding Miles of unbridled Centaurs as they stomped about this way and that, the dark edge of rebellion deep in their eyes; and, at the furthest end of the raised dais, Judge Laverty, Vinny McIntyre and the Father debated the sanity of Tomas' proposal like genteel Lapiths, all too aware they might soon have to make war upon their equine cousins.

Miles stared impassively between the two groups, before turning to regard Tomas, who was now moving unconcernedly down the centre aisle examining each Station-of-the-Cross. The vagrant couldn't believe it: Tomas had somehow persuaded Judge Laverty into presiding over an absurd midnight trial in this ill-lit chapel as a virtual Sword of Damocles hovered above them. Not only that, the other man had also had the audacity to propose jury duty for Miles and the other inmates without firstly seeking their permission.

Miles gritted his teeth together: What was Tomas thinking? As noble as his ideas were, how could he hope to win Craiglann's locals over? Didn't he realise that man's basic instinct was survival, or that people only ever willingly agreed to forfeit their lives en-masse for either great religious or political leaders? Similarly, how could he believe any sane jury–should it consist of the most honourable men on earth–might elect to place one ordinary man's life above those of many? True, Tomas possessed a certain charisma which might earn him a few believers over the next hour, yet he seemed to forget he was also a stranger in town, so how much empathy did he seriously think he'd muster? Furthermore, Tomas wasn't in possession of all the facts. While he now knew as much about Marie Devine as most people, he wasn't aware that Wing-Ding had also been on the Crissom on the night she'd gone missing – as, perhaps, had many others. The difference was, of course, that Wing-Ding's evidence and a further anonymous phone-call to the Guards had fully implicated the Stranger in Marie's disappearance. Not only that, Miles now suspected that particular call had been made by Brian, who, knowing Wing-Ding was under suspicion, perhaps did so to further incriminate the Stranger. If this was indeed so, there was no doubt which way both men would vote if elected onto the jury. Miles shook his head despondently: No matter what happened, the cards were stacked against Tomas, and the other man wasn't even aware of it.

Too, the more Miles thought about it, the more he realised those were only the initial problems. What would happen afterwards, he mused, when this farcical trial reached its inevitable conclusion? An unprotected esplanade of a field stood between the chapel and the farmhouse, and the Stranger had a gun. So, if the storm drew to a temporary cease, a plan would have to be forged whereby that killing-ground was made safe and the farmhouse taken with a minimum of casualties. And how would the locals achieve that? Would they construct a Trojan horse or fire combustible solutions of nitre, sulphur and naphtha from catapults at the farmhouse in the manner of the Byzantine Greeks until the enemy either succumbed or died? No, Miles mused angrily, they'd probably order a hoplite army in there first, brush-shafts and shovels in hand, with people like Miles and the other inmates at the head of it. Naturally, the Father would make a wee sign-of-the-cross over everyone before they all set off on their crusade, but that would hardly matter, would it? And there was probably no point in counting on Tomas for help. After stirring up trouble, he'd probably feign madness in the same way Odysseus had done when he'd been asked to help take Troy. Aye, Tomas would probably escape all harm, Miles thought coldly, because people like him always bloody did!

Miles stared venomously at Tomas, hating him then for putting everyone into such an impossible situation. There was now no doubt in the vagrant's mind that, as soon as the inmates delivered their verdict of guilt, they'd be called upon to do their bit. And how could any of Adullam's habitués–the least cherished members of their community, to whom such a task just had to be afforded–complain when they owed such great debts to both the Father and society? The inmate jury could, of course, declare the Stranger innocent, yet even that wouldn't guarantee their survival. The locals, incensed at such a call, might still elect to use that small group as cannon-fodder, and perhaps even threaten to kill them if they didn't do as they were ordered.

Miles shivered briskly before regarding Tomas through even tighter slits of eyes.

Tomas stretched himself fully at the furthest end of the chapel, before walking back up the centre aisle. He ignored a host of hostile glares and returned to his seat. Miles, now soberer than he'd been in years, waited until most of the minatory glares were again focused upon Judge Laverty, Vinny McIntyre and the Father.

'What the hell are you at?' Miles said, in a barely controlled screech. 'That's the most ridiculous idea I've ever heard. This is a chapel, for God's sakes. It isn't a fuckin' courtroom, and you aren't a fuckin' solicitor! How did you ever get anyone to fuckin' agree to that?!'

Tomas seemed startled at the other man's vehement display. He raised an eyebrow and moved back a little, waiting for Miles to stop fuming. 'Steady on there, Miles. I thought you didn't like people cursin'. What's that all about?'

'You bring it out of me. You, you're a fuckin'..!' Miles sighed deeply, gritting his teeth together hard in an attempt to regain his calm.

Tomas smiled broadly. 'This *is* a courtroom, Miles,' he whispered. 'It's the greatest courtroom of all! Here, men always judge themselves. Here, the truth is constantly unveiled. And here, durin' this midnight hour, we get to take over. Don't you see the irony in it?' There was a glint of mischief in Tomas' eyes and he rubbed his hands briskly together as if relishing what was about to come. 'Here we are with people who've judged us over the years, and now we get a chance to judge them. And here, for one whole hour, we actually get to change places with God himself.'

Miles clenched his jaw, debating whether to tell Tomas about the many flaws in his plan, about his loaded-jury and the cannon-fodder role of Adullam's inmates in the inevitable battle for the farmhouse which would ensue. But there was no point, he decided grimly, because Tomas wouldn't listen: It was there in the other man's eyes, in his voice, in his actions. Miles made himself a bleak promise then: He was going to hold Tomas tightly to his front as they were forced up the field to meet with death. He could do it, he knew he could, because despite the weakness brought on by his debilitating malaise, his anger would see him through.

'I thought we were goin' to judge the Stranger,' Miles said through thin lips. 'Nobody else. We…you…whoever…are supposed to judge one man, not everyone in Craiglann.'

'Aye, we'll judge him too, Miles,' Tomas grinned. 'You'll see soon enough.'

Miles skipped the cryptic answer, not in the mood for riddles. There was a shake in his hands and he felt nauseous, knowing he needed a drink. But there was no way he could get outside until the storm had subsided. Still, Tomas had seemed quite certain he could help earlier on. 'You said you'd get me a drink,' Miles said, accusingly. 'You said you'd get me a bloody drink, and that...'

'I told you that I'd help you,' Tomas reassured him. 'But you'll have to wait another few minutes. You can do that, can't you?'

Miles felt like snapping at Tomas, and he barely managed to restrain himself. He nodded uncertainly, even as he induced a voluntary shiver into his legs to keep them warm. 'Another surprise eh?' he said sombrely, trying to conceal both himself and his mood. *You just wait, Tomas*, he promised inwardly. *You just wait until I have my drink. Then you're on your fuckin' own!*

Tomas nodded with a grin. 'Aye, another surprise, Miles.'

Miles took a deep breath and down-turned his head, 'So, how do you know so much about courts and law. I thought you were just...'

'Just a nobody?' Tomas asked softly. 'Aye, Miles, that's exactly what I am.' He took his last two cigarettes from their packet, giving one to Miles before throwing the empty carton under the seat. Miles almost snatched it from him, making another silent promise never to return the favour, even if the other man was lying on the floor and gasping to death. Tomas lit his cigarette and shared the light, deep in thought. 'Or maybe I'm just like you, Miles. Maybe I once carved a niche in the world before life carved chunks out of me. Maybe I once had a wife and kids, and someone who believed in me. Aye, and maybe my true-love and I lay often beneath the stars, watchin' as they glowed fiercely in the obsidian night, our breath as one, shallow, almost tantric, and our hearts beatin' a dual rhythm that only couples know.' Tomas grinned facetiously. 'Aye, maybe that happened to me once, Miles. Do you think that might've been at all possible?'

'I don't recall ever tellin' you about my wife and kids,' Miles frowned.

'You don't remember much though, do you, Miles? Sure, you said that yourself. Hey, I bet you can hardly remember last night.'

'I would've remembered tellin' you that,' Miles said defensively. 'I told you – I remember some things very well.'

'Maybe you were drunk at the time. Could that be it?'

Miles shook his head vehemently. 'I never said it. I'm near certain of it. And what's with all of these fuckin' maybes?'

'Maybe you didn't say it then,' Tomas offered, seemingly undisturbed by the other man's anger. 'Maybe I'm just tellin' you about myself, and you think I'm talkin' about you. Like every man alive, you think you stand in the centre of the known universe at all times, no matter where you are. Perhaps you think you're the only one who ever had a family,' Tomas admonished him. 'How naive you are, Miles, to believe you're the only man to have ever loved and lost.' Tomas shook his head and smiled sadly. 'And how vain you are when everyone has known a similar pain to yours at one stage of their blighted existence. Of course, they'd share their pain with you, Miles, if you'd allow them – I'm near certain of that. But you – I doubt very much that you'd share your pain with them.'

'I didn't know that about you,' Miles snapped, ignoring the other man's riddled jibes. 'You never told me that before. I just presumed...'

Miles paused, unsure of what he'd actually thought. Because Tomas had arrived in Adullam on the day Miles had tried to commit suicide, Miles hadn't really questioned who he was, too preoccupied just then with trying to find a good reason why he should continue living. And, after eventually dispensing with the notion that the other man was a troublemaker, he'd actually begun to assume Tomas was just a happy-go-lucky adventurer who somehow managed to keep his more negative thoughts at bay by wandering the land.

That Tomas may've led a more normal life before his arrival in the Mission Home had never occurred to Miles, who'd by then fallen into the trap of thinking all the inmates were the same, that the past had betrayed each of them and that their sole purpose was to search out enough drink to help them survive the longest journey they'd ever take: That journey which led them, each evening, into the blackest realms of night. For it was there, at day's end, that men always met with their younger selves, and there they inevitably came to understand the futility of their existence, even as they ruminated over why the Gods–supposedly possessed of so much love and forgiveness–chose to inflict the cruellest lives upon those lonely, forgotten children who lived within the empty shells of men.

Miles shrugged brusquely. 'I just thought what I thought, that's all.'

'Maybe we never talked enough when I was here last,' Tomas shrugged. 'I'll take half the blame for that. I should maybe've been more of a friend.'

Miles shrugged again, not wanting to meet the other man's gaze. 'They say friendship can be as much a burden as a source of happiness.'

'Ah, Miles, don't say that. Friends bear witness to your existence, and are probably your best epitaph. Everyone need them at some time or another.'

'What were you before?' Miles asked blankly, not wanting to hear the other man's definition of that word, and trying to refocus upon his own dark promises of revenge. 'In the past, I mean. What were you?'

Tomas raised another eyebrow. 'I've always been a wanderer, Miles. And this time I just happened to wander into the middle of this storm, nothin' more.'

'That's hardly a bloody answer.'

'Probably not. Alright, I've defended people in the past. There really isn't anythin' more to know.'

'Good people or bad people?'

'What's the difference? The law defends everyone equally.'

'They say the Devil looks after his own,' Miles said, sweating coldly as pains flashed in his gut. 'They say he knows the law and sometimes speaks the truth.'

'Well, if it's clichés you want, then they also say inferior men are governed by law and wise men by decorum,' Tomas said seriously. 'So, as there are very few wise men in this chapel tonight, we'll have to use the law – even though it's often devoid of any real meanin'. Hey, are you alright, Miles? You don't look the best.'

Miles shivered deeply as a broadcasting wind laid full claim to his mind. He found his gaze drawn to the stained-glass windows and briefly envisioned a cluster of vengeful Harpies mutating from the brooding Cherubim, Seraphim and Thrones, their horrific faces and vulture-like bodies too repellent to behold. As yet another flash of lightning seared the sky, amorphous shadows clustered in the transepts and the vagrant tensed, inwardly swearing he'd just seen the figure of Pan flitting in and out of the umbra, pipes in hand and eyes red as ember. Miles groaned softly, his heart racing, the coldness in his bones deepening.

'Are you alright, Miles?' Tomas asked again. 'You look as if you've seen a ghost.'

'We can't win this,' Miles whispered. 'You can't change the way people think.'

Tomas shook his head. 'I don't agree, Miles. It has to be possible to change the way others think, because it's possible to change the way we ourselves think.'

Miles stared at the floor again. He was seeing Tomas in a new light now, despite not wanting to do so. The man had more faces than a many-headed Hydra and was causing more trouble than a wine-drinking, lecherous centaur. Why did you come here, Odysseus? he found himself wondering. Is this some mission of vengeance? Couldn't you have stayed on Calypso's island, where you were abandoned by the goddess Athena? Why couldn't you have let your ship be guided by the prevailing winds to north Africa, there to dwell in the Lands of the Lotus Eaters, there to forget about Adullam, your sometimes home? Why don't you go back where you belong? Don't you know that an army of suitors has invaded your palace, and that even now your wife, Penelope, weaves an embroidery...

'Are you alright, Miles? You're ramblin' on a bit, and you look pretty ill.'

Miles shook himself from his momentary torpor and opened his eyes to see Tomas staring concernedly at him. The cold was consuming him and he was definitely losing his mind. 'You can't make us do jury-duty, Tomas. We'll just give them permission to kill the Stranger. Then they'll blame us, or even kill us afterwards to keep us quiet...'

'You'll have to trust me, Miles. All men grow uncertain in the shallows of night, it's perfectly natural. But you'll be fine, I swear.'

'No, you'll be fuckin' fine!' Miles said shortly. '*What's that word again, Miles, for do-goodedness?*' he added mockingly. 'Aye, you pretendin' to be stupid all along, and you a solicitor. What was the fuckin' point of all that?'

Tomas seemed surprised. 'You're gettin' very fond of the cursin', Miles. Didn't think you were into that sort of thing, really I didn't.'

Miles stared coldly at him. 'Who the fuck are you?'

'I'm your Christ, Miles,' Tomas replied simply.

Miles shook his head and raised a hand as Tomas was about to continue. 'Don't say another word,' he snapped, shifting fast towards the furthest end of the pew. He was fuming and hadn't been as angry in a long time. This was a just joke to Tomas, who now sat there like some insane Caligula, calmly inducing strife and mayhem into a situation which, only an hour before, Miles wouldn't have believed could get any worse.

Tomas was the Devil–Miles was certain of it–and he was here to ensure everyone died a slow and painful death. It was time, Miles knew, to cut all ties with him and to relinquish their absurd affinity for once and for all.

'We'll talk later then?' Tomas called after him; the smile was still there, the sparkle in his eyes evolving into a teasing glint. 'You want to discuss it later then?'

Miles sat alone at the end of the pew, trying to control his panic, and a thought struck him that he might even die if he didn't get a drink soon. He began rubbing hard at his chest in an attempt to ease his unsettlement, and it was then he felt the coin in his shirt pocket, imagining in his confusion that he might only have kept it there in order to pay the ferryman, Charon, to carry him across the Styx into Hades. A fear-induced rush of adrenaline urged him to shuffle back along the pew. There, he grabbed hard at Tomas' arm, inwardly cursing the way his mind threatened to leave him each and every time he felt that compulsive urge for alcohol.

'You promised me a drink,' he snapped, ignoring a flashing pain in his arm, in his chest, in his mind. 'And, instead, you have me doin' jury duty. Why don't you just let them kill this Stranger and mind your own business? He probably did what they said anyway, so what is it to you?' Miles felt his breath leaving him all of a sudden, the pain heavy in his stomach and threatening to double him over. 'You said…you'd…get me a drink,' he wheezed, aware he was letting himself down, though unable to find the energy to care.

'I did,' Tomas replied, carefully helping Miles to sit upright. 'And I will, I promise. Now, I'm just goin' to the toilet. You follow me out there in about five minutes, and I'll get you your drink, don't worry.'

Miles nodded, deeply perplexed, and he watched as Tomas moved out past the other inmates and made his way up the aisle towards the toilets in the left-hand transept. Then, as the other man disappeared from view with a codified wink, Miles sank deeper into his coat, attempting once again to gain unagitated entry into his past in order to suppress both his physical and mental angst, even as he wondered exactly what Tomas had in mind.

.

TWELVE

Before falling for Sarah, a younger and more secure Miles Kivlehan had scorned the existence of true love, certain that no single emotion– outside, perhaps, grief impelled by a sudden close bereavement–had the power to strike as a supernal thunderbolt into a rational person's heart and leave them incapable of thinking logically thereafter. Upon his lonely walk back from the train station to the campus, however, he found himself recalling a snippet of ancient Greek wisdom:

To verify its own existence, Fate can never allow a man to become too certain in life, nor the world to revolve too slowly.

Only now did Miles understand the truth in this maxim. For years, he'd sought solace in his own definitions of love, trust, hope and faith; but, over the last few days, each of those constants had been thoroughly disproven. Naturally, this grave realisation unsettled him to no end, for never again could he truly justify any thought or deed for which he didn't firstly receive positive council from either his conscience or his heart. As importantly, he had to painfully acknowledge that logic and reason would always be inferior to intuition, for the human mind had an ongoing ability to thwart, rationalise and manipulate all actions and ideas to its advantage.

Now sadder but wiser, Miles used the next few days to fathom whether–this new knowledge aside–he'd learned anything positive about love. Could it be, he mused, that a person had to be prepared to fully embrace heartache before they could understand true love? And was it possible, too, that his own deep-rooted relationship fears stemmed from a dread of success rather than failure? After all, if one used mortality as the ultimate example, people seemed better equipped for dealing with failure than success, so less intense love affairs of shorter duration were perhaps better suited to men's fickle nature.

Upon deeper reflection, Miles supposed this was why many people were fascinated with love's inherent tragedy moreso than its positive benefits, or why others settled for the first person to show an interest in them instead of waiting for the right suitor to come along. Success, after all, was often more difficult to contend with, and perhaps only the very brave could deal with extended contentment and its natural counterparts, protracted heartache and failure.

As these ideas evolved, Miles also found himself debating whether the human heart was equipped to deal with perpetual happiness. Surely there had to be a way for it to do so, for how else could true love survive? Miles didn't know the answers to these questions, yet he instinctively felt Sarah might, and so he set off to her home two days later, filled with the almost terrifying comprehension that his future no longer felt as if it was directly in his hands.

The sky was heavy with rain that Saturday morning as the train pulled out of the station, and Miles was in an undecided mood. He knew there was a chance Sarah would instantly rebuff him upon his arrival, yet he had to tell her that he now instinctively understood that they were supposed to be together. Not only that, he was certain Sarah still wanted to be with him: This, he'd subconsciously learned not only from the way she'd touched the park bench to ever so briefly reclaim her past, but from the way she'd casually tossed an apple to him as she left for home, for at weddings the ancient Greeks had thrown apples to those whom they either lusted after or loved.

Upon arriving at Sarah's house in a taxi, Miles was struck by an eerie sensation that he'd finally arrived home. But, brushing aside this distracting thought, he walked up the rain-stricken path and knocked at the door. Briefly aware of the sitting-room curtains being pulled gently aside and then slowly replaced, he stood upon the doorstep awaiting a reply. But, as the minutes ticked by, there was no answer. Moving around to the side of the house, Miles tapped gently upon the window and called out Sarah's name, but again there was no response.

Despondently, he went and sat upon the damp garden wall, feeling a futility rise within him. For fifteen minutes or so he sat in silence, oblivious to the growing rain and allowing that brief despair to engulf him, until it struck him that, even though reason deemed he should now cut his losses and go, his instinct–which he was slowly starting to rely upon–told him Sarah was simply gauging his reactions.

Buoyed by these thoughts, he began looking around him, only to realise that the once unkempt front garden had been lawned and planted with a wide variety of flowers. Within moments, Miles found his gaze drawn to one yellow rose bush, now in full bloom, and an idea suddenly came to him. He got up, moved towards the bush and proceeded to snap one blossom low down the stem, gritting his teeth together as he allowed its protective thorny mesh to bite deep into the flesh of his palm. Then, with his hand bleeding profusely, he walked up the path and stood in front of the window, where he again called out Sarah's name. As she peered tentatively out through the curtains, Miles silently held the rose aloft, showing her he finally understood what she meant: Falling in love was easy, but unconditional and truly spiritual love required people to also accept and attempt to overcome the very necessary pain which was bound inseparably to that highest of virtues.

Seconds later, the front door opened and Miles felt his every worry evaporate as a smiling Sarah led him silently into her kitchen, where she took the rose from him and gently tended the wound in his hand with a disinfected cloth. But as he stood there in that relaxed silence, Miles was once more overwhelmed with doubt. He wanted to be with Sarah more than anything, he knew, but what if he was incapable of unselfishly loving her in the way she deserved? What if he couldn't drop his own barriers sufficiently and allow himself to be loved? How was he supposed to cope with the burden afforded by almost perpetual happiness? And, more importantly, could Sarah ever trust and believe in him–never mind love him–after the way he'd treated her in the past? For a moment, he felt like running away, but, as this conflict raged within him, his inner voice calmly urged him to talk to Sarah. And soon after, after haltingly explaining his fears, he found himself backing away from her in the expectation she might now tell him to leave because she finally knew the darkness in his heart.

But Sarah pulled him towards her, gently explaining that it was indifference and not concern which killed relationships, and that no affair was truly doomed when those involved expressed fears as to its future well-being. Nor did Miles have to worry about Sarah trusting him, she soothed, because her father had taught her a long time ago that trust had be given automatically, for to prejudge invited pre-judgement, which always led to mutual distrust, resentment and the eventual imprisonment of two souls. As for Miles' thwarted preconception of love, Sarah grinned, that too was a very different thing altogether.

When asked to describe true love, Sarah explained, most people defined it as a perpetual alliance forged in Heaven. But, even though it was a nice idea that love required nothing more than admittance and acceptance, man's inability to totally understand anything of an eternal nature often forced him to test not just love, but all strong emotions, via the medium of physical action and reaction in order to comprehend each more fully. For this reason, love closely mimicked Nature's formula for all life–this being one of varying degrees of chaos and disharmony acting as a catalyst for replication and survival–and so remained in periodic flux, thereby granting people a deeper insight into its meaning.

So, Sarah smiled, those who deemed true love a perfect union of two un-conflicting and exclusively attracted souls, were–in her opinion, at least–quite wrong. There was no formula for true love: In fact, most couples appeared totally unsuited at the start, argued sporadically and often had few outward interests. What did matter was that they had a commonality of purpose and identical goals. With these latter factors present, they could then savour and explore their complementary imperfections, even as they revelled in the ongoing mystery of their attraction. Moreover, Sarah shrugged, if you recognised true love as an ongoing process, then you'd find succour in its almost rhythmic existence, and take comfort in knowing that–like life itself–it would always have its ups and downs and forever ebb and flow.

As Sarah talked, Miles listened in silence, watching her intently. Now, he found himself viewing her in an entirely different light: What he'd once perceived as her slowness of thought, he recognised as thoughtful consideration; and what he'd once deciphered as her slowness of action, he understood as patience.

He kissed her deeply then, knowing that the chase wasn't always better than the catch after all. And, that night as they made love, he felt a different intensity stirring within his mind, body and soul.

Shortly afterwards, as he held her tightly in his arms, he remarked upon this to Sarah, saying their lovemaking had never felt as good. She simply smiled, before replying softly that he'd never truly been with her before; and, as she fell deeply asleep in his arms, he prayed he'd never lose her again.

***

Rending loneliness forced Miles back into the present, and he stared balefully around the darkened chapel. The town's law-lords as yet mulled surreptitiously over Tomas' bold ideas upon the dais, even as the more revolutionary of the male evacuees gathered around Con Logue in the third pew as if he were Ares, God of War, granting counsel go his chief-warlords Panic, Grief, Terror and Strife. Miles, now deeply agitated by the latter group's aggressive postures and certain they were set upon imminent insurgency, knew he'd best wait several more moments before joining Tomas, so he attempted to distract himself by listening into a muddled conversation several rows to his front.

There, some of the townswomen were now proposing remedies to the ongoing problem above the thrash of the storm, with Mrs Stewart and Mrs Malhaffey embroidering a fanciful scenario in which one volunteer was wrapped in a padded coat and helmet before being sent over to the farm with a rope attached to him so that he might be dragged quickly back if injured or shot. Miles smiled wryly, briefly reminded of

Poseidon's son, Theseus, using a ball of string to find his way out of the labyrinth of King Minos after slaying the Minotaur. Still, the vagrant couldn't help squirming as someone else intimately elaborated upon the bloodier injuries that same volunteer might receive as he was swiftly dragged around trees, through thorny hedges and up the hill into the chapel. So, with this idea wisely discarded, the Amazonian Mrs Daly and her cohort Mrs Stewart began unsubtly rousing the women to make a stand against their men, pointing out it was probably their testosterone-fuelled rage, and not the storm or the tree, which would get everyone killed. Instinctively aware that a male of sorts was listening in, however, Mrs Daly rounded silently on Miles, as did her confederates.

Upon being confronted by that spiteful nest of Furies, with their damp, snake-like hair and vengeful dispositions, Miles averted his gaze. He tried concentrating instead upon several candles burning to his left, watching as their Will-o-the-wisp flames were strobed by an animated breeze into sending blocks of shadow dancing across the ceiling's architrave. But, as the supposedly infinite attraction of the flames only increased his angst, he turned to stare up at the Father, who was deep in conversation. Almost instantly, the vagrant decided to take advantage of that moment to find Tomas. Walking briskly up the aisle, he passed the priest, saying he was going to the toilet and that he'd be back in less than a minute. The Father fixed him undecidedly for a moment, before nodding his reluctant permission.

As Miles approached the toilets, he noticed the nearby sacristy door standing slightly ajar. Moving warily towards it, he pushed it open, only to espy two dim candles burning at the room's furthest end. Closing the door softly behind him, he sought to adjust his vision, feeling the quickening of his heart as illusory amethyst shadows presented themselves as incorporeal shades in the badly interpreted light. But it was the raw sound of splintering wood which made him jump. Following the noise, he espied Tomas deep in one of the corners. The other man was hunkered down and grunting loudly as he tried to prise open the door of a locked cupboard with the attenuated end of a long metal candlestick.

'What are you at?' Miles gasped. He moved towards Tomas, only to jump back as the wood around the lock splintered into shards, after which one door drooped lazily open.

'Gettin' you a drink,' Tomas grinned, rising and briskly dusting himself off.

Miles stared into the cupboard and noticed an array of chapel wine upon the top shelf, before glancing swiftly back at the sacristy door: A world of danger and banishment lay beyond that portal, he knew, and a surge of fear ripped through him. 'But what if the Father comes in? He'll slaughter us both!'

'You wanted wine, didn't you?' Tomas lifted a bottle out of the cupboard and sniffed at it ridiculously–as if he could actually smell its sweet aroma through the glass–before offering it to Miles. 'Hey, this is no time for gettin' yourself a conscience.'

Miles licked nervously at his lips, his bunched shoulders sign-posting his angst. He needed alcohol badly, and the innate compulsion to close his hand around the bottle was near tangible. But Tomas was correct – something held him back.

Whether it was his conscience, Miles wasn't sure – and whether he believed he possessed one anymore was even less of a certainty. In his university days, he'd argued that the concept of conscience had been artificially invented by rational beings over the ages, who–deeming it an easy way of making lesser men review their own integrity–repetitively expounded its virtues to their descendants. A mainstream point of view, of course, held the conscience to be an inherent gift of God or Nature which asked men to realise the interests of the species above that of the individual. But, in the last eight years, Miles had increasingly found himself wondering if it was always correct to put the interests of others above his own. After all, if God or Nature were busy preserving humanity as a whole, didn't each individual have a moral and personal duty to keep themselves alive by whatever means possible? And, if men forever placed others foremost in their thoughts, wasn't that self-defeatist and generally detrimental to their individual rights?

Or, Miles thought wryly, by resurrecting these arguments now, was he simply seeking to justify the stealing of wine by rationalising his base desires? He shook his head dolefully, realising paradoxically that the existence of conscience–no matter its origin–was actually proven every time one asked oneself such questions. 'I'll wait,' he said through gritted teeth. 'I'll just .. wait.'

Tomas shook his head, and looked Miles deeply in the eyes. 'I don't think you can, Miles. Y'see, I understand your problem. I understand the *allurement*.'

'Who the fuck do you think you are, Tomas?' Miles snorted. He wanted to hate the other man then, yet he didn't think he'd the energy to sustain such venom at present. 'I can do anythin' I fuckin' want!''

Tomas extended the bottle even further, a malicious glint in his eye. 'Now, Miles, there's a darkness I never thought possible. What's that all about?'

Miles felt his mind crumbling: *Drink, Miles. Drink of my cup, and, like Circe the Enchantress, I shall see you turned to swine.* He swiped angrily at the bottle, knocking it flying from the other man's hand, and he watched as it hit the wall and exploded into innumerable shards, staining the grey stone black, even as it sprayed the wooden floor blood red in an evil lixiviation. 'I don't need it that fuckin' bad!'

'You do, Miles!' Tomas took another bottle out of the cupboard and held it to his front. 'You do, because it owns you. You need it – you're just afraid to admit it. But what's the problem here? You can't just show the world how to treat you and then refuse its assistance – what's that all about?'

'What's that supposed to bloody mean?'

'We show the world how to treat us, Miles,' Tomas grinned. 'In our actions, the way we speak, the way we display ourselves – after which we wonder why others abuse us. But then, we've all been doin' that since we begged for a chance at the beginnin' of time to savour life's brevity and cruelty, its triumph and defeat, and from the very moment we refused to be awarded clear insight into the consequences of our actions, in case they somehow dissuaded us from movin' in the direction of our chosen destruction.'

As Miles frowned his confusion, Tomas shrugged lightly, and his glistening eyes seemed to feed on the night, even as his smile brightened impossibly. 'Do you ever wonder if you asked for this experience, Miles? Is it possible, do you think, that your life unfolded exactly the way you wanted it to, so you could test yourself to the extreme? Was this your own idea, Miles? After all, haven't you noticed life usually delivers what we ask of it – it's just that we aren't always so sure of our expectations. At times, in our confusion, we even pray to a higher authority to help us understand the complexity of our desires, and our prayers are always answered, if rarely in the way we first imagine. Your prayers have been answered tonight, Miles. You asked the world to help you, and it did. So what's the problem?' Tomas extended the bottle further. '*In vino veritas*, Miles - there *is* truth in wine, believe me. Take it, because it will help you survive this ordeal. Take it and discover your truth at a later time, for, all too often, the present is hampered by over-contemplation.'

Miles shivered briskly, unsettled by the other man's words. He suddenly recalled how Aristotle had claimed the perfect friendship was between good men alike in their virtue, and the vagrant once believed this to be why he and Tomas got on so well. Now he knew Tomas and he were poles apart in their morality and that the other man was the Devil incarnate, for it was apparently the Devil's way to tempt men through their hopes and fears, and to seduce them into believing they were acting out their evil deeds for God.

Or, Miles thought coldly, perhaps Tomas was just a lesser demon, and what had Hesiod said of such demons? Didn't they live a mortal span ten times that of the phoenix, which itself lived nearly a thousand times as long as man? It was something like that. Still, if demons *were* mortal, they could definitely be injured or even killed. The vagrant narrowed his eyes thoughtfully, knowing then that he had to stop Tomas before he fell foul of his melodious seduction.

As Miles searched the small room for a makeshift weapon, the other man studied him questioningly. 'What's wrong, Miles? You're lookin' remarkably intent for some strange reason. Are you afraid of the Father? Or–ah!–is it *God* you fear? Remember, He only punishes the intention–man punishes the action. C'mon, take a wee drink. You'll hurt no one if you do.'

Miles ignored Tomas and focused instead upon the metal candlestick the other man had used to break open the wine cabinet. He moved towards it, hoping he'd only have to render Tomas insensate, not actually kill him. Still, because Tomas was a demon and possessed of superhuman powers, Miles knew he'd have to act perfectly normal until the exact moment he was about to strike. 'No, it's stealin',' he replied as he moved. 'I'll, ehm, wait.'

'You judge yourself too harshly, Miles, that's your problem. And you seem to believe God would further punish a man who's already spent years punishin' himself.' Tomas grinned broadly as Miles lifted the candlestick. 'Sure, if things are the way they say, He's all-forgivin' isn't He? And you probably forgive Him for everythin' He did against you and yours, so who's the bigger man, eh?'

As Miles moved towards Tomas, he heard a noise somewhere to his immediate left. He turned hurriedly and allowed the makeshift cudgel to fall limply to his side as he espied the Father looming large in the opened doorway. Beside him, an unperturbed Tomas allowed his own broad grin to droop into an almost comic frown. 'Ah, Father Joseph,' the other man said sadly. 'How nice to see you.'

The Father moved across the room at speed, snatching the bottle angrily from Tomas, before urging him away from the cupboard with a dismissive wave.

'Just helpin' out a friend, father.' Tomas continued easily, seemingly nonplussed at the apparent severity of his predicament. 'Just givin' Miles a small buoy to cling to as this veritable Eden drowns in the black of night.'

The priest shook his head and wagged a finger sternly. 'You're out of here first thing in the mornin', Tomas!' he blustered through gritted teeth. 'For good and forever!'

'You'll not want me to go ahead with the hearin' then, Father?' Tomas asked, distractedly patting his pockets one by one, and searching–Miles could only presume–for a cigarette. Several pockets later, he still hadn't found any.

'Oh, we'll have our hearin',' Father Joseph replied thickly. 'That's already been decided. You're an intelligent man, Tomas, and well read despite your appearance. But common sense has obviously evaded you throughout your life because you just can't see the reason behind certain things. You tell everyone you've no free-will here in Adullam, and that *the Father* is a *bad man* who deprives everyone of their liberties. But *this* is why I enforce strict rules, and it's people like you who'd have people like me exact that control. No, have your trial, for you've the same right to impart your doubts and fears as everyone else here tonight. But tomorrow you leave Adullam for good.' The Father shook his head, his eyes unreadable there in the gloom. 'Still, I can't say I'm really surprised – you haven't changed at all. You've only been here a few hours and you have the whole town goin' at each others throats.'

Tomas shrugged easily 'It's a knack I have, Father,' he sighed. 'I just have to walk into a room and I offend somebody. Though it's probably nothin' to boast about, right enough.'

The Father glared at Tomas as if he were a predatory pike which he'd just hauled up onto the riverbank, and one which he might soon have to cosh rather severely into submission with a large rock, maybe several times over. The priest turned to Miles. 'Still, I'm surprised at you, Miles…'

Miles stared at the floor, his shoulders slumped, pensively waiting for the words 'attempted murder' to escape the priest's lips. Inwardly, he knew that he couldn't blame the priest for declaring it. After all, his life had been going this way for a long time, and it was perhaps…

'Aye, I know the courage it took to say what you did there now, Miles,' the Father said, interrupting his thoughts. 'And, believe it or not, I'm not the Antichrist that Tomas makes me out to be. I actually see hope for you, Miles, because you obviously have morals and values. But Tomas isn't your friend – he never was. You should try and realise that before it's too late.'

As Miles slowly lifted his head to see if the priest was serious, Tomas winked at him. 'Now, don't go believin' that rubbish, Miles. I'm you're Christ–remember I told you that–and you're mine. It's the only religion, Miles. Every man should be Christ to every man, there to lift him when he needs elevated, and there to be comforted himself on those days when he feels he's little more than pitiful flesh. At least that's what I think, Miles, and I was only tryin' to help you. Really I was.'

'You're an agitator, Tomas,' the Father said angrily. 'And you should know that when men deny God, they bestow an enormous duty upon themselves. Besides, I can't believe you don't pray at times to a greater force than even you can comprehend, for all men are spiritual in nature. Still, that aside, you've no right to try and instil even the smallest of doubts in the minds of those who are tryin' hard to rediscover themselves.'

Tomas walked over to the sacristy window and surveyed the ruined night through the bevelled panes. 'Ah, Father Joseph,' he sighed heavily, 'we just have different perspectives. You go with the Nod from God theory, thinkin' yours the only true cause because you picked it. Me, I believe no true God would condemn anyone who chooses to live a peaceful life beyond the walls of your great religious carnival. You also think I'm bound for Hell because of my blasphemous ways. Me, I see a man who stands in front of his one-headed totem-pole every Sunday, believin'–because he partakes of bread and wine instead of cuttin' mistletoe or worshippin' a golden calf–that he's better than your average shaman. Your God asks men to constantly validate His existence, and I sense a bit of insecurity in that, never mind a bloated ego and sensational arrogance. And you see a God possessed of no sense of humour at all, while I can't understand how that can possibly be if we're supposedly made in His image. We just see things differently, that's all.'

'I see what I see, Tomas. I see what's in evidence before my eyes.'

'And there was me thinkin' you wanted us to look beyond what we perceive as real,' Tomas replied sardonically. 'Y'see, Miles, it's just the way I said – every man alive lives at the centre of his own universe, and his own perspective is the only one that truly counts.'

The Father regarded Tomas evenly, before waving a hand towards the door. 'Just go back out there and have your trial, Tomas. And, in one way, I wish you luck because you've set yourself an impossible task and you'll be playin' to a very erratic forum. But tomorrow...'

Tomas raised a hand to stall the priest. 'Say no more, Father. People like me know when people like you have said enough.' Tomas looked across at Miles, his consanguineous grin again fixed firmly into place. 'You haven't a cigarette, have you, Miles? I seem to have run out or somethin'.'

Miles stared at Tomas blankly. On this night that Atlas strained to hold a troubled sky above a trembling world, the vagrant felt he should now hate his former friend forevermore without reserve. True, he'd always admired the ways in which Tomas bravely–if somewhat argumentatively–pointed out the many holes in the dike of Christianity to whomsoever was present. But sometimes you had to go with the flow–

161

even Miles knew that–and sometimes you had to admit that old beliefs also had a place in the world because they provided succour to those unsettled by constant change. Besides, the Father wasn't so bad: If you listened to him and believed in him, there were times when he could set you at ease with an epistolic aspirin. Though the drawback there, Miles had to reluctantly admit, was that you had to want to listen to him, even when you really didn't want to listen, and you had to want to believe in everything he said, even when you didn't truly believe.

Still, Tomas didn't seem to comprehend any of this, lost, as he ever so ironically was, at the centre of his own universe. Furthermore, the other man often made out he was doing you a favour when he actually wasn't. Upon presenting Miles with that bottled gift tonight, he'd also fully reminded him of something he shouldn't have – the allurement. Or, if you were to say it straight, the dependence; the dependence Miles attempted, every single living moment of his waking life to deny even existed. Dependence: It was the vilest of words to those who knew its meaning, and it only ever served to remind you that you needed equally copious amounts of air and drink to survive, as the deprivation of either for any period meant relative forms of brain damage or varying degrees of death. For this reason, and this reason alone, Miles so wanted to hate Tomas just then.

And he believed, for one short moment, he could do so.

But the Father had communicated more than enough thinly-disguised hatred for the other man just moments before. The priest was excommunicating Tomas from Adullam once again, and Tomas had simply been trying to help Miles to exist without pain in this, his own perdurable limbo. Or, Miles thought wryly, had Tomas merely been feigning altruism in a bid to upgrade his own personal pension scheme, and trying to make himself feel better by recognising and responding to another man's weakness?

The vagrant sighed deeply in his confusion: How would he ever know?

Miles put a hand inside his pocket, pulled out his cigarettes, opened the packet and threw one haphazardly at Tomas. The other man caught it, grinned, and fished into his jacket pocket for a lighter. He then lit up the cigarette and inhaled deeply, before turning it carefully between his fingers and staring at it for long moments as if it were carved from precious gemstones. 'I love these bloody things,' he said then. 'I could really get myself hooked on them if I was that way inclined.'

Miles frowned heavily, the disgust completely overwhelming him once more. Momus was taunting him, taunting everyone, and Miles found himself ludicrously wishing that a man-eating Stymphalion bird would tear the roof off the chapel, carry Tomas away to Tartarus and dine slowly upon his flesh until one day beyond the end of time. Shaking his head in disgust, Miles moved towards the sacristy door, intending to return to the chapel proper. But, as he was about to leave, the priest called him back, even as he brusquely urged Tomas to leave the two of them alone for a few moments.

When Tomas had disappeared down along the aisle, the priest turned to Miles. 'He, ehm, doesn't know about *Wing-Ding* bein' outside Adullam on the night of Marie's disappearance, does he?' Miles regarded the priest neutrally for a moment, watching as the other man clasped his hands firmly together to relate the strength of his internal dilemma. 'It's just that things are complicated enough without lettin' anyone else know that – especially Tomas. Anyway, Vinny and I don't think the young lad had anythin' to do with her disappearance. From what we know of him, we don't think that's his form.' The priest paused, staring directly into Miles' eyes. 'You don't think your little friend had anythin' to do with it, do you? I mean, *you* know him better than most, and if you think he did, then go ahead and tell Tomas certainly.'

Miles frowned, trying to read purpose in the priest's eyes. He wanted to ask why Father Joseph was so readily standing up for Wing-Ding now and not the Stranger, yet he supposed it was a shepherd and flock sort of a thing, whereby you bonded with those you knew in times of danger, and to hell with the rest.

Miles shrugged uncertainly. 'I don't think Wing-Ding did anythin', Father. But I don't claim to know that much about him either. Still, do you think he should be on the jury?' Before the priest could reply, Miles added, 'I mean, if he did anythin'–which we *all* think he didn't–then he might vote the Stranger guilty just to lay the blame on someone else.'

'There are four men on the jury, Miles. Wing-Ding is just *one*.' The priest shrugged then, his thoughts lost in a helpless frown. 'Hopefully, the majority will make the correct decision. I personally think and *believe* that they can.'

Miles nodded uneasily once more, wondering if he'd now betrayed an already over-burdened Tomas by agreeing to omit Wing-Ding from the equation. Then the two men moved outside, where the Father keyed the door solidly shut behind them.

With his head down, the vagrant walked down the aisle and moved into the pew alongside Brian, Wing-Ding and Pele, pointedly ignoring Tomas, who sat smoking casually at the furthest end.

Miles was quick to note that Brian, Wing-Ding and Pele were huddled together in light-hearted conversation, a secret kuklos eagerly awaiting a chance to judge their betters. Miles frowned darkly, not in the mood to join in, and he stared up at the altar, watching neutrally as Judge Laverty sat rather uncomfortably behind it, cast in the insufficient light as an incorruptible Rhadamanthus, one of the Chief Judges of the Lower World. On either side of the dais, Vinny McIntyre and young Seamus Brown had positioned themselves, sentinel-like, grimly determined to quell any revolt. The Father joined the guardians of Craiglann there upon the dais a second later, standing to their front and facing into the first few pews. There, the townspeople had gathered once more in near silence, some with uncertain frowns upon their faces and others with their arms solidly folded.

Most, Miles presumed, had probably made up their minds as to what should be done already.

Moments later, Miles allowed his gaze to linger on the furthest end of his pew, where Tomas currently sat examining his fingernails. Again, the vagrant found wondering if the other man had actually been trying to help him in the sacristy or merely trying to tempt him into doing wrong. There'd been a definite glint of mischief in Tomas's eyes, that much Miles was certain about, because it was that dark glint alone which had stopped him from taking the wine. And the look may have been malicious, and it might even have been that of a demon – though Miles wasn't overly certain about that latter thought anymore, knowing the way his mind could sometimes overreact when confusion overtook him.

The vagrant shrugged inwardly: It hardly mattered because the trial was going ahead anyway. And it was all down to Momus, the evil God of Mockery, who'd just gone and got himself expelled from the heavens again for forever taking the piss out of the other gods. Fair enough, he'd been breaking into the wine-cabinet to get Miles a drink, but it didn't bloody matter – stealing from the house of God was wrong, no matter your reason.

No, Miles thought as he crossed his arms solidly across his chest, it's your own fault, Momus, and may that artificial, inner God of yours help you over the course of the next bloody hour!

THIRTEEN

'Are you ready to begin, Tomas?' Judge Laverty asked loudly from behind the altar. To his upper left, the stained-glass windows were brightly activated by forks of lightning, and, merely seconds later, there followed an alarming peal of thunder. Nonetheless–to Miles, at least–the elderly judge appeared as calm and impassive as anyone could possibly be under the circumstances.

'I am indeed, Your Honour,' Tomas replied pleasantly. He stepped out into the side-aisle and walked around to face Molly Devine 'If you wouldn't mind, Molly, I'd like you to take the stand first of all.' The senior-hairstylist seemed confused. 'Just so that we can get an overview, as it were, into wee Marie's daily routine, personal thoughts and general demeanour. Would that be alright with you?'

Con Logue stood up quickly. 'Now he's harrasin' the wee girl's mother, Father, and you're just sittin' watchin' as bloody usual!'

The priest regarded Con darkly and seemed set to reply when the Old Man gently intercepted him.

'Leave him be, Con,' the Old Man soothed. 'Let them have their trial and their hour. And if the Father, Vinny and Judge Laverty are content to leave the fate of everyone here within the hands of a makeshift jury, then let them.'

'What?' Con screeched. 'Are you losin' your bloody mind, too?'

The Old Man grinned sourly. 'No, it's just that I now know Tomas is simply tryin' to stall us from goin' anywhere.' The newsagent pointed back to the seventh pew. 'But those men are aware of this too. And who in their right mind would vote that we stay in this chapel as it turns to flamin' rubble? No, those men also want to live, so no amount of ethical debate will change that.'

'Aye, you'd imagine that's how it should be,' Con remarked, acidly. 'But then, you're forgettin' one important detail, aren't you?'

The Old Man raised an eyebrow. 'Aye, and what's that?'

'Those four layabouts–much like Craiglann's Guards–aren't *in* their right minds, and the promise of an early death is probably as attractive to them as a new fairground ride! They're mad–that's why they're in Adullam–and no one can get a sensible word out of any of them at the best of times!'

'Have you ever tried?' Tomas asked, neutrally.

'Aye, once,' Con said bitterly. 'But if you mollycoddle those already steeped in self-pity by tellin' them nothin's their fault because they have a disease, you relieve them of personal responsibility, and then they start thinkin' they can do whatever they want. No, it's better to be firm with your sort!'

'Well, Con,' the Old Man interjected calmly, 'it doesn't matter how mad anyone thinks they are, they aren't mad enough to want to die. I know Miles – he's a good man who often drops into my shop to keep me company, and he was one of the first to alert me to the Stranger's wicked disposition.'

'Correct me if I'm wrong,' Con snapped, 'but didn't *Miles* once jump into the brook?' Before the Old Man could reply, he added, 'So tell me, how can a man with no respect for his own life be trusted to respect the lives of others?'

As Miles lowered his head in shame, the Old Man nodded ruefully. 'Well, I did hear somethin' about that, but it doesn't mean he's mad. It just means he's never tried as hard as the rest of us to make his own way in the world. But maybe now, if we grant him this chance to act responsibly, he'll reward our trust in him.'

'And Wing-Ding isn't mad either,' Mrs Malhaffey piped in, unable to comprehend the sudden outburst of defamatory mutterings which followed that remark. 'People just don't understand him,' she expanded. 'He can talk for minutes at a time on several subjects at once–really, he can–and he's as sane and lucid as you and I.'

'And Brian too,' Dan McGinty piped in, sagely. 'He helped us out on the night of the fight and actually got hurt doin' so. Actions speak louder than words in my book, and that's as unselfish as it gets.' He winked at Brian, and Brian grinned broadly. 'He's just had a run of bad luck, like the rest of them.'

The Old Man patted Con Logue's shoulder. 'There, that's three out of four. You'll see how well this nonsensical trial of a man in his absence will go.' He regarded his watch, then turned to Judge Laverty. 'You'll agree to follow the judgement of these men then?' he said coldly. 'Or the majority of them, at least?'

Judge Laverty exchanged one final look of bewilderment with both Father Joseph and Vinny McIntyre, before nodding pensively. 'This is only an extrajudicial hearin', but aye, we've agreed to act accordin' to the wishes of this jury tonight.'

'Good, then let's get on with it,' the Old Man said sternly. 'And remember *exactly* what you said, no matter the verdict. Because, if somethin' goes wrong afterwards, then–despite what Vinny says–nobody in this chapel will be guilty of anythin'.'

Judge Laverty nodded grimly once more, and the Old Man winked at Con Logue before calmly regaining his seat. At this, Con Logue released an exasperated sigh, sat down alongside him and nodded in grim resignation.

***

'Well, that's nice,' Tomas grinned. 'Now we've found faith in the jury, I'll explain why I'm callin' Molly to the stand. It's just that–as Judge Laverty correctly pointed out–few people in this town have talked with the Stranger, yet most have formed an opinion of him. Now, I'm the first to admit that all societies thrive because of, and not in spite of, overlappin' perceptions, but I'd like to question both your view of this man, and, more specifically, your view of Marie Devine. Some of you knew the wee girl just to see, a few knew her quite well, and others just socially or from work. Still, by no two people anywhere are we perceived *exactly* the same, so I'll bet Marie was a different person to each of you.'

Tomas stepped up onto the dais and scanned the gathering. 'Of course, many of you have already told Vinny where you were on the night she vanished, as well as what *you* think may've happened to her. But then, when we establish what we deem as a fact in our mind, we usually look, even on a subconscious level, for evidence to verify our theories from *one* particular vantage, because, hey, we don't want to be seen as wrong, do we?'

'That's a good point,' Judge Laverty remarked sagely. 'Our egos often demand that our greatest contemplation is ourselves, and at times goad us into believin' what we desire to be true in order to inflate our own sense of self-worth.'

'Thank you, Your Honour,' Tomas said sincerely. 'And so, maybe if we all knew Marie in the way her mother knew her, we'd have gone to Vinny with somethin' different – somethin' which, because we were denied that special insight, we at first considered inconsequential. By learnin' more about the wee girl's daily routine, therefore, certain other facts could come to light. To keep things orderly, of course, it might be better if everyone waits until I've called all of my witnesses before they forward any questions they may have.'

'Another good point,' Judge Laverty agreed. 'Molly, would you mind?'

167

Molly Devine nodded gravely, before rising gracefully from the pew, making her way up onto the dais and sitting in the Father's chair. Composing herself, she then candidly admitted that the Devines were a private family, so it now scared her–as it would most people–to reveal details of their home life to others. Still, as it was in the public interest to do so, Molly said she'd begin by mentioning how she'd split up with her husband a few years back, and how he'd run off with a wee girl from her salon. That had caused something of a scandal at the time, of course, and rumours abounded in Craiglann for ages afterwards. What few people knew, however, was that Marie's father hadn't once tried to contact either her or her sisters since; and this hit Marie doubly hard, not only because she'd once been the apple of her father's eye, but because the other wee girl was the older sister of one of her best friends. Since then, of course, Molly had tried to keep her daughters on track: She was a strict mother-figure when required, but approachable as a big sister if need be, and this method had almost certainly helped the Devine family to cope with that acrimonious split.

Molly shrugged sadly then, before saying that everyone perhaps knew by now that Marie was her youngest daughter and that she'd been a secretary in Brendan Harper's accountancy firm for the past year, having begun there several months after leaving school. What they perhaps didn't know was that it was a tough enough job and not overly-well paid, though there were apparently good prospects for promotion within the company. Still, Marie was an independent person who valued the responsibilities that went with her work. She also got on well with her co-workers–even if she didn't mix with them socially, as they were all much older than her– and she did quite a bit of overtime, too, the same way she'd even done the week before she…

Momentarily lost in thought, the senior-hairstylist shrugged matter-of-factly, took a deep breath, and then said that that was all she had to say about Marie's public life. On a more personal level, Marie had moved through adolescence with relative ease. She'd tried smoking for a while, as most teens did, though gave it up soonafter, and she'd started taking the odd social drink a few months back, though she never drank to excess because she and Eddie had recently taken an interest in the gym. Molly smiled then and said she personally took credit for that, having constantly drummed the value of a healthy lifestyle into all of her daughters' heads from an early age, so much so that Marie was very picky about her diet. Of course, Marie was still a month or two off the correct drinking age, this was true, yet Molly said she firmly believed that, by accepting her daughter occasionally drank, she'd greatly diminished the chances of Marie using alcohol in a wrongful or rebellious manner. As to the ways in which she interacted with others, Molly said Marie was normal in that regard, too. Admittedly, the wee girl was strong-willed and stubborn at times, yet those faults were vastly outweighed by her intelligence and thoughtfulness, her ability to empathise and the fact that she was slow to judge. And, though not overly religious, she'd been attending Mass every week over the last few months in the build-up to her wedding in accordance with the Father's wishes. On a more private note, Marie had also been *taking precautions* for the last six months; which really wasn't anyone's business, Molly added pointedly, yet it was perhaps necessary to put paid to those dark rumours which suggested Marie was pregnant and had run off to have an abortion.

As for Marie's upcoming wedding, Molly then ruefully admitted that she'd been as concerned as any mother would be when Marie had first approached her about her plans to wed wee Eddie: After all, Marie had dated young Geoff Harkin for a year before he'd moved to Dublin, fully convinced at the time that they'd end up marrying one day; and, even though Molly had nothing really bad to say about Geoff, well, that would've been a match made in hell! Still, when Molly had sat Marie down to discuss it with her as an adult–asking her to perhaps postpone it for a year or two, and maybe concentrate upon her career–her youngest daughter's answer had surprised her. Marie had taken Molly's hands in hers, looked her straight in the eyes and said she'd known instinctively, from the moment they met, that Eddie was the one for her because he made her laugh and think, and he'd created a new world for her in which she felt able to grow and express herself as an individual, even as they developed together as a couple and as friends. And, upon hearing their love so profoundly expressed, Molly accepted they were very much in love, had more than enough in common and were fully aware that marriage was a lifetime's commitment of hard work.

The senior-hairstylist stopped speaking then and gazed maternally down at a now distraught Eddie Logue. Aye, Molly beamed, Eddie obviously missed Marie as much as she did, and the rumours had affected him terribly, though Molly said she was now going to put an end to that by revealing something about him: Eddie wasn't the sort of lad who felt comfortable on the phone–Molly said she recalled him telling her that once–yet he'd been ringing the Devine household constantly since last Tuesday, asking if everyone was holding up and if Molly believed something bad had happened to Marie in the way most now supposed it had. Molly admitted then that she hadn't quite known what to say to that: She'd simply told him that her daughter was a survivor and had probably just run off somewhere to get her thoughts together.

The senior-hairstylist frowned reflectively once more, before saying that Marie was also like any other young girl, in that she'd once had alternative dreams: Once, she'd dreamt of being either a hotel receptionist or a stewardess, and she'd also taken languages at school for a while in the hope she'd end up working in somewhere like France or Spain. In the last few years, however, Marie had put aside those fleeting fancies and matured enough to realise she'd rather fulfil her most attainable wish, that of marrying Eddie.

Molly paused, then sat there thoughtfully for a time, before shrugging despondently once more. There wasn't much more she could really say, she added lamely, though if anyone had any questions at the end of the hearing she'd answer them to the best of her ability.

The chapel had fallen relatively silent as Molly had spoken, with only the ferocious turmoil of the heavens in the background to be heard. Tomas waited patiently for the senior-hairstylist to return to her seat, before loudly addressing the gathering once more. 'The owner of this bar, The Drunken Duck, could we have a chat with him next, seein' as how he was one of the last people to see the wee girl around?'

Dan McGinty rose from the third pew and made his way up the altar steps. Once seated, he fixed Tomas with a belligerent stare. 'I'm not bloody happy about this,' he snapped. 'I told Vinny all I knew, and now it's the same old shite..!'

Tomas placed a finger against his lips and Dan fumed to silence. 'I'm sorry for troublin' you, Mr McGinty, really. But, if you'd just tell us about the wee girl's usual habits in relation to this bar of yours. We've heard she was nearly eighteen and about to get married, if as yet a little too young for enterin' licensed premises. Still, she was apparently mature enough to be gettin' married, and so...'

Dan McGinty had a lived-in face and shadows clung to the draw in his cheeks and beneath shrewd eyes. He turned to both Judge Laverty and Father Joseph as if imploring either divine or legal intervention–though neither was forthcoming–before scratching idly at two-day stubble. Aye, well, Marie was a nice wee thing, he admitted gruffly, and both she and Eddie had begun frequenting his bar a few months back, having outgrown the community-centre. They kept themselves to themselves, too, and usually just sat in the corner, snogged a wee bit or held hands, real private-like. Or, at times, the wee girl would come in with her female friends and they'd all have a natter and a giggle, buy a few drinks and play some of the machines; though Marie herself–and Dan said he hated saying this, as she'd been doing the exact same thing the night she disappeared–had an annoying habit of hogging the bar's only public phone, which tended to aggravate people who wanted to call taxis and such. Still, that was no big deal: She was an adult and had to be treated as such, even if she was only seventeen, as Tomas so self-righteously pointed out. But then, Dan sniped, it wasn't as if he was the *only* person in town who was letting under-age drinkers into his bar, was it?

Dan aimed a superfluous finger at Mullan then, as if the chapel was awash with publicans. Aye, Dan rasped, Mullan was no saint, even if many here deemed him so, and his bloody bar was a hotbed of crime in comparison! Firstly, Mullan was cheating the tax man on every level as most of his staff were taking wages *and* drawing state-benefits – which they wouldn't have had to do, of course, if he paid them a decent wage! Not only that, Mullan received a renovation grant for his bar last year, but everyone had yet to see what he did with the money. And how he got the grant in the first place was stranger still, Dan added solemnly, what with Mullan originally being an out-of-towner! Bribes must've been passed, and money must've been handed to the council under the counter. Aye, Dan stormed, grants were being handed to blow-ins above the heads of native-borns; and, as if that wasn't bad enough, those blow-ins hadn't the decency to spend the allocated funds on what they were supposed to! So, Dan sniped, was it any wonder Mullan had to walk around with a henchman forever at his side? And was it any wonder, too, that he'd chosen a brain-dead yes-man like Big Sean to perform that task? Aye, Dan snarled, the Tinker and the Thinker, they were two bloody cabbages in a bloody pod!

As a frustrated Judge Laverty once again called for order, Mullan stood up angrily. Bidding Big Sean to remain in his seat, the younger licensee pushed his way out of his pew and hurriedly approached the altar rail. 'Your Honour,' he snapped, 'it's not right that *he* can stand up there and slag me off in God's house. I should at least be allowed my own say in return.'

Judge Laverty sighed wearily. 'Mr Mullan, contrary to popular opinion, we aren't here to rip each other to pieces. I can only allow you up here if you're called as a witness. Tomas, do you plan to question Mr Mullan?'

'Only if he has somethin' relevant to add to the proceedin's.' Tomas turned to Mullan and smiled broadly. 'Well, Mr Mullan, have you anythin' to say pertainin' to the disappearance of wee Marie Devine?'

As Dan McGinty returned to his seat, Mullan tracked his nemesis through dark slits of eyes, before considering the other man's question in depth. 'Aye, I do,' he replied eventually. He made to climb the steps onto the dais, but Tomas placed a hand across his chest, barring his way.

'You aren't just tryin' to get up here and make a big speech because the local competition has challenged a few of your day-to-day ethics?' Tomas asked dryly. 'You wouldn't be doin' that, would you?'

'Of course not,' Mullan blustered. 'I'm goin' to tell you about the last few times I saw the wee girl. It may sound like nothin' much, but, as *you* pointed out, it might also be very important. So let me past!'

As an unnerving fusillade of rain pummelled the heavy oaken doors and surged violently against the windows, Tomas stepped aside and allowed Mullan to move onto the dais. For a few moments, the younger licensee bit thoughtfully at his lower lip before saying that, despite what everyone was thinking, he had seen the wee girl in town on several occasions in the week before she vanished, so there! Still, he'd never allowed her into his pub, because Big Sean–who wasn't a henchman, but a good man who was misunderstood in the main–always kept a tight watch on the clientele's age. But, aye, he'd seen the wee girl on either the Friday or Saturday before she'd disappeared. He'd been in Kelly's shoe shop buying a new pair of loafers for work, and, as he minded, she'd been trying on beach sandals. He recalled thinking she was probably getting ready for her honeymoon, and he'd said hello and she'd said hello back, civil wee thing that she was – although he hadn't stopped to speak as she looked really deep in thought. And then, about half an hour or so later, he'd been on his way back to the pub and he'd bumped into her again on the Crissom. It'd been raining heavily too, Mullan reflected, but the wee girl hadn't even put the hood of her coat up–which, he freely admitted, he'd thought very strange at the time–and, furthermore, she'd also been dragging deeply on a cigarette.

Still, Mullan exclaimed with a growing gleam in his eye, now he'd put that one to bed, he'd something else to add: Dan McGinty there–aye, him with the same shirt on he'd been wearing a week!–was as guilty of underhandedness as anyone in this town. He was selling *poitin* illegally for starters, as well as plying alcohol after hours, while telling everyone that Big Michael's off-licence prices were well over the top! *And*, Mullan continued above a growing furore, a few weeks back–around the time, *coincidentally*, that that big brewery yard in the next county was robbed– it was rumoured that Dan bought several hundred kegs off a few boys who found things long before they went missing!

As Dan McGinty raged in the background, Mullan innocently added that he'd no desire to get involved in a slanging match with anyone tonight, but then, this whole dark episode in the life of Craiglann was all Vinny McIntyre's fault, because if he'd done his job correctly, this mess would've been sorted by now. And Mullan liked Vinny too, he admitted sadly, even if the officer wasn't the sharpest dart in the set. Furthermore, because of the Chief Guard's inherent tendency to let things ride at times –like, say, facts–it was hardly surprising that they were all being held to ransom by the Stranger, was it? Of course, the bar-owner countered, Vinny was probably snowed under with paperwork, and maybe that was why his own entertainment's licence was being held up – the one he'd applied for six months back, no less. Aye, Mullan said finally, Craiglann's new judge was probably still waiting for Vinny to get off his big fat arse and sign the bloody papers agreeing to it!

As Vinny smarted under those remarks and Mullan returned smugly to his seat, young Seamus Brown moved to the centre of the dais. The trainee-Guard apologised instantly to Judge Laverty for the interruption, but said he felt he must say something in Vinny's defence. Above several unflattering heckles, he then loudly exclaimed that it wasn't fair everyone blaming Vinny or his men for everything that went wrong in Craiglann. Firstly, the Guards had known for a long time that Mullan allowed his staff do-the-double. They also knew that Dan McGinty ran a late pub, sold illegally-stilled poitin, and–although they couldn't prove it, or they'd have been over him like a rash–that he was probably peddling stolen liquor too.

No, Seamus reiterated, Vinny wasn't stupid, for one of the first things the Chief Guard had taught him was how the police in any democratic society had to differentiate between maintaining order and exerting a jackboot authority. The reason for this, Seamus expanded, was that all lawful societies maintained liberty by enslavement, in that they denied their citizens certain lesser rights in order to preserve more fundamental rights. Of course, if too many rights were taken away, people would deem the law too strict, start to believe they'd surrendered those less important freedoms in vain, and refuse to be freely governed. The only way to prevent that, according to Vinny, was to occasionally overlook certain lesser infringements and borderline discrepancies, thereby convincing the populace that the law was on the side of the just. So, Seamus said firmly, to everyone thinking themselves ahead of the Guards at every step, he'd one thing to say – they were treading a fine line and weren't half as clever as they thought! Seamus rounded on Mullan then, stating that the delay in his entertainment licence wasn't Vinny's fault, but due more to the overwhelming amount of public objections. And, if Mullan didn't believe that, all he had to do was look around him – most of the people who'd signed the petition against him were actually here in this chapel tonight.

'What petition?' Mullan frowned. 'Sure, most people here were all for the idea of a late licence when I put it to them months ago.'

Seamus Brown shook his head. 'The petition sayin' you were keepin' a noisy bar,' he replied evenly. 'The one statin' that people in your immediate vicinity don't want the late-licence, because the rowdiness is bad enough as it is.'

'You're makin' that up,' Mullan said accusingly. 'Just because I got onto you about your boss. Sure, there's a dozen here who were all for it when I spoke to them.'

'Am I?' Seamus retorted coldly. 'Then ask Mrs Malhaffey, Mrs Daly, Mrs Malloy and Mary Scullion. Lots of others signed it, too. Just look around and see who can look you directly in the eye. And Judge Laverty there will confirm it. He retired shortly after the petition went through. Besides,' the trainee-officer added lamely, 'your fire precautions aren't tight enough either.'

Dave Mullan stared about him, seeing the betrayal instantly. He nodded sourly, his frown deepening as each of the aforementioned people avoided his gaze. 'Well, that's fine,' he declared rather unconvincingly. 'But I'm a man tryin' to make a livin', and I won't be judged by others. Mrs Malhaffey there–angelic little do-gooder that she portrays herself to be–has no right to judge me. She used to drink like a fish until she woke up one mornin' and found God preachin' to her through the mouth of an empty bottle. And Mrs Stewart?' Mullan snorted. 'Christ, she's given many a dyin' rumour the kiss of life, yet she wouldn't be as keen to tell you about her own LSD-induced free-love sessions in the Swingin' Sixties – aye, that's right, *Twiggy*, I drank with your brother and his tongue was near as loose as your own!' Mullan ignored the growing babble of discontentment amongst the women. 'And we all know about the time Mrs Daly there went to England to get rid of a *package*.' The bar-owner pointed to his stomach and ran his hands into a bump. 'And Mary Scullion there, I think the whole of Craiglann knows about her and the *happily-married* Brendan Harper.' Mullan clenched one hand into a fist and slapped the other against his bicep in an Italian-type gesture, the meaning of which was swiftly apparent to everyone.

Miles' eyes widened at the uproar that followed. The evacuees rose en-masse, with many of the women loudly threatening to tear Mullan into shreds, and most of the men promising to do things to their one-time confidante that would've required the labour of a very good neurosurgeon to repair. Upon seeing this, Vinny stalked to the middle of the stage, produced his gun and fired a shot off into the air. The Guard then watched solemnly as a rain of crumbling plaster fell around him like Christmas snow. An immediate silence ensued and everyone sat again in a raggedly uneven Mexican wave.

All, that was, except Frank Devenney: The grey-haired man with the noticeable limp stood on, his head raised defiantly in the air.

Aye, Frank declared, that was right and brave of Vinny, firing his gun into a chapel roof. Aye, *Big Vinny* - you could've respected him if you didn't know *he* was one of those buying that illegal poitin off Dan, and that he'd been doing so for bloody years! And, Frank snapped, *if* anyone wanted to know how he knew that, sure, didn't Frank used to supply the stuff to McGinty himself! And young Seamus Brown was no man to stand in anyone's defence either, Frank added bitterly: If he wanted to defend anyone, he should defend his own family, for they all had police-records as long as your arm. Sure, that time Molly had her house broken into–aye that robbery about a week before the girl vanished –sure, Vinny had sent Seamus up to interview her the next day, and the chat about town was they were actually setting a thief to catch a bloody thief!

As Seamus dropped his head, Vinny stepped boldly across the dais, retorting hotly that his protégé was going to make a fine officer some day, and it was hardly fair judging him on his family-background. Besides, Vinny raged, Frank could hardly talk: That walking cane of his, for example–the one he only used when the Disability Allowance people came round to check on his *ever-deterioratin'* condition–was merely a prop. Aye, get up Lazarus, Vinny snorted, the Disability people have just driven off! *And*, Vinny added thickly, for those who didn't know *how* Frank came about his bad leg in the first place, he'd be more than happy to explain: Frank *took a lift* in a stolen car once, and the driver supposedly crashed it into a wall. Of course, despite never finding the actual driver, and despite finding Frank midway between the driver and passenger seats, the Guards could never prove he'd been the one driving, so Frank staked a very lucrative claim with the government shortly thereafter. Which was, Vinny mused, much the same sort of thing his friend Neil Martin used to get up to at times, as well, although the market-trader had actually paid for *his* crimes in prison.

'I was young,' Neil Martin fumed. 'And, alright, I was a bit of a wild man in my youth, but I've been above board on everythin' I've done ever since!'

'Aye, and that's slander, Vinny,' Frank snapped. 'If I live through this night, I'll be makin' sure that my solicitor has you in the dock for that one!'

'I'm just makin' a point,' the Chief Guard growled. 'And the point is that those who live under rocks in greenhouses shouldn't throw bloody stones!'

Judge Laverty slammed a latten candlestick heavily into the altar, before wincing apologetically at the Father for doing so. 'Gentlemen,' he shouted, 'let's get back on track. Tomas, is there someone else you want to call?'

Tomas looked calmly around the unsettled audience. 'I'd like to ask Molly another question, Your Honour.' As the elderly judge nodded his agitated consent, Tomas turned to face the senior-hairstylist. 'This burglary of your house, Molly, could you tell us a little more about it?'

'What relevance does that have on the case?' Con Logue barked angrily. 'Who are you now, Sherlock effin' Holmes?'

Tomas grinned easily. 'I've been led to believe there's not much crime in Craiglann,' he replied. 'Well, not on the surface, anyhow. So, if that's truly the case, I find it strange that two crimes–if you'd call Marie's disappearance a crime, and we've no evidence yet to consider it such–should be inflicted upon the same family within such a short period of time. I'm simply askin' because the first might bear slight relevance upon the second, you never know.'

'It might indeed,' Judge Laverty concurred. 'Would you mind answerin' the question, Molly, if only for the sake of maintainin' relative peace and quiet.'

Molly nodded. She stood then and said that one night, just over two weeks back, she'd been out for a drink with a friend. And, with her two eldest daughters away for the weekend in Wexford and Marie out on a date, there'd been nobody at home. Marie, however, was the first to return that night, and she'd discovered the kitchen window lying wide open and the house in complete darkness. Rather foolishly–and Molly had scolded her for doing so afterwards–Marie had entered the house, only to discover that thieves had stolen all of Molly's rent and electricity money. Still, Molly mused, they hadn't actually ransacked the place, thank God, though when the senior-hairstylist had phoned to report it shortly afterwards, Vinny told her that maybe this was because Marie disturbed them in the middle of their foul business.

'I'm guessin' you live in a fine house too,' Tomas smiled.

Molly Devine nodded easily, managed a thin smile. 'I like it, aye. I've worked hard over the years, and I'm proud of what I have.'

'And you have expensive furniture, and the like?' Molly Devine looked at Tomas and he smiled disarmingly. 'And a good burglar alarm, probably. If you've a house with fine furniture in it, then you've a good burglar alarm too, is that right?'

'I have,' Molly nodded. 'And it was turned on that night too – I'm sure of it, because I always turn it on, and have done without fail ever since my ex-husband threatened to beat me up again.' Molly shrugged weightedly, then raised her chin. 'Anyway, I was the last to leave the house that evening and, aye, I turned it on. But the alarm must've failed because it wasn't sounding out when Marie returned.' Molly shrugged dismissively. 'However, when I was chatting to Vinny, he said that sometimes even the best ones go on the blink. He said we were lucky really, so it was better to let the whole thing go and put it down to experience.'

Tomas regarded the Chief Guard bemusedly, before extending a hand in the direction of the chair now being used as a witness box. As he did so, Vinny bit hard at his lower lip, obviously riled by Tomas' informal manner. 'Aye, Mr McIntyre I'd like to ask you a few questions, if you don't mind.' Tomas smiled amicably. 'I mean, we're tryin' to piece together a chronology of Craiglann's current *crime-wave,* so maybe you can help.'

Vinny sighed audibly, fixed Tomas with a vexatious glare, then went to sit down in the chair, his actions a fidget. Tomas moved to the altar rail, leant against it.

'So, Mister McIntyre, they fail at times, these expensive burglar alarms, do they? And it was best to put the robbery down to experience, do you think?'

The Chief Guard fixed Tomas with a thin grimace. 'It might've failed,' he replied shortly. 'Or Molly might've forgotten to switch it on. Whatever – it was no big deal. Some money was taken, but it was hardly worth followin' up, as there was no way of tracin' it? Valuables maybe, personal property maybe, but money, and all of it in used and non-consecutive notes? Sure, that makes it untraceable, and I was hardly goin' to open an investigation on that one, was I?'

'Fair enough. So you waited until the next day to send Seamus around–say, some eight to ten hours after it was reported–and you personally told Molly Devine it was best to let it go, is that right?'

'It was pourin' down that night, the way it always seems to do around here, and the culprit or culprits were long gone from the scene of the crime. Molly told me that herself over the phone. So what did you want me to do?' Vinny blustered. 'Go over and dust a wet window down? Fingerprint and shoe-print the entire town? Bring out a squad of men and kick every door in Craiglann in durin' the middle of the night?'

'No, hardly that. But an appearance at the house shortly afterwards would've been nice, just to make sure everyone was alright.' Vinny seemed visibly anguished and Tomas frowned sternly, drawing the moment out. 'And you're sayin' you knew for a fact the culprit or culprits were gone, because…'

'Because Molly said they bloody were!' Vinny fumed. 'So I told her to lock the house up tight and to give me a ring if anythin' else happened. But nothin' did. She didn't phone back, so I presumed everythin' was alright.'

'And you didn't presume the culprits might've decided to come back and maybe finish Molly and her family off?' The Chief Guard looked angrily between Tomas and Judge Laverty. Before the elderly judge could interrupt, however, Tomas raised his palm-heels. 'Alright, that aside, you're sayin' that's the way it happened, so if you'll just confirm that for us now...'

Vinny bit at his lower lip, nodded sourly and then upturned his stony gaze towards the ceiling. 'That's the way it happened, aye.'

Mrs Stewart stood then, and, directing her gaze solely at Judge Laverty, she said she recalled that time of the burglary well because she'd been standing behind Marie in the bank queue a few days later and she'd asked the wee girl about it. But Marie had simply shrugged, saying she hadn't a clue what happened, although she was nearly sure that a few of the young lads who hung around the community-centre were to blame.

Mrs Stewart paused then, before adding that Marie had been drawing money out from the bank that day, although precisely how much she couldn't say, as she wasn't as nosy as *some* people made her out to be. Still, it was rather a lot, and Mrs Stewart recalled thinking that Marie was probably going to give it to Molly just to make up the loss. She was a good wee girl, y'see, Marie, just like her mother, and it would've been just been like her to do something as decent as that!

As Tomas was about to reply, the senior-hairstylist raised her hand. Tomas raised an eyebrow and looked over at her. 'Molly, is there somethin' you want to say?'

'Aye Tomas, I've been considering everything I've heard tonight, and there are one or two points I'd like to clarify as they don't seem to add up. Would you mind?'

Tomas moved down to the front pew and took the senior-hairstylist gently by the hand, leading her up the steps and onto the dais. Once there, Tomas politely asked the Chief Guard to surrender his seat. As Vinny did so, Tomas again smiled an alluring smile. 'Ask away, Molly,' he said. 'We are tryin' to set your mind at ease, after all.'

FOURTEEN

Angry flashes of lightning seared the sky and sonic booms of thunder imploded fiercely in the pitch night air. The storm was gathering in its intensity and a very agitated Miles Kivlehan laboured with every breath, cursing himself inwardly for not taking the wine from Tomas when he'd had the chance. As stark premonitions of impending havoc and carnage sought to unnerve him, he attempted once again to quell them with Greek fable. But, as that ever-frailing technique denied him even the slightest solace, he switched his ragged concentration towards the disconsolate figure of Molly Devine upon the dais, who was now preparing to speak.

'I'd like to ask Mr Mullan a question first,' Molly said pensively. She turned to face the publican. 'Are you sure Marie was trying on beach sandals, Dave?'

'Aye, I'm near positive about that, Molly. Is it important?'

'Well, due to the price of the wedding, and because they were saving for a house, Eddie and Marie cancelled their honeymoon in Portugal three weeks ago. That was their own affair, of course, and only those in our immediate circle would've known they'd decided to spend a week on my brother's farm in England instead.'

As Molly spoke, one of Mullan's barmaids raised her hand. 'Sorry for interruptin', Mrs Devine, but I also saw her buyin' bikinis and a few short skirts in Mrs Scullion's clothes shop just a few days before she vanished...'

'Aye, Molly,' the Amazonian Mrs Daly piped in, 'and I saw her fillin' in a passport application form in the Post Office around the same time. I didn't consider that a big deal either, as we'd all heard she was goin' abroad. But if she was only goin' to England, then she'd hardly need a passport, would she?'

Within seconds, Brendan Harper raised a hand. Three rows back and as intentionally diminished as possible since the revelation of his extra-marital affair with a local shopkeeper, the accountant didn't say a word until Tomas spotted him. 'Ah, Mr Harper, have you somethin' you'd like to add here?'

'I was also considerin' what Molly said earlier about Marie doin' overtime in my office,' the accountant mused. 'We do work a few weekends–when audits are due, or at the end of the tax-year, for example

–but we don't work every weekend. In fact, I haven't had anyone in on overtime for over two months now.'

Noticeably shaken by those revelations, Molly dropped her head. 'Marie told me she was working overtime on each of the three Saturdays before she vanished,' she frowned. 'And then there's this thing about the bank. Y'see, she and Eddie were saving, but only in the Post Office, and Marie didn't actually have a bank account. Unless it was yours, Eddie?' she asked Con Logue's son. 'Was it yours?'

Equally puzzled, an ashen-faced Eddie Logue shook his head.

'No,' Molly reiterated, 'Marie always saved in the Post Office. Though it's hardly a big deal. Still, I'll say one other thing – she didn't give me any of the money she withdrew that day either. And you say it was quite a lot, Mrs Stewart?'

The middle-aged woman nodded vigorously. 'Aye, there was well over a thousand in all.' She paused reflectively. 'In mostly tens and twenties. But mainly twenties.'

'Well, I don't know what that was about either,' Molly shrugged. 'But, then, it was Marie's private business. I suppose...'

Once again, Brendan Harper raised his hand. 'Well, I have asked Marie to withdraw money on occasion from our accounts, for expenses, wages and such. But, ehm, well, with me being away the last two weeks, she wouldn't have done that...I think.'

As both Brendan Harper and Molly exchanged uncertain gazes, Tomas scratched thoughtfully at his chin, before eventually turning once more to the senior-hairstylist. 'Have you a phone in the house?' he asked her suddenly.

Molly seemed puzzled. 'Why, ehm, yes. Of course I have.'

'Of course you have,' Tomas grinned. 'The reason I'm askin' is that Dan McGinty told us Marie was constantly usin' his public phone, to the point whereby she was actually makin' a nuisance of herself by doin' so. Don't you think that a bit strange? After all, the wee girl's best friends were usually along with her, she didn't actually socialise with any of her older colleagues at work, and young Eddie there wasn't into spendin' great amounts of time on the phone.'

'It's not too unusual,' Molly countered. 'People use public phones all the time, and Marie didn't want a mobile as she considered them too expensive.'

Tomas turned to Dan McGinty. 'On average, Dan, how much time would you say the wee girl was spendin' on your phone of late?'

The scruffily-attired bar-owner nodded thoughtfully. 'I'd have to give her a fair bit of change, so I'd say between half- and three-quarters of an hour at a time.'

Tomas turned back to Molly. 'Well, I suppose there's nothin' unusual about that in itself. But then, remember, Marie's only seventeen, she's savin' for her weddin' and she's not earnin' a lot of money in the first place. So why is she spendin' quite a lot of money on an expensive bar phone when she's got a perfectly good line at home? Is it possible her family afforded her no real privacy?'

Molly appeared mortally wounded by that remark. 'No, no, not at all. We gave her all the space she needed.'

Tomas smiled disarmingly. 'I mean you no offence, Molly,' he told the senior-hairstylist. 'I'm sure you gave her enough privacy. Besides, you're probably out workin' most of the day too, aren't you?' Molly nodded quickly. 'Mmm, so that guarantees her virtually all the privacy she wants. Still, we'll leave that for the moment. And then I'll ask you if you believe your daughter was happy of late?'

'She was very happy.' Molly frowned uncertainly. 'Well, she seemed happy. I mean, I think she was…'

'Maybe she was just puttin' a brave face on things,' Tomas pouted. 'A lot of people spend their time pretendin' to be happy for other people's sake, rather than actually doin' what makes them happy. Still, to be fair, you weren't the only person with a keen insight into Marie's recent state of mind.' Tomas turned to Eddie Logue. 'I can't force you to talk to us, young man,' he smiled. 'But we'd like to hear what you have to say on the matter, if that's alright.'

'He doesn't want to talk,' Con Logue seethed, placing a protective arm around his son's shoulder. 'Can't you see he's upset enough as it is?'

Eddie pulled himself gently away from his father. 'I want to do this, dad. Molly has said her bit, and she did it for Marie. I want to do my bit for her, too.'

Sighing heavily, Con relinquished his gentle grip and Eddie stood and made his way up onto the dais. 'Alright, Eddie,' Tomas smiled, 'I want you to let your mind drift freely back over the last few weeks to see if you can pinpoint anythin' out of the ordinary that occurred between you and Marie.' Tomas raised a finger. 'Were you unsettled at any time by either your girlfriend's actions or words, and did she more recently seem very guarded or defensive about anythin' at all?'

For a moment, Eddie sat gathering his thoughts, before haltingly admitting that the build-up to the wedding had disrupted everyone's daily routine over the last few months to quite a stressful level; and even Marie, who was usually easy-going and placid, found things quite intense. Still, despite work-commitments and wedding-associated chores having cut into their time, he and Marie had maintained a strained social life in order to preserve their sanity. They'd attended their local gym on a regular basis, gone into the Drunken Duck once or twice a week–where they'd had a few drinks and discussed their future–or, on occasion, Marie had gone out with her friends, and he'd gone out with his. And, in this way, Eddie said they'd both coped well with the pressure, content in the hope their lives would return to normal after the wedding.

Eddie frowned then, before saying that one rather strange incident did stand out in his mind, now that he thought about it. About four weeks ago, they'd been drinking in the Duck and Marie had been eating a bag of sweets. Eddie had started teasing her that she'd never fit into her wedding dress if she continued with that recently acquired habit. It had been a bit of a barbed jest, Eddie admitted, as Marie had sort of let her diet go a bit of late; although, having a great sense of humour, she took it pretty well. But, shortly afterwards, Marie had gone to the toilets, and Eddie noticed that she'd left her handbag behind, so he planned to take the sweets out of it and hide them as a bit of a joke. As he opened the bag, however, he noticed an envelope addressed to Marie in his father's distinctive handwriting. Still, as Eddie was trying to work out why his father would send his girlfriend a letter, Marie returned from the toilet and snatched it quickly off him, snapping that it was nothing important and scolding him for rummaging through her belongings.

Eddie bowed his head then, and said that, even though he'd thought it strange, he didn't pursue the matter, knowing Marie–who'd never forgiven her own father for submitting her family to so much physical confrontation–had a tendency to clam up for hours at a time in order to show her displeasure. And afterwards, despite his reservations, he'd simply reasoned that Marie would've divulged the contents of the letter to him if they'd been important. Eddie then said he'd considered confronting his father about the letter, yet Con was constantly preoccupied these days with trying to sell his garage, so there'd never been a correct time to do so. Anyway, it hadn't been necessary in the end –or so he'd imagined at the time–as Marie's mood picked up over the following weeks. And last Tuesday night, she'd barely left his side in the bar and she'd been as affectionate and loving as ever.

'And when you left her on the Crissom last Tuesday night, did she seem in any way different?' Tomas asked gently. 'I mean, was she actin' normally?'

Eddie pouted thoughtfully, his gaze locked in the past. 'Everythin' was the same as usual. But, before she left, she hugged me very tightly, as if she...'

'As if she might've known somethin', maybe?' Tomas offered.

Eddie frowned darkly. 'There was just somethin' different about it. Or maybe I've exaggerated it all in my mind, because that's my last memory of her – I don't know.'

'Alright, fair enough. But to recap, you found a letter in her handbag which you think may've been written to her by your father, is that correct?' Eddie nodded again. 'Alright, young man, thank you. You can return to your seat if you wish.'

As Eddie stepped down from the altar, Tomas momentarily assessed the new evidence, before turning to keenly regard Con Logue, whose arms were now firmly folded across his chest. 'Did you write the wee girl a letter, Mr Logue?'

'I did nothin' of the sort,' Con Logue rasped, fully aware he was now the focus of everyone's attention. 'I swear – I didn't write her a letter. Why would I?'

Tomas turned his gaze upwards, momentarily lost in thought. Seconds later, he brightened and turned to regard young Eddie. 'The envelope in Marie's handbag, how exactly was it addressed? Was her full name in use, or just her first initial?'

Eddie screwed up his eyes. 'As I mind, it was just her first initial.'

'And was the letter old or new? Was it sealed or opened?'

'I didn't see the postmark. But the letter was opened and quite soft and tattered, so it may've been in her bag a while, though I don't know for certain.'

Tomas turned to stare between Con Logue and Molly Devine, both of whom had now dropped their heads. 'Alright, let's assume the letter wasn't addressed to Marie, but to her mother, Molly. If this were so, then maybe Marie picked it up and read it by mistake. And, had the letter's contents been innocuous in nature, we might presume Marie's next step would've been to return it to her mother. Still, the fact she retained it and didn't even want Eddie to touch it, never mind read it, leads me to surmise she was somewhat shaken by its contents.' Tomas attempted to catch the garage-owner's gaze. 'It's probably none of our business, but...'

'Too fuckin' right it isn't!' Con Logue said abruptly, his arms drawn in tighter to his chest. 'It's nothin' to do with anybody. It's a private matter, a family matter.'

The Father stepped hurriedly towards the centre of the altar. 'Right, Con,' he declared solemnly. 'I've listened to enough profanity for one night. You're right – *your* business is your own and God's affair. But, I'll have no more cursin' in my chapel or else it'll be a long time before I allow you to make use of it again.'

'It's not *your* chapel!' Con snarled, ignoring the strange looks he was receiving from his wife. 'You work here, nothin' more! And I've had enough of you forever judgin' me too, Father Joseph – we all have! Why do you think people around here don't like attendin' Mass? Because they can't *relate* to you, that's why. Because you're a *robot*, and you give off the impression you've personally never sinned.' The garage-owner placed a hand firmly upon the Old Man's shoulders. 'But if you're lookin' for *real* secrets, then here's one man who knows a secret very few people in Craiglann could even guess at.'

The Old Man fidgeted restlessly for long moments and seemed set to speak when Deborah Logue waved a stalling hand, saying she'd more urgent business to attend to, and that it'd take no more than a moment. Anything that anyone had to tell the Father, she added, they could say after that. As she spoke, the Old Man nodded worriedly, seemingly quite relieved she'd intervened.

Deborah Logue turned to her husband. 'You're sayin' this letter you sent to Molly has nothin' to do with anyone,' she said, fixing him with penetrating eyes. 'But we've never had any secrets, Con, yet I don't recall you tellin' me anythin' about that. And why would you need to send her a letter anyway? You live minutes away from her home and we have her phone-number.'

'It was a *business* letter,' Con Logue replied sharply, his panda-like eyes trained firmly upon the tiled floor to his front. 'It's to do with the weddin', and I've no desire to divulge its contents with you in front of everyone here. If we live through this hell of a night, I'll tell you, but *only* in private.'

As Deborah was about to delve deeper into that mystery, Tomas raised a stalling hand. 'Alright, I suggest we forget that particular point for now and move on with our case.' He turned to Judge Laverty. 'Besides, I've only one more witness, Your Honour. And then, if you shall allow me, I'll tell you what I think may've happened to young Marie Devine on this night one week past.'

Judge Laverty regarded his watch in the pale light, before scratching hard at the grey stubble working its way onto his chin. 'Alright, Tomas, I'll allow you one more witness before your summation. But, from the little evidence gathered here tonight, I really don't see how you can deduce with any degree of certainty what might or could possibly have occurred.'

'We'll see.' Tomas bowed an exaggerated bow, before turning to face Father Joseph. 'Father – I'd like to you to now take the stand, if you would.'

With his eyes narrowing and his jaw firmly clenched, the Father seemed set to round upon Tomas, yet one look into the other man's twinkling eyes caused him to refrain. Instead, the priest exhaled deeply and then walked calmly towards his chair and sat down, watching neutrally as Tomas moved to his front.

'Father Joseph,' Tomas began, 'for a while now we've heard people debatin' the strengths and weaknesses of legislation, the policin' system, general Christian doctrine, and moral and ethical law. So, why now, after discussin' the pros and cons of each of these forms of restraint, do you personally believe that everyone here has finally agreed to use constitutional law to seek what Mr Logue might term a *utilitarian* solution to our current dilemma?' Tomas raised his palm heels. 'After all, Judge Laverty is no longer a judge, and so–and I mean this in the nicest possible way–we are very curiously referencin' what might be seen as the most invalid form of law in order to solve a potentially *fatal* problem. This bein' so, mightn't it still be a better option to run out into the night and do the Stranger to death? And, in truth, what is there to actually stop anyone here from doin' such? I mean, Vinny can't kill everyone with that little gun of his, can he?'

'Is this goin' anywhere, Tomas?' Judge Laverty asked, somewhat uncomfortably.

'It is, Your Honour. It's just that Father Joseph–like yourself and Vinny–is keenly aware of the ways in which the many can be governed by the few, and so I'd like him to inform us of why he thinks we've chosen this particular method over so many available others.'

Judge Laverty nodded a tolerant nod and the Father sighed wearily. 'I don't see the relevance of your questions either, Tomas, yet I'll indulge you with two replies. Firstly, I'll grant you a *spiritual* answer and suggest that this situation is *very* like life in general, in that we make the best decisions we can–be they ethical, moral, accordin' to spiritual doctrine, or in either vague or distinct reference to the written and physical and laws of the land–while livin' forever under the threat of death, which is arguably never more than a second away. And, as spiritual creatures, we need to reference *all* such laws, not just to raise our consciousness above that of the beast, but to ascertain and *strengthen* our security of thought and purpose. By doin' so, we live more *fulfilled* lives, and that sense of fulfilment usually increases tenfold if we choose a purpose which doesn't *conflict* with the purpose of others. We do this every day of our lives, so there is no true difference between our current situation and any other, except our heightened sense of awareness.'

The priest took a deep breath. 'Now, the second part of my answer is a *practical* response, and it is this: In any civilised country in the world, written and physical law *must* prevail, as morals, ethics and religious beliefs differ from not just person to person, but town to town and nation to nation, thereby makin' them more difficult to enforce. Nevertheless, because we are mortal, it might *seem* that the best way for a society to protect her subjects as best she can is by incessant *physical* policin'. But because those who maintain the law are also mortal, their methods–if left unchecked–might be whimsical, biased and unevenly served. For this reason, it is by writin' down a strong, *consistent* code of values and precepts that we ensure prolonged structure, guidance and harmony in society, and it is by consultin' the benchmarks of that same legislation that we ensure total equality and fairness for all.'

As Tomas mulled over his reply, the priest lifted his head and smiled thinly, as if content with the fullness of his response. 'And yet, all of that aside, what is your true reason for callin' me up here as a witness?'

Tomas moved directly to the front of the priest's chair. 'I want to know if you *truly* consider legislation stronger than morality, Father. Y'see, in the last half-hour, we've discovered that people never cease to surprise us. And it seems few people–despite what they once believed–knew Marie Devine very well at all. But you came to know her *very* well of late, Father, didn't you?'

'I don't know what you mean, Tomas,' Father Joseph blustered. 'And I'm not sure I know or like what you're tryin' to imply…'

'It's alright, Father, I'm not implyin' anythin' indecent,' Tomas grinned. 'It's just that we now know Marie Devine recently attended regular Confessions here in your chapel. So you knew her far better than most. You knew her fears, the way she thought, what was worryin' her over the last few weeks, and the state of her mind in general. Isn't that right?'

'We still operate a closed confessional in this chapel,' the Father declared coldly. 'You mightn't be aware of that, Tomas, seein' as how you've been away a time. But the new, open-confessional doesn't appeal to everyone.'

'Fair enough, Father,' Tomas smiled. 'But, even so, you live in a small town. You know the people here, their peculiarities and their inner minds. Moreover, you aren't a stupid man: You hear a voice and it doesn't take you long to figure out who's behind the screen. Of course, you've also undertaken a moral oath whereby you may never relay the contents of those same confessions to others. Still, there are exceptions to every rule: For example, when you believe a crime is about to be committed, such as an act of brutality or a murder, you're obliged to inform the police as to how and when this might occur. And so, therein is the conundrum,' Tomas said, turning towards the gathering. 'And I must ask you now if, due to our prevailin' situation–a situation in which someone may soon be murdered–you can morally justify it within yourself and before your God to withhold what was so worryin' Marie

186

Devine shortly before her disappearance.' Tomas raised his palms. 'And you *do* know what it was – I can see that in your eyes. We *all* can.'

Frowning darkly, Father Joseph sat there for a few moments, intently scrutinising the expectant faces before him. Then, taking a deep breath, he turned to face Con Logue. 'I'd just like to say you were wrong about people, Con. Despite perhaps thinkin' me robotic at times, they *do* trust me, and they *do* tell me their deepest secrets. And even though I don't want to break my sacred vows here tonight, Tomas is correct: I might be forced to do so if a man's life depends upon it.'

'What is it, Con?' Deborah asked her husband again. 'Is there somethin' I should know?' Deborah looked between Con and Molly, yet both refused to meet her gaze. As if suddenly illuminated, Deborah's face turned chalk-white. 'You aren't – I mean, the two of you aren't...' She shook her head slowly, her brow heavily seamed and her eyes moistening. 'No, no, that can't be...'

'Alright, Deborah,' Con rasped, unable to meet his wife's incredulous gaze. 'Molly and I ...we...'

'Molly and you?' Deborah gasped. 'Con, what are you sayin'?' Tears formed at the corner of her eyes, and she turned to Molly. 'Molly and *you...*?'

'Christ!' Frank Devenney remarked. 'No wonder the girl was upset – her bloody father-in-law-to-be was gettin' it on with her mother!'

With the pain heavily evident in her eyes, Deborah Logue stood up and stared at her husband as if he'd suddenly turned leprous. Then she took a swing at his face with an open palm and struck him squarely upon the cheek, before slumping heavily back into her seat. Soured, and with his face swiftly reddening, Con ground his teeth in distress as his son also granted him a glare of disdain before hurriedly moving further along the pew to comfort his mother.

'Aye, alright,' Con stormed defensively. 'But it's not as sordid as it sounds. About twenty-two years ago, when we were *young*, Molly and I dated for about a year or so. Then Molly met her husband and I met Deborah. But then shortly after Molly and her husband split up, we sort of...well, let's just say, things happen...'

'They split up over fifteen years ago,' Deborah screeched. 'Are you tryin' to say that you've been seein' each other again for *fifteen* years?'

'Aye, near enough,' Con Logue admitted sheepishly. 'Though Molly was tryin' to break it off – she'd been tryin' to do so since she discovered Eddie and Marie were serious about each other. Me, I found it harder to let go and I tried talkin' to her and phonin' her, but she insisted it had to end and she just stopped talkin' to me. So, I wrote her several letters in a bid to re-establish contact. The irony is, of course, that I wrote so many, Molly didn't even notice one had bloody vanished!'

'Fifteen years?' Deborah repeated in disbelief, staring coldly between her husband and Molly Devine. '*Fifteen years*?' She shook her head, unable to see anything other than the entirety of the tiled chapel floor at her feet.

Con Logue clenched his hands into fists. 'Right, so I fell by the wayside,' he fumed impotently. 'But I'm not the worst person in the world for doin' that.' He stared penitently at his wife. 'I'm sorry,' he told her urgently. 'I would've told you when we were alone, but these people persisted and now it's out in the open. I've sinned, alright, and I bloody admit it! But then, you've heard the rest of this lot comin' unravelled here tonight and I'm no worse than them. Still, if you want to judge me in relation to my so-called peers, then let's get *every* single skeleton out of the closet. If you want secrets, let's hear the biggest secret of them all.' The garage-owner once again proffered a hand in the Old Man's direction.

'We'd rather hear about what you and Molly have been up to the last fifteen years,' Neil Martin interrupted, gleefully. 'You've been sittin' there mouthin' off all night, Con, and there you are mixed up with your wee boy's girlfriend's mother. Christ!' he snorted indignantly. 'Things don't come any lower than that.'

'That's what you bloody think,' Con stormed, prodding the Old Man in the ribs. 'Go on, tell them.'

The Father turned to the Old Man. 'Well,' he said icily. 'Seein' as everyone is tellin' tales out of school, what exactly *are* you guilty of?'

The Old Man raised his hands feebly. 'I didn't do anythin' wrong, Father Joseph, not in the strictest sense. I was just lookin' to gain a competitive advantage, that's all. That's why I was sellin' my shop, because...'

'Because of what?' the Father asked, impatiently. 'What are you talkin' about?'

'I found a leak in the cellar of my shop several months ago, Father, and I thought it was a bit of damp and nothin' more. So, I got the builders in, hopin' they'd damp-proof the place. But it was worse than that, far worse. The foundations were givin', the whole place was subsidin', and apparently the only thing keepin' my shop up were the shops either side of it. So, I thought about sellin' up. I mean, you have to seek a competitive advantage if you're a businessman. At least, I think so...'

'And what's wrong with that?' the Father asked, raising an eyebrow.

'Nothin' much,' Con Logue remarked, bitterly. 'Only we later found out most of the town was goin' the same way. I was next to get the builders in. I found risin' damp under the petrol sumps and all the way through the garage foundations. The river, y'see, it's reclaimin' its natural course. So, along with Dan McGinty, we made a pact to keep the whole thing quiet until we'd sold up our businesses.'

'You mean that I went and bought myself a white elephant of a cafe which might be under water in a few years time?' Hugh Rafferty asked, thickly. 'What kind of people are you all here in Craiglann anyhow?'

'Who told you this anyhow?' the contractor called Gerry interrupted. 'And, sure, how would a buildin' contractor know from the damp under one or two properties about the intended passage of the River Hart? That's a load of nonsense, and you'd need the word of an expert to determine that.'

'Aye, we weren't goin' to take the word of any know-it-all builder,' Con Logue snapped, defensively. 'So, through a friend of mine, we hired an outsider to come in and do a few tests and he confirmed our worst fears. We did it on the quiet, of course, as we didn't want to start a bloody panic. Word would've spread and we'd never have got a fair price for our properties.' Con Logue shrugged as he surveyed the sea of frowning faces. 'We were just seekin' a competitive advantage, so fair's fair! And we were just doin' what you'd've done if you'd had the brains.'

'Aye, very fair,' Dave Mullan muttered. 'You three climbin' up on your soap-boxes tonight and givin' off to everyone about morals, even as you're stabbin' the rest of us in the back. Aye, very bloody fair!'

His comments were met with mumbles of angry agreement. Now the entire gathering were scrutinising the Old Man, Con Logue and Dan McGinty with disdain and distrust in their eyes.

'Well, now we're all in the same boat because no one has sold their property yet,' Con replied, refusing to capitulate. 'Of course, we were goin' to tell you all eventually, a couple at a time, so there wouldn't be a panic. You could've all sold up then, gradually, and said you'd got good offers to go elsewhere. We had it all figured out. Over the period of a few years there would've been a mass exodus, durin' which time we could've off-loaded Craiglann to a bunch of patsies from another town.'

'Like me you mean,' Hugh Rafferty snapped. 'A load of patsies is it? I'll be seein' you in the mornin,' Mr Logue, after Mr Martin and Mr Devenney have done you to death. We'll see who the bloody patsy is then!'

'Aye, that's very brave of you!' Con muttered, shaking his head.

'So, no doubt you'd've told everyone about this plan of yours in order of preference,' Big Michael Doherty snapped bitterly. 'And I suspect people like me and Mullan would probably have been the last two livin' in this ghost town!'

'Aye,' Con muttered, tersely. 'And even then the two of you probably wouldn't have caught on to what was happenin'!'

Vinny McIntyre raised his gun in the air as yet another insurrection threatened, and again the crowd faltered. Seamus Brown called for quiet then, and an uneasy calm took hold.

The Father sat down against the altar rail and shook his head. 'I can't believe it, Con,' he declared solemnly. 'You were goin' to watch me stick one-hundred-and-fifty-thousand euros into refurbishin' the chapel, knowin' it would hardly be worth it. And you were goin' to watch every other property in town rapidly devaluate day by day just so you could gain what you've the nerve to call a *competitive advantage*. If word of that had spread out of Craiglann–which it would've done–everyone would've lost out. People who've lived in this town for generations would've come away with nothin' and ended up with nowhere to go.'

'Well, the only difference now is we'll *all* end up with nothin', Con Logue rasped. 'I don't bloody care anyhow – I started with nothin', so I'll do the same again.' He stood suddenly, taking everyone off their guard. 'Anyhow, now we've all got our petty little secrets out in the open, it's time to make a decision. That storm's gettin' worse, and our lives are *still* in danger.' He pointed a finger at Tomas. 'We've heard this man defendin' the Stranger, and, in my opinion, it's been like listenin' to one disease tryin' to diagnose another. Alright, I'll agree he's brought a few facts to light, as well as one or two other things a few of us would've been best not discoverin'. Still, he hasn't convinced me that the Stranger *isn't* guilty of murder. So, unless he's anythin' else to add, I say we listen to his conclusion, then let those reprobates in the back row decide our fate. And then,' Con trumped. 'When they've all decided whatever they decide, *we'll* all go over to the farmhouse and take it off the Stranger. Because *that's* what they're goin' to decide anyhow, it's obvious! And, because I've a lot to make amends for, I'll lead the charge!'

Once again, Judge Laverty banged the latten candlestick down upon the altar, yet this time he made no apology for doing so. 'You'll adhere to whatever these good people decide, Con,' he said sharply. He took a deep breath, seeking to regain his calm. 'Still, I agree that we must see an end to this situation, if only to stem this diversity of opinion, for, while many here are controlled enough to obey what presently passes for law in Craiglann, others are seemingly too keen to dispense a more personal form of justice. The safest thing we can do now, therefore, is to remove all possible doubts from everyone's minds as to who exactly is who.' He stared blankly at Tomas. 'You have a concludin' argument for the defence, I presume?'

'I can only offer an alternative hypothesis, Your Honour, other than that which is generally agreed to be the main reason for wee Marie Devine's disappearance.'

'Then continue, Tomas,' Judge Laverty declared evenly. 'Because I too need to hear somethin' sane for a time. What I've listened to this night is–as ironic as it might now sound–enough to send any man to an early grave!'

FIFTEEN

Seemingly unaffected by the growing clamour of the storm, Tomas strode calmly across the dais. Then, rubbing at his chin, he stared at the expectant faces down in the pews, before loudly stating that most people had by now perhaps guessed he was about to suggest wee Marie Devine had orchestrated her own disappearance shortly after learning of her mother's involvement with her father-in-law-to-be.

Still, Tomas declared evenly, this wasn't idle speculation on his behalf, as several things seemed to back that idea up. The first thing to clarify was that Marie had *definitely* known of that illicit affair, and Tomas reiterated that Father Joseph had cleverly confirmed this without breaking his sacred vows. Of course, it was irrelevant whether she made this dark discovery by reading a certain letter: The important thing was that, upon receipt of this knowledge, she'd instantly known that confronting Molly or Con on the issue virtually guaranteed the dissolution of her imminent marriage, as well as an inevitable inter-family rift and maybe another very public scandal into the bargain. Nor, too, would brushing the issue aside make it disappear for good.

So, despite sharing this dilemma with Father Joseph, Marie still had a tough decision to make, and this was obviously wearing her down. What evidence was there to support this? Nothing distinctive in itself, but, just a few days before she disappeared, Marie was seen wandering around in a heavy downpour with her hood down–the sign of a distracted mind, perhaps? She was also seen smoking–something her mother thought she'd given up years ago. Moreover, according to Eddie, Marie had let her diet go a bit of late: Again, this was insignificant in itself, but wasn't Marie normally very picky about her food? And, as her wedding day neared, wouldn't she have been a little more diet-conscious, knowing she had to fit into her wedding gown, which was most likely pre-ordered and of a certain pre-selected size?

Here, Tomas waited for Molly to clarify if that was indeed so; and this the frowning senior-hairstylist did with a grim nod.

So, Tomas continued, the wee girl was obviously quite distracted. But, as Molly pointed out, Marie wasn't one for acting rashly. So, if one recalled the amount of time she'd been spending on the phone, it seemed she'd sought a second opinion from a trustworthy and objective friend.

This, again, no one could prove for certain, yet would a young girl overwhelmed by complex personal problems spend significant amounts of time on the phone without relating exactly what was going on in her own life? Possibly not. Moreover, it was unlikely that Marie had called any of her work colleagues as she didn't mix with them. Nor, for obvious reasons, had she been phoning Eddie. Of course, Marie may've confided her ongoing quandary to one of her local friends; but again, why talk on the phone if they lived nearby? No, the chances were this valuable friend –whoever it was–lived a considerable distance away. And when you took into consideration that Marie was young and had perhaps formed few, if any, friendships beyond Craiglann, probability suggested that she'd been in contact with either her father or her ex-boyfriend.

Tomas shrugged, then suggested that there was a certain amount of evidence to back this up, though Marie's father was the unlikeliest possibility: After all, by confiding in him now for lengthy periods, mightn't Marie have given him the impression she condoned the way he'd treated both her and her family in the past? Besides, as everyone had heard, Marie was aware that one of the strongest and effective reproofs possible was very often the judgement of silence.

Tomas pouted uncertainly, before stating that Marie's ex-boyfriend seemed a likelier candidate. Firstly, the use of an outside line suggested that Molly's phone-bill was itemised and that Marie was phoning someone of whom her mother disapproved. And, just a while back, Molly made it clear that she hadn't anything *really* bad to say about Geoff Harkin, yet her tone spoke volumes. Of course, young Geoff was, by all reports, now a responsible adult with a good job in the travel industry; and Marie may've felt this new-found maturity also made him quite approachable, objective and even empathetic. Besides, Geoff may've also been willing to take the odd Saturday off his work in order to spend quality time with his old flame, which might further account for those days when Marie was supposedly working overtime.

As Molly Devine dropped her head in confusion and Deborah Logue comforted her increasingly distraught son, Tomas said this still didn't solve Marie's problem: She was able to air her misgivings, yet her wedding day was drawing closer. What was she to do? Cancel it without telling anyone why? Sure, how long would it be before someone actually figured out the truth?

Tomas shook his head: No, Marie–a non-confrontational sort of person–decided to hatch a plan of escape in order to give herself some breathing room. And why not? Her most attainable dream had suddenly become unattainable, but she was very much a survivor. And wasn't that the difference between the strong and the weak? Couldn't survivors always visualise a future of sorts, no matter the troubles which befell them? Didn't the strong always retain hope and have a dream to fall back on? And hadn't Marie herself once entertained other dreams?

Sadly, most of Marie Devine's past dreams had been adulterated by time, yet it was likely the vestiges remained at the core of her being. Marie had taken languages, she'd wanted to be an air-stewardess, she'd once talked of living abroad, and didn't her ex-boyfriend work in the travel industry? Wasn't he, too, free from all ties in Craiglann? Didn't he know what made Marie breathe, how to quell her angst and how to comfort her? Of course, Marie was very independent, and would hardly have wanted to impose upon him. But what if she took all of her savings from the Post Office and bought a passport, short skirts, bikinis and slippers? And what if she perhaps made a secret and illicit withdrawal from a bank account to which she was granted almost daily access just to give her new life a kick-start?

As Molly Devine and Brendan Harper again exchanged uncertain glances, Tomas shrugged and said that of course it was possible. And it was equally possible that Marie provided herself with another small cash reserve – some rent and electricity money she'd taken from her own house just one week earlier.

And why not? Tomas asked, above several tetchy murmurs of disapproval. After all, wasn't burglary a risk-taking profession in which the thief tried to attain as many valuables as possible in the shortest time to lessen their chances of being caught? So, under such restrictive conditions, what burglar would break into an expensive house in a built-up area and ignore all manner of valuable objects in order to seek out– in the dark–a stash of money, the latter of which was hardly in plain view? Someone with inside knowledge, perhaps, or maybe not a burglar at all. So, wasn't it feasible, Tomas asked evenly, that an angry young lady with no other way in which to openly vent her wrath had actually done this? Because wasn't her mother responsible for the mess Marie was now in and actually forcing her to run away? And, after being hurt by those who should've known better, why should Marie even care that her actions or unexplained absence was going to cause a small furore in Craiglann?

Tomas raised his hands and admitted ruefully that everything he'd said was an alternative theory to those suppositions being levelled against the Stranger. Still, it wasn't any more unbelievable, was it? In fact, in light of everything they'd heard, was it inconceivable that Marie ran off to think things through? Maybe she needed time and distance to reconcile herself to the fact she could no longer be romantically involved with Eddie Logue. And wasn't it also possible that she was even worried–

given the length of her mother's affair with Con–that her boyfriend's father was actually *her* own father too?

'No, no!' Con Logue blustered. 'Now, I know for a definite fact that *she's* not mine!'

As suddenly aware of not only what he'd admitted but implied, the garage-owner rubbed at his forehead, blushed furiously, then slumped back into his seat under the increasingly troubled and weighted glares of both his wife and son.

Tomas shook his head and sat down upon the altar steps. 'Well, that might just be one sin too many, Mr Logue. And on the subject of sins, let's talk of *sloth*, and of how so many here are prepared to listen to rumour and innuendo instead of findin' out what others are like for themselves. Let's speak next of *pride*, and of how so many here are always right, despite all evidence to the contrary. Let's speak of *wrath*, and of the mental and physical wounds brother has imposed upon brother over the course of this last week. Let's talk of *envy*, and of how one man would see his profits turn to ashes just to see his competitor fall. Though let me quickly skip over *lust*, for by now we're all very much aware of the ripple-effects of that great sin. And let me bypass as quickly on *gluttony* – except to say I didn't get as many sandwiches as I should've done earlier on. But let me linger for an instant upon *greed*, for it's there I find myself wonderin' where true *competitive advantage* ends and where the last of all of these terrible seven sins begins.'

Tomas paused and keenly scrutinised the evacuees, many of whom now declined their heads shamefully. 'I could, of course, speak also about the spreadin' of lies, deceit, back-stabbin', thievin' and cruelty to lesser men, but I think you get my point. Because we now know that no one here is better than anyone else, and each is so caught up in their own world of malleable scruples that they're totally desensitised to the troubles of others. And yet, many here have the nerve to blame the Stranger–a man they've never met or spoken to–for their present troubles. Which is convenient, if logically unsound, as here we have a man who moves to Craiglann–maybe he's a killer, maybe he's not–and, instead of tryin' to blend in with the locals, the first thing he does is murder one of them. Does that adhere firmly to the laws of probability or what?'

Tomas smiled wryly and very slowly shook his head. 'Still, the decision about whether or not this man committed that terrible crime isn't mine to make. Court has been ordered, a judge appointed and a jury convened. Of course, this particular jury consists of four non-persons whom society has, until now, sought to constantly exclude from their pious day-to-day way of livin'. And yet, I'm sure these men shall soon pass a judgement to which the upper and not-quite-as-lower echelons of Craiglann will definitely agree to adhere.'

A frowning Judge Laverty rose from behind the altar and loudly cleared his throat. 'I have never presided over a stranger hearin',' he admitted grimly. 'And I'd like to remind all here that such an enactment would normally hold no validity in the eyes of the law. But tonight, we've all agreed to abide by rules we set ourselves. So, you've heard the primary supposition – this bein' that the Stranger is guilty of murder. And murder, I'd like to remind the jury, is defined as to kill with malice aforethought. In effect, this asks you to judge whether the Stranger elected–*compos mentis*–to kill someone at an earlier time, then followed through with that intention in succession to his original thought?' The elderly judge upturned his palms. 'The defence, on the other hand, suggests the girl ran away, perhaps firstly to Dublin, then to somewhere on the continent. And there's as much evidence–if you can term it such– to support that theory too. So, due to the precariousness of our position, our small jury must now decide how we should settle this affair.' He regarded his watch. 'It is now 12-40am, and I declare these men have twenty minutes in which to decide upon the best possible course of action. I shall, however, offer them one last piece of advice: Keep your minds clear and calm in order to obtain the highest benefit from your thoughts.'

Fidgeting restlessly in the seventh pew, and feeling as if he was about to succumb once more to panic, Miles took no comfort from that Epicurean guidance. Seeking to stay in the present, he stared briefly at the other inmates, wondering if Tomas' summation had affected the way in which they'd now vote. Pele, the most rational of the group, would perhaps be guided by common-sense; yet the problem there, Miles thought sadly, was how one defined common-sense. Wing-Ding's impassive face and his proximity to Brian told a more obvious story: The youth would mimic the stronger man's actions solely because he couldn't grasp the seriousness of their predicament. And Brian, of course, had that devilish glint in his eye, the one which said he was definitely going to find the Stranger guilty just to escape this questionable sanctity for one that offered warmth, food and drink.

Miles, though, had never been as uncertain about anything in his life. At first, he'd instinctively felt that, no matter the evidence presented, it would be safer to vote the Stranger guilty in order to prevent the evacuees from turning upon the inmates, although this particular strategy didn't fully negate the chance that he and his cohorts might still be forced to assist in the taking of the farmhouse. Shortly after the incident in the sacristy, however, Miles had decided to vote the Stranger innocent, simply because the Father had made him feel like a responsible person with the potential to some day overcome his malaise.

But now, the more Miles considered that brief exchange with the priest, the more he realised the Father had nothing to lose by declaring his belief in other men. In fact, when the priest had asked Miles whether it was necessary to tell Tomas that Wing-Ding had also been outside on the night of Marie Devine's disappearance, he'd simply relieved himself of an enormous responsibility, for, in truth, that one snippet of information was enough in itself to infer doubts upon the capability of the jury. Aye, Miles decided bitterly, the Father would be the only winner here tonight. If the chapel was divided in a schism and the priest died trying to prevent it, the papacy would later erect a shrine to him, canonise him or have some literary genius record his memory evermore in a glowing hagiology. But if the priest lived through this ordeal, they'd erect Phidean statues of gold and ivory to him, then possibly hook him into a book-signing tour of the entire Christian world.

Miles gritted his teeth hard at the thought of it. Aye, the Father had to do nothing now other than wait. Not so the inmates of Adullam – they had to make a black-or-white decision now about whether death should be visited upon the one or the many.

As yet another unsettling grumble of thunder shook the chapel, Miles glanced up to see Tomas strolling across the dais, seemingly unconcerned by the fact he might be one of the first to die if the Great Oak careened into the chapel. Miles narrowed his eyes, begrudgingly admitting to himself that Tomas had definitely administered a fine defence on behalf of the Stranger. But to what avail? If anything, Tomas had simply stalled the inevitable, for most of the towns-people were as recalcitrant as ever – you could see it in their faces.

You poor misguided fool, Tomas, Miles thought then. You'll need more than hope and that cheerful alacrity of yours to sustain you against the folly you perpetuate this night, so why bother? And what would possess a man–any man–to embark upon this futile odyssey?

Madness – that was the answer. Tomas was completely mad, and not temporarily so. Despite his intelligence and redoubtable courage, there was no balance in the man. His bravery wasn't tempered by even the smallest glimmer of fear, nor his intelligence checked by the limiting capacities of reason. He was truly Odysseus, the only man who'd dare to sail a black trireme into the depths of Hades. And yet Odysseus had been tied to the mainmast and given the herb *moly* by Hermes to render him immune to the call of Sirens.

You Tomas, Miles mused blackly, who or what shall sustain you on this darkest of all nights? Not I certainly, and you have no other friends.

And what happened to you in your lifetime to make you crave your fifteen minutes of fame amongst people who perhaps aren't even worthy of a madman's efforts?

Miles shook his head, realising that, for the first time in years, he so wanted to discover what lay behind an outer façade. Perhaps Tomas had once been an ordinary man, he decided then. Perhaps Miles wasn't the only one to have fallen weak-kneed to the incapacitating arrows of Eros after all, to have had his willpower slowly and inexorably drained away as desire possessed him, and to have had his mind pleasantly and joyously lost to true love, that illogical and illusory enemy of reason. Perhaps, once upon a time, Tomas had also found someone who hadn't just been there to press against in times of loneliness, someone who'd met him with the powerful union of her mind, body and spirit beneath a glittering of stars on so hauntingly beautiful a night that it could never have lasted long enough had it lasted forever. And maybe, ever since, Tomas had been searching for a night to equal that particular one in its delirious ferocity and in its simplistic beauty.

Of course, Miles mused grimly, Tomas might've deemed this unholy sabbat an obscene obverse to that particular time. And, despite having declared himself here on a temporary sojourn, he may've already decided to play out a final self-punitive chapter of his life in grandiose style. The captive audience, clearly unworthy of him, were an audience still. The peaked emotions were also there, albeit in perversely stark symmetry to that one superior moment in his past. And, in his madness, Tomas might now view this night as one in which–in spite of the overwhelming odds against him–to momentarily bloom like a prize-winning winter rose, before willingly giving himself up to death.

Miles shook his head, almost totally overwhelmed by despair. Then, at a whim, he rose quickly from his seat and moved out past the other three inmates into the aisle.

'Where are you goin'?' the Father asked him, almost nervously.

'The toilet, Father Joseph,' Miles said, clutching at his stomach and exaggerating a pained expression that would've been there anyhow had he time to nurture it fully. He felt the tectonic strain within his mind and knew his brain was about to explode into millions of shards with the build-up of pressure.

'Then be quick,' the Father whispered evenly. 'We must make a decision here.' The priest frowned heavily and reached out to hold softly onto the vagrant's arm, his vulnerability momentarily visible. 'You'll make the right one, Miles. I trust you will. You're a fair man – I think you all are, basically.' He nodded then, took a deep breath and released the vagrant's arm. 'Go on then, and please hurry up about it.'

Miles nodded resolutely, as if that was his sole intention. Then he made his way quickly out past the sacristy and into the toilet cubicle, where he locked the door and placed his foot heavily against it. And there, a few moments later, he realised that, if his life was about to end, he needed to revisit those last bitter-sweet years he'd spent with Sarah.

***

The day after they got back together for the final time, Sarah asked Miles to spend the summer on her farm, where she still had land and livestock deals to conclude. And, assenting that they were at last a couple, Miles happily agreed to do so, realising he'd felt emotionally unfulfilled until then, and that it was only now–because he'd freely decided to involve himself fully in someone else's life–that his loneliness had virtually disappeared. Upon deeper reflection, he also felt he'd chosen wisely in Sarah as she accepted him without expectation for all he currently was; she wasn't critical of the mistakes he'd made before meeting her, which meant he'd never have to defend his past; and she incessantly gave him hope for a future he'd once believed he didn't deserve.

Yet one of Sarah's impending plans did cause Miles some concern. Shortly after her business transactions concluded, she told him she'd purposely withheld the sale of those two-acres of land immediately surrounding the farmhouse. She'd done so because she intended to renovate the building and develop the fields into a sprawling garden, thereby transforming it into somewhere they might comfortably spend their future. But as Miles took stock of the ruinous building and the weed-choked and uneven land that encompassed it, he instinctively felt that she'd set herself too laborious a task. Despite this, he agreed to help Sarah fulfil her dream as best he could, even as he secretly prayed she'd soon tire of that enormous task.

It was the middle of June before Sarah hired a contracting team to initiate the reconstruction work, and by then she and Miles had begun bordering the land with a strong wooden fence, along the inner perimeter of which they closely planted a line of deciduous saplings. The work was physical and engaging, yet even Miles eventually agreed that he could see Sarah's vision slowly taking shape. And, as summer waned and they began their final year at university, they divided their hours between studying and adding the final touches to what was slowly becoming their home. The interior was painted and papered, the exterior walls were whitewashed and affixed with pergolas that would soon be suffocated by clambering hydrangeas, the long driveway was gravelled, and every outside sill was embellished with plant-pots filled with flushes of lilac, dark violets and salmon rose. The bulk of their gardening work would, of course, require the assistance of friendlier neighbours, who helped them turn and level the earth in readiness for the following summer, after which Sarah would begin seeding her lawn and planting low earth tors along its edge with effervescent sprays of summer roses, dense cushions of winter heathers, and thick carpets of spring bulbs.

As work on the house progressed–and as they both studied hard for their finals–Miles revelled in his growing compatibility with Sarah, often wondering just how he'd survived without her until then. Moreover, their love moved beyond acceptance and realisation–just as Sarah once suggested it might–and at last became a constant learning process in which success and failure regularly tipped the scales.

Still, even though Miles accepted their relationship would have to be worked at in order to evolve, he realised that he was still young and had other equally important goals to attain. One of those required him finding gainful employment, and this he achieved shortly after his graduation by securing a part-time lecturing post in a nearby university. Another goal involved him eventually earning a place on an inter-county sprinting team, which allowed him to further his sporting interests by travelling to meets all around the country. Nor did his occasional weekends away bother Sarah in the least, as she was now working full-time in a local primary school and often enjoyed those quieter periods to herself.

And yet, the more Miles involved himself in these sporting-meets, the easier it somehow became to let his relationship with Sarah transform into a secondary consideration.

In truth, Miles knew his love for Sarah should've deterred him from succumbing to the adulation of those female admirers who fawned over him when he won races, or who sought to intimately console him when he lost. But, like many young people at the start of a relationship, he'd thought to accentuate the positive aspects of his love for Sarah, instead of taking more time to minimise the extent of their differences through communication. As a result, on those days when his girlfriend revealed herself as a real person possessed of minor faults and complex emotions, Miles found himself wondering whether he'd even known Sarah at the outset of their affair and wondering why she'd changed; and, instead of trying to discuss their difficulties, he more often found himself avoiding the issue and reflecting instead upon whether he should settle for that which he already owned, or if he should once again attempt to actively pursue the life of a single man.

His indiscretions had started out as guilt-ridden one-night-stands at first, and he truly hadn't intended to let things go as far as they did. But, upon discovering he could somehow live quite comfortably beyond them, Miles gradually allowed one of those inconsequential couplings to turn into an affair which sporadically continued after he and Sarah married, and even for four years after the birth of his twin daughters. His lover was a mature-student, a vision of beauty who was only two years younger than Miles and infatuated with everything he seemed to be. Too, even though she knew his circumstances, she insisted she could eventually mould herself to suit his every need if he'd only leave his wife.

Miles knew this clandestine affair could never work as its roots were embedded in dishonesty; yet he was somehow drawn into thinking that transitory distraction enough to buoy him and Sarah through their rougher days. Besides, he knew he could walk away from this other woman at any time, so who was he harming if no one else knew of their relationship? Moreover, wasn't life often a process of elimination in which you gradually discarded everything you didn't want before finally settling for your heart's desire?

Deep down inside, of course, a nagging rejoinder informed Miles that he'd stumbled back into the disingenuous world of rationalisation. Still, now that he was married and the initial hormone-sparked passion of that situation had evened itself into mainly pleasurable companionship, he was also struck by the further realisation that he'd committed himself to Sarah for life. And, even though he loved his wife more than anything, he was aware that the rest of his life might be a very long time. So, unwilling to ignore, confront or run away from this stark revelation just then, he opted for the alternative of self-deception.

Exactly how much he'd deceived himself was revealed to Miles on a summer's day just over four years into his marriage. That afternoon, his daughters were playing with their toys within the cool shade of the patio, and Miles and Sarah were sitting in an agreeable silence upon the lawn, relaxed by the warmth of the sun and idly observing a host of butterflies and bumblebees weaving their way through what had almost become a veritable Eden. Soon after, Miles started to fondly reminisce about the garden's conception, and about how that first winter–when hoarfrost turned the soil iron-hard and a blanket of snow carpeted all but the saplings–he'd despaired for Sarah, believing he was watching the death of her creation. Of course, he needn't have worried, as the following spring–and, to his surprise, every spring thereafter–the intricate beauty of his wife's labours increased in both richness and intensity. Moreover, some five years on, he admitted that it still amazed him as to how and why she put so much time and effort into the garden, despite knowing that the ravages of time would make it an endless chore.

As he talked, Sarah regarded him searchingly, before dropping her gaze and replying that the hardest part of the any garden's construction–as Miles now knew from experience–was digging out the foundations and ascertaining the boundaries. A small respite then came during that interim period when the stronger trees and the more easily-maintained perennials were planted, after which the rather monotonous, yet generally more fulfilling work began. To some people, that next phase appeared to be a simple matter of planting seeds and then liberally spraying fungicides and pesticides over their labours in order to prevent Nature from stealing the flowers away; and still others found it easier to bed the frailer blooms beneath constrictive cloches in nitrogen-enriched soils, or in greenhouses when the winter often promised to asphyxiate their gardens with its icy breath. And yet, Sarah said gently, most people didn't understand that fungicides and pesticides had a tendency to weaken or even destroy flowers if applied too harshly; and, while the flow of Nature could be briefly stalled by locking seeds and bulbs protectively away, this process also served to produce far weaker flowers with no individual qualities that only lived a little beyond their natural span.

Therefore, Sarah smiled, if you wished to maintain your garden in accordance with Nature's seasonal plan, you had to incessantly find more natural methods of protecting your blooms from the ravages of the weather, plaguing insects and those weeds and ivies which were often able to thrive impassively alongside other plants, only to smother and consume them over time. Of course, while this labour appeared time-consuming to others, there were many benefits to be had. Wild flowers were actually more resistant to disease, their fragrance was truer and lasted even beyond death, and they produced healthier seeds in order to continue their line of survival, thereby living fuller lives overall. Besides, while man laboured to produce uniformity in Nature, Nature abhorred stereotypes in everything; and, for this latter reason alone, wild flowers were more aesthetically pleasing because of their imperfections and because no two ever looked exactly the same.

Of course, it was quite sad to watch your own flowers reach their allotted time. And yet the most beautiful flowers were like the most precious of moments in a sense, in that their natural brevity and beauty made them live forever in your memory, giving you something to hold onto beyond their existence, and making you hope other flowers of a similar ilk might one day bud in their place. So, Sarah said finally, maintaining a garden was often very hard work at times, requiring love, sacrifice, hope, visualisation, patience and an ability to accept change. But if you accepted those facts beforehand, you could look beyond the natural flaws, derive happiness from savouring those flowers in bloom, and thereby grant your garden almost perpetual life.

As she stopped talking, Miles stared sorrowfully off into the distance, struck by the realisation that Sarah now suspected, or was very aware of, his ongoing transgressions. Nevertheless, she'd chosen to very courageously relay the extent of her pain to him on this most ordinary of summers days through the medium of intelligence, perhaps knowing he'd never admit to anything under a host of emotional accusations.

Dumbfounded, Miles sat there in silence as the fullness of his and Sarah's past encroached fully upon his mind. Over the years, they'd both idled away many hours together in that garden, sometimes writing silly love poems to each other in the dactylic hexameter of Homer, then laughing until they thought they'd never stop at the result. In that garden, too, they'd often exchanged apples after an argument, or lay beneath the stars holding hands, both aware just then of exactly where the earth met heaven.

Despite its many imperfections, life with Sarah had been everything for Miles, and very often much more than he imagined it could be, yet he'd been blinded by his own unrealistic expectations and an inability to progress beyond youth into manhood. But just then, as they sat there in that garden and the truth of this struck deeply into him, Miles understood that Sarah was providing him with an opportunity to grant himself his own ultimatum. Turning to face her, he took her hands firmly in his and he kissed her as if it were she and not the world that provided him with oxygen. And, as he did so, he made a silent promise never to hurt her or his baby daughters ever again.

Despairingly, less than twelve hours after that fateful epiphany, the idyllic future that Miles Kivlehan had promised his wife and family in that lingering kiss would come abruptly and savagely to an end.

Startled abruptly back into focus by a tumultuous crash of thunder, Miles nervously clasped his head in his hands and made himself small in the toilet cubicle, peripherally aware that a lightning flash had engorged the arched window above him, flooding the entire room briefly in dazzling light. As soon as the consuming darkness returned, however, he began to shake violently, so much so that he had to jam his foot against the door and wrap his arms tightly around his chest in an attempt to bring it under control. But it was then that several loud thumps upon the partition wall nearly sent him into orbit.

'You'll have to come out now, Miles. You've been in there almost five minutes, and you've a *really* important decision to make.'

The Father's stressed voice was all too recognisable above the thrash of the storm and Miles shifted uneasily on the toilet seat, feigning the groan of a man engrossed fully in his business. 'It's the stomach, Father. It's a bit, ehm, watery, y'know...'

'Well, you'll have to pull yourself together,' the Father returned shortly. 'Just come out and give your verdict, then you can sit in there all night if you wish.' Upon receiving no reply, the priest sighed in exasperation. 'Look, Miles, you can't keep runnin' away from responsibility. Remember, the rest of your friends are doin' their bit too. And if you're feelin' that bad, maybe I can give you all a small drink of wine later. But only *after* this thing is over...'

Miles gritted his teeth, wondering why those words didn't instantly buoy him up. But then the answer hit him: To be truly altruistic, a person had to give without expectation of either immediate or future reward. By promising him the wine now, the Father appeared to be bribing Miles, while further suggesting that the other inmates would never act morally or ethically without similar incentive.

'I just want to talk to Tomas for a moment,' the vagrant snapped, wishing the priest had phrased his offer even a little differently. 'That's... that's *all* I want, nothin' more!'

'Very well, Miles, I'll give you a few minutes with him. But then we *must* put an end to this madness. Because if we don't–and if everyone out there starts believin' we've wasted this last hour–there'll be *chaos*, and someone may even get hurt. All you have to do is make your mind up, one way or the other, then Vinny, Judge Laverty and myself will take it from there.'

The vagrant didn't reply. Instead, as the Father walked away, he upturned his gaze, wondering if there was now actually anyone in the chapel who wasn't set upon following a personal agenda. About a minute later there was yet another knock upon the cubicle door, this time softer and nowhere near as prolonged. 'You in there, Miles?' Tomas whispered. 'The Father said you needed to see me.'

'I didn't ask for any of this fuckin' shite!' Miles seethed, purposely skipping the formalities to let the other man know he hadn't forgotten exactly who was to blame for his ongoing predicament. 'So why doesn't everyone just leave me the fuck alone?'

'I think we should probably talk,' Tomas replied easily. 'I mean, that's if you *want* to talk to me. I could send Brian or someone in to have a word, if you'd prefer.'

As yet another myalgic pain shot through his gut, Miles didn't reply. Instead, he attempted to focus all of his remaining energies upon controlling the spasmodic shakes of his body. As he did so, he suddenly recalled how Odysseus had once tried to persuade the beggar Philoctetes to return with him to Troy, which couldn't be taken without him. That persuasion had failed, however, and it had been left to Heracles to remind Philoctetes that it was the will of the gods they all play a part in the city's downfall. Now, as Olympians brawled loudly with Titans in the heavens on this bedevilled night, Odysseus was once again threatening to send Heracles in to convince him that Troy had to be taken in the next few hours. Miles shook his head in despair. Had Odysseus somehow forgotten it had taken Agamemnon twenty years to take the city after the first rape of Helen? Besides, who was he to convince anyone of anything when he too had once feigned madness in a bid to avoid that same war?

'You're ramblin' again, Miles,' Tomas said, almost sadly. 'Don't you want to talk with me, then?'

Miles frowned deeply, aware that he was shifting intermittently between two ever-blurring worlds, and wishing he could somehow lose himself in the more preferable of those existences. 'We can't win, Tomas,' he said wearily. 'Even I know that, and I'm havin' real difficulty thinkin' straight at the moment. Seriously, no matter which way we vote, somethin' bad will happen. And why the fuck did you drag me into this shite anyway!?'

'Ah, Miles, you're just bein' negative because you're afraid to die,' Tomas replied calmly. 'But we don't know if that'll happen yet, so what's the point in worryin'? Besides, it's very likely we'll all be fine.'

'Jesus, Tomas, you live in a fantasy world!' Miles wrenched the cubicle door open angrily and stared accusingly up at the other man. 'And don't you realise that those who aren't afraid of death always destroy the lives of others around them? Is that what you really want to do tonight?'

'Questions, questions,' Tomas sighed, kneeling down on one knee and countering the other man's serious gaze with an uncomplicated smile. 'Look, Miles, I'm just tryin' to do what I do best. But to be honest, I'm not certain we can win this one either, because it's not in my hands anymore. What happens next is actually down to you. And you mightn't want to make a decision, but then life's all about doin' things you don't want to do at times. That's how we become men. We make decisions, we follow dreams and we stick it out until the end – no matter what!'

'I used to follow my dreams,' Miles replied hollowly. 'And all I ever wanted was to live out the rest of my life with my wife and children. But God took them away.' He dropped his head, aware of the sudden warmth of his tears as they traced along his cheek towards the corner of his mouth. 'Why did He do that, Tomas? I wasn't the greatest husband, I know, but was I *that* bad?'

Tomas shrugged uncertainly, his gaze both empathetic and solemn, and Miles wiped his eyes with trembling hands, dropping his head as he was suddenly overwhelmed by sorrow and regret. For some reason, he wanted to tell Tomas all about his past just then so that he might repair the ragged affinity that had grown between them before this most terrible of nights had begun; that same affinity which would instantly evaporate the moment Miles delivered the verdict he now felt he must deliver – the easiest verdict, the one that would save the lives of the majority, the verdict of guilt.

But then, re-establishing that affinity required telling the truth, and how could Tomas ever understand that Miles now felt doomed to exist forevermore in something akin to Hesiod's Age of Iron, an era in which men reputedly never ceased by day from toil or woe, nor by night from feeling worn? Could Tomas comprehend that Miles wasn't even sure at times he'd known anything but his present Spartan life, because the nine drink-addled years he'd been forced to exist without his family were now interspersed with all too many moments when he believed they might've just existed within a beautiful dream? And in what way could Miles ever hope to describe Sarah, the intelligent woman who might eventually have convinced him of the empathetic workings of Destiny and the benevolence of Fate had her own life, and that of their daughters, not been taken so suddenly and tragically away.

Now, Miles raised his head and studied Tomas from under a furrowed brow, wondering yet again if the other man had experienced similar tragedies. Had he also had his nearest and dearest taken from him unexpectedly, only to lose his friends and job in quick succession because he'd sought solace in drink? Had Tomas also abandoned his home and taken to an unplanned and chaotic pilgrimage of the land because he couldn't slightly comprehend why Heaven would even consider stealing children away, when logic dictated that a just God would revel fully in the joy those innocents brought to their parents on earth? And had Tomas ever felt like offering himself daily to Neptune, having grown heart-sick of offering himself daily to Bachus, who tortured men by drowning them more slowly? It was possible, Miles supposed wearily, so who was he to say what the other man could or couldn't understand?

'They tell you to grow and chase a dream, Tomas,' Miles said softly. 'In your youth, they tell you to do that. But what if your dreams die and refuse to take you with them? What do you do then?'

'Some dreams are supposed to die, Miles. That's one of the Four Consequences of Bein'.'

Miles rubbed at his eyes, suddenly feeling very drained. 'I don't understand.'

Tomas regarded the other man seriously for a few seconds. 'I'll tell you, Miles, but I'll have to be quick, and you'll have to concentrate. Is that alright?' Miles nodded dismissively. 'Right, there are Four Consequences of Bein', the most important of which dictates that, at some time durin' your life, you're obligated to try and fulfil a specific task which will either instantly or eventually contribute to the maintenance or the betterment of all humanity.'

Miles smiled despite himself, momentarily reminded of the similarly disarming manner in which Sarah used to try and convince him of her beliefs. 'Are you tryin' to tell me you believe in Destiny and Fate, Tomas?'

'No, because if you believe in Destiny, Miles, you believe somethin' will *definitely* occur, no matter what else happens in the world. And the intrinsic flaw of Fate is that it controls every single path in life, except those we *freely* walk upon. Admittedly, time and circumstances often force each of us onto paths we'd rather not tread, but you *always* have an alternative choice, in that you can either accept that new situation or move onto another path of your choice, thereby regainin' full control of your future.'

'But what if you're trapped in a chapel at midnight durin' a terrible storm and about to die?' Miles asked dryly. 'What are your choices then?'

'Choices of conscience–bravery, acceptance, fear, rejection–stuff like that.' Tomas raised a finger. 'But back to the First Consequence, which requires that we each make a promise–before we're born–to try and fulfil certain personal goals within the span Life allows us. Of course, durin' that same span, we must work *with* Life, which is man's greatest ally and departs him only with the greatest reluctance; we must work *around* the trials conceived and exacted by Nature, which abhors stagnation and holds no interest in anyone after they reproduce; we must *avoid* bein' waylaid by, or too ensnared in, certain distractin' and time-wastin' enticements; and we must, at all times, attempt to *disentangle* ourselves from the ploys of those who'd blatantly set their own welfare above that of others.'

Miles snorted derisively. 'And I suppose we promise this to God?'

'No, we promise it to ourselves.' As Miles frowned in confusion, Tomas smiled broadly. 'So, to the Second Consequence, which deems that you must also place the steady advancement of mankind above your own interests at all times, even insofar as that–if necessary–you'll destroy yourself or others who are set upon impedin' that same progression.'

'That just sounds like a very warped version of Survival of the Fittest?'

'No, it's *very* different. The Survival of the Fittest theorises that you'll use all tools at your disposal to ensure that you–or some aspect of you–survives the encounter. But the Second Consequence deems it at times necessary to *fully* destroy yourself or others for the overall benefit of mankind, as doin' so for correct and moral reasons shall inevitably aid in the positive progression of our species.'

'Aye, well, if you don't mind me sayin', that particular one could also be the barbaric defence of a mass-murderer,' Miles replied dryly. 'Not only that, it also sounds very like the rather cruel argument presented by Con Logue.'

'Barbarity and cruelty are merely perceptions, Miles, and concepts such as those don't exist within Life or Nature. Life's only concern is that it receives an equal input of energy for the energy it expends. And Nature has been tasked by Life to indiscriminately cut away all dead-wood in any way it deems fit so the world may continue to thrive at its optimum best. Contrarily, the species of man has just one main goal–continuous re-population–and spiritual awareness tells us we can't just dispense with either our own lives or the lives of others without providin' ourselves with a virtuous reason for doin' so. And this is where most people fail in life: Too caught up in doctrine and processed thought, they can't see that injurin' either ourselves or others in the short-term for reasons that are unconscionable can only destroy all humanity in the end.'

Miles shrugged evenly, trying to withhold judgement despite his reservations. 'And these other two Consequences of Bein', what are they?'

'Well, they involve the eternal conflict between Free Will and the responsibility men must assume for their actions, each and every single one of which ultimately affects everyone, everywhere.'

Miles raised an eyebrow. 'My every single action affects everyone, everywhere?'

'Naturally,' Tomas grinned. 'Every action instigates a reaction of a sort, that's a basic law of physics. Furthermore, despite what you may believe, every single action in the world affects you. You may feign indifference when a bird sings or a leaf floats softly by, for example, but you can't be truly indifferent, for you too are affected by those actions, should it be in the future when a storm blows and you momentarily recall the calm you knew when a particular bird sang or a certain leaf blew by.'

Miles shrugged lamely. 'Alright, I might concede that one.'

'Good.' Tomas grinned. 'Anyway, because Life has expended energy in the First Consequence by allowin' men to set out personal goals before they enter the world, it now requires an input of energy in return. The Third Consequence, therefore, asks every single person to settle this debt by fulfillin' one task of Life's choosin' – a task which shall instantly or eventually further the progression of all mankind. The task is different for everyone, can appear meanin'less to others, is rarely presented in an obvious form and can manifest itself at any point in a man's lifetime – meanin' the person for whom it's conceived may live an otherwise ordinary existence for years before or beyond its appearance. But, the main thing to remember is this task is fashioned specifically around the experiences and abilities that individual has accrued by then, and it's for them *alone*, even though it may often appear to belong to others. All that's required after its arrival is that the recipient attempts to fulfil it to the best of their potential.'

'And if they don't want to, or if they fail to recognise its existence?'

'The moment their task arrives, a person's conscience and spiritual awareness will make them aware of its existence. But, if a person chooses to ignore its presence, they only fail themselves. For this task–although it may strike immense terror into the recipient–is secretly a gift which, if completed, takes man to a higher level of spirituality, thereby allowin' him to instantly accept both the positive and negative facets of the Fourth Consequence of Bein' with no true fear in his heart.'

Deep in thought, Miles nodded that he had a very vague grasp upon what the other man was saying. 'And what's the fourth?'

Tomas smiled wryly. 'The Fourth Consequence asks man whether he is prepared, after receivin' all of Life's gifts, to place his complete trust in Death. Y'see, in the same way men choose the general pattern of their lives before they're born, they also choose the general manner and timin' of their own demise. Although–don't ask me why–only those who agree to be great religious or political leaders actually get to choose the exact place and time they pop their clogs.'

'So, you're sayin' I chose this life, and that I've already chosen the way in which I'm goin' to die?' Miles attempted to keep the sarcasm out of his voice. 'Well, that's one less thing I have to worry myself about, isn't it?'

'It is,' Tomas agreed eagerly. 'Of course, as very few people would face life if they knew what was comin' next, all of our general choices are placed deep into our subconscious the moment we enter the world. Subsequently, we then live out our lives carefully avoidin' all sorts of harm, until we're instinctively alerted that it's either time to instigate our own deaths through our own actions or inactions, or time to accept the quite normal medium of random repercussion...'

Miles raised his eyebrow even higher. 'Random repercussion?'

'Well, while most people wish to perform specific tasks durin' their lives which will benefit mankind, there are braver individuals who offer to make a positive impact upon others through the manner or timin' of their own demise. And, although such deaths seemingly have a negative impact at first, their more positive benefits become obvious over time. Of course, just because such people are brave, it doesn't necessarily mean they'll always be objective enough to know when their demise will achieve the highest impact upon others. For that reason, that cold, dispassionate observer known as Death is employed to oversee the task when he sees fit. And this he does through random repercussion, whereby he takes their lives away by usin' certain tools within Nature, or by manipulatin' either the direct or indirect actions of others.'

Miles rubbed hard at his forehead. 'So, now you're sayin' we all make a pre-arranged agreement with both Life and Death, is that it?' Tomas nodded once again, and Miles sighed deeply. 'Right, well, supposin' your strange philosophy had any merit, why would someone make such a gory agreement with Death?'

'So others might accrue the enormous knowledge to be gained from that dark experience and perhaps use it to fulfil their own allotted task,' Tomas continued softly. 'After all, even though experiences like that aren't the nicest, they are experiences, and each can change someone else's perception of the world.'

'And where does God come into this? Don't you believe in a God, or Gods?'

'If the Gods do exist, Miles, they're probably nothin' like the divine creators many believe them to be,' Tomas shrugged. 'They may be cold and dispassionate observers who created men merely for sport, and who's to say they don't even envy humankind, for the brevity of our lives grants us many experiences they could never own. I mean, when we know love and happiness, we savour it more fully because we realise it can be taken from us at any time. But how can the Gods feel that if they know the eternity of all things? What does a joyous moment truly mean to them if they can replicate it endlessly? How can they know the precariousness of those dark hours precedin' a storm, and the amazin' feelin' of relief experienced afterwards? And what do they know of dreams, for what wish may they not grant themselves?' Tomas smiled thinly. 'They're cursed with eternity, *if* they exist. And if I were a God, I'd envy men their mortality, too. Still, I don't have all of the answers. I just know my own truths – and one of them is that you can't destroy another person's life without virtuous justification.'

'I've never destroyed anyone,' Miles replied lamely. 'Not intentionally, at least.'

'You can destroy people by inaction, too,' Tomas smiled, rising up from his hunkers. 'Because not makin' a decision is also a decision. Anyway, a man's life depends upon you, so maybe it's time to make a stand. And it doesn't really matter what your decision is, because the balance of life corrects everythin' in the end, although it does matter that you make one.' He winked at Miles then, before turning and making his way back into the chapel proper.

***

'Where were you, Miles?' Wing-Ding asked, looking him deep in the eyes as he made his way back into the pew. 'And your face is all wet. Have you...?'

'I fell,' Miles snapped. 'I fell against the toilet door and hurt my eye, so let's just leave it.' He took a deep, composing breath. 'If you would. Please.'

Wing-Ding, halfway to being offended, smiled bashfully before directing his wide-eyed gaze up towards the shadowed roof. Miles sat beside him and took a quick glance around the chapel. Nothing much had changed since his departure, although Tomas was now employing the Father, Judge Laverty and Vinny McIntyre in muted conversation upon the dais. As Miles reviewed the enforced assembly of townspeople in the first three pews, he noticed quite a few of them were staring darkly in his direction, a fact which also hadn't gone unnoticed by Brian.

'Could we have a bit of privacy?' the broad man solemnly asked Judge Laverty, waving offhandedly in the direction of the offending viewers. 'You don't have to go outside, of course, but it'd be nice if you'd all stop bloody gawkin' at us!'

Upon hearing this, Judge Laverty nodded and asked everyone to turn and face the front of the chapel, solemnly reminding them that it would now be no more than five minutes at most before a verdict was delivered. As if to reinforce his request, Vinny McIntyre walked to the centre of the dais, where he raised his chin and gently tapped two fingers upon his gun-holster. For a few moments, Miles scrutinised the Chief Guard intently, wondering if the officer could actually shoot someone if he had to. As the vagrant was doing this, he was interrupted by Brian.

'We've made our decision,' the broad man remarked suddenly. He fixed Miles with an uncompromising glare. 'When you were away in the toilet, we reached our verdict.'

Miles raised an eyebrow. 'I thought we were all decidin'. All of us. Between us, y'know. Isn't that how it's normally done in court?'

Brian grinned a feral grin that was just on the correct side of tolerant. 'We don't really have a choice about how we vote,' he replied through thin lips. 'I mean, it was alright them makin' us a jury for a bit of a laugh, Miles, but we're not *really* men to them, are we? We're here to take the blame if it all falls buttered-side down. And they know we want to live too – it's only natural.' He shrugged lamely. 'So, we have to give them the vote they want. Then, if they want to fight over the bloody farmhouse in the middle of this storm, it'll be none of our concern.'

'I don't want to vote the Stranger guilty,' Miles frowned. 'I just don't want to do it. I don't think I could live with myself if somethin' went wrong.'

'They're just told you the worst possible scenario,' Brian rasped shortly. 'The chances are that, if this storm keeps up, no one will be goin' anywhere. But, sayin' Vinny does manage to reach the farmhouse, who knows what'll happen? I mean, if the Chief Guard *has* to shoot the Stranger, he might only wound him. Sure, what's the problem with that? The Stranger can then sue him for tons of compensation.'

Miles licked nervously at his top lip. 'So that's your decision then?' he sighed, supposing he'd perhaps been expecting a little too much from this aggregate of peculiarities. 'You, Wing-Ding? You're happy with that?'

'I don't want to die,' the callow youth said, dropping his head. 'I don't think it's my time yet, y'know?' He twisted knots in his trouser leg with two fingers of each hand. 'And I don't know the man – he might've done it.'

'*You* might've fuckin' done it!' Miles rasped venomously. 'You were outside that night, too, lest you forget! What if we all voted to kill *you* just because you went for a walk in the rain? How the fuck would you like that?'

Wing-Ding stared at Miles sheepishly, his owl-like eyes widening as a forerunner to his denial. 'I didn't do anythin' to anyone, Miles. You know that.'

Overwhelmed by the innocence ingrained in the youth's gaze, Miles felt his stomach dropping. Wing-Ding was Cassandra, doomed always to tell the truth, though never to be believed – except, for some unfathomable reason, Miles always seemed to believe him. 'Mmm, right. Well, Pele, what about you?'

The gaunt man sat thoughtfully for a time. 'I don't mind dyin',' he replied eventually. 'I've been alive thirty-six years, and if I die here in this chapel tonight it wont matter a damn, because at least there'll be someone to watch me go.' He regarded Miles kindly. 'Still, if I have to choose between one man dyin' or a whole lot, I'd choose the one. It isn't fair, I know, especially now Tomas has told us what may've happened to the girl. But I think it might be the best decision of the two.'

Brian nodded and stared obdurately at Miles. 'And you, Miles, what do you have to say?'

Miles regarded Brian neutrally for a moment, before directing his questioning gaze up at Tomas and wondering why he felt he actually owed the other man something. Alright, Tomas had tried to steal a drink for him earlier that evening, and he'd also tried to comfort Miles in the toilets. But had the other man been genuinely trying to help, or had he also been trying to buy the verdict he wanted to hear?

Miles frowned thoughtfully, before eventually deciding that it wasn't really that important whether or not Tomas had offered him the wine as a philanthropic gesture. What was more important, perhaps, was that Tomas had freely offered both his time and his ideas, before telling him it didn't really matter what his decision was in the end. Of course, the other man's debatable neology wasn't quite what Miles had expected in the way of comfort either. But then, did the structure of Tomas' peculiar belief system truly matter if all he'd wanted to do was non-judgementally help another man in any way he could? After all, everyone lived by a philosophy of sorts, no matter how base and egocentric, for men were basically creatures of reflection and therefore mainly what they considered themselves to be. Yet how many people were as aware as Tomas that action was the highest achievement of any philosophy, even as protracted thought was its greatest resistance? And how many people truly understood that those who framed themselves in a passive existence died all too quickly, even as those who resigned themselves to a life elected for them by others weren't actually living?

As the howl of a draining wind tore at the husk of the chapel and lightning ripped through the heavens, the vagrant calmly returned his gaze to Brian, certain he was now indebted to Tomas and equally sure he was indebted to the Stranger for much the same reason. Now, there was only one way to release himself from both kindnesses. 'Do you mind if I tell you somethin'?' he asked Brian.

Brian sighed an exaggerated sigh. 'Go ahead, Miles. But don't be too long.'

Miles nodded compliantly. 'I just want to tell you that I met this woman once – and I suppose most of us have met her. The one who can turn your life around, and the one upon whom I came to rely so much I actually lost a great big part of myself while doin' so. She's dead now, as are both of my children. But when I look back, I realise she was far stronger than me because she'd always face whatever came her way. There are a few things I forget about her, too, I won't lie, but there's one thing I always seem to recall which showed itself in every instance of her life–such as durin' her father's funeral, or durin' the birth of our fine, twin daughters–and that was her dignity, grace and composure. And I always envied her that, y'know. Even though she was my wife, I bloody envied her...'

'We've all been there,' Brian interrupted firmly, but not unkindly. 'But that was then, Miles, and this is now. And I don't mean to be nasty, but your past has nothin' to do with this situation. What we really need is your decision – though, in truth, it hardly matters anymore because it's three against one. We're goin' to give them what they want. We have to, Miles, because we really don't have a choice.'

'I don't agree with you there,' Miles said. 'Though I can see why you'd think that. But I was talkin' about my wife because I want to show her that I remember.'

'Aye, well, I'll repeat this once more just in case you didn't hear me – that was then, and this is now! You're clearly confusin' the two issues.'

'I'm not,' Miles smiled. 'Y'see, I have this strange feelin' I can bring the past back if I just try. It sounds mad, I know, but I need to start makin' decisions again, and the first is that I just can't do what you want.

I can't condemn a man to death, or even to be hurt, just because everyone else wants to. It's not in me, y'know. I want my dignity back, even if it's only for a single moment in time. I hope you all understand.'

Miles looked down at the floor for a time, very much aware of the ensuing silence. After a few moments he dared to look up at Brian, feeling a strength growing within him that he hadn't known in years. He knew it would perhaps vanish again within moments, yet he wanted to hold onto it so badly while it was there. It was a moment of life to grasp solidly onto even as he faced death, a fleeting moment of stark realisation under the threatening Sword of Damocles. Absurdly, he somehow felt it might even be enough to tide him over as he wandered evermore through infernal Tartarus.

'I agree,' Pele said then. He smiled a transitory smile at Miles from under hollow cheeks and much atrophied musculature, not having the energy to exact it for very long. 'I want that too. They might say we're mad, Miles. They will say that, won't they? But I want it too.'

Miles nodded solemnly and then regarded Brian evenly, feeling stronger by the second. As he did so, he recalled Tomas' words: *It has to be possible to change others, Miles, because it's possible to change ourselves.*

'Two against two,' Miles said, regarding the broader man evenly. 'But let me just say one last thing here, Brian, please. It's just that I remember you tellin' me somethin'...'

Brian raised an eyebrow. 'Oh, aye?' he said dryly. 'What's that?'

Miles ignored the sarcasm. 'You told me once that you used to believe in yourself when no one else did. You said it was comfortable and you only ever had problems when others started believin' in you. You said they started doin' that when you became successful, and then it was *you* who had problems believin' in them.'

Brian smiled ruefully. 'And I thought you had a terrible memory too, Miles.'

'I remember some things,' Miles replied, softly. 'I remember some things very well. So now–now everyone believes in you–how do you feel?' Before Brian could reply, Miles added, 'and they didn't believe in you before tonight, did they? Not really. They hardly knew your bloody name, never mind believed in you.'

Brain sat thoughtfully for a time. After a moment he sighed, 'I don't feel comfortable with their belief, Miles, if you want the truth. You'd almost think they wanted somethin' off me, wouldn't you?'

Miles nodded and shrugged a small shrug.

Brian sighed ruefully. 'Aye, you'd almost think that, right enough. Tell you what, Miles, I'll go with you on this one.' He raised a quick hand. 'Not because I want to, you understand. It's more of an anti-social sort of a thing and nothin' to do with what you're sayin'. Y'see, I don't need *you* believin' in me either, because I'm doin' fine in this world all by myself.'

'I know that,' Miles grinned. 'Sure, we all are.'

Brian nodded as impassively as he could manage, before turning to Wing-Ding. 'And I suppose you'll be changin' your mind too, then?' he asked with a barely tolerant sigh.

The youth nodded eagerly, his lips curling up into a gentle smile.

'Aye, I thought so,' Brian said with a sigh. 'But sure, that's you all over, isn't it? You're as fickle as the fuckin' weather!'

'You want me to tell them, Miles?' Brian asked, a refractory glint in his eye. Having briefly reconsidered the situation, the broader man now seemed to relish the prospect of having a dig at those who'd feigned new-found belief in him.

As the windows trembled loudly in their lead-lined casements and forked lightning reaved the sky, Miles swiftly deliberated over whether anyone would truly blame him if he now rescinded all responsibility, claimed his prize from the Father and then raced to the toilets to replenish the thinning alcoholic ichor which pulsed weakly through his veins: After all, malevolent Zeus had charged Pandora to visit innumerable sorrows upon Craiglann without refrain, and each was a foul harbinger for Death, whose imminent scythe might yet be slightly blunted by anaesthetic.

Still, as the vagrant stared around the dimly-lit chapel, he knew it wouldn't be quite so easy. The kerosene heaters were now surrendering their last ranks of heat, dozens of candles had been tenebrously doused by the consuming wind, and lines of grimly impatient faces in the foremost pews seemed all too aware that the full wrath of the storm was nearly upon them. If Brian were to now relate the verdict in his usual thoughtless manner, therefore, chaos would perhaps ensue within moments.

Frowning dismally, Miles shook his head. 'No, I'll do it – if you don't mind, that is. I think, unfortunately, that this is *my* time.'

Brian shrugged easily. 'Here,' he grinned, extending a cigarette. 'You should always have a last smoke before facin' the firin' squad.'

Miles smiled thinly, took the cigarette and accepted a light, bleakly aware of the truth in that dry jest. There'd never been a pan-Hellenic solution to their problem, that was obvious from the start. Nor was there any guarantee the evacuees would await the full delivery of the verdict, darkly distracted as they were by the coarse squeals of those grotesque wind-spirits currently intent upon prising open the husk of St Augustine's with their shearing talons. But Miles still had to try and say something, if only because the gentler spirits of Sarah and the twins might have skilfully concealed themselves in a nearby perjury of shadows, not wanting to miss the brief resurrection of a man they'd once known. Seeking one last look of reassurance from Tomas–who now sat propped against the altar, his hands in his pockets and his coat collar upturned to warm his neck–Miles rose to his feet and steadied himself against the pew in front, hoping his legs wouldn't deny him before he finished speaking.

'We're sorry for keepin' you,' he began, dragging consciously at his cigarette. 'And I know you're all tired, but in the next few minutes I'd like to briefly explain who we are, the way we view this situation and which factors influenced our final decision. We know, of course, that the more empathetic amongst you view us as withdrawn, hurt and lonely men. Crueller critics, of course, regard us as drink-addled tramps, devoid of logic and morals, who'll say anythin' if the price is right. Naturally, we understand each of those opinions, yet both are completely wrong. We're just four ordinary men who've chosen to withdraw from the world, even though we're very aware that the world rarely withdraws from anyone makin' a conscious effort to become involved. That said, after what we've heard tonight, I think I'm speakin' for all my friends when I say we're not too worried about how you perceive us anymore, yet I'd still like to challenge those particular views.'

Ignoring several gruff comments, Miles forced himself further upright. 'To begin with, we didn't always live in Adullam. Once, albeit a while ago, we mixed with ordinary people and led ordinary lives, which is somethin' you can't do without becomin' at least aware of how society views right and wrong. Furthermore, while most people here in Craiglann reserve judgement when their peers commit borderline sins, they're always quick to remind us when we fall even slightly by the wayside. So, if we four appear morally bereft, the opposite is true: We have morality thrust in our faces seven days a week. And so, in askin' us to judge this case, you've made a very wise decision.'

Miles tapped his fingers uneasily upon the pew. 'Now, before I deliver our verdict, I'd like to tell you somethin' I've never told anyone. It'll take a minute and has an indirect bearin' upon this case. Many years ago, I taught history and philosophy in a university in my home town. I had a house, a wife and two very beautiful daughters. But I also had a habit of rationalisin' my every action and word, and I did so as well as any man alive. Because of this, I perhaps wasn't as nice to others as I might've been, but more especially my wife, who must've found me quite hard to live with on occasion. I'm not proud to admit that I was also caught up in a very long affair throughout my marriage – one which my wife, Sarah, eventually took me to task over in an intelligent, yet non-confrontational manner. I won't go into details, but her honesty and dignity that day touched me so deeply that I made a silent promise never to hurt her or my daughters ever again. And I thought I'd have plenty of time to do that, but I was wrong. Because later that same night, around eleven o clock, I went on an errand, durin' which time a burglar broke into our home, stole a few things and then set the place on fire. That night...was the last time I saw my wife and children alive...'

Miles swallowed hard, praying the tremble in both his legs and his voice wasn't audible above the lament of the wind. 'The burglar was a local youth of eighteen or so, and he claimed in court that he'd imagined the house was empty because he'd seen my car drivin' off. So, he broke in and fumbled about in the kitchen, lightin' a few matches as he did so because he didn't want to turn the lights on and attract undue attention. Apparently he then panicked upon hearin' a car drive past outside, threw one of the matches away and made his escape, only to realise too late that he'd tossed it into a pile of papers.'

Miles shrugged solemnly, finding it an effort to keep his head raised. 'That may've been what happened, I don't know, but my friends kindly advised me that it was perhaps best that I view the entire situation as a tragic twist of fate. And they'd no doubts that, due to my studies in philosophy, I'd soon order my thoughts: I just had to take one day at a time, grieve when I felt the need, and try to slowly move on with my life. But what I never told anyone about that night was that I'd just popped out to tell my latest lover our affair was over. I could've phoned her, y'know, but somewhere at the back of my mind I thought that, as we'd spent so long together, she deserved more than a quick call...'

Miles took a deep breath and raised a stalling hand as Con Logue was about to intervene. 'So what, you ask, has this got to do with our verdict? Well, most people might say I did nothin' legally or even morally wrong that night. I was, in my own mind, tryin' to do the best for all concerned – or, as Mr Logue might say, seekin' a utilitarian solution. But I take no comfort from that, as terminology and definition mean little when you're forced to eternally revisit one moment of your past every night in your dreams, and awake each mornin' to the grim realisation that one wrong choice was enough to change your life forever.

'And therein is the lesson: There are certain fateful moments in our lives when our choices can drastically affect not only our own future, but the futures of other people. If we're lucky–which, as you've heard, isn't always the case–we'll have time to correctly weigh our options. But if we aren't lucky–and if we make the wrong choice–our decision can have far-reachin' repercussions, the consequences of which will haunt us forever. And everyone suffers – no one escapes. Shortly before I left home, the youth who burgled my home killed himself before the case went to trial. Maybe guilt drove him to do that, or maybe a fear of jail – I don't know which, but it hardly matters: As a result of his actions that night, he also brought about his own untimely demise. As for me, I bear my remorse more openly, yet I now realise that the self-loathin' I wear as a second skin wasn't inflicted upon me by God–much as I've conveniently blamed him over the years–but by myself, for, as my good wife once said, all men have a tendency to judge themselves more fiercely than any god ever can.'

Miles cleared his throat. 'But that's enough about me. I speak now on behalf of the appointed jury, and I'll begin by sayin' that, despite our demeanour, each of us is as conscientiously aware as anyone that it's very dangerous to consider a man guilty until proven innocent. And all of the so-called evidence aside, what no one here has done tonight is judge the defendant for the qualities which make him a man and not a stranger – somethin' that I'm as guilty of myself, because I also said a few things about him just to stay on the right side of a few people.' Miles shrugged weightedly. 'Anyway, havin' listened to what has passed as evidence, and havin' consulted both our consciences and each other, we adhere to the old adage that ten thousand probabilities do not make one truth. The Stranger may well be guilty of somethin' – but then, we all are, and I don't need to remind any of you of that. We find him *not guilty*, however, of the charge bein' levelled against him.'

As the verdict registered with everyone present, Judge Laverty swiftly mustered a reply. 'And this, Miles, is the decision of you all?'

'It is,' Miles nodded, aware of the gathering tension. 'That is the verdict of us all.'

'Then there's little more to be said,' Judge Laverty said firmly. 'I dismiss this case.' He shrugged uncertainly, before rising from his seat and staring solemnly out through the stained-glass windows behind him. As yet another crack of thunder resounded loudly overhead, he added, 'The only viable solution, therefore, might be to sit here and pray to God we all emerge from this night unscathed.'

The Old Man stood up sharply. 'No, it isn't the end of it,' he barked. 'It's just plain silly to return a verdict like that. What's goin' on in your head, Miles?'

'I'm just a man who's had a few problems,' Miles replied grimly. 'You said it yourself. But I still know what I'm doin' most of the time.'

The Father, clearly expecting such an interruption, stepped quickly down off the dais. 'Now, you all *agreed* to abide by the decision of these men,' he soothed, pointing to his watch. 'Look, it's just after one-o-clock, and nothin' catastrophic has happened so far. All we have to do is have faith.'

'Do you really believe that this storm's just goin' to blow over?' George Harkin shouted above the din. 'And have you *that* much faith,

Father Joseph, in this hulkin' wreck of a chapel of yours, with its worn-out columns and its leakin' roof?'

The Father took a deep breath, before nodding rather unconvincingly.

'Well, I agree with George,' Frank Devenney remarked coldly. 'I'm not sittin' here in Hell's waitin' room any longer while we could be in somewhere safe from the storm!'

'Aye, and I agree too,' Neil Martin agreed. 'That verdict is sheer nonsense!'

As both Vinny and Seamus Brown moved supportively in behind the Father, they should perhaps have been aware that Con Logue hadn't said a single word. As the arguing grew increasingly vexed, the garage-owner crept furtively up behind the Chief Guard and snatched the gun from his holster, before taking one quick step back, raising the weapon and firing a single shot into the chapel roof.

'Right - everyone, sit down!' the garage owner barked, before examining the gun as if it were a foreign prosthetic he wasn't so sure he liked. 'I swear, I'll fire this effin' thing into someone if I bloody well have to!'

Nearly everyone swiftly did as they were ordered, except for a very fraught Deborah Logue. 'Con, this is madness!' she cried. 'What in God's name are you goin' to do?'

'You know what I'm goin' to do, woman, so sit down!' As his horrified wife slowly regained her seat, Con inched his way down the side-aisle, the purloined gun covering every conceivable angle and his narrowing gaze intent upon seeking out the enemy within. Stopping at the seventh pew, and now fully gripped by a paroxysm of rage, the garage-owner then pointed the gun directly at Miles. 'Look at these inebriated fools,' he snarled, retreating ever so slightly as the vagrant rose quickly to his feet and stared him directly in the eyes. 'Do you really think I'm goin' to let these maladjusted sots decide whether *we* live or die?'

As Miles stood there wondering why he'd risen to his feet, he became peripherally aware of Vinny McIntyre attempting to sneak up behind Con Logue. Alerted by the vagrant's momentary shift of focus, the garage-owner pivoted nervously and pulled the gun's trigger, only for his jaw to drop in disbelief as a bullet tore through the Chief Guard's right shoulder.

'Jesus, I fuckin' warned him!' Con thundered, visibly aghast as the officer slumped to the chapel floor. 'You heard me – I warned all of you! And I don't know why you're all lookin' at me like that, because I'm doin' this for you! Now, I'm goin' over to the bloody farmhouse – does anyone want to go with me?'

As even his hitherto confederates either turned away or shook their heads in abject disbelief, Con nodded his sour resignation. Then, without uttering another word, he rushed down the aisle and unlatched one of the main doors, momentarily bracing himself against the bludgeoning wind as it tore through the chapel, before firmly launching himself out into savaged penumbra.

As Miles made to move after him, he felt a firm hand upon his shoulder and he turned to see Tomas standing beside him. 'He's made his own pact with Life and Death, Miles – let him be.'

Trembling visibly, Miles nodded his consent. And, by the time Neil Martin, Big Sean and Dave Mullan had forced themselves down the rainswept aisle to shoulder the door shut, Con Logue had vanished into the darkest reaches of the night.

***

'Aren't you goin' out there after him?' Mrs Stewart demanded of Seamus Brown as a few of her more level-headed peers began administering first-aid to the stricken Chief Guard. 'You're what's left of the law around here, are you not?'

'And what would you have me do?' the younger Guard snapped, wincing as yet another lightning strike surged from the midst of an explosive hurl of thunder and filled the chapel window's with a voluminous escapade of light. 'Chase after him, and him with a gun? Uh-uh – no way!' Seamus shook his head firmly, and he was just about to further justify his reluctance when a very loud cracking sound forced him to silence.

It sounded very much like a gunshot, and, as before, the Father was the first to call for calm, before straining his ears for more distinctive clues above the cacophonous din of the caterwauling winds and intermittent crashes of thunder. 'The tree,' the priest at last declared in a strangled whisper. 'That wrenchin' noise – do you hear it?'

'Aye, it's been struck again,' Vinny said, clasping at his bloodied shoulder and pushing himself weakly back up onto his feet. 'And it sounds as if…it's fallin'!'

As if suddenly disembodied, Miles found himself staring numbly up at the altar wall and listening impassively as the Great Oak splintered with the resonance of a sheering hulk, resounding sharply above even the robustious wind. At the same time, the vagrant's encompassing awareness took stock of the evacuees, who–having found no solution in either moral, physical or legislative law–had once again had devotion thrust upon them by the immediacy of peril. Many had dropped to their knees in prayer, others had been shocked into paralysis, and still others fastened adducently onto friends or neighbours in trembling huddles. Only one man moved amongst them–Tomas–and he was smiling broadly as he stepped calmly back up onto the dais with his arms outstretched as if parodying Christianity's greatest effigy

In those arrested moments, Miles found himself feeling sorry for the other man, aware theirs was but a Pyrrhic victory. Nemesis, God of Retribution, had again awarded cruelty with power, granting Con Logue his every boon. And the Sirens–slyly sensing there were no oarsmen to tie Odysseus to the mainmast and sedate him, nor an Orpheus to drown out their enchanting lures with a lyre of sweet incantation–had finally tempted Odysseus to sail unaided into their darkest realms.

For a split second, Miles so wanted to call Tomas back, to warn him that it wasn't right to greet Death with outstretched arms, no matter his beliefs. What did it matter if the Gods, in their impossible hatefulness, had orchestrated this dark affair in order to provide themselves with questionable sport? Life still had to be fought for, and what victory was there in dying? Besides, who truly wanted to end up like Achilles, who'd believed he was going to an afterlife of purpose and reward for his heroic ventures, only to later confide in Odysseus that he'd surely swap his bleak and wearying existence in Hades for the life of a servant's serf, rather than be proclaimed Lord of all the Dead?

But Miles couldn't speak, for Time was wrenching hours from moments and had all but ceased to move its unilateral march. And, just as swiftly, he found himself gripped by a sudden selfishness, realising that he truly didn't want to die, despite the fact he lived in an age which was complex and often painfully unrewarding.

As Miles was coming to terms with this latter revelation, Time wrenched free from its momentary paralysis and the vagrant's attention was accosted by an almost sickening groan as the Great Oak at last tore itself from its tendrilled moorings. Miles closed his eyes quickly, praying Death would strike quickly and fairly, despite its tendency at all times to do otherwise.

But nothing happened.

A final ugly wrenching had signified the tree had fallen – he was as sure of that as anyone within the chapel. Unless, of course, he was now totally delusional – and he wondered then if his mind was still playing tricks upon him. But he couldn't be sure. At least, not until the Father confirmed his suspicions.

'It fell,' the priest whispered. 'But it must've fallen the other way.'

'You're right,' the Old Man grinned. 'What else could it be?'

'We're goin' to be fine,' Mrs Malhaffey smiled, grasping Mrs Stewart solidly by the hand. 'I knew we would be,' she added buoyantly. 'I told you, God never lets you down if you believe in Him enough. That's a well known fact, sure, isn't it?'

Tomas turned around, his arms still outstretched. 'Sure, isn't He the greatest there ever was?' he proclaimed loudly. 'Where did you ever hear of the likes of Him?'

He was mainly ignored, with most too busy congratulating and hugging each other to examine his ongoing eccentricity. But Miles nodded warmly up at his truest peer, that small movement relaying his respect and appreciation. Within moments, however, both men were distracted by the sounds of bitter squabbling emanating from the Centaurian gathering of Neil Martin, the Old Man, Geoff Harkin and Frank Devenney; and, for a small time, the empty drumbeats of that argument grabbed their attention.

But then Miles noticed the Father approaching Tomas, and, sensing something less than congratulatory was in order, he moved hurriedly towards them.

The priest stared neutrally between the two vagrants. 'Tomas, Miles – you did a very good job here tonight, and I'd like to thank you both for that.'

'We just confused them for a time, Father Joseph,' Tomas agreed with a grin. 'Sure, it was hardly all that serious anyway, was it?'

As if still unable to weigh Tomas up, the Father narrowed his eyes, before nodding evenly. 'Still, I can't go back on what I said earlier.'

'Tomas tried his best, Father Joseph,' Miles interrupted. As the priest's eyes accrued gentle resistance, the vagrant gathered his strength. 'Let him stay in Adullam for a while. You could both work somethin' out, I'm sure of it.'

'I can't,' the Father frowned. 'It's not that I don't appreciate his efforts. But we need rules–everyone does–and if I allowed everyone to act as they wished, how would I ever keep order?'

Tomas raised an interjecting hand. 'I wasn't for stayin' anyway, Miles,' he grinned. 'I was just passin' through and I got myself caught up in a storm, as usual. Anyway, I've things to do and places to go.'

Miles nodded sadly, even as he took out his crumpled packet of cigarettes and gave one to Tomas. The other man smiled appreciatively, rolled it between his fingers and seemed set to make a comment. 'Don't say anythin', Tomas. Please.'

'Now, Miles, I was just goin' to say thanks,' Tomas grinned. He placed the cigarette in his mouth, accepted a light, and then pointed towards the evacuees. 'Listen to that lot, Father Joseph. They're as happy as a load of pigs in...' He paused, then grinned wryly 'Stuff, Father Joseph. As happy as a load of pigs in stuff!'

The Father pursed his lips as if contemplating whether to wrangle further with this predatory pike or cut the line and set it free. But then he merely nodded a vacuous nod before walking off in the direction of Judge Laverty and Vinny McIntyre, the latter of whom was now sitting upright in a pew and being tended by Mrs Daly.

Tomas grinned widely at Miles, even as he ushered him back down the aisle towards the seventh pew. 'C'mon, Miles, we'll sit and chat about the old days, eh?'

'What about Con Logue?' Miles asked, wondering what chance the garage owner now had of surviving any storm powerful enough to topple the Great Oak.

'Fate, Destiny or Random Repercussion,' Tomas shrugged. 'I'm sure one of those three fine ladies will make him see the error of his ways. We'll just have to wait and see.'

'Great job,' Brian smiled as Miles sat down beside him. 'You spent a little longer than I'd have done, but you nearly got the message across as effectively.' His pupils contracted sharply as he stared over at the evacuees. 'And, by the way, you were right in what you said about that lot – they're a bunch of fuckin' tossers!'

Miles chuckled under his breath, wondering which part of his intonation during the delivery of their verdict had even hinted at such a derisory opinion. Then he shrugged dismissively and warmly accepted Pele's outstretched hand, shaking it firmly and wordlessly until Wing-Ding gently nudged the ex-footballer aside so that he too might extend his own sycophantic congratulations.

'Some laugh that, wasn't it?' Tomas smiled, granting Brian a begging stare as the broader man took out his cigarettes and lit one. Aware of that abrupt intrusion, Brian sighed deeply, before reluctantly giving cigarettes to everyone present – even to Wing-Ding, who didn't normally smoke, but who now appeared eager to start.

Tomas graciously accepted a light, before saying, 'Hey, Miles, you mind the time I stuck a cat's paw into that horrible rabbit stew Nan used to make?' He feigned a pawed hand. 'Claws and all, mind? God, it looked disgustin', didn't it? I don't think she ever had the nerve to make it again after that.'

Miles nodded warmly, partially distracted as Brian and Pele allowed yet another one of their disjointed debates to loudly inherit the night, and trying not to laugh as Wing-Ding, ever the crowd-pleaser, agreed with each and every diverse opinion.

'And the time I sent the Father a Valentine's card from Nan,' Tomas grinned, staring amiably into the past. 'You mind that, Miles?'

Miles smiled and nodded again, allowing all sounds to blur into one as an unexpected weariness suddenly relaxed both his body and his mind, dragging him ever downwards into the comforting arms of Morpheus, there to dwell for the shortest of times in a comparatively dreamless sleep.

***

The storm had all but ceased when Miles startled awake several hours later. Staring tiredly around him, he noticed that many of those who resided upon Craiglann's elevated periphery had already left for home, leaving her more local residents to await their uncertain fate. The other inmates were still asleep, however, and Miles glanced at Brian's watch, which indicated that it was nearly 5-30am. Then, noticing that Tomas was standing just outside the partially-opened chapel door, the vagrant crept out of his pew and walked slowly down the aisle, shivering briskly as he stepped outside.

Above him, a darkly veiled Selene, Goddess of the Moon, looked set to shortly retire her powers to Aurora, Goddess of the Dawn, and the last traces of raven storm-cloud were now being truculently frayed by the wind, with dismembered striations still aswirl in the leaden sky. In the surrounding grounds, the leaves on the ravaged hedgerows and trees were sheened with silvered raindrops, and the lawns replete with patinas of jade and lime.

Staring down towards Adullam, Miles realised the elms and silver birch shivered only slightly now, yet the willow was still danced by the shallowest of breezes and had seemingly lost none of her energy. The flower-beds, however, had all but been washed away, and a dark mulch of broken stalks and torn petals deeply worked into the sullied gravel, though the hardier thistles and wilder flowers beyond the Mission Home's gateway had seemingly weathered the storm. The vagrant took a deep breath and an effluvium of scents drifted towards him upon a stiff breeze.

'Did you ever imagine the Great Oak would fall the other way?' Miles eventually asked the other man. 'I mean, all of that bloody worryin' for nothin'!'

'Maybe no one wanted it to happen,' Tomas chuckled. As Miles smiled cynically at that reply, he added, 'Oh, and they found Con Logue.'

'Is he dead?' Miles felt his heart skipping a beat. He wondered if the garage owner had been granted a fitting rejoinder to his perpetual eschatology of death and destruction.

'Nah, men like that never die,' Tomas trumped. 'He was pinned down by one of the tree's heavier branches when it fell. Ironically, that actually protected him from everythin' else blowin' around. Big Sean and a few others are over there now, tryin' to haul the damned thing off the top of him.'

'You think we should go and help?' Miles asked, sincerely.

Tomas shook his head. 'There's enough help there. Besides he's only broken his leg, and I don't think I could stomach listenin' to him cryin' for his Last Rites.'

Miles laughed dryly. Seconds later, he said, 'You didn't impress the Father tonight, did you?'

Tomas shrugged indifferently.

'He thinks you're evil.' Miles suppressed a blush as he recalled what he'd been about to do to the other man in the sacristy. 'But then, how can you blame him, what with all the agitation you stir up?'

'I don't blame him, Miles,' Tomas grinned. 'It's the task of every priest to make us feel disgraced by the existence of our dark side. Because, havin' achieved that, they can then feed leech-like upon our fears and use pious rhetoric to manipulate us into the people their God supposedly intends us to be. But they don't realise that everyone is basely savage, so nobody's dark side can be fully expelled, only tamed as their spirituality awakens. Also, if we didn't have that black side of our nature, we'd become insipid and weak, so we actually depend upon it to keep us alive.'

Miles nodded easily. 'I can understand that, but I don't think the Father does. He thinks you hate him and God, and that you don't care about anythin' or anyone.'

'Do you think it's just his crowd I've a problem with?' Tomas asked pointedly. Miles shrugged uncertainly, and Tomas shook his head firmly. 'Uh-uh! Alright, I'll always have doubts about any religion that uses the chantin' of archaic verse to draw you into a virtual trance before the shaman drinks a cup of blood – that's too much like vampirism for me! But any organised faith which requires men to live as wretched slaves under a vengeful God–who needs to be worshipped with austere routine, who is particular about his idols and fetishes, and who seeks such unquestioned devotion that his earthly warlords are forced to besmirch or destroy all unbelievers–nah, that's too controlled for me!'

'And your God – who or what is He?' Miles smiled. 'And is He the one who issued those Four Consequences of Bein'?'

'I created my own guidelines after a lot of thought.' Tomas smiled, pointing to his chest. 'And my God's in here. He's not hidin' in a chapel or a mosque or in the sky. I mean, do you ever wonder why most people who follow organised religions are still afraid of life and death? It's because they're brainwashed into adherin' strictly to the word of ancient religious texts–vague scriptures which can be interpreted any way at all–without questionin' why they should actually do so, and without listenin' to their hearts.' Tomas raised his palms. 'So, in what way do these so-called modern men of God differ from the duplicitous politician who maintains an electorate by promotin' fear of political rivals and their terrible policies? In what way do these so-called spiritual leaders differ from the tyrannical ruler who promotes patriotism by spreadin' dark tales about the evil deeds other countries would perform against his people should they gain even the smallest foothold upon their shores? And how different are these holy men to those who sought enlightenment by worshippin' a golden calf?' Tomas pouted almost sadly. 'There is no difference, none at all. Most modern religions lead chiefly by fear, and they all promote the lie that strict external rule is far more important than the need for total self-responsibility!'

Miles frowned introspectively, wondering when his temporary lucidity would expire and return him to the ravaged man he'd let himself become. 'You seem to know the answers to a lot of things,' he sighed sadly. 'I wish I did.'

'You do, Miles,' Tomas chided, his eyes flashing brightly. 'You know all the answers. You just haven't asked yourself any of the right questions yet.'

Miles looked at Tomas, then upturned his gaze to watch the sky tinge a pale pink on the periphery of the world. 'I think I've forgotten what it's like to feel alive.'

'But when you stood up to Con in the chapel, you must've experienced that feelin'. You must've felt more alive than you have in a very long time.'

'Aye, maybe,' Miles replied uncertainly. 'I know I was prepared to die just then, even though I didn't want to. Still, I don't know what that means.'

'Maybe it means you're ready to live again,' Tomas shrugged. 'Anyway, do you want to know what keeps me alive?'

Miles nodded, before dropping his head and swallowing hard.

'I view life as a game, a game that I perhaps agreed to play before I was born, and one in which I set out every adverse condition for myself, just so I could see how much I could both learn and overcome. To me, this is just one of many journeys I'll take, and my life's simply a continuation of a more prolonged existence which doesn't begin at birth and end with death, but which is simply split by the two.' Tomas smiled gently. 'Sometimes, I even imagine I might've made a bet about just how much I could take, and, in that way, I take responsibility for all my own actions. In that way, I don't blame God–should He exist–nor can I accuse Him of bein' cruel or terrible.' As Miles lifted his head, he noticed an indefatigable glint in the other man's eye. 'And I'm set to win, because I'm still here. Hangin' on by my fingertips, maybe, but still here.'

'I suppose that's one way of lookin' at things,' Miles said, frowning. 'Though I don't see the point of thinkin' like that.'

'It's what gets me through the hard times, Miles,' Tomas said solemnly. 'It's my fairy-tale, my Bible, my Quran. But it asks nothin' from anyone else, and, sure, what's the worst that can happen to a man who takes responsibility for his own thoughts and actions? Besides, is my story really any worse than the rest?'

'The Father thinks you're the Devil.' Miles repeated with a wry smile. 'I'm beginnin' to think he might have a point.'

Tomas smiled. 'I might be, Miles, because there's definitely a dark lure in my creed. But remember, a messenger of a true and lovin' God would probably forward exactly the same arguments as me.'

Miles decided to get off that subject: Either the other man's dizzying logic, the early morning air or a lack of sleep was making him vertiginously dizzy. 'You made a good decision tonight,' he admitted then. 'You saved the Stranger's life.'

Tomas shook his head. 'It was you who saved a man's life, Miles. You convinced four downtrodden men that Fate is their servant, not their master. I couldn't have done that, because they didn't know me well enough. I just made a few more-ordinary people stop and think about what they were goin' to do. You saved a man's life, Miles. I just bought the Stranger some time.'

Miles didn't reply, caught up in deciphering the other man's reply. Four men? Perhaps Tomas was right. Perhaps Miles had saved a life tonight – by standing up for what he believed, he might possibly have saved his own. As this thought struck him, he became peripherally aware of Tomas lifting a rucksack up from the corner of the step. Miles regarded the hold-all curiously. 'How did you get that?'

'You were all sleepin',' Tomas grinned. 'I went into Adullam before you awoke. No trick, no devil's magic. I just tip-tied in and out again, nothin' else.'

'Are you leavin' already?' Miles sighed. 'I thought that...'

Tomas extended a hand. 'Nah, I've outstayed my welcome, and I'd best be off now before the Father slaps a bus or a plane ticket in my hand as a further hint.'

Miles smiled sadly and shook the other man's hand solidly, even as he attempted to preserve that moment forever in his memory. Tomas, standing there with the poverty and austerity of a dervish, though with fire and life as yet in his eyes. Poor outside, though wealthier than most because he was all too aware that a man was rich in relation to the amount of illusions he could dispense with in life.

'Farewell, Miles. I'll meet you again at our journey's end.'

The vagrant nodded sadly, then watched as Tomas walked down the drive and turned onto Pheasant's Crest. From there, the other man took the first side road which led off to the east, and Miles smiled knowingly to himself as Tomas was framed tall against a sky which had all but been subdued by the approaching pink and scarlet wash of morning.

Most of the night stars had vanished from their heavenly firmament by now: The Pole Star and the Great Bear had long since disappeared, as too had the Plough and the yellowish-red Betelgeuse in the constellation of Orion. Each of the night stars had relinquished their hold upon the night – all but one. A pale star still shone in the east – Lucifer, the Morning Star, the last star of morning, and the star that heralded the rising of the sun. Miles shook his head and smiled. Two-hundred-million stars in the galaxy and Tomas had chosen to vanish with that one. A dramatic entrance, an equally dramatic exit – that was seemingly the only way Tomas had ever known.

As Tomas ascended to the top of the rise, Miles watched as the sloe sky was traced with blood-red streaks, which signified that Helios, the Sun God, was now set to begin his daily journey across the heavens in his golden chariot. Then, as both Tomas and the Morning Star faded into temporary oblivion, the vagrant turned and noticed Wing-Ding standing umbilically at his side, laggard and quiescent, the sleep still in his eyes and his hair once more a cordage.

'Who was he, Miles?' the youth frowned. 'I mean, he wasn't really one of us, was he? So, who was he *really*?'

Miles shrugged uncertainly, returning his gaze to the crest of the hill. Tomas was beyond it now, probably holding out his thumb and smiling amiably, even as he strode in the general direction of the county line. He'd turn west as night fell, of course: West towards Hades and Tartarus, to where Sun sank into a Golden Bowl upon Ocean to rest the night away. Still, whether he was a messenger of the gods, a devil, or simply a man, Miles wasn't sure.

'I d'know,' he grinned. 'Maybe he was just Tomas.' Wing-Ding nodded his vague understanding, before frowning and stretching lazily. 'Anyway, I'm goin' for a walk. Do you want to come?'

Wing-ding smiled and nodded quickly, before frowning again. 'Where?' he asked cautiously.

Miles pointed to the farmhouse across the way. 'Over there.'

Wing-Ding shook his head quickly and Miles smiled easily. 'You sure?'

Wing-Ding nodded a determined nod.

'Alright, well, you wait here and I'll be back shortly.'

Drawing his coat tight into his shivering body, Miles walked down the gravelled drive, out through the chapel gates and onto the rain-washed rise of Pheasant's Crest. Then, with one largely disinterested glance back at those attempting to free Con Logue from under the Great Oak's sundered carcass, he moved towards the rusty iron gate in the middle of the briar fence which surrounded the old farmhouse across the way.

Closing the gate behind him, the vagrant raised his arms in a semaphore of surrender and stepped warily up the broken path, uncertain as to what now compelled him. After all, Guards from the neighbouring county would soon have the Stranger safely within custody, which meant that his role–if any–in the disappearance of Marie Devine would soon be revealed. But Miles walked on, slightly unnerved as he neared the farmhouse, though finding it hard to shake the idea that this was now somehow personal. Still, his heart nearly broke free from his chest as he heard the sound of a dog barking loudly, and he suddenly recalled that the Stranger owned a large mastiff. His senses heightening, the vagrant stopped several yards from the farmhouse door, nervously tightening his hands into fists as he noticed a curtain being quickly displaced.

'H…hello, I'm Miles. I'm from Adullam across the road…'

Miles felt his legs almost collapsing beneath him as the door was cracked open and a shotgun pointed in his direction. Breathing fitfully, he tried to discern the Stranger's outline in the shadowed room beyond it, yet he could see nothing. Then, as slowly as he could, he dipped a hand into the breast pocket of his shirt, pulled out the coin and held it up high.

'You probably don't remember me,' he said, conscious of how foolish his words and actions perhaps seemed. 'But you, ehm, gave me this when you first arrived in Craiglann.'

The door opened a fraction more and the Stranger was gently cast against the backdrop of a rather ordinary farmhouse kitchen by the birthing sunlight. For a moment, Miles felt his every tension evaporate, yet his heart leapt once again as the snarling black mastiff bounded from the kitchen towards him, its pearl-white teeth flashing under drawn lips and its intentions as darkly clear as those of Cerberus, the three-headed dog who denied the unworthy access to Hades.

'Caesar – lie down!' The Stranger's authoritative voice had an instantly pacifying effect upon the dog and it dropped to its haunches just inches from Miles, yet its intense gaze never left him for an instant. With the shotgun gripped tightly to his side, the Stranger then stepped from the farmhouse, furtively scanning the path and the rise in the road. After a moment, he nodded. 'Aye, I remember you. Is this some sort of a trick?'

'No, I came here alone. I was wonderin' if you'd like to talk?' As the Stranger shook his head assuredly, Miles added, 'Well, I can't really blame you. So, would you like me to tell you what's goin' on instead?'

The Stranger regarded him indecisively, before stepping back towards the farmhouse door. 'Are you sure you're the only one here?' he rasped. 'Because they're all mad, y'know. Everyone in this town is mad in the bloody head!'

'Aye, I know,' Miles said, as agreeably as he could. 'But, no, really, it's only me.'

The Stranger bit hard at his lower lip. 'Well, if it's just you, you can come in.' He took another distrustful glance around the farmyard, before ordering his dog inside. 'But there'll be no one else comin' in, mind, no one else at all!'

Clasping the coin solidly in his sweating palm, Miles nodded hesitantly, before following the man and his dog into the building's dimly-lit kitchen. Five or six candles now burned at various places around the room, and yet the formless remains of many more indicated that the Stranger had undertaken an all-night vigil. A worn teak table and six chairs dominated the room's centre, and, at the furthest end, a scorched kettle hung from a spit above a log-fuelled fire, the water within it hiccupping the lid into a chattering frenzy.

As the dog trotted to his basket in the corner, the Stranger told Miles to take a seat at the table. The vagrant did so, very consciously choosing the one nearest the door.

Moments later, the Stranger sat directly across the table. 'Sorry about the lack of light,' he said, setting the shotgun down at his side. 'The electricity's off, and I ran out of coins for the gas-meter, so I can't use the cooker either.'

Shrugging evenly, Miles gently pushed the coin along the table, at which the Stranger nodded gratefully, lifted it and went over to the cooker, where he slipped it into a meter at the back. As he did so, Miles briefly considered lifting the shotgun; but, as the mastiff stared coldly in his direction, he smartly dropped his gaze.

'Thanks,' the Stranger said, returning to his seat. 'That'll save me from puttin' the kettle on the fire.'

'No problem.'

'I know what you're goin' to say,' the Stranger said then. 'The locals think I'd somethin' to do with the disappearance of the girl, don't they?'

Miles nodded lamely, seeking to discern the man's guilt or innocence from his eyes, yet he was unable to do so in those briefest of moments. 'Some of them think you'd somethin' to do with it, aye. But a lot of them now believe otherwise.'

'Oh?' the Stranger regarded him quizzically.

'They've changed their minds,' Miles continued, as if that were explanation enough. As the Stranger nodded dubiously, he added quickly, 'Did you have anythin' to do with her disappearance, then? It's just that someone saw you down at the river on the night she disappeared, and they thought...'

The Stranger stared at Miles in disbelief. 'You mean *that's* what they based their theory on?' Miles nodded worriedly and the Stranger shook his head. 'I mean, I knew they suspected me, but I didn't know exactly why. Y'see, when that Guard came up here the first time, he just asked if I'd seen anythin' strange and I said no, after which he started rantin' on about certain people in the town. The second time, he searched the place but said it was routine, so, again, I thought nothin' of it. But when he came up yesterday and that big fellah along with him tried to rough me up, I thought they were takin' the law into their own hands, so I ran inside and locked the door.' The Stranger shook his head again. 'Christ, I knew I shouldn't have done it!' Aware that Miles had paled and was about to vacate his seat, he grinned nervously. 'No, not *that!* Look, I know you deserve an explanation, so why don't you join me for a cup of tea.'

Miles nodded that he would, supposing that if the Stranger had wanted to harm him, he'd have done so by now.

'Trust me,' the Stranger said, moving towards the fire. 'I can explain what I was doin' down at the river that night.' He regarded Miles through piercing eyes. 'You do trust me, don't you?'

'The, ehm, gun,' Miles winced. 'I don't think it helps.'

'Ah, sorry about that.' The Stranger lifted the shotgun, then placed it in a cupboard beside the hearth. 'Do you trust me now?' he asked easily.

Miles shrugged, a bit wary still. 'I suppose.'

'Mmm, well, I'd be the same in your position, I guess.' He moved towards the fire, drew the spit out with a poker and suffused several teabags in the kettle. Seconds later, he poured two cups of tea and offered one to Miles along with a jug of milk and some sugar. Miles waited until the other man had taken a drink of his own tea before sipping gratefully at the steaming drink.

'So, I suppose I'd better begin, though where....'

234

'At the start,' Miles offered lamely. 'That'd probably be the best place.'

'Right, well, I'm a limnologist,' the Stranger began. Noting his guest's frown, he added, 'Simply put, I study the physical, chemical, geographical and biological aspects of inland freshwater systems such as rivers, lakes and swamps.' He pointed to an assortment of mechanical equipment in the corner. 'It's all quite borin', really. It's about assessin' the characteristics of water and the interactions which take place between organisms and their environments.'

Miles regarded the cumbersome machinery and smiled wryly, sensing where the story was going and feeling strangely elated by the irony of it all.

'Still, I haven't worked in a while. There just aren't too many posts available in my business, as you can guess. So, when a friend offered me a temporary contract he'd received from a third party a while back, I took it. But I made a rather hurried job of it–basically because I'd nowhere to stay–so I came back to do it correctly. The only drawback was I needed to find some accommodation in order to...'

'...see if the River Hart was tryin' to reclaim its old course,' Miles interrupted with a small grin

The Stranger regarded Miles suspiciously. 'That's right. But...?'

'It's a long story,' Miles replied, smiling at the irony of how Con Logue and the Old Man had been unwittingly trying to get Vinny McIntyre to kill the very man they'd secretly hired to help them gain what both had termed a 'competitive advantage'. 'So, you rented out the farmhouse?'

The Stranger nodded evenly. 'It was the only place available, and it was cheap. Apparently no one has put an offer in on this place for years, and I can see why. It's like somethin' from the last century, and you'd probably think it was haunted if you believed in that sort of thing. Still, the land's full of rabbits, which is good, because I do a bit of huntin' on occasion.'

Miles smiled thinly, recalling the first day the Stranger had arrived in Craiglann: The man had been carrying a map and resembled a confused tourist, which should perhaps have instantly indicated he was new in Craiglann and so had hardly purchased the farmhouse without viewing it. The vagrant shook his head, cursing himself inwardly for missing that vital detail. 'But didn't the Chief Guard ask you if you'd bought it?'

The Stranger shrugged sheepishly. 'He presumed I had and he didn't ask me for too many details–he didn't even ask me my name, now as I mind–so I played along. Y'see, I didn't want to tell him exactly why I was here, in case he told everyone. Still, if I'd done so, it might've saved me one hell of a lot of bother.'

'It might've, indeed,' Miles grinned.

'Of course, when everyone started snubbin' me, I thought they'd found out what I was here for anyway. Then, when they came up here and started callin' me a murderin' bastard, I wanted to tell them everythin', but no one gave me a chance.'

Miles nodded empathetically. 'I'd say you've been through quite a lot.' He took another few sips of his tea. 'So then, is the river reclaimin' its old course?'

'No, not at all. A few buildin's have damp under them, but that's normal for older properties. And it's been a bad winter, which means that water levels beneath the soil are runnin' higher than usual, so that's normal too.' The Stranger smiled wryly. 'Of course, I was paid to do a job, so I simply gauged the river's depth a few more times and drew on the soil in various places, but I couldn't find anythin' extraordinary. To be honest, I was more interested in the local ecology, though that seems healthy enough too, to be honest.'

'But why is the Crissom so badly flooded then?'

'I'd say it's to do with poor drainage,' the Stranger pouted. 'The council will probably have to widen the catchment and interception drains, and maybe broaden the natural streams and ditches surroundin' the Hart to provide it with the required discharge capacity.' He shook his head firmly. 'No, the river is runnin' along the course it was given many years ago, and it'll probably do so for hundreds of years to come.'

'Then you'd nothin' to do with the girl's disappearance?'

'Heavens, no!' the Stranger frowned. 'I know that, in a sense, I deceived your Chief Guard about why I was here, so that was wrong. And I may even be guilty of takin' money for this job under false pretences the first time around. But then, I did return and carry out the tests properly, so maybe I earned it. Still, I've always believed in karma, so maybe I was supposed to learn a lesson from all of this.'

'Maybe,' Miles agreed, finishing his tea and rising up from his seat. 'But, if it's any consolation, the storm taught a lot of people a lesson last night. We had to spend the night in the chapel because the town's so badly flooded.'

'All of you?' the Stranger asked incredulously. 'The whole town?'

'Well, about forty or fifty of us. There's a lot of damage down there. Apparently, it'll take weeks to repair, maybe even months.'

'It was a bad one, alright,' the Stranger agreed. 'Someone could have died out there.'

Miles regarded the man thoughtfully. 'Someone could've died last night, and that's a fact,' he replied, unbolting the door and stepping outside. 'But no one did, as far as I know, and that's the main thing.'

'Aye, definitely.' The Stranger followed quickly after him. 'Listen, will you explain to everyone why I came here? I asked the other fellah to do that for me yesterday, and he said he would. But I don't know if he did.'

Miles, now halfway down the path, turned around to face the man. 'Who?'

'The fellah who came by yesterday just shortly after I locked myself away. No offence, but he looked as if he lived in that Mission Home, too.'

Miles nodded, not offended in the least.

'Anyway, he was as friendly as you, so I told him everythin'. He just smiled and said he'd have a chat with one or two people. But I think...'

Miles smiled broadly. 'His name's Tomas, and he did as much as he could, believe me. Anyway, I'll explain everythin' to the others, I promise. They're in a more tolerant mood now, and they might just listen to me.'

The Stranger nodded gratefully and made his way back inside. Then Miles walked down the path, chuckling to himself as he locked the gate, crossed the road and walked back towards the chapel. An ambulance was there when he arrived, and both Con Logue and Vinny McIntyre were being ferried into the back of it. Miles waited for the vehicle to speed off towards the county hospital, before calling the Father and Judge Laverty aside. Then, in a low whisper, he told them everything he'd just learned about the Stranger, though he omitted to inform them that Tomas had visited the farmhouse the previous day, believing then, for some strange reason, that no one else actually had a right to know.

***

The sounds of hammers, drills and saws resounded loudly throughout Adullam as Miles took one last glance into the mirror. An ordinary man now stood before him, a freshly shaven man with many of his frailties hidden away beneath fresh clothes, and that tell-tale hint of flint now removed from his eyes. Miles recognised this new man vaguely and he smiled easily at him, before moving out of the bathroom and into the dormitory, content that he could now actually see himself for what he was, and not for what he once allowed himself to become.

The dormitory was filled with a knot of labouring carpenters and glaziers, and Miles politely squeezed his way through them towards his bunk, listening, as he did so, to their idle assessment that it'd be several months before Craiglann even resembled the picturesque and friendly little town it once was. As he pulled on his coat and finished placing his few remaining belongings into a small hold-all, Miles turned to find Wing-Ding once more at his side.

'Are you goin' too?' the youth asked above the din, his trembling voice relaying his sadness. 'I thought you'd stay a while longer.'

'I think I've stayed long enough,' Miles replied softly. He allowed Wing-Ding a few moments to take that in. 'It's time for me to move on, y'know.'

'I'll move on someday,' Wing-Ding replied, his eyes widening even further. He turned and frowned darkly at the contractors–suddenly, the posse–before stepping quickly aside as three of them pulled the sodden carpet up from the wooden floor beneath him. The youth looked set to scold them, but then he stepped closer to Miles, smaller, his nerve lost. 'Some day, Miles – you'll see.'

'I don't doubt it for a second,' Miles said warmly, moving back downstairs with the youth in his shadow. Upon opening the front door, his gaze was instantly drawn to the ruined flower-beds and he wondered silently to himself if the blooms would ever return. He smiled softly, believing they might, for he'd seen evidence of similar revivals in another garden many years before.

'You'll come back, won't you?' Wing-Ding said, slowed by the boundary of the front door

Miles shrugged uncertainly. 'I might. For a visit, maybe, but I don't think I'll be back for good.' He took Wing-Ding's hand firmly in his, induced a shake into it. 'You'll say good-bye to everyone for me, will you? To Brian and Pele.' He paused thoughtfully for a second. 'To Nan and the Father, too. And to anyone else who might ask.'

Wing -Ding nodded sadly, and then he watched in a fretful silence as the other man stepped casually down the drive and onto Pheasant's Crest.

Miles walked to the top of the hill, then stood there staring over Craiglann. From that vantage, he could see the flood-damage was immense. The Hart still ran with a swell that would take days to disappear, the Crissom was as yet lost beneath several feet of water, and most of the buildings within the town-centre now required repair. But, as a rainbow girdled the earth in the distance and a pale sun crept weakly to its zenith, he suspected it wouldn't be long before the town reverted to its former glory, and perhaps even benefited overall from its ordeal. Whether the storm had been a natural phenomenon or sent as some form of karmic lesson to teach the locals a lesson was a matter of conjecture, though Miles preferred to think that Gaia, Goddess of the Earth, had granted temporary reign to Chaos for the simple reason that, without such sporadic intervention, the world would never know growth and rejuvenation.

The heavy whirring of a chain-saw drew his gaze to the lifeless torso of the Great Oak, and he saw two workmen almost sacrilegiously setting to work upon her fallen frame. For some reason, he felt saddened by that sight moreso than any other, and he wondered where the birds would settle in the future, and where the Dryads which once inhabited her mighty breast might now reside; though he wryly supposed that, despite their supposedly lower consciousness, their more willing acceptance of the laws which governed their lives would perhaps see them through this terrible transition all the sooner than much superior man.

Miles turned and began walking slowly along the rise. Then, with his thumb held out to catch a lift, he found himself wondering why Tomas hadn't explained the reason for the Stranger's presence in Craiglann to the townspeople in the community-centre the previous day.

Had the other man simply wanted to toy with the lives of those gathered in the chapel, or had the trial merely been his way of revealing those inconsistencies within the laws which governed men when mortal danger threatened? Had he been trying to underline the inadequacies of all conventional religions, each of which purported to level inequalities, even as they furthered the disparities between men by declaring theirs the only true belief system? Or had the other man just wanted to test and share his own beliefs?

Miles wasn't sure. All he knew for certain was that Tomas had shown Craiglann's inhabitants that no single philosophy, conventional or otherwise, had all the answers.

Of course, when Tomas had told him that they'd meet at their journey's end, his tone had also implied that all men had similar journeys to undertake, and this Miles could accept. In one night, he'd learned to live again and he no longer sought justice from the world, for it was now all too clear to him that no one had ever made a pact of immortality with Life. The ultimate realisation to which Miles would have to submit, naturally, was that he was possessed of a destructive compulsion which wouldn't be mellowed by age. From the moment he left Adullam, therefore, he'd have to undertake a strict prohibition, and maintain–if possible–a desire for daily renewal; although again, he supposed that most people would benefit greatly from such recurrent repair.

He would, of course, require the help of others during that initial period, mainly those who understood his particular form of malaise. But, as importantly, he'd need to develop an edifying creed in order to bolster his spiritual needs. The Father's stalwart doctrines no longer appealed to him, however, for the priest was too much a textualist who appeared convinced that human action was not entirely free, but determined by external forces acting upon the will, as well as motives directly or indirectly imposed by a higher source. Though nor was Miles fully inclined to the beliefs of Tomas, for the other man was too much a Gnostic who forever sought God within himself, instead of at times accrediting life's more miraculous achievements to a divine hand which acted unerringly for the best of all possible outcomes from somewhere within a theocentric universe.

Miles shrugged those thoughts aside, understanding that they were perhaps the beginning of a personal belief system, but checking himself with the reminder that action was the greatest philosophy. He took a deep breath and smiled, realising that he had a house to return to six counties distant, in which there were some bad memories, yet many good ones. Of course, Fortuna, Goddess of Fortune had once deserted it, as too had Flora, Goddess of Flowers. But then so had Miles, and yet he'd soon attempt to entice those goddesses to rejoin him and, hopefully, learn to live again.

A car pulled up on the rise and Miles stared in the window. A woman, small and beaming a friendly smile, pushed the passenger seat door open to him. 'I'm takin' this road for another thirty miles or so,' she said easily, her eyes searching his. 'Is that any good? Are you goin' far?'

'I hope so.' Miles climbed into the front passenger seat, pulled the rucksack onto his lap and closed the door behind him. He regarded the woman's kindly yet puzzled frown. 'I mean, aye. I am.'

'That was a bad storm last night,' the woman said, after a moment. She released the hand-brake, and drove slowly down the Crest away from Craiglann. 'Wasn't it?'

Miles nodded politely and forced a smile. 'It was, aye. But I think you have to live through things like that now and then to appreciate the tranquillity of the next day.'

'I think so, too,' the woman beamed. 'Still, it's an ill wind that blows nobody any good. Did you hear about that wee girl who went missin'? It was on the news there now, just a second or so back.'

Miles felt his heart skipping a beat. 'No, I didn't, sorry.'

The woman smiled contentedly. 'She's fine. It seems she ran off with an ex-boyfriend of hers because the pressure of her upcoming marriage was just too much. That storm must've scared the life out of her, though, because she apparently contacted the Guards in Dublin last night and asked them to get in touch with her mother. But the phones were down and they couldn't get through.' The woman sighed easily. 'Anyway, I think that's great, isn't it? A happy endin' like that, I mean. You just hear so much bad news all the time that sometimes a happy endin' like that is just nice.'

Miles returned her smile and relaxed back into his seat. Then he took a deep breath and realised that his smile wasn't in the smallest way forced. 'It is, aye. It certainly is.'